PRAISE FOR FRA

"Nantucket and its impenetrable, secretive fog and characters come to life in Mathews' capable hands."
—Diane Mott Davidson, author of *Prime Cut*

AND HER NANTUCKET ISLAND MYSTERIES
DEATH IN A MOOD INDIGO

"Outstanding . . . Mathews is a dazzling talent indeed. This book has it all—fascinating, beautifully drawn characters, such a realistically rendered setting that you can hear the waves as you read, page-turning suspense, the struggle of good vs. evil so skillfully brought to the forefront that I'll be thinking about the issues that the book raised for a long time to come. . . . A must read for those who appreciate fully realized, believable characters and a strong sense of place."
—*Mystery News*

"An exploration of the very nature of evil. . . . Bright, determined, and yet vulnerable, Merry is an appealing heroine . . . sensitively drawn . . . memorable."
—*The Denver Post*

"A smart, savvy, appealing heroine who's definitely worth getting to know . . . One more fine entry in a series that just keeps getting better."
—*Booklist*

"The detection is first-rate, sadly a rarity in many crime novels these days. Mathews dares you to guess the killer, and so do I."
—*The Plain Dealer,* Cleveland

DEATH IN ROUGH WATER

"Refreshing island atmosphere, believable villainy, and down-to-earth sleuthing."
—*Kirkus Reviews*

"An enticing read."
—*The Denver Post*

"Mathews offers a nice blend of island lore and contemporary connivers, a . . . twisty plot and a dogged heroine."
—*The Armchair Detective*

"Mathews skillfully incorporates close-knit relationships, small-town gossip and a salty Nantucket flavor as she steers this intricate tale to a satisfying conclusion."
—*Publishers Weekly*

Other Mysteries by Francine Mathews
Featuring Merry Folger

DEATH IN THE OFF-SEASON

DEATH IN ROUGH WATER

DEATH IN A MOOD INDIGO

and

The Jane Austen Mystery Series
by Francine Mathews
Writing as Stephanie Barron

JANE AND THE UNPLEASANTNESS AT SCARGRAVE MANOR

JANE AND THE MAN OF THE CLOTH

JANE AND THE WANDERING EYE

JANE AND THE GENIUS OF THE PLACE

Look for THE CUT-OUT *by Francine Mathews*
coming soon in hardcover from Bantam Books!

Death in a Cold Hard Light

Francine Mathews

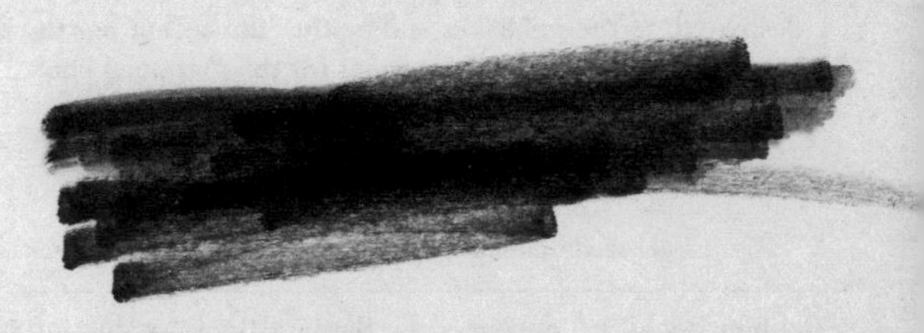

BANTAM BOOKS
NEW YORK LONDON TORONTO
SYDNEY AUCKLAND

This edition contains the complete text of the original hardcover edition.
NOT ONE WORD HAS BEEN OMITTED.

DEATH IN A COLD HARD LIGHT
A Bantam Book

PUBLISHING HISTORY
Bantam hardcover edition published June 1998
Bantam paperback edition / May 1999

Library of Congress Catalog Card Number: 97-44253.

ISBN 0-553-57625-9

Published simultaneously in the United States and Canada

Bantam Books are published by Bantam Books, a division of Random House, Inc. Its trademark, consisting of the words "Bantam Books" and the portrayal of a rooster, is Registered in U.S. Patent and Trademark Office and in other countries. Marca Registrada. Bantam Books, 1540 Broadway, New York, New York 10036.

PRINTED IN THE UNITED STATES OF AMERICA

OPM 10 9 8 7 6 5 4 3 2 1

Dedicated with love to my sister,
Patricia Anthony,
who always knew the Cape was home.

Death in a Cold Hard Light

Chapter One

The cold hard light of a December dawn hung heavily over Nantucket Sound, turning the sea opaque and alien. It clung to the church spires and curled like smoke along the gray-shingled eaves of the huddled houses. It flew on the spines of maple leaves as they skittered lonesomely down the length of Main Street, and cast a rime of frost over the lettering carved deep in the cemetery's timeworn headstones. The sadness at the edge of the blanketing clouds made the few scallop boats in the harbor seem even dingier and more futile as they dredged less with every cast from the slowly dying shallows.

Beyond Brant Point and the stone jetties thrusting bravely out to sea, a curtain of freezing rain obscured the approaching ferry. It was the first boat of the day—the first boat of a holiday weekend—but there was no one, really, to observe its arrival. Just a log half-submerged in the harbor's chop, seaweed streaming from one end like a tangle of human hair.

The captain of the Steamship Authority's M/V *Eagle* sighed deeply at the last of his coffee and dabbed an ineffectual towel over his fogged windows. Ted Moran had been awake since three A.M. The wife he had left behind in Hyannis was habitually unkind to him. His wool socks were damp and his toes were chilled. He was worried, as usual, about money. And as he gazed out over the dispiriting Sound, he felt the weight of that hard cold light settle as quietly as a gull on his slumped shoulders. It folded its wings and prepared to stay.

Captain Moran expelled a deliberate breath against the glass. The sourness of his own coffee churned with the odors of dust and exhaust and burning rubber that pervaded the ship. He grimaced and thrust open a porthole to one side of his control panel. The briny wind dispersed the interior funk. The captain turned his face to the sky and looked out over the tourists' heads grouped in the bow below his perch. They were craning, inevitably, for the first glimpse of Brant Point Light. Moran's gaze moved beyond them, and registered the log.

It bobbed with a sharp, wooden gracelessness in the waves, as though attempting to keep time to another man's music. And it was drifting directly in the steamship's path as it approached the harbor channel marked by the stone jetties.

Moran swore aloud, then adjusted the *Eagle*'s controls a hairsbreadth. The ferry's massive hull would hardly register the impact of even a sailboat thrown in its way, but he preferred to avoid obstacles when he could. The *Eagle* began its turn to port, nosing into the channel, and the bow wave shoved the piece of driftwood sideways into the starboard jetty. Spume broke over the jagged breakwater. The log rolled upward—and showed a pallid, mortal face beneath the streaming weeds of its hair.

"Jesus," Moran whispered; and at that very moment, the tourists began to scream.

The chief of Nantucket's police, John Folger, usually awoke a few seconds before the first car ferry of the day rounded Brant Point and blared its horn into the stillness. Like the ebb and flow of the tide, the ferry horn was a predictable sort of chaos. The sound came and went at scheduled intervals, punctuating the island hours in much the way that the Angelus had once divided the devotional day. As if in genuflection to that thought, Chief Folger said a fragmentary prayer into the cold hard light that filled his bedroom, closed his eyes, and waited. The blow of the ferry's horn came just as he ceased to expect it—a long, multitoned, earsplitting bray. When the last note had died away, he swung his feet to the bare plank floor. And at almost the same moment, like the ferry's strident echo, his bedside telephone rang.

"Hey, Chief," Terry Samson said. The bosun's mate greeted him from the doorway of the Brant Point Coast Guard station, his mouth set in a thin line. "Sorry to pull you out of bed. I thought I'd get your daughter."

"Meredith is off-island. Boston trial lawyers, again." John shook Terry's hand, unwilling to say more. For the past eight months, the prosecution of the worst killer in Nantucket's history had dominated Merry's life, and the burden showed little sign of easing. They would all be relieved when the trial—with its white glare of publicity, its endless prevarication and legerdemain—was at long last behind them. John no longer hoped desperately for justice; that was something for the victims' families to pursue. What he wished for now was far more elusive—a measure of forgetting, for himself and Meredith. "And everybody else is assigned to *something* today," he added. "Christmas Stroll, you know. So I thought I'd handle this myself."

"Right."

The Chief looked beyond Terry Samson to the gray water of the harbor. Santa was due to arrive on-island by boat tomorrow. If they had to find a body, thank God they'd found it today.

For the past twenty-odd years, the first weekend in December had brought Christmas to Nantucket. What had begun as a Chamber of Commerce gimmick—promote the island off-season, and lure a boatload of tourists to do their

Yuletide shopping on historic Main Street—had quickly turned into a cheerful community extravaganza, so that now John wondered what they had ever done for the holidays before Christmas Stroll began. There were tours of venerable houses and candlelight walks, roving bands of costumed carolers and concerts in the naves of churches. The local inns mulled vats of cider and kept their fireplaces roaring; art galleries mounted special shows; and shop windows gleamed with Christmas balls spilling artfully from dories and sea captains' chests. Tourists arrived by the plane- and boatload, to walk the deserted lanes in heavy sweaters, gaze out at the forbidding sea, and tramp back over the dunes for bowls of steaming quahog chowder. They nursed single-malt Scotches from the depths of their armchairs. They spent far too much money on lightship baskets and antique brass barometers and hand-loomed throws. They bought Nantucket Reds baseball caps and twill trousers and wore jackets embroidered with small blue whales. And then, like a flock of migratory fowl, they left—as though, John Folger thought, money could buy what was precious about Nantucket, and sustain the exiles through the doldrums of winter.

The first of the tourists had probably already arrived on the morning ferry, and witnessed the *Eagle* captain's frantic call to the Coast Guard—had witnessed, perhaps, Terry Samson's retrieval of the body. Old news by lunchtime.

"Where is he, Terry?"

The bosun's mate gestured toward the water. "Out back at the boat dock. We didn't want to unload him under the eyes of the entire town. Particularly *this* weekend."

"No. Poor bastard. We'll take him off your hands as soon as we can."

Terry led the Chief through the station's central hall. Beyond the double doors at the back lay a patch of grass, dirty brown and unlovely in the late autumn wind. The two men crossed it and came to the Coast Guard's working dock—a couple of slips for cutters, a boat ramp to one side, and beyond it, the horseshoe curve of the island's harbor. On the deck of the far cutter lay a tarpaulin-shrouded mass.

"Any identification?"

"We didn't look." Terry shoved his cap upward and fingered his hairline. "I guess I thought you'd want to do that yourself."

John Folger grunted. He sprang from dock to gunwale, reaching haphazardly for the support of a stanchion. Despite living awash in the seas for nearly sixty years, he had never been a sailor. He wavered for an instant, fell heavily into the body of the craft, and steadied himself. Then he made his way to the corpse and pulled back the tarp.

"God damn," he said. "Holy mackerel."

Terry jumped into the boat beside him. "What's wrong?"

Other than a kid lying dead who shouldn't have died—nothing at all, Folger thought. *Nothing to speak of, in fact. Oh, Christ.*

The police chief stood silent and frowning over the body for a moment, just taking it all in. Long wet hair the color of old rope hung in hanks about the blue-tinged face. He usually wore it in a ponytail, John remembered, but the hairband must have disappeared in the water. A dark mole punctuated the right cheek. One hazel eye stared remotely, but the other had been torn from its socket—by a crab, probably, near the wharf pilings where the body might have entered the water. His nose had been chewed up, too. But there was no other visible sign of violence. John Folger closed his eyes, shock giving way to anger, and felt suddenly sick.

"Chief?" Terry Samson prodded.

"I've got to use your phone," Folger said.

And called the Water Street station.

"Such a *sweet* girl." Julia Mason set down her coffee cup and smiled brilliantly across the breakfast table at Meredith Folger. "So *ambitious*, too. But then, the sort of woman who survives a Princeton education is of a different breed—wouldn't you agree? Beauty and brains, with spirit into the bargain. A certain *je ne sais quoi* in her air and address, her familiarity with all levels of society. Where did you say you attended college, dear?"

"Cape Cod Community." Merry's jaw felt stiff, as though it were slowly turning to stone. But then, her entire body was tensed for the receiving of a blow. Her neck ached from the effort of keeping her head upright, her eyes fixed on Peter's mother.

"And that was for—two years?"

"Yes. I went to the police academy afterward."

"Ah." Julia dusted her manicured fingertips with a linen napkin. "Yes—we all thought that Alison would have been perfect for Peter. I simply do not understand young people today. They seem to consider no one but themselves."

Merry had to agree with Julia; for her part, she had barely spared a thought for Alison Miller in the four years since she had saved the woman's life—but in Julia Mason's mind, at least, Alison was the standard against which Merry should be judged. Probably, Merry thought, because Alison had been wise enough to quit the Mason field rather than tackle Peter's mother.

"So very sad in every respect that things fell out as they did," Julia continued.

"Particularly for Alison." Georgiana Whitney reached for a scone and then passed the pastry tray to Merry. Like everything in the Greenwich house, it was a study in elegance. "That girl had a talent for making lousy choices. Peter, however, generally makes brilliant ones. I haven't seen him so happy in years."

Merry managed a crooked smile. She had instinctively liked Georgiana Whitney from the moment Peter's sister had opened the door of her Round Hill home the previous afternoon. George was lithe and dark, with glowing eyes and a glossy cap of hair that reminded Merry of a mink. She moved with an almost feral grace—years of ballet lessons embedded in the bone—and a contained energy that might have powered the space shuttle. Her four children roared about the high-ceilinged rooms and clattered up the back staircase, leaving heaps of winter clothing, ice skates, and dog leashes in the front hall; but George moved serenely through the chaos like the very best of good witches. Her love for her family, and for her world in general, was obvious. And yet there was hidden strength in the woman's whipcord body, Merry decided. She certainly managed her mother the way a New York tugboat guided a barge.

"So tell me," George said now, leaning forward conspiratorially. "Are you planning a summer wedding? On the island?"

Merry shifted uneasily in her chair. "We haven't actually decided."

"But none of Peter's friends will be there!" Julia protested. "None of the ones that count. His old friends, the people he knew before he met—" She hesitated, and studied Merry for a long moment. "None of his *real* friends, I mean."

"Since when is Nantucket a backwater in August?" George asked the table in general. "Half of Manhattan would kill for an excuse to fly in. The other half will already be there."

"But why not save all that effort and have the wedding here? Or better yet, at the Plaza downtown?"

"I doubt Peter would be comfortable with the Plaza, Mother."

Julia said nothing in reply; then she shrugged her indifference. "Oh, well, if you insist on making it a horrid little shotgun affair . . . perhaps at least Sky Tate-Jackson and his wife—what *is* that creature's name? Maymay? Chinese or Korean or something?—might manage to attend."

"I only asked, Merry, because of the house," George continued, ignoring her mother.

"The house?"

"Cliff Road. *You* know. We're there every summer with the kids. And Hale and I were thinking—if you wanted to use the backyard for the reception, tent it over with a dance floor and everything—we'd be delighted. But we should start planning now. Those sorts of services get tied up quickly in the summer months."

The Cliff Road house. With its narrow clapboard facade and divided front steps, it had sat for one hundred seventy years behind perfect lygustrum hedges, a masterpiece of the Federal style. Crushed quahog shells lined the drive and the path to the door, and in summer, hydrangeas welled over the lawn in every shade of blue-pink, like a Laura Ashley photo shoot. The back terrace ran straight to the bluff's edge, and below it lay the crowd of cottages near Jetties Beach, the long smooth expanse of Nantucket Sound. Merry had been inside the home only once, the previous January, when she and Peter had stopped to check the pipes. Chinese red walls in the hallway, black and white marble on the floor. A treasure trove of export ware. Mahogany and Chippendale. Turkish carpets strewn over the heart-pine floorboards. A house in the Potentate style.

She tried to imagine Peter's foreman, Rafe da Silva, kicked back with a beer on one of the Cliff Road house's lawn chairs—and failed.

"So lovely," Julia Mason sighed, "when we held the engagement party there. Tubs of hydrangeas around the tent poles, and Alison a *picture* in white organza—"

"Excuse me," Merry said, rising abruptly from the table. "I think I hear Peter coming in."

"Pity," Julia remarked to George as her prospective daughter-in-law beat a hasty retreat, "that she has so little to say for herself. Peter used to *love* witty women."

He had just returned from his morning run. He stood in his sister's back hall with his face flushed from the cold. At the sight of Merry, he grinned and enfolded her in an exuberant hug.

"You stink," she said, "and I don't even care. That says something, I think."

"About your love for me?"

"Or my hatred of your mother."

"That bad, huh?" Peter released her and busied himself removing his shoes and sweatshirt. "Isn't George any help?"

"She's trying. But this is Julia Mason we're talking

about—the Rommel of the Social Register. And the assault on North Africa has only begun."

"I see. You're ready to leave."

"Pretty much," Merry replied equably. "If she mentions your lovely and talented ex-fiancée again, I may just settle for drawing blood."

"Three days." Peter looked at her then, his gray eyes brilliant beneath his sharp brows. "Three days of touring my childhood haunts, making friends with George, and ignoring Mother. Then we hit the city, take in a few shows, and pick a china pattern at Tiffany's."

"You despise the whole subject of china."

"So I'm being selfless. Look—nothing my mother can say will change how I feel about you, Merry."

"But it's having a dreadful effect on my feelings for *you*," Merry objected. "I can't help wondering what sort of nightmare I've talked myself into. She wants to have the wedding in New York, Peter! With the reception at the Plaza! I mean—that's just not *me*. It's not what I signed on for."

"And now you're wondering whether the whole thing is a mistake," he concluded, with the resignation born of long familiarity.

"Of course. I mean—no, of course not. I love you. I do. I just don't love . . . your baggage."

"I'm not asking you to." He shook her shoulders gently. "I'm asking for three days here in Greenwich, and then a whale of a good time next week in Manhattan. I'm not trying to add any pressure to your life, God knows—I saw what those depositions in Boston did to you."

"And the trial will only be worse," Merry said hollowly.

"I know. I brought you here to have some fun, not to be judged by yet another jury. Try to ignore my mother. Ignore the whole lousy year, if you can."

Would she have used the word *lousy* to describe the past eight months? Probably not. What came to mind were words like *painful*, and *bruising*, and *unremittingly bleak*. Her giddy relief at having survived last April's terrors had turned swiftly to remorse—for the lives she had failed to save—and anger at her own gullibility. Had she been less easy to impress, a killer might never have clouded her mind. Had she relied more on objective study, and less on gut instinct—which had urged her to suspect an innocent party—two people at least might still be alive today. Self-loathing consumed Merry whenever the subject of the Osborne investigation arose; and for most of the past week, it had been forced unremittingly down her throat. First by the prosecution, who should have been her allies, and then at the hands of the defense—a gaggle of lawyers baldly calculating how Meredith's testimony might be turned to their client's advantage. She wanted nothing so much as to put the debacle behind her—but some nights, staring wakefully into the darkness, she knew she never would. It was now of a piece with her successes and failures, written like a growth ring into the trunk of her life.

"You need and deserve a vacation," Peter said, comprehending much that had filled her silence.

Before she could reply, Georgiana poked her head around the hall door. "Merry?" she said. "Telephone. It's your father."

Chapter Two

"Dad," Merry said into the phone. "What's up?"

"Hello, Meredith." Her father cleared his throat. She could feel his indecision across twenty-seven miles of sea and one hundred fifty of land.

"Is everything okay?"

"Yes. Well, not exactly. How are things in Greenwich?"

"Fine. Great." She raised her eyebrows in exasperation at Peter, who stood in the middle of Georgiana's kitchen with a loaf of bread and a jar of peanut butter, his approximation of breakfast. "Is . . . Ralph okay?" Ralph Waldo Folger, Merry's grandfather, was approaching the age of eighty-five, and his right hip was threatening to give out.

"Ralph's just fine."

"Well. Then we're all fine." She worried at the diamond solitaire on the third finger of her left hand, its band too loose past the knuckle, and waited for her father to come to the point.

Peter stabbed a knife into the peanut butter jar, pulled out a chair, and draped his feet inelegantly over George's kitchen table. Trace odors of sweat and running shoe drifted toward Merry. She fought the impulse to reach out and tickle the ball of his foot.

"Meredith—"

"Yes?"

"We found a body floating in the harbor this morning."

"Whoa." Merry turned her back on the dirty socks and bent her blond head protectively over the receiver. "So . . . what is it? A drowning?"

"On the face of it."

"Accidental?"

"I don't know."

They were both silent for the space of several heartbeats. "Why shouldn't it be accidental, Dad?"

"Hell, it might be. But it just feels . . . weird. We've got an ID on the guy and he was working a scallop boat. Jay Santorski. All of twenty-one."

"And it doesn't make sense to you that a scalloper would simply fall into the water and not come out."

"Does it make sense to you?" John Folger asked.

"Water's pretty cold this time of year."

"Thirty-eight degrees, this morning."

"Hypothermia wouldn't take long."

"Few minutes, maybe. And he was wearing a ski jacket, shoes. All that would drag him down." Her father's voice seemed to gain confidence with every sentence exchanged, as though he had moved from hostile terrain into familiar territory.

He really wants to believe it, Merry thought, *but in his heart he can't.* "Any idea when he went into the water?" she asked him.

"The cold makes it hard to tell, but Fairborn is saying he's probably been dead around eight hours." Dr. John Fairborn volunteered as medical examiner for the Nantucket force. "Coast Guard pulled the body out about eight A.M."

Merry glanced at her watch. Nine-thirty. "So we'll say midnight or thereabouts. You think he fell over the side of a boat or off the wharf?"

"Who'd take a boat out at midnight in December? Besides, there's none floating around empty in the harbor. We did find a bike that may have been Santorski's submerged in the shallows of the Easy Street Basin. I've got Seitz checking for a registration now."

Merry could imagine it—the rusted frame of a beat-up old three-speed, hundreds like them on the island, skittering off the edge of the boat basin near the renovated fishing shanties of Old North Wharf. It was one of the more historic places to call home on Nantucket, almost prestigious. But at this time of year, a lot of the seasonal cottages would be deserted. It was unlikely, she thought, that anyone would have heard a cry for help.

"Did Santorski live at Old North, Dad?"

"Nope. He had a room in a group house out in Surfside."

Where some unfortunate member of the force was probably parading the dripping bike even now, and informing the young man's roommates that he was dead. "You might want to get a crew to dredge the basin for evidence," Merry suggested. "Or maybe send the Pottses down." Tim and Phil Potts, brothers and officers of the Nantucket police, pinch-hit as the force's diving team whenever necessary.

"They're a little busy right now."

So am I, Dad. "Chief," she temporized, "this really could have been an accident. You know how close the Rose & Crown is to Easy Street."

"Yeah," he said doubtfully.

"Santorski would hardly be the first twenty-one-year-old to go drinking on a Thursday night." And even a scalloper—a *drunk* scalloper—might not crawl out of December water once he rode his bike in.

Peter squeezed her shoulder and mouthed, *Taking a shower*. She waved at him distractedly. "Any sign of violence on the body?" she asked her father.

"Not violence, exactly. Abrasions on the wrists and ankles that could have come from a rope—"

"Bound and gagged and sent in on a bicycle? Then where's the rope now?"

"—or they might be nothing more than posthumous cuts from the jetty's rocks. The corpse was first sighted rolling in the channel."

"It should be easy enough to decide which." Merry was thinking out loud. "Postdeath trauma doesn't bleed."

"And predeath abrasions would be washed clean of blood after eight hours in salt water," her father retorted. "I'm no coroner, Meredith. I'll wait to hear from the state crime lab whether the corpse got these cuts from the jetties or . . . something else."

Again, Merry felt John Folger's tension singing down the telephone wire like an electrical shock. She frowned in irritation; it was unlike him to offer only half his mind. "What's really worrying you, Chief?"

For an instant, while he debated what to tell her, she could almost track his evasion in the way he drew breath. "The kid had needle holes in his left arm, Mere. Probably an intravenous drug user, Fairborn says."

Merry closed her eyes and leaned against the kitchen door frame. "This guy was mainlining drugs, and you're wondering whether he died by *accident*? Come on, Dad! He died from his own stupidity!"

"We don't know that," her father objected sternly.

"Why are you even calling me? This is a job for the state crime lab's forensic pathologist. It's not a case of murder."

"Meredith—it might actually be heroin. I'd like you to come home. Look into things a little."

There was a dubious silence.

"Heroin isn't just any drug," he persisted, as though she had suggested otherwise. "If it's being dealt here on Nantucket, among the twenty-something crowd—if this drowning was an overdose—I want to know about it *now*. Before it trickles down to the high school kids."

"And the kindergartners. Right." She paced to the end of the phone cord's length, turned, and paced back. Peter would not be happy if she ruined his plans for the coming week. He might even think she had arranged the summons just to escape his mother. "What do you expect me to do, Dad, before the autopsy report is in? As you said—we don't *know* that this Santorski was shooting heroin."

"Oh, Meredith—" He sounded too weary for nine-thirty in the morning. "Find out who the kid hung out with.

What he was doing the night he died. The usual scut work. You should learn fairly quickly whether this was an isolated incident, or just the tip of the iceberg."

At which point, she would be expected to dry-dock the iceberg. "Are you asking as my dad, or my chief?"

"Both." John paused, and then added grudgingly, "I'd feel better if you were here."

Merry sighed. "It's that important?"

"I wouldn't tear you away from the Masons for anything less."

"Okay. *Okay.* I'll cut short my first vacation in years because some junkie got himself drowned. But why can't Matt Bailey make a fool of himself over this one? It's about his speed."

"Bailey has disappeared."

"*What?*" Merry stood straighter, fingers clenched around the receiver. Her distinguished detective colleague was habitually late for work, but even Matt Bailey took Christmas Stroll somewhat seriously. "Maybe he's still in bed."

"We checked. Before I decided to bother you in the middle of your vacation, I sent Howie Seitz over to his house. Bailey didn't come home last night. His son is frantic."

For the first time in her long acquaintance with Matt Bailey—whom she resented, despised, and rarely acknowledged was even breathing—Merry felt a spark of sympathy. Bailey's son, Ryan, was only twelve. Bailey would never have left the boy without a word. And even though Bailey's disappearance surely had nothing to do with the death by drowning of a drug-addicted scalloper—

"I'm on my way, Dad," she said, and hung up the phone.

"Merry—what are you doing?"

Peter loomed in the doorway of George's guest room, and she could see immediately that he was angry. Which meant that he already had a fair idea of what she was doing. He resembled nothing so much as a hawk—long, thin nose, prominent cheekbones, a sharp brow jutting over cool gray eyes—but when he was angry, the raptor in him fairly screamed aloud. Facing him now, Merry felt like a rodent cowering beneath a shadowed wingspan.

"I'm packing." She reached for a sweater, attempted to fold it, then tossed it in her suitcase. "That was my dad."

"I know. Why are you packing?"

"There's been a—a death. He wants me home right away."

"A death? You mean a murder?"

"He's not sure. It looks like a drowning, actually—"

"Oh, for God's sake, Meredith!"

Peter never shouted. And Peter never called her Meredith. He glanced over his shoulder guiltily, aware of the speed with which argument travels, then eased her door closed behind him.

"The last time I checked," he said in a more reasonable tone, "there were three detectives on the Nantucket force. *Three.* One of whom is presently on vacation and unavailable."

"And another of whom has completely disappeared," Merry retorted. "Matt Bailey has gone AWOL."

"Matt Bailey has been AWOL most of his life."

She tried not to smirk, and failed. "Admittedly. He's a complete chucklehead. But Dad sounded pretty upset."

"You are *not* leaving twelve hours into your vacation. *Our* vacation. I absolutely refuse."

Merry leaned pleadingly across the expanse of down comforter. "Don't bully me, Peter. I've got to go back."

He blew out his breath in exasperation and turned toward the window. The gray eyes roved over the backyard, where Georgiana's two boys were engaged in constructing a snow fort. Peter barely saw them, Merry knew. He was marshaling his arguments.

"Where's Fred McIlhenney?"

Fred McIlhenney was the force's third detective—and like Bailey, technically senior to Merry. Unlike Bailey, he had earned the respect of the entire force.

"Fred's on loan to the DA's office in Barnstable through March. You know that, Peter. Or at least, I've mentioned it before. I suppose there's a possibility you weren't listening to me." The words came out more sharply than she had intended, and when Peter looked at her, she found she could not meet his eyes.

"Am I in the habit of ignoring you?"

Merry shrugged. "When I talk about my work—yes."

He sat down on the edge of the bed and gripped her wrist. She shook him off angrily and tipped a collection of mismatched socks into the lid of her suitcase.

"I'm the only one who *does* listen to you anymore, Merry. Everyone else has had enough."

She zipped the bag closed and pulled it off the bed. It dropped like a lead weight directly on Peter's foot. He yelped in outrage.

"Oh, God, Peter—I'm really sorry." She sank to his side. "Are you okay?"

"I'm just fine," he said, cradling his instep and glaring at her. "Aside from the fact that you never seem to see me anymore, I'm just great."

"That was an accident."

"I'm not talking about my foot. I'm talking about—everything."

"Everything?"

"Oh, Merry—" He stroked one hand gently along the curve of her blond head, then pulled her against him. "I've spent the past year trying to get your mind *off* your work, at the urging of everyone who cares about you. You've been walking around in a fog. Whether it's the stress of the trial—or something worse—I can't begin to say."

"That's ridiculous." She reared away from him stiffly. "If you can't handle my job, Peter, you should have said so long ago."

The patent unfairness of this was obvious to them both.

Peter regarded her silently, a crooked smile hovering on his lips. "All right. We'll call that a different topic. Let's talk about your vacation right now. So what if McIlhenney and Bailey are out of commission? There must be someone who can cover for you, Merry. The Nantucket force shouldn't fall apart every time you leave the island. You're good, but you're not that good."

"I didn't say that I was," she shot back, stung. "I said that my father—my *chief*—ordered me to return to work, okay?"

"You're actually trying to tell me you had no choice?"

"Of course I didn't! Do you think I *want* to ruin our vacation?"

The gray eyes met hers without mercy or quarter. Then he said, "Yes, Merry. I do."

"What does that mean?" She gripped the suitcase and hauled it, staggering, to the door.

Peter threw up his hands. "It means you've resisted meeting my family for months. You refuse even to *talk* about a wedding date, much less make any plans. And now that I've finally got you to Greenwich, you're packed and leaving twelve hours after you arrive. A far stupider guy would have figured this out long ago, Merry. You don't want to marry me."

Heat flooded her face and her breath came suddenly short, as though throttled by a blow. "*Peter.* Never think that. It's just . . . it's been such a terrible year."

"I suppose it has been." Merry saw the pain in his face before it faded behind a protective mask. "For both of us. You've been struggling with your . . . demons . . . and I've been trying to pretend that they don't sleep in our bed and eat away at our dreams. But they do, Merry. They do. And it's time to talk about it."

"You don't understand," she attempted helplessly.

"I understand more than you know." He took her firmly by the shoulders, his gaze intent. "I understand that you feel responsible for too many deaths, and that even my love can't absolve you. I wish that it could. You did all that was humanly possible last spring, and no one could have done more. But what I think or say doesn't count. Only John Folger, as your boss and your dad, can let you off that hook."

"Maybe it's not his job." She had meant to say it lightly, but the words were strangled and bitter.

Peter released her. "You have too much ability to need his good opinion quite so much, Merry. There's more to life than running errands for your father."

"I don't run errands!"

He laughed harshly. "No—you single-handedly manage every burglary, arson, and homicide on Nantucket Island. You're at John's beck and call, regardless of how little he appreciates it, or how much it costs you. Well, it's cost us both, this time. And I'm not going to take it quietly."

There was no hint of refuge in the gray eyes, nothing but ice when Peter looked at her; and she understood suddenly how much she had worn him down. She managed a smile.

"I think you're exaggerating just a bit—"

"What a relief to hear your father's voice this morning," he continued, as though she had never spoken. "He gave you a reason to leave. You've been looking for one for months. Haven't you?"

Chapter Three

It would have been nice, Merry thought callously, if Jay Santorski had died a day earlier. Then she could have gone straight back to Nantucket after her depositions in Boston, and never have known the depth of dislike it was possible to feel for Peter's mother. It was hardly Julia Mason's fault, of course, that a dead scalloper had divided Merry from Peter; but Julia exulted so much in the sudden constraint between them that Merry might almost have suspected her of murder.

"How very unfortunate," Julia said with grateful insincerity when Merry ventured downstairs to explain that she was leaving. "And must you go, too, Peter? It hardly seems necessary."

"No," he said briefly, "I'm going on to New York. I've made too many commitments to cancel the trip now."

"Commitments?" Merry's voice was cool and skeptical. "Or reservations?"

"Then we'll have you all to ourselves for a few days!" Julia exclaimed brightly. "Such fun! It will be like old times!"

And which old times were those? Merry wondered. When Julia's favorite son, Rusty, was destroying his father's business and seducing Peter's ex-fiancée, she of the hydrangea-tubbed tent poles and angelic white organza? Or the time when Rusty had fled under indictment to Brazil? Or when he was finally murdered, and Peter suspected of the crime?

But Julia seemed entirely free of unpleasant memories. The past had cast a golden haze over even the traitorous Alison Miller, who would never have passed up New York for the claims of duty. It was *Alison this*, and *Alison that*, for the entire hour remaining to Merry in the bosom of her future in-laws; and it was with very little regret that she shook off the elegant dust of Round Hill, and headed toward La Guardia.

It was a little before noon, but the sky was so lowering it might have been dusk. Gusts of wind scattered handfuls of rain across the windshield. The rawness of the day had invaded the car's interior, where a chill silence predominated, rife with uncomfortable thoughts. Merry kept her eyes fixed on the lower rim of the passenger side mirror, studying the red-painted flank of Peter's Range Rover as though it were the latest Grisham thriller, while Peter scowled at the highway and doggedly tailgated carpooling housewives.

Was she resisting marriage, as he claimed? Could she possibly prefer a life of dutiful service on the force, to a life with Peter Mason?

Her mind shied away from that gulf, and attempted an easier leap.

Was she thrilled to be free of Peter's mother? Yes. Would she have left Greenwich if her father hadn't called? No. Should she have argued the Chief out of ruining her vacation?

Here she balked. There were only unpleasant answers, after all. Peter had touched bone when he said she was desperate for her father's good opinion. It was true.

She could never say how much John Folger respected or valued her. At most, Merry thought, she was a convenient substitute for the son her father had lost to Viet Nam. Billy was frozen forever in the amber of death, an eighteen-year-old flush with promise and sacrifice. She might step into her brother's job, but never into his place in her father's heart.

Work, then, had become her touchstone. She had fought for the right to handle every one of her cases; and when she successfully closed them, she won something more than justice—she had proof of her father's good opinion clutched tightly in her hands.

John Folger had almost assigned her first homicide investigation to Matt Bailey. If he had, Merry might never have met Peter. It was his brother, Rusty, who had lain drowned in the Mason Farms cranberry bog four years ago, as much a burden in death as he had been in life. Then the following year, her childhood friend Del Duarte had been brutally murdered. The Chief actually assigned that one to Bailey, and put Merry on administrative leave. She had defied him and found the killer. It was only natural, Merry thought, that John Folger had asked her to investigate the death of Elizabeth Osborne last spring. She had spent years destroying her father's prejudices and defenses, his fear of favoritism, and his desire to protect.

And then her luck had run out.

Afterward, when the brutal reckoning came fully home, and her sleep was riddled with nightmares, Merry had almost resigned from the force. Why she continued to report for work, and handle the endless stream of minor thefts, petty larcenies, and domestic disputes that made up the island's caseload—the errand-running, as Peter put it—was a question she was afraid to ask. It might broach the subject of failure.

John Folger had every reason to criticize her roundly for the Osborne fiasco; he might even have requested her badge. That he did neither, she thought, was a testament to his love for his daughter.

It said nothing whatsoever about his professional opinion of her.

Merry shifted her gaze from the mirror rim to Peter's profile. His brows were knit and his jaw was clenched. A muscle twitched along his cheekbone like a second heartbeat.

"I'm sorry," she said again.

"I'm sorry, too." His eyes never left the road. "But neither of us is sorry enough to back down. There are choices, Merry, and you've made one of them."

"Peter—"

"You realize you're never going to get over there this afternoon, don't you?"

"Christmas Stroll." Merry uttered the words like an imprecation. She had completely forgotten what the holiday weekend would mean for travel. She had intended to catch the New York–Boston shuttle, and connect to a commuter flight for Nantucket—but the little prop planes seated only ten people. They would be booked solid for the Stroll.

"Never mind that," Peter said brutally. "There's a nor'easter coming. I can barely keep the car on the road."

And indeed, the heavy recreational vehicle was shuddering in the crosswind sweeping the highway. As she watched, the steering wheel jumped in Peter's hands.

"If I can't fly standby," Merry attempted, "I can always rent a car at Logan and drive to Hyannis. Then I could catch the ferry."

"Good. You can sail by the scene of the crime. I know how you love to reenact these things."

"Don't be petty, Peter. It doesn't suit you."

He sighed, looked harassed, and then braked suddenly to avoid a crawling truck. "I can't help it, Merry. I've been worried about you for months. And now you're running away again."

"Let's just . . . not talk about it, okay?" Her face ached with the effort of looking normal.

"If I could move you forcibly off-island, I would. Maybe then you'd put your nightmares behind you."

"You would never leave Nantucket, Peter. It's your home."

"*You* are my home, love. Everything else is just so much landscape."

It was almost a plea for peace between them.

"I wish that I could have stayed," she said, and felt the force of her lie like an inner violence. "But, Peter—whatever you think of my father—Dad would never have asked me to come back if it weren't very serious. We could be talking about heroin."

"I can't believe heroin has come to Nantucket."

"Why? Are we somehow immune?"

"Heroin is just so—"

"Deadly," Merry supplied. "I know."

"So *glamorous*," he countered. "It's too urban, too New York. Supermodels and rock stars. It's as though the dealers have confused Nantucket with the Vineyard."

"Or New Bedford." She glanced sideways, and saw that the shot had gone home. They had driven through New Bedford only the day before. Merry's trip down memory lane, on the way to Peter's.

It was the place where she had spent her first tour out of the police academy, a once-prosperous seaport brought low by factory closings and the scarcity of fish. Merry had taken Peter to her old neighborhood, where both she and his foreman, Rafe da Silva, had once lived. It was a working-class street, filled with the families of Portuguese fishermen and newer immigrants from Southeast Asia, more derelict now than it had been eight years ago. On one corner was a Vietnamese restaurant; on the other stood Martha Ligueira's Laundry. They'd had spring rolls at a dimly lit table and then crossed the street to look for Martha.

The small, strained woman had remembered Merry, and her face lost some of its sadness when the detective walked through the door. Martha threw her arms wide and enveloped Merry in a rocking hug, with exclamations of surprise and joy. She wiped her hand on her cardigan before shaking Peter's, and assessed him thoroughly from shrewd blue eyes. Merry inquired after her grandchildren. Martha asked after Rafe. And then they began to swap memories and names.

Peter had listened at first, a polite smile on his face, but then the tide of reminiscence had cast him adrift. He wandered idly about the laundry room amid the vibration of the rolling dryers, the shuddering gait of an unbalanced washer. And came to rest before a bulletin board overflowing with newsprint.

Merry joined him there, her hand sliding under his elbow. It was then she saw that every column was an obituary.

The deaths they detailed had an eerie sameness—a man or woman in the mid-thirties, gone "suddenly," or "after a long illness." As she scanned the boardful of faces, Merry felt the hair rise slowly along the back of her neck. She had known at least half of these people.

"It's the needles," Martha said quietly at her side. "There's so many of them gone now, you wouldn't believe."

"Heroin?"

"Those are the 'sudden' ones. 'After a long illness' means AIDS. But it's the needle that gets them all, in the end."

Merry and Peter hadn't lingered very long with Martha after that. She offered coffee, and they refused, pleading traffic and the hours of travel still ahead. There was little of comfort they could tell her, after all; Martha was fixed in the midst of a battle zone, with her grandchildren growing up beside her. Merry had uttered false promises of a longer visit, sometime soon, and offered her home if Martha ever came to the island—

Peter touched her knee lightly now, the first sign of affection he had shown in hours. "Nantucket is hardly New Bedford. I can't help thinking that drugs are a summer-people problem. Something to do with free time and boredom."

"But that's where you're wrong. When we roll up a drug network—and the Nantucket force manages to bust somebody nearly every year—it's the same sort of people over and over again. *Islanders.* The ones who have no choice but to stay, while the wealthy and privileged follow the sun." She said this carefully—Peter himself was wealthy and privileged, and might hear her words as criticism. "The only difference between our economy and New Bedford's, really, is tourism. It keeps us swimming in revenue for four months of the year. But the other eight, when jobs are scarce and money's tight, people can give way to despair."

"You've never found a heroin ring on-island before," he objected.

"No. It's usually pot or cocaine. This is ten times worse. Which is why I'm going home."

"Oh, is that why?" Peter downshifted for the off-ramp, his mouth set in a thin line. "What a relief. I thought it was to win your father's good opinion. It'll always mean more to you than mine."

One of the things Merry found most annoying about Peter, she realized as she battled her way down the rain-lashed belly of Route 6, was that his predictions had a nasty way of coming true. By the time she had caught the shuttle into Boston, learned she would have to wait five hours to fly standby to Nantucket, rented a car, and sped down Highway 93, it was well past three o'clock. The two forty-five Steamship Authority ferry was a distant memory. The nor'easter had settled in for the weekend over New England. Her rental car shook in the frigid gusts of rain, traffic crawled, and whole hours ticked by without a significant change in the view beyond her streaming windshield.

It was now five P.M., and she was in danger of missing the high-speed Hy-Line boat at five-thirty. (These usually ran exclusively during the summer season, but had been pulled back into service for the Christmas Stroll weekend.) Merry screamed like a maniac at the sea of automobiles clogging the road before her, cut right onto the shoulder, and barreled toward the Hyannis exit. Just *watch* anybody try to stop her. She had her badge, and for once she was prepared to abuse it.

She arrived at the Hyannis Airport with half an hour to spare—just time enough to return the rental car and grab a taxi for the Hy-Line ferry. But when her taxi pulled up to the Ocean Street dock, Merry discovered that the high-speed boat was canceled. So was every other type of surface conveyance between the mainland and Nantucket. Peter's nor'easter buffeted the Cape and islands with such fury that thousands of hopeful Christmas Strollers were stranded on the docks. Captain Ted Moran's M/V *Eagle*, the ferry that discovered Jay Santorski's corpse, had been the last boat of the day.

Merry did not even bother to tear her hair or curse

aloud, kick stray dogs or mutter darkly at complete strangers. The day's bad luck was so firmly entrenched that all form of protest seemed futile. She merely picked up her bag and stood in line with the hordes awaiting the next available taxi, intent upon the airport and a standby seat, keenly aware that somewhere Peter was probably laughing.

There were times, John Folger thought, when he hated what he did for a living—when the necessity of simply going on, headfirst into the unpleasantness of other people's lives, was too much for his soul to bear. Right now he wanted nothing more than to be strapped into the passenger seat of an airplane, headed into daylight, a magazine in his lap and someone else at the controls.

His worst days had followed hard on Anne Folger's suicide, over twenty years ago. There had been months of remoteness, of self-loathing and recrimination. A turning away from the depth of his own pain. A denial of it, even, and of all that Anne had meant. What he felt now was nothing like the desperate wounding of his wife's taking off; but the edge of something similar—a chill hard light just beyond the range of sight—sat heavily on his heart.

Such times were few and far between, of course. John Folger was a fortunate man, and wise enough to recognize it. If he carried any scar from Anne's death, it was perhaps a desire to run from what was terrible.

He felt it aching now as he studied the mess on Matt Bailey's desk.

It was after five o'clock, and the stormy December dusk had already fallen around the town. It seeped into Bailey's office like smoke. On the verge of lighting the desk lamp, John Folger lingered a moment in the rain-filled twilight, staring through the streaming station window. The nor'easter was lifting elm branches, brightly strung with lights, and flinging them to the cobblestones; Christmas trees bravely stationed along the length of Main Street were swaying in the gale. The brick sidewalks were unnaturally bereft of holiday crowds, and in the back of his mind, John wondered how much of a hit the shopkeepers were taking. The few Strollers who had arrived before the storm's full fury were now huddled head-down against the sleet pelting the island. Their clothes threw bright splashes of red and green and blue against the dark canvas of the street. Despite the wind, John caught a burst of laughter. For these people, even the storm was festive. They knew they were proof against it, and that a roaring fire awaited them at bedtime. The morning would probably dawn a little brighter; and if it didn't—well, rain was always an excuse to go shopping. They had no unanswered questions or nagging doubts, no difficult choices beyond the restaurant menu.

The wind howled like a cat at the second-story windows. The old brick police station shuddered once and subsided.

John snapped on the light. It fell, sharp and uncompromising, on the welter of papers. *All our sins remembered,* he thought. *All our faults revealed.* What business did he have throwing Merry into it? Why not leave his daughter comfortably in Peter Mason's care, high and dry on the mainland? Cowardice. That denial, again. The weakness of running away.

"I'm sorry, Anne," he muttered, and began to sort through Bailey's trash.

Chapter Four

At nine o'clock that evening, Merry's Island Air flight out of Hyannis finally touched down in Tom Nevers field. She crawled from the body of the plane, bruised and thankful, and sank in a heap on the wet tarmac. Her legs were completely nerveless, her entire body trembled. A fellow passenger kissed the ground; another stood over a garbage can and vomited.

For Merry, the twenty-minute flight had been nothing short of an encounter with her God. The plane had bucked, plummeted, shuddered, and careened through the hurricane-force winds, a fragile bird blown wildly off course, and even seat belts had seemed futile. What Merry wanted was a full body harness.

For once, she decided, Island Air's lack of in-flight catering was not such a bad thing. Rather than dulling the tide of fear washing through the cabin, alcohol would only have inflamed hysteria—and tonight, hysteria had needed no help. The man directly behind Merry had burst into a frantic pleading somewhere over the Sound, promising never to cheat on his wife again; and his wife, one seat to the rear, had not been amused. All Merry could think was that Matt Bailey was somehow responsible for her imminent death, and that she would never forgive him; and that if she died, Peter would never forgive himself. The latter thought should have comforted her. Instead, it made her feel guilty.

So she made a bargain with God. If she landed safely on Nantucket, she would never leave Peter without a backward glance or a kind word.

In fact, she would never leave Peter again.

"Jay's mom says he didn't use drugs."

Patrolman Howie Seitz had actually met Merry's plane, and after dragging her to his car, had produced a thermos filled with hot buttered rum and ordered her to drink it. He was sitting now in her living room, a box of takeout balanced on one knee.

"Jay?" Merry looked up from the case file Howie had brought over from the station, her black brows furrowing. "So we're on a first-name basis with the deceased."

"Actually—now that you mention it—yeah. I knew him. That's why the Chief asked me to call his mom."

Jay Santorski's death had changed the tenor of Howie's weekend. He had expected to spend it walking a beat from Main Street to Broad. Instead, Chief Folger had appointed Howie as his personal errand boy, and the patrolman had battled snarled roads, foul weather, and irritable islanders for hours in pursuit of the dead scalloper's history. In the process, Howie had discovered the true meaning of Christmas Stroll—he was better off walking than trying to navigate the island. Now, fourteen hours after he'd reported for duty, he was finally eating a real meal.

And trying to banish the memory of Jay's corpse lying ravaged and mute on the Coast Guard boat ramp. Jay was three years younger than Howie. Nobody that age should die.

"I didn't know you hung with scallopers," Merry said.

"I don't, really."

"How'd you meet him then?"

Howie felt the constriction in his throat ease at the question, and swallowed a mouthful of hamburger. "Jay was Owen Harley's mate. You know Owen."

"Never heard of him."

"I thought you knew everyone, Mere. Harley plays tenor sax in a band I mess around with. I met Jay through him."

"A band? *You,* Seitz? Don't tell me you're developing character."

"Well—a personality, at least." He picked at a forkful of cottage fries. The odors of grease and carbonized protein rose uninvitingly in the air. "We don't get much time to practice, or anything, and we only play Open Mike nights at the Rose & Crown—"

"What do you play?"

"Swing." Sudden embarrassment. It was Howie, after all, who had introduced the detective to Seattle grunge.

Merry patted his hand maternally. "I think that's great, Seitz. By summer, you'll be headlining, and you'll leave this sordid island of murder and mayhem far behind. So tell me what you thought of Jay Santorski."

"I liked him a lot." Howie set his food to one side and reached for a napkin. "He was smart without being stuck on himself, and he cared about what he did."

"Scalloping?"

"That, and the harbor in general. What else?" Howie rarely analyzed the people he met; he either liked them or didn't, and saw or avoided them accordingly. "Jay didn't brag. He didn't try to hit on a lot of women. He was a good athlete—I shot hoops with him once or twice. And he never let his partying get out of hand. He was the kind of guy you gave the keys to after a late night."

"So how'd he end up dead in the harbor?"

Howie shrugged. "Dumb fucking luck."

She was silent at this—not, he thought, because his profanity had shocked her, but because it echoed the assumptions in her mind. "Did you see the corpse?" she asked.

"Yeah. I had no choice. The Chief called over to the station from Brant Point and wanted Clarence and the Doc." Clarence was the Nantucket force's crime scene chief, their resident forensics expert. The Doc was John Fairborn, the medical examiner. "Clarence wasn't in yet, so I left him a message, took the evidence bag, and met the Doc at the Coast Guard station."

"Exactly what I would have done."

Howie took the tacit compliment in stride. "I won't go into what Jay looked like. It's not important, except for the needle marks."

Merry's green gaze sharpened as she looked at Howie over her hot buttered rum. "Ever notice them before, Seitz?"

"No. And I think I would have noticed."

"They must have been dramatic enough for the Chief to have called in Clarence." Merry said it reasonably.

"I don't think your dad had even seen them. Jay's clothes weren't disturbed at all when I got there." Howie shoved his hand through his ragged curls. "I don't know what made the Chief think it was anything other than a straightforward drowning. But maybe he would have called Clarence and the Doc anyway. Just to be certain. Your dad always goes by the book."

"Could be," the detective conceded.

"When Dr. John and I got there, we helped the Chief look for some identification. I found Jay's wallet in his back pocket, where it should have been—so he wasn't held up for his cash . . ."

". . . and then hit over the head with his bicycle and tossed in the water," Merry finished. "I didn't think so."

"Anyway, that's when we took off his coat, so the Doc could examine him better. Your dad wanted to be sure there were no marks of violence."

"What else was Santorski wearing?"

"Mayhew House waiter's uniform—he had a part-time job at Ezra's. Black dress shoes—laced, they stayed on his feet. Dark blue socks, black pants, black vest, white oxford cloth shirt. The sleeves were rolled up to the elbow."

"Helpfully revealing the aforementioned needle marks."

Howie nodded. "On just one arm, the left, so I guess he was right-handed. It would make sense, wouldn't it?" He pulled up his sleeve and stroked the pale flesh of his inner elbow. One violent green shadow of a vein pulsed and relaxed. "But I gotta say, Detective, there weren't a whole lot of marks. If Jay had a habit, he didn't have it very long."

"You're not convinced."

"Neither is his mom."

"Of course his mom says he never used drugs," Merry retorted impatiently. "What is she supposed to say?"

"She's a nurse, Mere. I think she would have noticed."

Merry registered this without comment. "When did she last see him?"

"Thanksgiving."

"You mean—last weekend?"

Howie nodded. "He went back to Boston for the holiday. Saw friends from college. Did a little shopping. Had a great time, she said."

"No sign of addiction? Chills, vomiting, wild mood swings?"

"Not according to Mom."

"The poor woman." Merry rested her feet on her coffee table and flipped open Santorski's file. "Heartbroken?"

Howie shrugged, looked away. "I guess. Yeah. He was her only child. She wanted to know when we'd release the body for burial, and I couldn't tell her."

"Father?"

"None that came up."

Merry settled down to skim Howie's cursory notes. He could have recited them from memory. *Deceased born 10/19/75 and raised in Quincy, Massachusetts, only son of Mary Anne Simpson, a registered nurse. Deceased attended Catholic grade schools, public high. Took leave of absence from Harvard U. in 1996 following junior year.*

Merry looked up from the file. "Why would a Harvard boy drop out of college to go scalloping?"

"Guess he liked boats better than homework."

Deceased moved to Nantucket in July 1996. Past two months worked days as scalloper, nights as waiter at Ezra Mayhew House. Lived in group house at 110 Pilot Whale Drive, Surfside. Roommates: Dave Haddenfield, 25, assistant football coach, Nantucket High; Dr. Barry Cohen, 28, resident, Nantucket Cottage Hospital; Sue Morningstar, 24, editorial staff, the Inquirer & Mirror.

Merry waved the file folder. "Did you know any of these roommates?"

"Just to say hi to. I met 'em once, when Jay had us over to practice at his house. The doctor came home early and threw us out."

"Have you talked to any of them yet?"

"All of them. I woke the doctor—Cohen—this morning when I took the bike out to Surfside. He wasn't happy about it, and he said he hadn't seen Jay in days. But he identified the bike."

"I suppose that confirms where Santorski went into the water, at least. Anything obviously wrong with the bike?"

"The brakes are lousy, but it's a thirty-year-old Raleigh three-speed, Mere, and a little rust shouldn't be surprising. Clarence called in a technician from Olde's Bicycles to look the thing over. He said it was basically sound. And I rode it around the block a few times."

"Did you wear gloves?"

"Yes. And the bike's already been dusted for fingerprints. Couple of different sets on them, one of them Jay's."

Merry flipped back through the file. "Did the Chief send a dredging team to the Easy Street Basin, Seitz?"

"Not that I heard."

She muttered something under her breath; it might have been an oath. "Okay. Back to the roommates. How did this Cohen guy take the tragic news?"

Howie shrugged. "Stoically. I guess doctors are used to death."

"Or think it no longer applies to them. What about the rest of the house?"

"The football coach—Dave—just looked amazed. He kept saying that it wasn't possible."

"Where was he around midnight?"

"At his girlfriend's." Howie anticipated Merry's next question and added, "I called. She says he was there."

"And the reporter?"

"Sue." Howie's brow cleared. He liked Sue Morningstar, and he knew that Jay had liked her, too. "She was pretty devastated, I'm afraid. Almost hysterical. She spent last night at home, watching some Jane Austen movie. Bathrobe and slippers until bedtime."

"But no witnesses."

"Not unless you count Emma Thompson."

"I doubt she pushed Jay and his bike into the harbor just to get a story," Merry said thoughtfully, "but you never know. If he *was* pushed. If there *is* any malice aforethought outside my father's head."

"Any what?"

"Never mind. Did Sue know where Jay was last night?"

"She said he was working at Ezra's, same as always."

"And what does Ezra's say?"

Howie wiped his mouth and crumpled the napkin. "Actually, this is where it gets a little interesting. Jay was sent home early because it was a slow night. He was out the door by ten."

"Time enough to have a few drinks—or shoot up—somewhere in town," the detective mused. "Did anyone from the restaurant notice anything odd about Jay's behavior?"

"The dining-room manager wasn't entirely surprised he'd gotten into trouble."

Merry's eyebrows lifted. "Did he know the guy was using needles?"

"*She.* A Miss Laurie Hopfnagel. She never said anything about drug use—but to be honest, Mere, the Chief asked me to keep that part of the business quiet until we have the autopsy results."

"Cautious of him," Merry commented. "I guess Dad's learning discretion in his old age. Why did Hopfnagel dislike Santorski?"

Howie took a sip of his iced tea before answering. "She thinks he was stealing from his coworkers."

"Stealing what, exactly?"

"Tips. From their tables. Hopfnagel says she was planning to give Jay the boot once Christmas Stroll was over."

Merry laughed abruptly. "Well, he denied her the pleasure. What do you think, Seitz? Was Santorski the type to steal from his friends?"

"No. Why would he? He worked two jobs. And he never seemed hard up." With a ready source of cash at the Ezra Mayhew House, Howie thought belatedly, why should he? It was a point Merry Folger was not likely to miss. But her expression never changed as she considered his words.

"Was Hopfnagel plausible?"

"Plausible enough. But I didn't like her."

"Sorry, Seitz. Personal attraction means nothing in a court of law. Maybe Jay needed some extra cash to pay for his habit. A small bag of heroin sells for about twenty dollars. A night's tips would more than cover it."

"If he *had* a habit."

She looked at Howie searchingly. "You're really not convinced?"

"It'll take an autopsy report to change my mind."

Merry set his report carefully on the coffee table, as though it had nothing more to reveal. "If Dad swore you to silence on the subject of drugs, I suppose you didn't query Jay's roommates about them either."

"The only person I asked about illegal drug use was Jay's mom."

"With the Chief's blessing?"

Howie reddened. "Without it, actually. I had to ask, Mere. I figured she'd know."

"Most parents never do."

"Jay loved his mom. He kept her picture in his room."

"Seitz—" Merry began, but the patrolman hurried past her words.

"Not all drug injections are illegal, Mere. Maybe Jay had a legitimate health problem."

"Did you ask his doctor-roommate?"

"Cohen said he thought Jay was as healthy as a horse. But he really didn't know much about him, if you ask me. Guy lives at Cottage Hospital most of the time."

"I suppose Santorski could have had a different doctor on-island."

"Or maybe he saw one while he was home last weekend."

"Did his mother say so?"

"No."

"Although he told her everything immediately, as evidenced by the picture he kept in his room," Merry shot back sharply. "Look, Seitz—it's always hard to think the worst of a friend. But maybe Jay was experimenting with something he'd never done before. Maybe his luck ran out, and he used too much, and died before he could get help. Overdoses are commonplace. There's so much heroin coming out of Turkey these days, the dealers don't even bother to cut it very much. The street dose is far too pure."

Howie was from a generation that had put heroin back on the map. He'd seen the fashion magazines glorifying emaciated girls, their eyes ringed in black; he'd gone to school in the city that dealt in drugs daily; and he was trained as a cop. But he would never feel as conversant with drug culture as Merry sounded now. "Where'd you learn about all this?" he asked her curiously.

"Heroin was the drug of choice in New Bedford, where I did my rookie tour. I logged a lot of hours busting dealers and the kids they employed to push the stuff. It's only gotten worse since I left." Her clipped words didn't invite much comment; and Howie felt suddenly awkward. Too aware of his relative youth.

"I guess that's why your dad wanted you home today," he attempted.

Merry's eyes came up to his. She smiled faintly. "God knows why the Chief bothers with any of us, Seitz. But Jay Santorski wasn't from New Bed. He was a Harvard boy dabbling in risk—*if* he had heroin in his veins when he went into the Easy Street Basin. What was he doing here, anyway? And why did this Owen Harley hire him? I'd have thought an established scalloper would prefer a seasoned mate."

"I never thought to ask. I know that sounds stupid—"

"Then I will. Are you on duty tomorrow, Seitz?"

"I am now."

"Good. Let's make a list."

Howie reached for his notebook obediently.

"I want to see the body, first thing. It hasn't been sent off-island yet?"

"In this weather?" Howie grinned, remembering the color of Merry's face as she extricated herself from the Island Air plane. She had already forgotten it.

"While I'm out at the hospital, I want the Pottses diving in the basin. Or at the very least, a couple of scallopers dredging the bottom. Dad should have arranged for that this morning."

"*Weather,*" Howie whistled under his breath.

"Did you search Santorski's room?"

He looked at her over the edge of his notebook. "I sealed it. Thought you'd want to search it yourself."

"We'll have to hope the housemates respect police barriers. I might as well interrogate them while I'm out in Surfside. And Owen Harley, of course."

"Want me to come?"

"I'd rather you supervised the dredging. And asked the residents of Old North whether they heard or saw anything unusual last night."

Howie wrote these instructions down, although that hardly seemed necessary, and closed his notebook with care. "One more thing about Owen Harley, Mere. It's in the report, but I don't think you got to it."

"Shoot."

"Harley feels—responsible, I guess."

"For Jay?"

"For his death. Harley lives on Old North Wharf. Jay was probably going to see him when he fell into the water."

Chapter Five

Merry sat quietly for perhaps a quarter hour after Howie Seitz had left, nursing the last of the buttered rum. Her relief at being once more in the comfortable arms of her own living room was exquisite; she wanted nothing so much as to slip into a viciously hot bath and then into bed. The ease of the moment was transitory, however; she could feel the sharp edge of unrest slicing just beyond conscious thought. What lurked there, exactly? Awareness of Peter's absence? The shadow of the morning's ugliness, and a fear of all it presaged? Or the death of the young scalloper, whom she had dismissed out of hand as a drug user like so many others—lost, foolish, hell-bent on self-destruction. But nothing Seitz had said tonight could really confirm those assumptions. Jay Santorski refused to lie down and play a statistic. Perhaps *this* was the cause of her father's palpable discomfort over the phone; he could not pigeonhole the death.

Then why hadn't the Chief ordered the basin dredged? And why the embargo on intravenous drugs—a desire to speak well of the dead until forced to do otherwise?

Why exactly had John Folger called her home?

At that thought, the last shred of transitory comfort dissipated and was gone.

Merry pulled on a sweater and a rain slicker and forced herself out into the gale that was Fair Street. Her garage apartment was just a few blocks from the old Folger house on Tattle Court, but tonight the narrow stretch of macadam, with its sodden piles of leaves and streaming gutters, was endless and lonely. Majestic old Federal houses lined both sides of the street, exquisite in white-painted clapboard and moss-rimmed shingles; most of them looked blankly into the middle distance as she passed, their windows dark. Owned by summer people who had failed to make it back for Christmas Stroll, Merry thought; and missed Peter with every atom of her being.

Tattle Court, at least, was ablaze with light. Someone—Ralph Waldo, probably—had hung a fir wreath on the door. The raw cold turned the acidic smell of evergreen more piercing. Merry pressed the bell and waited.

"Meredith Abiah!" Ralph Waldo cried as he flung open the door. "You're just in time for dessert." He peered over her head into the rain-lashed darkness, hoping for a glimpse of Peter, then ushered her inside.

"I thought you two would be done with food hours ago," she said, shrugging off her coat. "Where's Dad?"

"Phone call. He'll be down in a minute. I'm surprised to see you, my dear. I thought you'd be stranded in Boston."

"I should have been. It's no exaggeration, Ralph, to say I nearly died tonight. One woman on my flight was actually treated for lacerations, the turbulence was so bad. We were bouncing around like eggs in a carton."

Her grandfather never wasted time on exclamation. "Need a drink?"

She shook her head, and followed him into the kitchen. "Seitz took care of me. But I'd love some dessert."

"It's Nantucket cranberry pie."

"Perfect."

"Your father will be glad you came."

"You mean I had a choice?"

Ralph understood, and grinned. "Sorry about your vacation. Has young Peter retired in a funk to the farm?"

"Peter has retired into deepest Greenwich." There it was again—a faint anxiety snarling her entrails. "If he had a ring to return I'm sure it would be in my possession right now."

"Bosh," Ralph said comfortably, and reached for his coffeepot.

Merry threw herself into a kitchen chair and glanced around the familiar walls. Very little had changed at Tattle Court since her departure last spring, but she could see that the house was growing dingy. It might only be an illusion heightened by her present mood and the early December dark; or then again, it might be the bald truth. Her father had never spared much time for the place, and Ralph's attention was given over wholly to his garden. On one kitchen counter alone sat a pile of unsorted socks, last week's supply of mail-order catalogues in imminent danger of sliding to the floor, a crumpled box of cat food, three burnt-out lightbulbs, a packet of California poppy seeds, and the remains of a ham sandwich. What her grandmother Sylvie would have done at the sight of it, Merry shuddered to think.

Her mother, on the other hand, would hardly have noticed.

Tabitha, the calico cat, twined like a ghost around Merry's right ankle and mewed soundlessly. She reached for the warm weight of fur and buried her nose in Tabitha's neck, imagining her father growing older, with or without Ralph, and the house falling down quietly around him. Merry stroked the cat's chin and wished, suddenly, for an outside influence. A nice sort of woman who could take care of both the Folger men. Another Sylvie—only her father's age, this time.

"Hello, Meredith," he said, interrupting her thoughts. He bent to kiss her cheek. "Thank you for coming home. I'm sorry it was necessary."

Tabitha pounced from Merry's lap to the floor and skittered into the shadows of the empty dining room.

"*Necessary?*" Merry said, brushing a few stray hairs from her sweater. "What a definite word. I've never thought of myself as necessary. Useful, perhaps; convenient, sometimes—but the *without which, nothing*, in your life? I'm shocked, Dad. I thought you were sufficient unto yourself."

"You still have your sense of humor. That's something," he replied, and inhaled the scent of Ralph Waldo's coffee. "That's decaf, I hope."

"Of course it is." Ralph poured him a mugful. "You have enough on your mind to murder sleep tonight, son, without the java jitters."

"What an original mangling of Shakespeare, Ralph." Merry was amused, but her father appeared unmoved.

He cocked an eyebrow at her over the rim of his mug. "You abandon poor Peter tonight?"

"I was denied the privilege. Peter has abandoned *me*." She had intended the words to sound carefree or, at the worst, self-mocking; but they came out forlorn.

"Whoops." John took a swig of coffee. "Sorry."

"No, you're not." Merry reached for the plates and pie forks and dealt them out like cards around the table. "You're absolutely complacent. I might almost think you summoned me home out of sheer loneliness."

"But I'll never give you the satisfaction of knowing, will I?"

"Among other things. Why exactly *am* I home, Dad?"

"Because a scalloper fell into the boat basin last night."

"Did he? Is that what you think happened—or what you *hope* happened?"

"You'd prefer something worse?"

"I'd like to think I came home for a reason. A routine drowning is something Seitz could have handled." She studied her father acutely. "Howie says you hadn't even seen the needle marks when you called the station for evidence collection. What raised your hackles, Dad? Did you know this guy?"

"Of course not," he said quickly. "I just thought the death was . . . suspicious."

Across the room at the sink, Ralph Waldo cleared his throat ferociously. The set of his back and shoulders screamed skepticism.

"I'd be inclined to call in Fairborn and Clarence at any unexplained death." John Folger set his mug on the table with all the force of an ultimatum. "It's the best policy, Meredith. You can't record observations once a body's been flown across the Sound."

"Admittedly. Did Clarence or the Doc share your concerns?"

"Fairborn is never concerned about anything. He lit a cigarette over the corpse and flicked the ashes into the sea. Clarence didn't make it to the scene."

Ralph Waldo ran a knife under the tap, blunting conversation for an instant. Then he turned and leaned heavily against the countertop, arms folded and bright blue gaze fixed on Merry's face.

His hip is hurting again, she thought, *but he'll never say so. He won't say what he thinks of this business, either.* "So tell me, Dad. Why did you call Connecticut and order me home?"

"I think that's fairly obvious. The needle marks."

"—and their implication of illegal drugs. Which you then ordered Howie not to mention to anyone."

Her father flushed. "Has Seitz been complaining?"

"Of course not. He simply answered my questions."

"And just what sort of questions were you asking, Meredith?"

He gripped his mug so tightly, his knuckles were white. Unreasonable, this degree of anger—unless she had touched a nerve. Merry glanced at her grandfather. Ralph's gaze was unreadable.

"I'm simply trying to pin down my role in this case. It's pretty nebulous until we know what was in Santorski's system—if anything. Am I looking for a murderer? Or a drug dealer? Or just the reason this kid drowned?"

John Folger opened his mouth as if to speak, then took a sip of coffee instead.

Buying time, Merry thought; her uneasiness deepened.

"I don't know what to say, Meredith. If your years of training and experience don't lead you through this case, then I certainly can't. It seems simple enough. Find out why Santorski died. Period. End of story. Are we ever going to eat that pie, Ralph?"

So now it was her problem—her failure to handle the job, again. Merry felt her throat constrict with anger, and swallowed hard.

"If it's that simple, Dad, why did you have to ruin my vacation?"

"So that's what this is about. Your *vacation*."

"I almost wish it were." She regretted the bitterness before it was fairly well out of her mouth. This was not the time or place to confront her father. Not before Ralph, who still stood too rigidly against the bulwark of his kitchen counter. For safety's sake, she retreated into the case. "Everything Seitz told me tonight raised more questions than it answered."

"Such as?" Ralph interjected.

Merry turned to him with relief. "Why a Harvard boy dropped out of college, and what he studied while he was there. Why, having dropped out, he chose to spend the cruelest months of the year in an open boat dredging scallops. Whether the saxophone-playing Owen Harley, his scalloping captain, invited him to Nantucket. Whether they had a falling out—over drugs, or women, or money, or something more obscure. And," she concluded, "what the distinguished and sadly absent Matthew Bailey might have had to do with it all."

John Folger choked on his coffee.

"Don't tell me," Merry exclaimed. "You've found Bailey."

"Actually, no." He reached for a napkin and blotted the front of his shirt distractedly.

"Well, then?"

"Well, what?"

"Why are you looking like a kid caught out with a copy of *Playboy*, Dad?"

"I don't know what you mean."

"Oh, come on—"

"Matt Bailey is not your priority right now, Meredith."

"His son might disagree with you."

"His son is happily eating pizza with the Pottses."

Of course. Tim and Phil were the closest things to friends Bailey could claim on the force. When they should have been diving in the Easy Street Basin this morning, they'd been saddled with little Ryan. That explained one thing, at least.

"And what do the Pottses think about Bailey's disappearance?" she asked her father.

"They think we should wait a few days before we call his ex-wife."

"They have no idea where he might be?"

"None. Or none they're willing to reveal."

Ralph pushed himself away from the counter as though suddenly reminded of his duties, fetched a second mug, and poured Merry's coffee. She took it from him gladly. "Was there anything in his daily calendar?"

"Of course not, Meredith." John was at the end of his patience. "If he'd made an appointment somewhere, he'd have told his son. Bailey has simply gone AWOL in a poor attempt to get fired."

Her grandfather drew a sharp breath, then expelled it almost immediately, as though the act might cut the tension knotting the room. Merry pitied him; he'd expected a festive holiday evening, and she'd turned it into an interrogation.

"Have you made any effort to find Matt, Dad?"

"I will," John said defensively, "once Christmas Stroll is over."

Ralph Waldo reached for his pocket handkerchief and began to mop his brow. For his sake, and the sake of the cranberry pie growing colder by the minute, Merry almost conceded the fight. She took the plate Ralph held out to her, then set it on the table deliberately. She hadn't come all the way home from Greenwich to concede. "Do you actually know where Bailey is?"

Her father kept his gaze on the depths of his coffee cup and shook his head.

"But there *is* some connection with this drowned kid."

"No!" he exploded. "For God's sake—can't you just do your job and stop asking questions?"

Merry raised one eyebrow and sat back in the chair. "I think I'll just let the idiocy of that statement reveal itself, over time."

"Try a little food, Meredith," Ralph suggested. "It usually makes the difficult more palatable."

"Meaning me or Dad, Ralph?"

"I refuse to be drawn into this." He sat down, with a faint gasp that might have been stiffness or pain—then planted himself firmly in the middle of the mess. "But it's clear that you two have more to settle than Merry's ruined vacation."

"What does that mean?" John Folger spluttered.

"Ask your daughter." Ralph's blue eyes, darker than his son's, gave no quarter. "Ask her how she feels about working for a man who doesn't trust her judgment enough to acquaint her fully with the facts of a case."

"I've told Merry all she needs to know."

"Have you?" The bushy white eyebrows rose like an inquisitorial Santa's.

"Look." John Folger slapped his broad hand down on the tabletop, sending plates and forks abruptly skyward. "Merry's been trusted with more responsibility than any other officer on the force. She has no reason to complain, by God. Some people would say I've been *too* indulgent toward her."

"Since I mismanaged the Betsy Osborne investigation so royally?" Merry demanded, flaring.

"I've never suggested that, young lady! And I'm not the reason you're living with those memories."

"No. I am. That's clear enough. I'm the reason those people died. Even you can't take that away from me, Dad."

There was a pained silence.

"I'm sorry, Meredith."

"So am I."

He sank back into his seat, and unfurled his napkin. The

constraint between them settled like mud on a river bottom. Merry lifted her fork, then set it down again. What exactly *hadn't* her father told her about Bailey and the dead scalloper?

"How did the depositions go, by the way?" he asked, with an effort at carelessness.

"Let's just say they went." Merry felt suddenly limp with exhaustion, and wished she were back home in bed. "The defense team did its best to suggest I had a personal grudge against the defendant, whom I somehow framed in the victim's living room. All of which I naturally denied, and sounded ridiculous in so doing."

"Christ," her father muttered. "*Lawyers.* Our job would be a lot simpler if we never had to deal with them. I just got off the phone with McIlhenney. He's getting the same treatment."

"Fred?" Merry clutched at the subject of the force's third detective with transparent haste. "What could Fred possibly have done wrong?"

"It's what he didn't do," John retorted, "if you believe the defense team for Marty Johansen. Fred thinks they're planning to discredit Joey."

Merry whistled under her breath. Marty Johansen was Nantucket born, the last of a large family of plumbers and fishermen who lived out on the small islet of Tuckernuck, a half mile off Nantucket's western shore. Marty was also a thoroughgoing screwup who had an inordinate fondness for cocaine. On three separate occasions he had generously offered to sell some to Joey Figuera, a long-haired, goateed part-time bouncer at the Rose & Crown. Joey had favored Johansen with the sales—and had turned over the cocaine immediately to Fred McIlhenney. Despite his nose ring and his indolent approach to conventional workplaces, Joey was a highly trained narcotics officer detailed from the mainland. McIlhenney was one of only two people (the other being John Folger) aware of Figuera's true purpose on the island, and he was the only member of the force permitted to make personal contact with the man. Even Merry had been unaware of the operation conducted for months virtually under her nose.

Throughout the previous winter, McIlhenney had spent successive midnights parked in the desertion of the Miacomet Golf Course, waiting for Joey to make contact. Joey brought his drug buys to Fred, who bagged the white powder and sent it on to the state crime lab for chemical testing. Once verified as cocaine, the drugs were returned and stored in the blue mailbox that served the station as an evidence file.

Fred's discretion and patience were rewarded with the island's most significant drug bust in years. He had rolled up an entire network of seventeen people in the predawn hours last April, including Marty Johansen's principal supplier. The trials were scheduled for May.

"What didn't Fred do?" Merry asked her father now.

"According to Johansen's defense team, he didn't control Joey Figuera. They've decided that Figuera was a freelancer—that he set his buddies up. And that McIlhenney was nothing but a pawn."

"Fred filed an affidavit after every report," Merry protested. "He wrote receipts for the police funds he paid to Figuera."

"—For both the drug buys and Joey's salary. I know." For the first time that evening, John Folger looked unswervingly at Merry, and she saw the sick defeat in his eyes. "But the defense says they've got somebody who'll testify Joey routinely did cocaine with Marty Johansen."

"And did he, Dad?"

"He denies it."

"Then it'll come down to a jury. In the best tradition of American justice."

"Figuera better lose the beard and the nose ring, that's all I can say. We can't afford to look stupid twice."

Merry caught the reference immediately, and reared back from the table. From John's sudden flush, she guessed the gibe was unintentional; but it told her volumes about his true opinion of the Osborne case.

"No, Dad," she said dryly, "we can't have McIlhenney tarred with my brush."

"I didn't mean—"

"Oh, I think you did."

He hesitated, then dropped his head and shoved his fork into his pie.

Ralph Waldo reached across the table and squeezed Merry's hand. A fleeting touch, like a dry leaf brushing her palm, wordlessly comforting. His confection of cranberries and almonds was lodged stubbornly in her throat. She was long past tasting it. But she smiled at her grandfather, feeling she owed him that much.

Matt Bailey was not mentioned again.

After the dishes were done, Merry kissed Ralph good-bye and nodded awkwardly to her father. He stood with his arms hanging stiffly at his sides, and watched her trudge down the front path in the driving rain. Then he opened the storm door a crack and leaned out into the wet.

"Sure you don't want a ride?"

"Don't bother, Dad," Merry called over her shoulder, and heard the click of the doorjamb a moment later. It was a trifling exchange, but it buoyed her spirits. She knew that he had tried, in that last moment, to show his concern. Whatever else he had withheld tonight, that much had slipped past his defenses.

She splashed toward town through the driving rain, hood drawn up over her white-blond hair. And tried not to notice that everyone else had a warm hand to hold.

Main Street was awash with brave lights flickering in the wind, as though desperate to sustain a holiday note despite the worsening gale. The raw damp brought out the pungency of decaying leaves and the mesquite burning on restaurant grills. There was loneliness in the air, too—autumn dying, Merry thought, or maybe Peter's absence.

She turned from the carnival of town into the tree-lined quiet of Federal Street. Candlelight glowed in the windows of the restaurants on either side; evergreens and sodden ribbon fluttered maniacally in the wind. There were shadows here, lurking pools of black that mirrored the soulless sky; and emerging from one of these, transfixed by a windowpane of warmth, was the idea of a face. Remote, disembodied, with heavily ringed eyes; a girl's face, frightened and ethereal. As Merry watched, it whirled and went out. An instant later, she heard footsteps running.

She stopped short, vaguely uneasy. There was something about the image that recalled a scene from Dickens—the spectre of Christmas Future, dooming the happy present. Then Merry shook herself abruptly and plunged across the soggy lawn between post office and police station. Both she and the vanished girl were well beyond the reach of revels.

Night Reception nodded when she came through the door, and went back to reading her novel. The 911 response officer was bent over his panel of lights. Merry slipped upstairs to her office corridor, went past it, and switched on the light in Bailey's.

And surveyed the appalling order of his desk.

Not a scrap of paper was visible. Even the trash can had been emptied. She crouched down and pulled open the metal file cabinet's drawers, one by one. The hanging green files were devoid of paper.

Bailey's quarters were generally squalid. He was an indolent being, without taste or a genius for order. His clothes looked slept in, and his furniture always held dust. Orange peels grew mold before Bailey thought to discard them; a permanent ring of nondairy creamer congealed on his coffee mug's bottom. Two dead houseplants had held a mournful pride of place on his windowsill for the past three years. He put red bows around their pots at Christmastime, and never seemed aware of the gesture's futility. The mildewed pots and their sagging bows were the only recognizable things in the room.

None of Bailey's characteristic disorder had been tidied before Merry's Tuesday-morning departure for the depositions in Boston; and she doubted that the detective had been spurred to housekeeping in the last hours before his disappearance.

Someone had cleaned up after him. Someone who knew the station inside and out. Her father, perhaps?

Chapter Six

The girl Merry Folger had glimpsed in the light of a restaurant window ran on through the storm-bludgeoned streets until her breath came in tearing gasps and the tears streamed down her cheeks. They left dark trails of kohl in rivulets on her skin. Her canvas sneakers were soaked through, and her long silk dress clung to her legs like weeds from a lake bottom. Her hair was wet and long, too, and twined drunkenly about her shoulders. She was shaking from cold and something more visceral, but she did not slow until she had turned off Main Street and managed the gentle incline of Orange. Cars flashed by her, headlights pinpointing the gale. Their tires spun whirlwinds of wetness against her ankles.

Margot St. John had been crying for most of the day, until the tears seemed almost volitional. She felt she could probably cry as readily as she might say hello to a stranger, which was often enough. Hellos were free. It was the goodbyes that always cost her.

She was walking now, trying not to look over her shoulder for the blond-haired woman who had seemed, in the light thrown out by the restaurant, so much like her dead roommate. An apparition and a warning. Margot had half suspected Katia's presence on the island. Katia had come back, of course, for Jay.

"One day they'll come for me."

She stopped still on the sidewalk by the steps of the Unitarian Church, then closed her eyes. Margot was tired unto death; tired of life, and of the mess she had made of it. Katia was gone. Jay was gone. There was no one left.

And she was desperate for a fix.

She had gone in search of Owen Harley tonight, needing somebody to cry with. Owen wasn't home. But Margot had stood for a while on the edge of the Easy Street Basin, looking out at the water churned white and restless by the heightened nor'easter. The sea and the wind were unappeased by Jay's sacrifice. Margot was afraid and seduced at once, like a vertigo sufferer at the edge of a cliff. She wanted to give way, and jump.

The shaking and the nausea overcame her a few minutes after she turned away from Owen's darkened windows and walked blindly up Federal. The need for the drug—the restless fever of craving—left her crouching against the shingled wall of a carefully restored house, her hands pressed against her head.

It was when she had stood up, dazed in reflected window light, that she had seen the blond woman. And ran like a refugee from war.

Margot forced herself to go on now, to Paul Winslow's house. Paul would understand; Paul would help. He had been Jay's friend, too. When she found the ramshackle rental with the decaying gingerbread in the peaked roof, she hammered on the door. No answer. The windows were as black and unlit as Old North's. Maybe Jay's friends had all gathered somewhere without her, for a sort of wake. Margot felt a sharp dread of the night and her own loneliness, and hammered again.

"Open the door! Please, Paul!"

A window was thrown up. A tousled blond head peered out into the rain.

"What're you doing out there, Margot?"

"Please—I need to talk. Let me in."

He disappeared, and a few seconds later the front door swung open.

"You look like hell," he said.

She walked inside, shaking off the rain on the worn pine floorboards. The hallway smelled of wet coats, and something that might be either old fish or oil. A miasma of stale warmth. Her nausea resurged.

"I need a fix, Paul."

"Of course you do." He said it bitterly. At barely nineteen, he was too young to sound so old. "Come on up."

She followed him, trying not to tremble, her palm drawing splinters from the worn banister. And when Paul turned before his bedroom door and kissed her brutally, she didn't bother to protest. His pupils were like pinpoints.

"You should wash your face," he said. "Your makeup's a mess."

She wiped her hand across her cheek and tasted the tang of blood. He had bitten her lip. "Have you got any smack?"

"I thought you were trying to quit."

She felt her face crumple and dissolve again in grief. "That was before Jay."

"He wouldn't want you to make his death an excuse, Margot. He'd want you to transcend. Jay was big on transcending things, wasn't he? Only it didn't work last night."

"Don't, Paul."

His hands tightened on her shoulders. "I mean it. He'd hate to see you here. Get out, Margot. While you can."

"I'll quit tomorrow. Only I need some help right now. I don't think I can make it through the night."

Paul pushed open his bedroom door and led her into the twilight. She followed, her heart beating faster at the coming salvation, the centering of the syringe.

"Give me thirty bucks," he said.

"I only have ten."

"You're kidding."

"Paul, you've got to help me!"

"This isn't a charity, Margot. I barely make enough to eat."

"I'll get you the rest tomorrow."

He said nothing, and tossed her a rubber band. She tied it around her bicep, her eyes following the movement of his hands. The small spurt at the needle's tip.

"Is it clean?" she asked, meaning the needle.

"Do you care right now?"

No. She cared for nothing at all. The needle bit at her arm, found the vein. Sent a sweet relief coursing through her body. She sighed, and closed her eyes.

"I can't believe he's gone, Paul. I just can't believe he's gone."

Paul fetched a warm washcloth from the bathroom down the hall. And very gently, as though bathing a baby, he began to wipe the black smears of kohl from her cheeks.

Chapter Seven

Saturday dawned cold and gray, like so many days throughout that long, wet, despairing year. There had been too much rain altogether, Will Starbuck thought as he turned his stepfather's battered old Ford into the dirt road that led to Pocomo. His right hand was draped carelessly over the wheel and the collar of his denim jacket was pulled up against the raw cold. He jolted his way toward the water at a steady eight miles an hour, thinking not so much of the road or the weather as of the New England Division 5 Superbowl Game scheduled to start at Burnham Dell field that afternoon.

It was the Whalers' second superbowl appearance, but their first one at home; and Will was quietly pleased that the nor'easter had abated. Boston English, the opposing team, would fly in on time. Will's coach had told the team to defend their turf as though pirates were coming to town—a hokey metaphor, maybe, but entirely suited to the Whalers' sense of purpose.

Will played halfback and punt returner, second string. He would probably spend most of the game on the sidelines stamping his freezing feet—but anticipation alone was causing his heart to beat a little faster. How many hours? He glanced at his watch. Nine o'clock. A while to go, then, but he had enough to distract him. He stole a glance at the girl sitting silently in the passenger seat beside him.

The girl's name was Marjorie Daugherty. She envied the Brookes and Ashleys of this world and told everyone to call her Jorie. She was pretty in the way of many seventeen-year-olds: honey-colored hair drawn back smoothly from her high forehead, brown eyes wide as Bambi's. When she spoke, however, it was with such calculation—such determined intelligence—that her listeners inevitably did a double take and quickly revised their opinions of her. She had yet to grow into her intelligence, and for the moment was half ashamed of what she saw and knew.

She was huddled into a ski jacket with a broken zipper, and her jeans were worn through at the knees. She had bought them this way from the J. Crew catalogue, to her mother's perplexity and distress. Jorie's striped knit polo was fashionably too small, and it rose up from her waistband to reveal a curve of velvet stomach. Will trained his eyes away from that waistband, but Jorie seemed as unconscious of it as of her ears, or the soft curling hairs at the nape of her neck, which he also knew enough to avoid. Jorie was taken.

The cigarette held negligently in her French-manicured fingers trailed ash from the open window of his cab. It was essential that Rafe da Silva, Will's stepfather, never have occasion to find smoke in his truck interior. Jorie understood that without Will having to say it, and left the window down despite her jacket's broken zipper. The raw damp of a Christmas Stroll Saturday was like a third person between them.

They were on their way to AquaVital, a shellfish farm and laboratory in the marshlands off Pocomo. Ten hours of volunteer work a week and a final paper on scallop culture—their senior-year science project.

"Is Paul gonna be there?" Will asked.

Jorie shook her head. "He's working the Horseshed." This was a spit of land across the harbor, and what she meant was that Paul Winslow was dredging scallops along the nearby bottom. He was nineteen, a year out of Nantucket High, and betting he could make a living on the water. Will Starbuck saw this as the triumph of romance over reason, or maybe just stupidity—but then, Will was the son of a scalloper who had drowned years ago. There would never be a future for Will in fishing.

He eased the Ford into the long drive that led to AquaVital. A venerable old house with wide porches, dormers in the third story looking out over the harbor, mildewed shingles in need of replacing. A peeling red door. Shutters so green they looked black. A very faint air of neglect, of purpose shifted elsewhere, of distracted attention. A multimillion-dollar estate declining to fixer-upper.

And then the lab complex behind the house swung into view. Three efficient Quonset huts were hunkered down like enormous barrels near the water, with the spawning nets and barrier rafts in the marshes beyond. There was a generator in a separate building. Beside it, a series of docks with several high-powered craft bobbed in the scatty wind off the water.

Hannah Moore stood waiting for them on the gravel walk near the first of the huts, hands on her hips and face unsmiling. Impatience screamed in every line of her body. Hannah was the shellfish farm's resident marine biologist, thirty-eight years old, nearly six feet tall, and as fit and angular as a triathlete. She wore lean black clothing summer and winter, making everyone around her look overdressed. Will had never heard Hannah offer a word of praise or thanks to anyone. She was complete unto herself. Men saw in this a blatant challenge, something to pursue and attack. Women simply saw danger, and gave Hannah a wide berth.

Occasionally, Hannah intimidated even Will, who had nothing to gain or lose by knowing her; but this morning she had pulled a hood over her long dark hair, and it somehow diminished her self-sufficiency. Made her look miserable, in fact. Will sat behind the wheel of Rafe's truck, unable to avoid feeling superior to Hannah getting soaked in the rain—and when he glanced at Jorie, he read the same inner mirth on her face.

"You're late," Hannah called over his dying engine.

"Sorry." Will shoved the keys in his pocket and thrust open his door. "Traffic out Orange Street was terrible."

"Christmas Stroll," Jorie added. "Town's crawling with tourists."

"In this weather?" Hannah's eyes drifted upward to the clouds, as thick and smudged as cappuccino foam. "I thought the storm would keep them away."

Will shrugged and adjusted his cap. "What're we doing today?"

"I want you two out on the water in the Whaler. Sample for tigerbacks and see how our population's doing."

"Alone?" Jorie looked askance at Will. "Water's pretty rough."

"I've got to work in the lab today. I've got a grant application pending, and the data just aren't there yet." Hannah turned abruptly away from them and strode toward the Boston Whaler moored at the dock. Will raised an eyebrow at Jorie, and the two of them followed slowly in the biologist's wake, hands in their pockets and heads down in the heavy mist. Last night's raging wind had dropped, and with it the horizontal rain and sleet; but it was cold, and the sea beyond the dock looked dispiritingly choppy. If there *were* any scallops in the head of the harbor, Will thought, they were probably huddled down over cups of coffee, with nary a tiger stripe in sight.

The tigerback was a Nantucket Bay scallop Hannah had bred in the controlled conditions of AquaVital's labs. It had a distinctive band of orange and brown running as jagged as an electrocardiogram across its corrugated shell. Hannah hoped that by propagating her tigerbacks, and releasing millions of their young into the harbor each year, she would eventually be able to market a scallop genetically identifiable as Nantucket's—a boon to fisherman and buyer alike. Now, with the project in its infancy, she simply tracked her spawn's fortunes in the harbor's population. For every sample dredged from the bottom, a certain percentage would be tigerbacks—and their distinctive markings tagged them as AquaVital produce. Over the months and years, Hannah charted the percentages of tigerbacks in the samples she took, and got a fair idea of survival rates. Lately, the numbers had been sobering. Two years after Hannah's arrival on-island, she'd had three million young tigerbacks ready to release in the waters of Nantucket Harbor. Hurricane Edouard had wiped them out.

Fishing was like that, Will thought as he climbed over the Whaler's side and moved forward to the controls. Death caught you with your head down.

"Did you hear about that scalloper?" Jorie sprang from the dock to the boat's gunwale, her question intended for Hannah rather than Will. "The guy who drowned?"

"No." Hannah tossed her the mooring line. "Work your way from the Gauls to the Jetties and back, okay?"

"Got it," Jorie said cheerfully, and began to coil the rope.

Will turned the engine key, feeling the Whaler roar to life beneath his sneakered feet. Eelgrass and tiny shells churned in the engine's wake as he slowly steered the boat away from the dock. He had heard about the drowning; he had been pushing the fact of it to the edge of his mind for the past twenty-four hours. To Jorie the drowned scalloper was simply a sensation, as unreal as a Hollywood marriage. She had no idea what a body pulled from the sea could look like after a few hours. But when Dan Starbuck was washed overboard in a nor'easter years ago, it was Will who had found him. No kid of fourteen should have to do that, or live forever with the memory.

"He wasn't a local," Jorie said at his elbow. "Only been here a short time. My friend Ashley worked with him at Ezra's. And I think he hung out with Paul."

The Whaler picked up speed as it left the shallower waters of the marshland and headed toward the Gauls, tidal flats that ran along the island's northern arm. The tide was running out and the wind was coming in; heavy chop bucked like an untamed horse and slapped the boat sideways. Jorie shivered in the wind. A wisp of hair worked free from her ponytail and streamed across her face. Will brushed it aside. Her eyes grazed his face a moment, expressionless, and then she turned her head toward the gray water. They were both braced in the cockpit, hands gripping the dashboard's rail, and the shooting spray felt cold and clean. After a moment, Will took one hand from the wheel and stuffed his baseball cap in his jacket. The wind tore through his fine dark hair. He had taken to cutting it very short, so that it stood up like a brush. With his high cheekbones, the effect was almost exotic.

He pulled back on the throttle and the whine of the engines declined an octave. The boat circled a bit, while Jorie craned over the side, her eyes straining to make out something of the bottom. "Okay," she said finally, the boat slowing, "we'll do a test tow here. Let's throw out the dredges."

They grabbed the purse-shaped dredges by their steel frames and tossed them over the side into the sea. Will was enough Dan Starbuck's son to make sure that the dredges' lines were clear of the Whaler's engine before he eased away. He gave the wheel to Jorie, and when the boat moved forward, kept his hand lightly on the lines. He was waiting for a sensation he could feel but could never adequately describe, a sensation embedded in childhood. The feeling of unseen scallops slipping into a steel-framed purse.

Jorie towed the dredges several hundred feet, then cut the motor. "Winch," she said.

Will said nothing, but he already knew what she would find. There were few if any scallops in the dredges; the lines had told him as much.

They hoisted one dredge after the other and tossed their contents onto the culling board amidships. Eelgrass, stones, an outraged crab. One scallop, too junior to be legally taken by a waterman, and *not* one of Hannah's tigerbacks.

They moved on. Another mile of harbor, the chop growing stronger across the bow; and another mile, and another. An hour passed. They were close to the Horseshed, where Paul Winslow was supposed to be dredging in his beat-up twenty-footer, but not a craft was in sight.

"Maybe he hit his limit early," Jorie said hopefully.

On their seventh test tow, they finally found scallops. Out of the twelve in the dredges, three were Hannah's tigerbacks, two-inch juniors without a growth ring. Jorie was pleased as punch as she swept them off the culling board and back into the sea. Will moved the boat perhaps a hundred feet, and they tossed out the dredges again. His hand on the controls, he eased the boat forward, shading his eyes and studying the harbor jetties. The starboard breakwater was quite near now, and rain-spattered waves churned whitely against its massive rocks. Will imagined a body tossed like a log, sodden and defenseless, while the prow of the M/V *Eagle* sliced coldly through the channel.

"Grab this," Jorie ordered, and started the winch.

Will reached for the dredge as it came up over the side, lowered it to the board, and upended the contents. More tigerbacks. More eelgrass. A crumpled can that had once been a Budweiser, probably off a transient power boat. And at the last, a slick plastic bag spilling out like a defunct jellyfish.

Jorie counted the scallops and rubbed the screen of brown algae from their shells. "Eight in this one, five in the other."

"Tigerbacks?"

She shook her head. "Just four of those."

Will picked up the plastic bag and frowned. Someone had weighted it to sink with several smooth brown stones the size of ostrich eggs—stones found on most of the island's beaches. He tore open one end of the bag and looked closely at what it held.

A crumpled pair of latex gloves. A small black oblong that upon examination revealed itself as a tape cassette. And at the bottom, fouled in the plastic, the spine of a hypodermic.

Chapter Eight

Elsewhere on the island that same morning, Merry Folger thrust her legs out of bed and deep into the sheepskin covering the bare wood floor. She had no need to glance out the window; the dim light filtering through her roman shade declared that the storm had settled down over Nantucket for the weekend. The weather had been bleak for the past year, in fact—raw summer giving way to a howling fall—as though Merry's internal depression must be echoed in the upper atmosphere. She longed for a clearing trend.

She glanced at the clock and saw that it was nearly eight. Peter was probably already back from his morning run, with a knife handle deep in a peanut butter jar. Perhaps he was wondering how she was. Thinking of calling, even.

And if he did? What would she say?

I gave up my vacation, Peter, for what looks like an accidental drowning. And yes, I did it to win my dad's approval. He actually called me stupid last night.

She fumbled her way toward the kitchen and her coffeemaker, wishing profoundly that she could spend the day indoors by the fire at Mason Farms, with a good dog and a good book for company. It was fortunate that Peter was off-island, Merry told herself; a holiday spent working in the miserable wet was somewhat more bearable without an enticing alternative.

The thought had no sooner formed itself in her mind than she knew it for a lie. On-island or off, Peter would always be preferable to work of any kind. But she had somehow failed to convince him of that. If he ever decided to get back in touch, she had some apologies to make and some habits to mend.

If he ever got back in touch. Her eyes strayed to the silent phone at her bedside, then slid away. Good thing she had a date with the Cottage Hospital morgue. Otherwise, she'd be waiting for his call for the rest of the day.

"Good marnin', Marradith." Clarence Strangerfield leaned against the wall of the hospital corridor, a cup of coffee in his hand. Just beyond him was the door to the small room that served as the island's morgue—a temporary berth at best, with a swift dispatching to the Cape or Boston. "I din' expect to see ya back heyah so soon."

"Me neither. What's your opinion of this mess?"

Clarence shrugged. "Sad set o' circumstances all 'round, don'cha think?"

"Ayeh." Merry fell into Clarence's comfortable way of speech, as familiar as the island's weathered shingles. "Dad tells me you're flying to Boston. Attending the autopsy."

"Orduhs o' Dan Peterson. Old Dan wants everthin' done by the book, case it's not just a drownin'."

Dan Peterson was the DA in Barnstable under whose jurisdiction the various law enforcement branches of the Cape and Islands fell. He rarely allowed the local force to handle a murder, preferring to let the state police take over; but in a probable drowning, why not give the locals a little fun? In the DA's estimation, the Nantucket force was just about capable of witnessing an autopsy, Merry thought irritably—no matter how many cases they had managed to close for him. Peterson was still smarting over her insertion in the Osborne investigation last spring—justifiably, Merry thought. And because of her incompetence, the DA would be unlikely to let the Nantucket police within a nautical mile of another murder.

"Have you seen the corpse yet?" she asked Clarence.

"O' cahrse. I came ovuh yestiddy with Dr. John. Missed the scene, but Howie handled that. He's learnin' fast, is Howie."

"Do you mind if I go in?"

"I figgared yah din' come all the way out heyah just to wave good-bye, Marradith." Clarence crumpled the coffee cup and tossed it in a trash bin. "But I'll wahrn yah—he's not a pretty sight. Wait a minute while I get a nurse."

Merry waited. The nurse—a gangly young man with a shaved head—ambled over genially enough and fumbled with a set of keys.

"Who ID'd him?" Merry asked Clarence in a subdued tone.

"One o' the roommates. The doctah fellah."

She did a mental review of Seitz's notes—Cohen, wasn't it?—and turned to the man unlocking the morgue. "Is Dr. Cohen around?"

"Sorry. Went home at six." The nurse flipped on the fluorescent lights and waved her through the door.

Jay Santorski, as Clarence said, was not a pretty sight. The bluish tinge to his skin was unsettling. A single eye stared blankly at the ceiling; the other socket showed gorily hollow.

"Why didn't somebody close his eyelids?" Merry asked irritably.

"Couldn't," the male nurse volunteered. "They're stuck that way."

"Rigor?"

"Nope. Rigor's passed off. This is some sort of paralysis. Dr. Cohen has never seen anything like it, he says."

Merry leaned over Jay Santorski's body to stare straight into his remaining eye. "Clare," she said slowly, "the pupil is dilated."

"So?"

"So, if he'd shot up heroin or even cocaine, you'd expect it to be a pinpoint. Score one for Howie."

"But look at the color of his skin, Marradith. I've seen that in overdoses befarh."

So had Merry. Santorski's skin was almost luminescent, as though a cold hard light—his soul, perhaps—was struggling to break free of his body. Heroin worked as a depressant on the central nervous system, creating transient euphoria—and in fatal cases respiratory collapse. Deprived of oxygen, the extremities grew cold and lost the flush of life. Breathing became shallow, and eventually ceased altogether. Nothing about Jay Santorski's appearance was at variance with a death from heroin.

Except his dilated pupil.

Merry scanned the left arm, looking for telltale marks, and frowned slightly. "Where *are* those needle tracks, Clare?"

"Above and to the right of the crease. Yah have to look pretty hahrd. Doctah John wasn't sure what they were until he pulled out his magnifyin' glass."

She peered more closely, and saw what might have been an enlarged pore, slightly reddened. And another. Maybe four in all, scattered around the shadow of a vein. Had Merry been the investigating officer, she would have missed the needle marks entirely. So, she thought, would Howie Seitz.

"Good thing Fairborn had that magnifying glass," she said dryly. "Although I don't remember him examining a corpse with one before."

Clarence grinned. "I suspect it had somethin' to do with yahr fathah, Marradith, and the good doctah not wantin' to appear slipshod. The Chief saw the mahrks furst, yah see, and made poor Fairborn look foolish. So he whips out his little glass and makes a production o' the business."

It was as though her father had been expecting needle marks, Merry thought, from the moment he saw the body. Didn't Clarence think it strange? Was she the only critical eye in the entire station?

Last night's uneasiness returned with a vengeance. To

quell its insistent voice, Merry resumed her study of the corpse. Forensic observations, as her father had rightly pointed out, could not be taken once Santorski was flown across the Sound. If he had been killed outright by a malevolent hand, his corpse might share the secret.

"There's chafing at the wrists," she said abruptly, "as though his hands were bound. Dad mentioned that, but he never said how obvious it looked."

"It's on the ankles, too," Clarence told her, "but remembah, Marradith, he came out o' the watah neah the jetties. His clothes were tahrn in places from the rocks. You can see a scratch on the side of his thigh, if you come ovah heyah. Cut clean through his pants."

She looked, and was forced to agree. The mounting chop of yesterday's nor'easter must have slammed the corpse repeatedly against the rocky breakwater, while the direction of the gale would probably have kept the current from carrying Santorski out to sea.

"Hard to say whethah the cuts are death-trauma or posthumous, what with the watah cleaning the wounds," Clarence added.

"Let's ask the state crime lab to check the wrists and ankles for fibers, all the same," she countered. "I want to be able to rule out . . . coercion."

"You mean murdah, dontcha?"

"I suppose I do." She paused, considering. "You think I'm making more of this than I should?"

Clarence shrugged. "Stands to reason. Yahr fahther gets all hot undah the collah and drags yah home. Yah want it to be fer somethin' more than an accident."

"Why do *you* think Dad is hot under the collar, Clare?"

His honest brown eyes held hers for a fraction of second, then slid away. "Holiday weekend, maybe. Bodies in the harbah have got to be bad for business. And there's the mattah of needle mahrks, don't forget."

The needle marks. Which nobody should have seen.

"What I'd like to know, Marradith," Clarence continued, "is where the ropes went. If this fellah was tied up."

"If he *was* bound," Merry said thoughtfully, "it was

probably so that somebody could inject him with an overdose of heroin, in the hope of making his death look like a stupid mistake. For that to seem plausible, he'd have to be untied before he was dumped in the Easy Street Basin."

"Followed by his bike."

"But why would anybody do that to a young scalloper?"

"And *who* would do such a thing?" Clarence added.

"A heroin dealer, maybe? —Who was afraid of Santorski for some reason?" Merry shook her head. "We're getting ahead of ourselves, Clare. We need to know more about this guy's *life*, before we can speculate about his death."

"Shouldn't be too long, Marradith, with the autopsy scheduled for this aftahnoon."

"How soon do you think we can get the bloodwork results?"

Clarence's lips moved soundlessly as he surveyed his mental calendar. "Wednesday, maybe?"

Merry took a last critical look at what had once been Jay Santorski. His body was as perfect and lifeless as a Michelangelo. "He took care of himself," she couldn't help saying.

"Up to a point," Clarence amended.

"But he must have worked out. He's got the body of an athlete."

"Athletes have died of overdoses befarh."

"Oh, Clare," she said. "He had his whole life ahead of him. What a goddamn waste."

They stood in silence under the fluorescent glare. Then Merry nodded to the nurse, who leaned against the room's sole windowsill. His eyes were focused on a gull pacing the unpaved Mill Hill Lane, a soggy french fry clamped firmly in its beak. "Thank you. We're done here."

As if by mutual consent, she and Clarence stopped in the corridor outside the morgue's door. "Did you find anything unusual among his effects?"

"Wallet, keys, couple o' packs of matches—phone numbahs on those, hard to make out. They're so waterlogged, the ink is as good as gone. Ah've got 'em down to the station drying. When I get back from the autopsy tonight, I'll turn some infrared on 'em and see what I can find."

He grinned, and Merry smiled back. Clarence loved what he called "the Sherlock end o' the business." He'd probably spend the bulk of Christmas Stroll in his small evidence room, pipe between his teeth and lights turned on Jay Santorski's matchbook covers.

Her own weekend would be a little more diffuse. There were the victim's roommates to interview, his room to search, his last moments to relive. Anything was preferable, Merry reflected, to waiting for a phone call that never came.

Margot St. John set her coffee mug on Paul's plain pine kitchen table, then pressed her fingers against her eyes. The buoyant tide of poison had receded, leaving her like so much driftwood on the rainy shore.

She was twenty-two years old this morning, although only her parents were left to remember that. It was months since they had known where she was.

And this morning, like last night, Jay was still dead.

In the uncompromising glare of eight A.M., Margot looked both defenseless and old. Her skin was chilled, and raked with the occasional shudder; her lips had a bluish cast. Dark shadows smudged the transparent skin beneath her eyes. The faintest web of lines had begun to map the terrain of her face, branching like veins from the corners of her mouth, the creases near her sherry-colored eyes, across the plane of her brow. An idle observer might have thought she laughed too much. Her friends knew otherwise.

The kitchen smelled of mildew. Margot clenched her fingers, drew the terry-cloth robe more tightly about her body, and then turned to retch in the sink. Painful dry heaving—there was nothing, after all, in her stomach but a little sour coffee. She doubled over, arms folded across her abdomen, and let the tears slip down her cheeks.

She felt Paul's hand in the small of her back. "You need some food."

"I can't eat."

"Neither can I, but we ought to try." He leaned closer, supporting her. "I've decided to quit, Margot. Starting today. I need food to do it."

"Oh, right." She stared at him from under the curtain of her hair, her gaze as dark as death. Paul looked this morning like what he was—a kid with a nasty habit. "Have you got any money?"

"Some. Get your dress on. We'll walk into town, have some bacon and eggs at Fog Island. Then I'll drive you home."

She could almost smell the overripe interior of a close-packed restaurant on a winter morning—bacon grease, the spat of frying, the funk of wet dogs fresh from a run on Jetties Beach. Promiscuous air, unshaven faces. The vision induced more retching.

"Come on, Margot. I should do *some* work this weekend."

"I can't face eggs."

"Toast, then," Paul said gently. "Tea and toast. Maybe you could quit, too."

And despite everything, laughter bubbled in her throat. It was not a joyous sound.

Chapter Nine

"Low-pressure systems," Dr. Barry Cohen said, as though that explained everything in life, and took a sip of his coffee. "They induce labor. Look into any hospital on a stormy night, and you'll find the maternity ward filled to overflowing. I haven't slept in two days."

The doctor, if Merry judged rightly, had been attempting to amend that situation when she had blasted his dreams with a ring of the front doorbell. He had hardly been pleased at the disturbance—a repeat of Howie Seitz's the previous morning—but when he saw that Merry was female, he summoned politeness. This was perhaps more insulting than undisguised annoyance; it suggested hypocrisy to Merry, and a latent sexism, and above all, a habit of disguising feeling.

"What's really going on?" Barry had asked, his eyes bleary and one hand fixed firmly on the door handle. He was short and spare, a wisp of a man with shoulders hunched like a question mark; his hairline was receding. She had difficulty thinking of him as *Dr.* Cohen; he was younger than she, and that fact alone destroyed his authority. "I thought Jay drowned."

"He probably did. But there's a possibility of a drug overdose."

Barry had whistled, and gestured her inside.

Like so much of the new construction in Surfside, the place where Jay Santorski had lived was an upside-down house—bedrooms on the ground floor, kitchen and living room located above, where it was possible to glimpse the Atlantic. Merry had followed the doctor, who was barefoot and still dressed in teal-blue hospital scrubs, upstairs to his waiting coffeepot. Presumably the scrubs served Barry as pajamas; but Merry would not have been surprised to learn that he had fallen from the emergency room straight into his bedsheets the previous evening. He wore the hollow-eyed grimness of the sleep-deprived like a POW insignia.

"So Jay was using," Barry said. He was standing now in his kitchen, seemingly held upright only by the vertical force of his tile-topped counters. "I gotta say I'm surprised. And then again, I'm not. He hung with a strange crowd. Scallopers. Musicians. Blue-collar grunge."

"I was hoping you could tell me about his friends." Merry slid onto a bar stool next to the kitchen counter and fumbled in her over-large handbag for her notebook and half-glasses. "I'd like to talk to them."

"I can't give you any names, unfortunately."

Merry opened the notebook casually and uncapped her pen. "Can't—or won't?"

"Can't. I may have seen a face or two in the living room, Miss Folger—"

Merry winced at the *Miss*.

"—but I never met any of them. Jay kept his friends to himself."

"You didn't socialize with him?"

Barry shook his head, and poured more coffee. Took a long draught, eyes closed, and then sighed like a swimmer emerging from the deep end. "That's better. God, what would I do without caffeine? What would *America* do without it? We're all drugged, if you ask me. No, I didn't socialize with Jay. Not that I disliked him—"

Merry believed this about as much as she trusted Cohen's forced geniality.

"—but I don't really socialize with anyone. Well, unless you count the woman in transition at three A.M. But she wasn't exactly socialized herself."

"I understand." Merry jotted something on her pad; it might have been the word *putz*. "Dr. Cohen—you're a trained medical observer. Did Jay's appearance or behavior ever suggest drug use?"

Barry swallowed another mouthful of coffee while he considered her question. "Contrary to popular belief, addiction is not that noticeable if it's well maintained."

"So the answer would be . . . no?"

"I suppose so."

"Did you ever notice needle tracks on Jay's arm?"

"Should I have?"

"The medical examiner—Dr. John Fairborn, do you know him? No?—found what he thought were needle marks on the deceased's left arm. We should await the results of an autopsy, of course, before drawing any conclusions about that . . ."

"Of course."

"I understand you were asked to formally identify the body."

Barry grimaced and looked away. "I've never seen somebody come out of the water like that. I hope I never do again."

"The one remaining pupil was dilated. Does that seem consistent with a death by overdose, Doctor?"

"A lot of things about death are strange. Not everybody reacts to drugs—or drowning—in a textbook fashion, Miss Folger."

"So you're willing to write it off?"

He shrugged. "I guess so. Until a pathologist comes up with a different explanation."

There was little hope of enlightenment or revelation here, Merry decided; and so she abruptly reverted to her first topic. "Would either of your roommates, Dave

Haddenfield or Sue Morningstar, be better acquainted with Jay's friends?"

At the mention of Sue Morningstar's name, Barry Cohen stood a little straighter. His slightly bored expression turned perceptibly more careful. Something to remember, Merry thought, like the doctor's ill-concealed dislike for Jay Santorski.

"You'd have to ask them," he answered. "Dave's over at the school. There's a big game today."

"And—Miss Morningstar?"

The guarded expression deepened. "Sue went into the office early. She's ambitious, is Sue. Practically lives at the *Inky*."

"It must have been quite a shock for all of you," Merry ventured.

"Yes," Cohen said curtly. "Particularly for—particularly when they made me identify his body."

He had been about to say something quite different. Someone—Sue Morningstar? Dave Haddenfield?—had been singularly affected by Jay Santorski's death.

Merry glanced around the kitchen. A cathedral ceiling soared above; the cabinets were something she thought might be pecan wood; and the counters were gleaming white tile with a design of blue waves and fishes painted on their surfaces. "Nice place," she offered. "New?"

"Two years old. I own it. The others rent from me."

"Ah. I see. How does that work, exactly?"

"What do you mean?"

"Did you choose them, or did they choose you?"

The doctor sighed. "A little of both. When I first moved on-island, I had more time. I interviewed people, tried to judge their personalities, asked for references and all that. But lately, I've just gone with any available warm body."

"Is that what Jay was?" She thought of the corpse lying cold and blue in the morgue.

"Yeah. A woman originally had his room. She moved back to Boston to get married."

"So how did you find Jay?"

"I put a notice up on the Finast bulletin board. He called at the right time."

"And how was he, as a housemate?"

Barry shrugged again. "Okay. I guess."

"Did he pay his bills promptly?"

This drew a grudging smile. "Better than my friend Dave does. He's always a month behind, and I've decided he'll never catch up. But what can I say, I'm a softie. I like the high school coach type. Dave's just an overgrown Labrador puppy, you know? Good-hearted and bright enough, but nuts for a ball. He lives and dies for that ball."

Jay, presumably, had lived and died for more complicated things; and they had never won Barry Cohen's affection.

"So you wouldn't have thought Jay was hard up for money?"

"Nah." The dismissive word was followed by an equally disparaging wave. "He's a Harvard boy. They've all got trust funds hidden somewhere, no matter how much they slum around in fishing boats."

Jay's mother, the single parent, might have disagreed.

"Any idea why Jay chose to slum around, as you put it, in *Nantucket*?" The question had an edge of sarcasm Barry Cohen completely missed.

"It's part of the program, isn't it?" he retorted. "Part of the whole liberal-education guilt thing. Self-indulgence masquerading as noblesse oblige. If he hadn't dredged scallops, Jay would've been teaching English in Hanoi, or building houses in Appalachia. They're all alike."

Since when, Merry wondered, was scalloping a charity venture? "I see. Did you have any reason to dislike Jay, Dr. Cohen?"

"Dislike him? *Me*? I didn't think about him enough to dislike him."

"No disagreements? No undercurrents? On your own part, or perhaps Dave's or Sue's?"

The stiffness in Barry Cohen's demeanor—the palpable unease—increased perceptibly. "What is this, Miss Folger?

The kid died by accident. Who cares what Sue or I thought of him?"

"*Detective* Folger, Doctor." Merry underscored the word *putz* on her notepad and flipped it closed. "I'd like to see Jay's room now, if I may."

It was neat and spare, an almost perfectly square space, with a narrow bed made up in the corner, and a trio of milk crates stacked by the door. These had apparently served to hold Jay Santorski's odds and ends—textbooks, rolls of film, a couple of photo albums, a ragged stuffed bear. A catcher's mitt with a torn flap in the palm.

Merry had donned plastic gloves pulled from her car's evidence kit for the purpose of searching Santorski's room. She shifted the crates first, frowning at the weight of a marine biology text holding pride of place in one of them. She thumbed through a notebook—mostly blank, ruled pages with a few math equations scrawled in the front section—and set it aside. Next, she found a bundle of envelopes from the Pacific National Bank—account statements, dated for each of the past three months, and some canceled checks. Merry stacked these on top of the notebook and glanced around the room.

Hanging upside down from a pair of hooks bolted to the ceiling was a gleaming racing bike in an outrageous shade of green. "Quintana Roo," Merry murmured, craning her head sideways to read the brand name scrawled on the bike's frame. It screamed speed, from its carbon-fiber beam to its aerodynamic handlebars; and Merry, who knew something about these glorious machines from Peter Mason, thought it shed an interesting light on Jay Santorski. She walked slowly toward the machine, assessing the Shimano derailleurs and the clipless pedals. He would have used special bike shoes with interlocking bindings, like Peter did when he raced. She had flipped through enough articles in Peter's triathlete magazines to guess that the Quintana Roo had cost the scalloper upwards of four thousand dollars. The perfect tone of his lifeless body again rose unbidden before Merry's eyes. She thrust the vision aside and concentrated on the bike.

What had he used it for? A piece of modernist sculpture suspended from the ceiling? Or triathlon training, perhaps?

A formidable U-shaped lock was attached to the frame, near a slim air pump. Merry stood on tiptoe and examined the tires. New, but not *too* new; the treads were somewhat worn. Her eyes traveled over the frame; the paint was nicked here and there by the impact of stones thrown up from the street. Mud spattered the front fork and caked the teeth of the back wheel's chain. He had ridden it recently before his death, then—although *not* to Old North Wharf on Thursday night. Everything about the racing bike was in stunning contrast to the aged three-speed retrieved Friday morning from the boat basin's shallows. But Santorski would hardly have used this sleek thoroughbred to bump his way over the cobblestones of town.

A small canvas bag was strapped snugly under the rear of the seat, well within reach of Merry's probing fingers. It was faintly damp; seawater. She unzipped it and withdrew a single key—for the bike lock, no doubt—a blowout repair kit, a plastic case with tiny wrenches in different sizes, a high-energy protein bar, two five-dollar bills, a folded piece of paper, and a ticket stub for round-trip ferry passage to Hyannis. This last she studied immediately—it was dated Wednesday, December 4. Jay had gone to the mainland the day before his death, and from the price stamped on the ticket, he had taken his bike. *This* bike, since the stub was in the seat carrier. Had he been entered in some sort of road race?

She unfolded the sheet of paper. It had probably been torn from the ruled notebook she'd found in the crate. Written with haste across the paper's surface were a few lines, almost incomprehensible. Jay Santorski's handwriting? The words, once Merry deciphered them, made absolutely no sense.

Albatross IV, Wednesday @ 2.

This was underscored heavily, as though it were important. The reminder of an appointment, perhaps. Three lines below was: *Larval tigers. Viral morph/unobserved phenomenon. Spectrometer? Rinehart Coastal?*

After this, nothing but a scrawl of pencil, as though the writer's hand had trailed away in thought; or perhaps it was an abstract drawing, a phone call's doodle, a fragment of the moon.

At this stage, nothing should be thrown away. Merry looked around for the notebook and tucked the slip of paper inside.

The dresser held a quantity of ragged sweatshirts, three pairs of jeans in various states of disintegration, some underwear, and six pairs of socks. Pressed khakis and a navy-blue sports coat hung in the closet, along with a surprising quantity of ties. On the closet floor were two empty duffel bags, a tennis racquet, a can of balls, a pair of running shoes, a set of strap-on weights, and a hamper full of dirty laundry. Some of it smelled bracingly of fish, oil, and the sea. Merry stepped back, her hand to her nose, and thought again of the mundanities of death. Jay Santorski's mother would still be washing his clothes, and weeping over every piece.

There were two framed photographs on the dresser top. One was of a middle-aged woman with striking cheekbones, direct blue eyes, and a firm mouth—the registered nurse, Merry decided, as she assessed the woman's sleek head. She looked like the sort of woman to raise a Harvard student, and do it alone.

The other shot was almost less interesting.

A group of kids barely in their twenties, slack-legged and sunburned on the steps leading up to a building—collegiate gothic, by the looks of it, and probably at Harvard. All giggled for the camera, except one—a girl with white-blond hair and a thousand-mile stare. She seemed to see something beyond the field of the camera's lens, beyond Jay—who was probably taking the picture. Merry felt the hair rise along the back of her neck, and knew, with sudden conviction, that Jay Santorski had been haunted by this girl.

And knew with equal force that she was dead.

Merry dropped the frame as though it burned her fingers, and stood there, amazed and doubting, in the middle of the silent room.

Chapter Ten

If a man nearly six feet five can be said to huddle, then Howie Seitz was huddled into his rain slicker as he stood on the edge of the Easy Street Basin. It wouldn't be so bad, he thought, if he could have worked up a sweat like the guys with the dredges, or worn a wet suit like Tim and Phil Potts; but he had nothing but his regulation blue uniform beneath the slicker, and a police cap on his head. The shower-cap contraption intended to shield his hat from the full effects of the rain only depressed him further.

The basin was one of the most picturesque spots in the harbor area, with its scattering of dories moored up near the houses of Old North. The gunwales of one of the boats were strung with colored lights. A diminutive Christmas tree sat amidships, the single spot of cheer in an overcast day.

"Whoa!" shouted one of the scallopers as he dumped his dredge onto a culling board. "Got somethin' here!"

Howie jerked himself out of self-pity. The guy who had yelled was one of two hired that morning by the Potts brothers, who knew almost every waterman on the island. He was young, not much older than a teenager, with a shock of blond hair and what Howie privately thought was a bad hangover. Howie had seen him around before—leaning against the brick wall of the Brotherhood, hands shoved into his jeans, or shuffling toward the Town Pier on a weekday morning. He'd said he was a friend of Jay's, although Howie didn't remember that; regardless, he had jumped at the chance to make a quick buck. And he handled the boat well enough.

Dredging must be warm work. The blond-headed kid—what *was* his name?—had thrown aside his jacket and was working in just a sweatshirt, the sleeves rucked high above his elbows.

What a life, Howie thought as he shielded his eyes with his hands and tried to make out the object on the distant culling board. *Just a kid, already stuck in a dead-end job.* The scallop boat was a good fifty yards away, and the slight fog that had followed the nor'easter turned everything—particularly the light—flat and gray. Howie gave up trying to pick out the contents of the upended dredges, and rubbed angrily at his eyes. "What have you got there . . . Paul?"

"A bike lock," he shouted back excitedly. "Chopped off in the middle. I think it's Jay's!"

"A bike lock?" Merry Folger said at Howie's elbow. "Now that *is* interesting. Why cut the lock if you're already riding the bike?"

Paul threw his boat into gear and nosed toward the Easy Street end of the basin, as though intent upon handing the chain directly to Howie. About fifteen feet from the edge, he gave up. "Too shallow," he called, and cut the engine.

Howie cupped his hands around his mouth and yelled, "Yo! Tim, buddy!"

A wet-suited diver poised on the gunwale of the second scallop boat slid into the water. A few seconds later Tim Potts surfaced amidships and shoved his diving mask high on his forehead. Paul handed him the bike lock—a length of green plastic that ended raggedly in a trail of chain—and Tim walked the last few yards to the basin's edge.

"There's no telling if it's Santorski's, of course," Tim said by way of greeting.

"No," Merry conceded, "but we might check it for prints. That plastic should hold something." She looked over the police diver's head toward the scallop boat. "What's that boy's name?"

"Paul Winslow." Tim dropped the ravaged chain at her feet. She ignored it.

"Use him for this sort of thing very often?"

"This sort of thing doesn't *happen* very often. But no. He volunteered. He was a friend of Jay's."

"That explains it, then."

Howie glanced at Merry curiously. She was still staring at Paul Winslow, and the expression on her face was forbidding. A mix of pity and anger.

"Explains what?" Howie asked.

"The turkey tracks on his left arm. Don't you see them, Seitz?"

Paul Winslow was backing the scallop boat carefully—the dories moored in the basin's shallows made maneuvering difficult—and Howie studied the boy as he worked the controls. Below the rumpled sweatshirt sleeve of maroon fleece Paul's forearm was dotted with needle marks, dark and inflamed against the pale flesh.

"He's been shooting a hell of a lot of something," Merry said. "Who sells him his drugs, Tim?"

"If I knew that," Tim retorted, "he wouldn't still be buying. You gonna take that chain back to the station?"

"You must have heard that Santorski had needle marks on his arm, Tim. Nothing's ever confidential on the Nantucket force."

"Maybe I did hear something about that. What are you driving at, Mere?"

"If that boy"—she nodded toward Paul Winslow, whose boat was now well out into the basin—"was Santorski's friend, maybe they used the same dealer."

"You want me to pump Paul? Find out how he gets the stuff in the middle of the Atlantic?"

"Well, you *are* a cop, Tim."

"Not after five o'clock," he said, and settled his mask back over his face.

"The Chief might be surprised to hear that."

Tim's snub-nosed face, so suggestive of a koala, turned pugnacious. "So now you're going to run to Daddy?"

"Don't be obtuse, Tim." Merry's mouth set in a thin line. "If this drug thing gets out of hand, a lot of people are going to be asking questions. Particularly when the summer season hits, and the population swells by a factor of eight. You might think about that, sometime."

He ignored her, and prepared to slide back into the cold gray water.

"Heard anything from Bailey lately?"

Tim Potts checked in midmotion. "If I had, you'd be the last person I'd tell," he replied. "There's never been any love lost between you two."

"None in the least," Merry agreed equably. "Glad to see you're such a team player, Tim. Let me know when I can do you a favor. It'd be a pleasure. Really."

A flip of the fins was her only reply.

"What an insufferable jerk," she muttered, gazing after him. "As though he owed Bailey something."

"He probably does." Howie was busy stowing the bicycle lock in a plastic evidence bag. "Bailey's been prepping him for promotion to sergeant. Tim wants to be a detective. He always has."

"And I'm blocking his upward mobility. Meredith Folger, the Female Quota Filler who runs to Daddy. I can hear Bailey preaching the gospel now."

"It might have helped if you hadn't made him feel like an idiot, Mere," Howie said gently.

She seemed about to snap his head off, but smiled crookedly instead. "It's one of my specialities—didn't you know?"

"Actually, you make me feel that way all the time."

She squeezed his shoulder. "I'm sorry, Seitz. You've done a good job here. How much longer do you think it'll take?"

"Two hours, maybe. They've covered about half the basin, but it's a little tough working around those dories."

"Then ship 'em," she said immediately. "Get Tim to help. And tell him to concentrate his dives in the water out near the jetties."

"Anything else?"

"Yeah. Take that chain over to Clarence's office. He's gone to Boston for the autopsy, but he should be back tonight."

"Okay," Howie said, and secured the evidence bag. "What then?"

"Start interviewing the people on Old North. I'm going to talk to Owen Harley right now—but I'd better hit Fog Island first. I need some coffee, and the last guy I interviewed didn't offer any."

"Barry Cohen?" Howie asked, on a hunch.

Merry nodded. She was eyeing the rear windows of Old North Wharf's cottages. "Which one of these is Harley's?"

"Second one in."

"That old wreck? Geez! Make that *two* cups of coffee."

"He keeps his gear on the ground floor. The upstairs is better."

Merry's gaze traveled from the tumble-down facade of Owen Harley's home, to the narrow strip of dock that ran along the back. There was space to moor a boat, but it was vacant now. "I'm surprised he's not out on his slip getting a ringside view."

"Give him some credit for feeling, Mere. Harley was Jay's buddy."

"Was he, Seitz?" she asked idly. "I wonder."

"Mr. Harley?"

Merry pounded once more on the massive sliding doors of the fishing shack and strained for some hint of life within. Perhaps Owen Harley was taking a shower—the sound of running water trickled over the noise of the throttled scallop boats and the slap of waves against the wharf pilings. She peered through a porthole-sized window and made out a huddle of darkened shapes: enormous blocks and tackle, coils of rope, heaped tarpaulins, a snare of fishnet.

Where did someone perch in all that clutter? Upstairs? Howie had promised it was an improvement over the present view. Merry set her steaming coffee on the ground and cupped her hands around her eyes, shutting out peripheral light. A circular staircase curved upward in the room's far corner and disappeared through a hole in the ceiling.

The rest of Old North Wharf turned a prosperous front toward its gravel drive. Directly across from Harley's was an artist's studio and gallery—austere, well-tended, and obviously above the meaner concerns of money. Brass ship's lanterns swung majestically from its painted roof cornice. Several doors down stood a beautiful little one-room cottage with a postage-stamp lawn and window boxes that in summer thrust unruly flowers to the sky. The Wharf Rats—a loose fellowship of storytellers and old tars—had their clubhouse here; a fortunate few of the seasonal tourists rented cottages opposite. In the midst of such order, Harley's dereliction seemed almost eccentric, like a bag lady muttering on the fringe of a theater crowd. But, Merry reflected, his was the only part of Old North that recalled the vanished days of whaling. Built as a fisherman's working warehouse, it was a working warehouse still. There was a certain truth in its decay, a Lear-like nobility.

She picked her way around the shack's foundation and homed in on the sound of running water. It led her to the strip of dock hugging the house's rear wall, and below it, a scallop boat that hadn't been there the last time she had looked. It bobbed in the harbor's chop. The fishing shack's neighbors, stridently residential, sported neat white balconies above the Easy Street Basin. Owen Harley was more prosaic.

He looked up from the hose he had trained on a gleaming black wet suit, registered her face, and spat tobacco juice from one corner of his mouth. He was standing on the broad planks of his boat slip, wearing nothing but a pair of long johns aged the color of old love letters. His unruly black hair was grizzled, and his face was so mapped and trenched by weather that it resembled the eroded facade of a cathedral, gargoyles lurking in the crags between nose and chin.

"Mr. Harley?"

"Ayeh?"

"I'm Detective Folger—Nantucket police." She pulled out a badge in a plastic case, feeling slightly foolish as she did so, and fought the impulse to stare at the seat of his long johns. It sagged and gapped like an empty pillowcase. With the air temperature running at about thirty-one degrees, the scalloper should be freezing; but Owen Harley seemed impervious to cold.

"You responsible for all this hoo-hah in my backyard?"

"Yes, actually. I'd like to talk to you, if I may."

"Just a minute," he said, and dropped the spouting hose. It snaked backward, dousing Merry at knee height. She did a little dance, mouth open with dismay, and caught a flash of amusement working its way across Owen Harley's seamed face.

"Sorry." Two sharp turns of the spigot. Deliberate movement, frugal speech, averted eyes. Merry knew another New Englander when she met one. Harley was unlikely to volunteer much about the dead Santorski.

"It's about your mate," she attempted. "Jay Santorski."

"You mean my *late* mate." He straightened and looked away from her, toward the dogleg in the channel that led to the jetties. The Hyannis ferry, up and running again, was just rounding Brant Point. "I didn't think you dropped by to talk about parking tickets."

"Have any you'd like to get off your chest?" Merry asked idly.

Owen Harley grunted. He shook out his wet suit and hung it on a hook apparently reserved for that purpose. Then he stepped around her. Merry had no great desire to follow in the wake of those sagging long johns, but after a moment she did.

"Coffee?" Harley suggested. "Just about to make some."

"I've got some, thanks." Her foam cup from Fog Island was still sitting in the gravel below the shack's front window. "But you go ahead."

He shoved aside one of the massive sliding doors and stepped inside. An indescribable smell rolled outward—part salt, part moldy wood, part rotting scallops—and engulfed Merry. She choked and slapped a hand over her nose. Owen Hurley ignored both the atmosphere and his guest's reaction, and shambled toward the stairs. When her senses had stopped reeling, Merry stepped after him.

As Howie had promised, the second story was a revelation.

Clean, whitewashed walls; expanses of sea-reflecting glass. Skylights in the ceiling flooded the room with light. Braided rag rugs the color of pomegranates. A few pieces of clean-lined furniture, a sofa upholstered in sailcloth. Merry touched a fingertip to the Windsor back of a chair, recognizing the work of a local craftsman. "These are Stephen Swift's, aren't they?"

"Ayeh. Guy's got great hands." Owen Harley scooped some coffee into a maker. "Mind if I shower real quick before we talk? Give the coffee time to brew."

"Go ahead," Merry said, suddenly content to sit down and absorb Harley's million-dollar view.

But in fact she remained standing. And when the scalloper had disappeared through a doorway and she heard the sound of streaming water, Merry set about disturbing Harley's peace.

The first thing she registered was the tenor sax, propped in a corner. She hefted the instrument with all the comprehension of a primate; it might have been so much stick. The next thing she saw was a flowered silk dress lying discarded over the seat of a chair. A small cosmetic case rested near it on the floor. Merry considered these expressionlessly for an instant, then lifted a sofa cushion and peered below. A pull-out couch. So Harley had company.

The corner of the room—the farthest from the windows—was arranged as a home office. A substantial desk, a filing cabinet, computer equipment, and a fax sat competently in front of a rank of bookcases. Photographs of what Merry concluded was marine life were tacked at random on the walls, and scribbled over with black marker showing measurements of various kinds.

Harley also owned a lot of books. But the copyright dates seemed to trickle away in the mid-70s, as though he had never entered a bookstore afterward. Noam Chomsky on linguistics; Leo Tolstoy on peasants. Stephen Cohen's study of Bukharin. Derrida and Foucault at opposite ends of a shelf, and on another, nothing but marine biology. Books on music theory. And several decrepit volumes of A. A. Milne.

"We have an anarchist," Merry said softly, "with a weakness for Pooh." She recognized only half of the names and titles, but it didn't matter; she had caught the general drift. Owen Harley had been an angry young man. What had he grown into?

A block of sunlight materialized on the bookshelves, then faded quietly, a ghost. Merry turned to the window facing Steamboat Wharf, and saw the gray sky unraveling. Saw the approaching ferry, no longer a toy, its prow awash with people, and the small dory strung with lights that carried a blazing Christmas tree through the winter season. And saw, finally, that Owen Harley had a clear view of the channel's dogleg and the barrier beach of Coatue. Impossible, however, to make out even a stone of the harbor's jetties, a half mile away, much less a body rolling against the breakwater in the flat light of a stormy morning.

If Owen Harley had gone out scalloping yesterday, however . . . but perhaps the nor'easter had kept him at home.

A gull cried beyond the window, then veered and hovered near the pane, searching for a perch. The bird caught Merry in one crazed eye, reminding her for an instant of Jay Santorski's ravaged face; and she laid a hand against the glass. Cold to the touch—poorly sealed. A true frame in a cockeyed building. All manner of sounds filtered in from outside. The sound of a fight, perhaps, or even a scuffle? A cry in the dark, and then a splash?

The shower suddenly ceased.

On impulse, Merry turned to the narrow galley kitchen and peered through the window over the sink. Old North's gravel drive, and a patch of Easy Street beyond, the jumbled roofs of town. In the offseason, few lights shone here at night; but it might have been possible to see a man on a bike pedaling down the street. Particularly a man one expected.

"Looking for a mug?" Owen Harley emerged fully dressed from his bedroom doorway. He was wearing clean, pressed khakis and a blue striped shirt; he looked nothing like the waterman of a quarter hour ago. "They're in the lefthand cupboard."

"Kitchen windows are a weakness of mine," Merry replied evenly. "I don't have one myself, and I miss a view when I'm washing dishes."

"Every window should frame something. And every wall should have a window."

"Not exactly possible, in most houses," Merry observed.

"But then I never cared for most houses." Harley reached up for the mugs, poured a neat cup of coffee. "Cheers."

Merry raised her foam cup in a gesture of cordiality. "Are you celebrating, then?"

For the first time, the scalloper's eyes met hers fully. They reminded her of the gull's—too pale and expressionless. The right one had a cast in the iris, green on gray.

"No," he said after a moment. "I can be a cold-hearted bastard, but not *that* cold. Jay was a good kid. He didn't deserve to die the way he did."

"I wasn't referring to Jay. I wondered whether you were celebrating Christmas Stroll. You look like you have company." She took a sip of coffee and wandered back to the harbor window, giving him time to think.

He followed her slowly. "I offer the sofa to friends when they need it."

"Ah," Merry said, letting it hang. Harley didn't elaborate. She watched the M/V *Eagle* nose into its berth and throw out its anchor. A crowd of reddened faces peered over the bow, eager despite the rain. She wondered how many of them had slept on the floor of the ferry terminal last night.

"Is there something you'd like to know about Jay?" Harley asked.

"Oh, probably everything there *is* to know about Jay. I haven't the faintest idea who he was, or how he came to drown in the boat basin Thursday. I thought perhaps you could help me."

He sat down on the sofa and balanced his coffee mug on his knee. "Jay was probably coming to see me. He fell off the edge of the wharf in the darkness."

She noticed Harley had dropped the laconic "ayeh." "Could he swim?"

"Like a fish. But that water is cold enough to kill a man in minutes. That's why I wear the wet suit—" He paused, uncertain. "I'm sorry, I'm terrible with names."

"Detective Folger."

"Thank you. I wear a wet suit, Detective, and I'm only working on *top* of the water. When you're in it, you go numb pretty fast. It makes perfect sense to me that Jay died."

Merry frowned. "Whereas it makes no sense whatever to *me*. Were you expecting Jay Thursday night, Mr. Harley?"

"No. But he often dropped by." A slight stiffness, as though the scalloper had braced himself for a blow.

"And were you here around midnight?"

"As it happens, I wasn't. I was rehearsing with some friends out in Sconset."

"Ah, yes. The swing band." At his look of surprise, she said reassuringly, "I'm not clairvoyant. I have a friend who plays bass for you."

"Of course—Howie. He's a great guy," Owen said, with unforced enthusiasm. "He's completely honest, you know? In his dealings with people, and in his music. He can coax more from a bass than I'd have thought possible."

"I'll have to come hear you play sometime. So you were with Howie that night. And your . . . temporary guest?" she inquired idly.

"Was also with us." The stiffness hadn't dissipated. "Is

there some reason to check everyone's movements, Detective? Jay's death was an accident, after all."

Ah, the betraying anxiety, so suggestive of guilt. In almost every detective novel Merry had ever read, Owen Harley would be immediately pegged as the murderer. If this *was* a murder.

"Well, Mr. Harley," she said, sitting down in an armchair across from him, "you tell me if this seems normal. As your scalloping mate, Jay Santorski has been coming to Old North day in and day out for the past two months. He's gotten pretty comfortable with your slip and the Easy Street Basin it services; he knows the deck of your vessel. So it doesn't seem likely he fell off your dock. He must have gone into the water where we found his bike—right beyond this house, down there in the basin." She gestured over her left shoulder toward Harley's beautiful, broad window.

"Is it likely Jay would overshoot the gravel drive into Old North—a fairly wide drive, I might add, and not entirely unlit, even in the off-season—just to careen into the water and drown there? It's not very deep at the wharf's edge. I checked. Between two and five feet, on average, given the tides. And you've just told me he was an accomplished swimmer."

"Well—when you put it that way—" Harley set his mug on the coffee table and propped his chin on his hands. "Poor bastard. He must have been wasted."

"Drunk?"

Merry let the word hang between them, and waited.

"It happens to everybody, sometime."

"Did it happen much to Jay?"

"Actually—no. He was a very moderate person."

"Were you aware, Mr. Harley, that Jay Santorski was an intravenous drug user?"

Something flickered in Harley's eyes, then vanished. "Why do you think that?"

"We found needle marks on his left arm."

Harley set his coffee mug deliberately on the table before him, his fingers lingering an instant on the rim. "Oh, *Jay* . . ."

"You didn't know?"

He shook his head. "He never showed any sign of it on my boat."

"Interesting. We won't have an autopsy report for several days, but we think it is possible Mr. Santorski was drugged when he went in the water."

"I understand." Harley stood up restlessly. Crossing to the harbor window, he gazed out unseeing at the car ferry's superstructure just visible above the wharf buildings opposite. "That would explain it. I wish I had been here! I might have heard something—been able to help."

"Yes," Merry said evenly. "It was unfortunate that no one was here." The silence hung between them, and Merry waited for Owen Harley to fill it. He disappointed her. "Tell me, Mr. Harley. How did you come to hire Jay?"

"I worked with him at Woods Hole last summer," he said.

"I'm sorry?"

"We're both—*were* both—marine biologists." He didn't turn away from the window. "Jay was studying mollusc habitats at Harvard. I study them here. After the summer, I invited him to join me for the scalloping season, and record the devastation at close hand. He agreed. He was good at what he did, Detective, and he cared about his subject. He wanted to know the harbor as intimately as the lab."

That explained a great many things, Merry thought, remembering the textbooks in Jay's room. It also raised a host of further questions. "So you're not really a scalloper," she said.

"What do you mean?" Harley shot back contemptuously. "Can't scallopers be educated?"

Merry's anger flared at the ridicule in his voice. "You know what I mean. You have an alternative. You have a career. You don't depend on a dying resource for your livelihood. I'm a native Nantucketer, Mr. Harley, and I grew up with watermen. I've seen what the decline in the scallop harvest has done to people. There's not much you can tell me about that."

"I wonder," he replied, amused. "Do you know *why* the scallops are declining?"

"No," Merry admitted, somewhat chastened. "But fish

populations have always run in cycles. Some years are good, some are bad."

Harley snorted. "Well, that explains a hell of a lot."

"Okay. You're the biologist. You tell *me*."

"Nitrogen," he said flatly. He sat down again on the sofa. "Woods Hole did a big study of the harbor in '95, and another report is due out next spring. According to their findings, the harbor water is polluted from two main sources—decomposing sewage leaching from the island's septic systems into the groundwater, and fertilizer runoff from the summer people's lawns."

"And the scallops are poisoned by it?"

"Not exactly. Nitrogen causes a bloom of phytoplankton in the water itself. The phytoplankton block sunlight from the harbor floor and decrease the oxygen supply in the water. Vegetation on the bottom dies and rots, sending even more nitrogen into the water. Which spurs all the phytoplankton, that take all the oxygen . . ."

". . . that live in the house that Jack built," Merry finished impulsively. "So the scallops are suffocating?"

Harley shook his head. "Not exactly. But their habitat is. Scallops set—or affix their young shells—to eelgrass growing on the harbor floor."

"And it's the eelgrass that is dying."

"Exactly. So the scallop spawn has nowhere to go. Worse, the septic seepage has encouraged a particular type of phytoplankton, known as brown tide, that fouls the feeding systems of shellfish. It literally chokes them. You don't dive, by any chance?"

Merry shook her head.

"If you did, you'd be appalled at the state of the harbor bottom. There's a creeping mat of brown algae, most of it trapped in the bends over on Coatue." This was the barrier beach that formed the upper hook of Nantucket harbor, once a breeding ground for the great scallop beds of old. "We're bringing it up all over the scallop shells."

"How bad is the die-off?"

"Pretty devastating." Harley rose, crossed to one of the bookshelves, and pulled out a file folder. The remoteness was gone from his light-colored eyes; they were intent and focused. "In the early eighties, Nantucket averaged close to forty-four thousand bushels of scallops per year. In 1995, the harvest plummeted to just under thirty-four hundred. God knows how bad it'll be this winter. It's looking thinner every day."

"But that's terrible! If the scallops are dying, so is everything else!"

"Naturally. Or unnaturally, I suppose."

"Do people know?" she asked, groping.

"It was in the paper last May," Harley said grimly, "but I'm never convinced that people read the newspaper, or believe it, if they do."

Last May, Merry had been able to spare very little time from Elizabeth Osborne's skeleton. An article on leaky septic tanks would hardly have caught her eye.

"The Shellfish and Harbor Advisory Board is trying to discourage the use of lawn fertilizer on properties surrounding the harbor—Pocomo, Monomoy, Shawkemo. But most of the problem is due to septic fields, and they're difficult to police. So many of the properties are seasonal, with high use four months of the year and complete disuse the remainder. Most septic problems go undetected."

"This makes me ill," Merry said. "I swim off Jetties all the time. Am I swimming in sewage?"

"Not really." Harley shrugged. "It's the harbor—the more contained water—that's at risk. There's a plan under consideration to dredge it, and improve the tidal flow. The Sound near Jetties is less affected. I wouldn't worry about swimming. This is *nitrogen* we're talking about, not feces."

"Still," Merry argued, "I'm never going to feel quite the same about eating a scallop."

"Enjoy them while you can. Your children may never see them." He smiled sadly. "Hey, I understand how you feel. I grew up here. My dad owned a trawler, back in the fifties."

"When it was still possible to fish out of an island port. Did you ever know the Duartes? Captain Joe, and his daughter Del?"

Owen Harley frowned. "I can't say that I did. But we

moved to Gloucester when I was ten. If I remember anyone, it's the men who crewed for my father. The Duartes were friends of yours?"

"Yes," Merry said heavily, "but they're both gone now." She thought of Del's strong-featured face, the competence of her hands when they held a harpoon, and felt a surge of pain. At least Del's daughter, Sarah, had escaped. She would be almost five now, Merry realized—starting kindergarten on the mainland next fall.

"I never forgot Nantucket," Harley was saying. "Everything—my work, my inclination—led me back here. But I wouldn't want to depend on fishing for a living. There's not much of a future in it."

With an effort, Merry turned her thoughts once more to Jay Santorski. "So your mate was studying the decline of the harbor."

"Ayeh." Harley pored over his file folder once more, scanning and turning pages. "We were scalloping, of course, and selling the mature ones we found—but we never hit our limit. The limit, by the way, is five boxes a day, or about fifty pounds of shucked scallops, and nobody has hit it in weeks. Jay and I spent a lot of our time taking field observations and data. Charting the destruction of the eelgrass beds. And the data are pretty depressing."

Merry reached in her purse and withdrew a plastic bag. Inside was the piece of paper she had found in the dead man's bedroom, unfolded so that its words were clearly visible. "Would this have anything to do with Jay's work?"

Owen took the bundle and squinted at the paper it contained. "It's his handwriting, certainly. Where did you find this?"

"In the canvas carrier strapped on the back of his racing bike."

Harley looked bewildered.

"The bike was in his room. Did Jay race, by the way, Mr. Harley?"

"He liked to enter triathlons in the spring and summer, but lately he only used the bike to train. He didn't have much time to ride, and the weather's been pretty lousy."

"Would he have raced this past week? On the mainland?"

"I doubt it. Why?"

"I also found a stub for round-trip ferry passage to Hyannis, dated Wednesday."

"Hyannis? Jay went to *Hyannis* on Wednesday? I had no idea."

"He didn't mention it?"

"No. Although he asked for the day off from scalloping. I figured he had to work at the Mayhew House."

"You'll notice that *Wednesday* is written on that paper, as well, in reference to something called the *Albatross IV*."

Harley glanced once more at the sheet of notebook paper. "The *Albatross IV* is a research vessel—operated by the Fisheries people out of Woods Hole."

"Woods Hole. That's a fair piece from Hyannis."

He shrugged. "Fifteen, twenty miles, maybe. A good training run for Jay."

"You think he went to meet the boat?"

"Or someone on it." Harley's brow furrowed. "Maybe Mel Taylor."

"He's with—Fisheries, did you say? Is that part of the Oceanographic Institute?"

"Institution," Harley corrected. "No. Fisheries is under the Department of Commerce—part of the National Oceanic and Atmospheric Administration. The Woods Hole Oceanographic *Institution* is private money—lots of it. The Rockefellers started WHOI, I think, and it's always had a slightly elitist air." He tapped the plastic-covered paper. "That'd be what Jay means, here, by Rinehart Coastal. The Rinehart Coastal Research Center falls under WHOI."

Jargon, like the paper itself. Merry shook her head. "You've lost me. What has that got to do with the *Albatross IV*?"

Harley grinned apologetically, his first suggestion of good humor. "Woods Hole is confusing. Probably on purpose. There are four different organizations doing biology within a half mile of oceanfront, all of them claiming to be *the* Woods Hole, and vying for grant attention. But I can clarify Jay's interest at least. His senior thesis advisor, Mel Taylor, is on sabbatical from Harvard this semester—at the Rinehart Coastal Research Center. Taylor spent the last month at sea, on the *Albatross IV*, by special arrangement with Fisheries."

"A light breaks," Merry replied, with an air of disappointment. "So this was just a reminder to meet Taylor's boat. It's not significant at all."

"But Jay must have had a reason for going to Woods Hole," Harley objected. "Nobody spends four and a half hours, round-trip, on a ferry—and several more on the back of a bike—just to say, *Welcome back*."

"Does the rest of that paper mean anything to you?"

Harley studied the cryptic lines again. "Larval tigers—that *might* refer to tigerback scallops. But as for the *viral morph* business, I've no idea what he means."

"Probably the senior thesis," Merry mused, "and he needed to discuss it with this Mel Taylor."

"I don't think so." Owen ran his finger over the penciled scrawl at the paper's lower edge. "That looks to me like a sketch of the Horseshed—that's a bit of land across the harbor, where there used to be major scallop grounds. And tigerbacks—if that's what Jay meant—are specific to Nantucket. They were bred here."

"Are tigerbacks found in the Horseshed?"

"And elsewhere around the harbor." Owen continued to stare at the paper, brows knit, his face wearing the same intent expression his scallop file had demanded.

"Well—thanks. That's some help." Merry held out her hand, and after an instant, he returned the plastic bag. But she could see he did so only reluctantly. Half his mind was worrying at the puzzle.

"You called the data about the harbor depressing, Mr. Harley. Was Jay depressed?"

"Jay? Not at all. He was nursing a broken heart, of course—but what college kid isn't?"

"For someone here?"

"Someone at Harvard, I think. He jumped at the chance to leave when I offered it to him. But here on Nantucket—he seemed pretty happy to me."

"Did he intend to go back to Harvard next year?"

"Yes. And to graduate school at MIT after that. They have a joint program with the Woods Hole Oceanographic Institution."

Merry considered this. "Any idea, then, why he might have turned to drugs?"

The eyes slid away and the stiffness returned. "None whatsoever."

"One last question, Mr. Harley," Merry said as she rose to leave. "How did you feel about Mr. Santorski?"

He hesitated. "I respected him. He had a good brain. He was a hard worker."

"Did you like him?"

"I must have. I asked him to come over here for the winter, didn't I?"

But even Owen Harley didn't sound convinced.

Chapter Eleven

Howie was waiting for Merry in front of Old North Wharf. The patrolman was reducing a spherical bullet of ice cream to something like soft-serve through the consistent application of pressure from the back of a spoon. Merry shivered at the sight.

"How can you eat that stuff today? Is it from Crazy Quinn's?" This was her favorite ice cream place, conveniently located a few steps from the police station on Water Street. "Give me a bite."

He complied obediently, and she shivered again. "Thanks. Now tell me what you learned."

Howie set down the ice cream cup and pulled out his notebook. "Talked to five people, all told. Probably three more houses on the wharf are occupied—weekend renters spending freely on Main Street at the moment. Nobody heard anything, except one woman who lives all the way at the wharf's end in the cute little cottage with the Dutch doors. *Whirled Away,* according to the quarterboard. Name's Irene Curtis." He paused, reached for his spoon, and took a gargantuan bite of ice cream.

"And?" Merry prompted.

"Didn't hear a fight. Didn't hear an accident. Heard a boat, though, at three o'clock in the morning. Says she sleeps with her window open, winter and summer, and the noise of the engine woke her. A boat engine being unusual at this time of year and that time of night."

"To say the least."

"She thought it must be morning, and the scallopers going out, because it sounded like that kind of boat—so she put her glasses on and looked at her bedside clock. Two fifty-three A.M. exactly."

"By which time," Merry mused, "friend Jay was probably already dead, if we believe Dr. John."

"And friend Owen was presumably back from his practice session, leaving him without an alibi. I know I turned in by one-thirty that night, and I quit when Harley did."

She looked at Howie, one eyebrow raised. "Was he in bed—or at the scallop boat's controls, dumping his dead mate's body over the side?"

"That might explain how the corpse got as far as the jetties," the patrolman observed, "but it begs a question. If somebody went to the trouble of dumping Jay from a boat, why not take him well out into the Sound? With that nor'easter coming, he might not have been found for days. If ever."

Merry mulled this over in silence. "Could Irene Curtis identify the boat from the sound of the engine, Seitz?"

"Wouldn't want to bet on it," Howie replied dryly. "But she did say it came right back. Only out about twenty minutes, if that. Irene thought it might be somebody getting dropped off at a vessel moored in the harbor."

"Or just . . . dropped off."

Glumly, Howie nodded.

"Any hope that she might recognize the engine if she heard it again?"

"I wouldn't call Irene mechanically minded." Seitz sounded almost apologetic, as though it were a personal failing. "She makes lightship baskets for a living. Carves the ivory plaques, too, with little tiny drill bits, worn down from drilling teeth."

"Teeth?"

"She has a dentist friend in Minnesota who sends them to her. Nothing else carves a delicate bit of ivory half so well, Irene says. And man! What she can make with those bits! An entire whaling ship, Mere—sails and masts and everything!"

"How long did you spend with this woman, Seitz?"

"What I mean is," he supplied hastily, "Irene's a real nineteenth-century type. She doesn't know engines. But she thinks the boat could have been Owen Harley's."

"Harley's boat must go past her cottage twice a day," Merry observed.

"And has for years. Right. That's why I asked about it."

Merry sighed. "Harley never suggested he'd taken the boat out in the middle of the night, Seitz. That has to look bad." She glanced at her watch and frowned. "I can't go back in there today. Do me a favor, would you? Ask a couple of follow-up questions later this afternoon. Phone 'em in, if you have to."

"Like whether Harley went for an early morning jaunt, and what he saw if he did?"

"And where the boat keys are kept. Whether someone else might have access to them." Merry stole the last of Howie's ice cream. "So does Irene know the woman who's camping out on Harley's couch?"

Howie stared. "I have no idea. We're not *that* good friends."

"Harley said that whoever she is, she was out with you guys, practicing, the night Santorski drowned."

"Margot was the only woman around. We were at Bill Johnson's, our trumpet player. He's house-sitting out in Sconset. Margot lives a few streets away from him, and walked over."

"Why? Is she a friend of his?"

"She's our singer. Sort of a white Billie Holiday."

"I thought you guys played swing."

"We do. Margot's very . . . versatile."

Merry's eyes drifted over to Paul Winslow, who was still busy dredging the Easy Street Basin in his scallop boat; he was well out in the channel now, almost to Brant Point. "What was this Margot wearing that night?"

Howie shrugged. "Same as usual. A long flowered silk dress. Doc Martens. An old army jacket."

"Sounds lovely."

"Oh, she is." There was a note of something like regret in his voice.

Merry studied Howie. "Tell me about her, Seitz. Harley didn't want to, and I find that interesting."

"Harley didn't want to talk about Margot because he's obsessed with her. And she was more interested in Jay." Howie crumpled the ice cream cup and looked around for a trash can. Finding none, he stuffed cup and plastic spoon into the pocket of his slicker. "Can we discuss this while we walk back to the station? I'm freezing out here."

"Sure." Merry shoved her hands in her jacket pockets. "So Margot was interested in Jay. He interested in her?"

Howie nodded. "They were sort of an item these last few weeks."

Merry whistled. "That *does* make my heart beat faster, I'm afraid. How does this sound, Seitz? Your friend Mr. Harley and his Margot show up at Old North together Thursday night after your jam session, and run smack into Jay. There's a fight, and Jay ends up in the boat basin."

"At which point, Margot goes happily to sleep on Owen's pull-out couch?" Howie protested. "Even *she* isn't that heartless. Besides, your scenario doesn't explain the bike chain."

"We don't even know if the bike chain belonged to Jay. But let's say it does. That's dealt with quite simply. Jay had already locked his bike somewhere on Old North, and once Harley killed him, he made it look like an accident by cutting the lock and throwing bike and chain into the basin."

"He should have thrown the chain into a restaurant dumpster," Howie argued.

"Admittedly."

"And what was Margot doing all this time? Cheering from the upstairs window?"

"Okay," Merry said in exasperation, "how's this? Jay and Margot have a lovers' quarrel. She runs to Owen Harley for sympathy and the loan of his couch. He gives her both, and she's in bed by two A.M., snoring soundly. Jay shows up at Owen's already high on heroin, and his mood is a little volatile. He hammers on the door, Owen comes down into the street, and we have the fight and drowning as before. Owen drops the body well out in the harbor and cuts Jay's bicycle chain to fake the accident."

"I don't know, Mere." Howie shook his head. "It's pretty speculative. Jay's body didn't look bruised, as it would have if he fought. He wasn't knocked unconscious with anything."

"But Harley's protecting *something*, Seitz. He quite obviously didn't want to discuss the nature of his late-night visitor. And every time I tried to probe his feelings for Jay, I got a polite and distant whitewash."

"Did you happen to mention drugs?"

"Yes. Harley insisted Jay showed no signs of heroin abuse while working on his boat."

Howie did not reply, and as they turned into Water Street, his eyes were fixed firmly on his shoes. Merry glanced at him, saw the morose expression on his face.

"What is it, Seitz? Tell me."

"You probably scared the hell out of him, Merry. The girl he loves is a heroin addict, and you just told him Jay died of an overdose—Jay, who most of us are certain never used drugs before. Where else would he have gotten the stuff, but from Margot St. John? *That's* whom Harley is protecting."

"Wait a minute." Merry shaded her eyes with her hand, as though the gesture might aid her comprehension. "You *knew* Margot was taking drugs, and you never charged her with possession?"

Howie looked away.

"You're as bad as Tim Potts, Seitz! What do you think law enforcement is—an occasional hobby?"

"Are you always on duty, Merry?" he asked brusquely. "When you quit work for the day and leave the station, do you pull out the Explorer's lights and haul over every speeding driver between here and Mason Farms? Or do you let it slide and keep going?"

"A speeding ticket is hardly heroin, Seitz."

"What do you do?" he insisted.

Merry sighed. "That depends. If the driver is just enjoying the call of the open road, and I'm on my way to Peter's for a Friday night dinner, I'd probably ignore it and speed along with him. If he's weaving uncontrollably and looks like he's about to run head-on into the opposite lane, I'd probably pull him over. You know how many DUIs we charge on this island. Particularly in the off-season. It's our most common violation."

Howie raked a hand through his black curls in frustration and looked unconvinced.

"If someone is endangering another person, I have to intervene," Merry added gently. "But I agree that it's no fun to feel like the perpetual Enforcer. Okay? Does that help?"

"A little." Howie shrugged, still unwilling to meet her eyes. "It's just kind of hard to adjust. I mean, if I'm out at a party with somebody, and I see something, do I necessarily have to report it? Maybe according to the book—but how does anybody live by the book, anymore?"

"You don't want to be playing swing at a club and have everybody say, 'See the bass player? He's a cop. So watch what you do and say around him.' "

"Exactly." Howie looked relieved. "I'm barely twenty-five myself. Margot's even younger. It's like tattling to your parents about a kid sister."

"It's nothing like that at all, Seitz," Merry countered without hesitation. "This is heroin we're talking about. And your parents are giving you a paycheck to stop its distribution and general social destruction."

"You're very sure of yourself, Merry."

"I have to be. I've lived with the same problem for years."

"You don't seem to find it too hard."

"Actually, I find it tougher than you ever will." She turned away from him and walked the last few feet to the station entrance. "You didn't have to go through high school branded as the police chief's daughter. Do you know how many parties I *wasn't* invited to? And you didn't have to start policing your neighbors a few years out of the Academy. I hated that part of it for a long time. There are always going to be people who assume a mask when you're only fifty feet away, and who never feel comfortable in your presence."

"So how do you deal with it?"

"I have fewer friends. I stick with the real ones—the ones who stuck with me."

"But that's just it, Mere!" he protested. "I don't have many friends here! It's really hard to make them, sometimes, when you've got this badge on your chest. Particularly off-season, when the island only seems to get smaller. Harley's band has been the one thing I could count on."

"It'll get easier, Seitz."

"It better," he muttered, "or I'm heading back to the mainland."

"A different place won't give you a different life."

"What will?"

"Growing up," she said, and pulled open the door.

Chapter Twelve

As he paced the edge of Burnham Dell field that Saturday afternoon, Rafe da Silva looked like he was braced against the pervasive chill of early December. He certainly felt the edge of the vanishing nor'easter through his windbreaker; but the real reason for his crossed arms and stony look was an almost painful exhilaration. Will Starbuck, the boy Rafe loved, was suited up and in formation at the most critical game of his senior year.

Any other day, Will would have warmed the bench and thumped the backs of his teammates at the game's end, hiding his disappointment behind a wider grin. But the Whalers had bobbled their first possession of the superbowl game, and watched Boston English score on the turnover. Rafe cared nothing for who won or lost at this exact moment—what mattered to him was that Jason Eppley, the first-string punt returner who normally edged out Will, had twisted his ankle thirty seconds into the day. Coach Victor (as the venerable Nantucket football god was known) had sent Will into the fray with a wordless nod and a clap on the back.

Rafe paced a bit and wished that Tess were here. Any

other game, she would have stood with the rest of the island's parents and cheered the Whalers on; but this was Christmas Stroll weekend, and she couldn't leave the Greengage. Thirty plucked geese were even now drooping on various prep tables in the restaurant's kitchen, their chest cavities stuffed with sage and oysters.

At least a thousand or two people were crowding the sidelines today, blocking Rafe's view. He craned on tiptoe to look for Will, and caught a distant flash of helmeted head. Impossible to read anything of his stepson's expression—but Rafe saw that Will was poised like a runner at the start of a race, eyes riveted on the Boston English kicker, his taped fingers flexing. Rafe could feel the boy's nervy anguish as though it were his own.

The Bulldogs punted. The ball soared high, a purposeful bird rocketing through the damp air, then plummeted toward Will. He stepped back, waiting, and leaped to meet its fall. Raced perhaps eight yards, or ten, to the thirty-two-yard line, before a Bulldog brought him down with a tackle to the legs. He rolled away as though nothing had even hit him, and shook his head slightly—that head, that had once been damaged enough to require physical therapy. Craning again, Rafe saw his boy's wide-mouthed grin, saw him fuss with his jersey in embarrassed triumph. Unable to restrain himself, Rafe cupped his hands around his mouth and shouted Will's number, *twenty-nine,* with every particle of his being. Will looked over his shoulder at Rafe, then turned away. Like every other eighteen-year-old embarrassed by a father's pride.

"Hey, buddy," Merry Folger said at his elbow.

Rafe lifted her off the ground with his hug. "Wasn't that great, Mere? Wasn't it just incredible? Did you *see* that play?"

"Missed it," she replied. "Did we score?"

"Will just returned a punt!"

"Yeah? Hey. That's wonderful, Rafe."

"I can never get over it, Mere, the way the kid always bounces back. When we had to fly him out to Mass Gen a couple of years ago—" Rafe stopped. "What the hell are you doing here? I thought you were on vacation for ten days. Is Pete back, too?"

"No." Merry zipped her parka, shivering, and Rafe was suddenly aware of the cold. "I'm here because a scalloper drowned in the boat basin yesterday, and Dad thought I should handle it."

"That drowning? You gave up the Mason Family Weekend for a *drowning*?"

"I know, I know. Peter was not amused."

She said it lightly, but Rafe read the truth in her expression. Wisely, he kept silent.

"You wouldn't happen to know the assistant football coach by sight, would you?"

"Dave Haddenfield? He's just beyond the bench, by the Gatorade cooler. Tall guy with glasses."

Merry looked in the direction Rafe pointed, her black eyebrows furrowing slightly. "Thanks."

"No problem, Girl Scout. Listen—"

"Yeah?"

She managed to smile at the familiar childhood nickname, but Rafe wasn't convinced. For months, Merry had been laboring under a cloud. Her shadowed eyes, the strain about her mouth, betrayed another sleepless night; and if she had agreed to investigate this drowning, it wouldn't be the last. What the girl needed was time off. Couldn't her father understand that? And where was Peter Mason, when Merry needed him most?

The thought of Peter recalled the reason for Merry's trip to the mainland—those Boston depositions. Rafe considered asking her how they had gone, then decided against it.

"If you aren't doing anything tomorrow after dinner," he said quickly, "come by the Greengage. Tess is having a closing party for a few friends. She'd love to see you."

"Great," Merry said. "I'll be there."

Dr. Barry Cohen had described his tenant Dave Haddenfield as an overgrown Labrador puppy—a type unlikely to shed much light on Jay Santorski's character. Merry privately thought she was certain to learn more from the reporter, Sue Morningstar; but since the high school fell right in the middle of Merry's route back to town, efficiency dictated she stop.

The lean, professorial figure Merry finally located at the far end of the Whalers' sideline looked nothing like the enthusiastic ball-chaser Cohen's description had promised. Haddenfield was more of a whippet than a Labrador, with a skittish, hungry look to his bony frame. He was well over six feet. His nose was sharp and his wrists protruded bonily from his team jacket. He swayed slightly as he followed the action of the game.

Merry edged around a knot of second-string players and tried to attract the coach's attention. "Dave Haddenfield?"

He looked down at her through his tortoiseshell glasses as though she might be a Football Mother, come to plead for her son's chances in the game.

She held out her badge. "I'm Detective Meredith Folger of the Nantucket Police. I know this isn't the best place to talk about your roommate, Jay Santorski—"

Haddenfield lost his distracted look immediately. "God, yes," he said. "You're here about Jay?"

"That's right. Could you spare a few minutes at halftime?"

"I guess—that is . . . Coach Victor will expect me to talk to the guys . . . and we need to go over stats—"

"Would after the game be better?"

"Yes." Palpable relief.

"I'll look for you in the gym, okay? We could sit on the bleachers and talk there."

A roar went up from the surging home crowd, and Merry completely lost Dave Haddenfield's attention.

"Touchdown!"

He jumped skyward, fist in the air, and came down pounding the back of anyone within reach. He was shouting something incomprehensible, a guttural rush, every line of his body straining. A man transformed by joy, or a similar violence. Merry drew a deep breath and stepped backward.

"Dave!"

Coach Victor, shouting from his position twenty feet down the line. "Where's our kicker, for crying out loud! What a time to visit the john!"

The fierce exultation died abruptly from Haddenfield's face. He looked around for the hapless kicker. A flushed-faced boy, his helmet tucked under his arm, sped mortified to the coach's side. Only then did Haddenfield relax, and remember Merry.

"I'm sorry—what were you saying?"

"When would you like to talk?"

He glanced at his watch. "Let's say, four o'clock. The post-game should be over by then, but the party isn't until six. Do you know the school?"

"I graduated from it."

"A few years ago, I'd guess." Haddenfield grinned. "There's a coaching office now that wasn't around in your time. In the corridor behind the gym."

"I'll see you around four."

Will was standing next to Rafe when Merry struggled back up the sideline. The boy had traded his helmet for a Whalers baseball cap with an impeccably rounded brim. Although the rain had ended, he had draped a poncho carelessly over his uniform. Merry had no idea who he was until she was almost upon him; and this, more than any transformation of height or voice, told her how much Will Starbuck had grown in the past few months. The uncertain kid was gone, and in his place was a too-thin, too-tall teenager on the edge of being a man.

He stood with his arms crossed, unconsciously mimicking his stepfather, and his eyes were riveted on the game. Since his fortuitous return of the Bulldogs' punt, the Nantucket team had crushed the despairing English. The superbowl was turning into a rout.

"Great play, Will," Merry said, and kissed his cheek.

"You saw it?"

"Yep," she lied. "I was *very* impressed."

He grinned and went uncharacteristically red. Then his eyes strayed to a ponytailed girl in a torn pair of jeans who sat in the stands a few yards away. She smiled, great doe eyes crinkling at the corners, and gave a little wave. The sleeves of her ribbed polo were pulled down over her fingertips for warmth. She was huddled against none other than Paul Winslow, who must have finally finished his dredging of the Easy Street Basin; and Merry felt a stab of worry as she looked from the pair to Will Starbuck.

"I should get back," Will said hurriedly. His eyes dragged unwillingly away from the ponytailed girl. "We're not supposed to leave Coach during game time. I just came to ask Rafe to catch you if he saw you again."

"Me?" Merry asked, surprised. "What do you need?"

"I found something in the harbor this morning. Dad thought you might want to see it."

Dad. Merry had never heard Will use that word for Rafe—it had belonged for too long to the dead Dan Starbuck—but from the effortless way the boy now tossed it out, Rafe had clearly earned it. She smiled.

"You go on," Rafe told Will, with a little push. "We don't want to get you in trouble. I'll take Merry to the truck."

Will nodded briefly and looked suddenly stern, as though he had no desire to enter the game again and would never burn with hope for a second chance at glory. Then he shoved his way through the crowd of Whaler fans. They parted for him with glances both affectionate and proud.

"So let's go, Girl Scout." Rafe was staring after his boy. "Will seems to think this is important."

Merry thought it was pretty important, too, when Rafe pulled the damp plastic bag from the bed of his old truck. She stifled an exclamation and ran hurriedly to her car for a pair of latex gloves, just in case. Then, holding the bag aloft like a kid with a carnival goldfish, she checked each end. One had been torn open, then knotted shut.

"Did Will do this? Or did he find it that way?"

"He opened it. Sorry. When he saw the needle, he got more careful. But by that time it was too late."

Natural, in a boy who had no reason to find anything sinister about a bunch of trash; but it meant two sets of fingerprints to exclude if necessary—Rafe's and his stepson's. Merry flattened the bag with her fingertips and stared at the things it held. A thimbleful of translucent ocean, a few grains of sand, an olive-green tendril of seaweed drifting on a lost current.

Latex gloves and a microtape.

And the hypodermic needle, of course.

Her green eyes flicked up to Rafe's sober brown ones. "Do you know where he found this?"

"Somewhere off the jetties, I think. The *actual* jetties, mind—not the beach."

"Right." Where Jay Santorski's body had been pulled from the harbor, as Will and Rafe probably knew. Bad news traveled like the Spanish flu around the island off-season. Did they know, as well, that the scalloper was familiar with hypodermic needles? Or had they made a lucky guess? One thing Rafe *did* understand, Merry thought, was that the strangest things turned out to be important—turned out to be evidence, even, in a serious crime. Years ago in New Bedford, lack of evidence had nearly killed him.

"Will said there were a couple of fair-sized pebbles weighting the bag. So it would *sink*." Rafe emphasized the last to convey what Merry already knew—that someone had hoped this bag would never be found. "He threw the pebbles back. Hell, he might've thrown the whole thing away. It wasn't until he showed it to me that we thought of you."

"I'm glad you did, although I have no idea whether it's important."

Rafe eyed the microcassette showing darkly through the clouded plastic. "For that, you might need a tape recorder."

Chapter Thirteen

A tape recorder Merry certainly had—buried deep in a miscellany of Post-it notes, rubber bands, paper clips, and half-empty packets of gum that lived forgotten in the middle drawer of her desk. The voice-activated microrecorder was a standard police item, easy to conceal, for use in delicate situations. But before it could be of any use, the waterlogged tape from the harbor bottom would have to be thoroughly dried. Still wearing gloves, Merry carried the cassette and Will's interesting plastic bag downstairs to Clarence's evidence room.

It was empty. Even if the crime scene chief returned from the Boston autopsy that evening, he was unlikely to report to the station until Monday morning. But Clarence Strangerfield was a man of method. He had strung a length of clean, new fishing line from one gray filing cabinet to another; and clipped neatly to the line were two matchbooks, blotched and crinkled with seawater. Jay Santorski's matchbooks. Completely dry, by this time. Merry peered at them idly. Nothing but chicken scratches and a blur of faded ink.

She tore off a length of paper toweling and set it on

Clare's desk. The cassette and plastic bag went carefully on top. Now she needed another clip, or some more fishing line. Her eyes roved vaguely along the narrow counter that ran down one side of the room. Its surface was covered with an astonishing variety of instruments—Clare was something of a pack rat where evidence collection was concerned. In addition to boxes of black, gray, red, and white fingerprint powder, there were several cameras—some handheld, some mounted over slides; a microscope; three infrared lights cocked at varying angles; calipers in graduated sizes; wood frames for molding footprints and tire treads with plaster of paris; a sketchpad; a boxful of loose vials with disposable eyedroppers in the lids; and three rolls of screaming yellow police barrier tape.

And these were only the supplies he kept at the station. Never mind the back of his van.

All this, Merry thought, *for a murder a year. Poor old Clare. He's wasted on us provincials.*

She found the roll of fishing line next to the fingerprint powders, and cut a length. Another instant, and the cassette was suspended from one of its reel openings next to the matchbooks. A drop of seawater gathered at one corner, trembled, and fell dismally to the linoleum floor.

Merry glanced at her watch. Two o'clock, and she was due back out at the high school to interview Dave Haddenfield around four. She was suddenly aware of a vast and unrequited hunger. Where to find lunch, after two on a Christmas Stroll weekend?

A simple association of ideas suggested the Ezra Mayhew House. But first, there were those matchbooks of Jay Santorski's, hanging under her nose and delightfully dry. They presented a considerable temptation. Clare could hardly object if she examined them under his infrared lights for an instant, and copied out the ghostly numbers thus revealed. Her stomach growled insistently. Without pausing for debate, Merry unclipped the matchbooks, snapped on the infrared, and threw the room into darkness.

One number had the Boston area code, 617. She could leave that for Clarence to trace. The other began with the Nantucket exchange—228. Merry copied it down on a piece of Clarence's notepaper, turned off the infrared, and clipped the matchbooks once more to the fishing line. Then she discarded her plastic gloves and left the evidence room.

"Gerri," she said to the uniformed officer behind the 911 response bank. "Can you plug a number into that thing and give me the address?"

"Sure. It's designed to work the other way around—"

"I know how it's designed." So that when somebody dialed 911, his home address immediately flashed across the screen, with a locator signal on an electronic map.

Gerri held out her hand for the slip of paper. "Give me a minute."

Merry stood by her side and watched as Gerri manipulated the panel's buttons. A few seconds later, a red light flashed out on the locator screen.

"That's 87 Sparks Avenue, Mere—the condo complex. Phone's registered to a Jennifer Bailey."

It was like Matt, Merry thought irritably, to have left his phone in his ex-wife's name three years after the divorce. That way, when he missed payment, the bill collectors harassed *her*. But what was his phone number doing in a drowned scalloper's pocket?

"Thanks, Ger."

She walked the short distance to her father's office with more than simple hunger churning in her stomach. The idea taking form in her mind was too disturbing to ignore. Her father's reticence about Bailey's disappearance—his entire demeanor since Merry's return from Connecticut—shouted an obvious warning. She was about to tread on some heavily corned toes.

But the Chief, as it happened, was nowhere to be found. His secretary, Janelle Taylor—a slight woman in her mid-forties with hair the color of gingersnaps—was barring the door to his empty office and looking singularly harassed. In front of her stood a stocky young woman dressed in pine-green corduroys and a cranberry-colored pullover that reached to her knees.

Christmas colors, Merry thought irrelevantly.

"Why can't I wait?" the girl cried in exasperation.

"I told you—Chief Folger is tied up all afternoon with the Stroll." The righteous indignation in Janelle's voice suggested to Merry that her father was sampling some Christmas cheer somewhere with an old friend.

"Then what about his daughter? When's she going to be back?"

"I have no idea. I am *not* the detective's assistant." Janelle reached behind her and pulled John Folger's door firmly shut. Then she slid smoothly behind her desk and picked up her reading glasses. "If you would like to leave your name and number, perhaps someone can return your call on Monday."

"Oh, I'll bet," the girl retorted, flaring. "I have a Monday afternoon deadline on this thing. Do I have to get my editor or the publisher to call?"

"Excuse me." Merry walked purposefully toward the small cubicle that held the secretary's desk. "I'm Detective Folger. Can I be of any help?"

"Oh, thank *God,*" the girl burst out. "Somebody intelligent for a change." She proffered a hand, and Merry took it. "I'm from the *I & M*. I'd like to talk to you about the death of Jay Santorski. You're responsible for the case, right?" She pulled open a large shoulder bag and reached distractedly for a notebook and pen.

"I'm not sure I'd call it a *case,*" Merry replied genially. "You wouldn't be Sue Morningstar, by any chance?"

Pen in hand, the girl looked up. Some of the frenzy in her face softened and died away. Under the fall of silken brown hair, her eyes were blotched and reddened with old tears. "Yes, I would."

Merry looked over at Janelle Taylor. "I take it Dad's not going to be back for a while."

"I really couldn't say."

"Then if you don't mind, I'd like to use his office. It's a little more private than the conference room."

Janelle shot to her feet in dismay. "Detective—I really don't think—"

"Fifteen minutes, max. Then I'm off to lunch at the Mayhew House. Can I bring anything back for you?" Merry threw the secretary her most winning smile.

"Well . . . maybe some chowder and a fish sandwich?"

"Done." Merry threw open her father's office door with one hand and ushered Sue Morningstar inside with the other.

"So," the reporter said, "you're the famous Merry Folger."

"Famous?"

"Around the *I & M*, at least. I covered the Roxie Teasdale story last spring. You were pretty impressive, Detective."

You don't know the half of it, Merry thought. She looked at the girl settling into the Chief's uncomfortable guest chair. Around twenty-four, if Seitz's notes were correct, and still sporting her college puppy fat. But her brown eyes were direct, and her chin was square and determined; nothing in her manner suggested immaturity. "Are you here as Mr. Santorski's roommate, or as an *Inky* reporter?"

"Both." Sue Morningstar's lips compressed in a thin line. "I asked to write the story on the drowning—we'd have covered it in any case, and as Jay's friend I owe it to him to get the piece right. But Barry Cohen called me after you left the house this morning. He says you think Jay died of an overdose."

Oh, Christ. He would. "That's something of an overstatement, Miss Morningstar," Merry said evenly. "We're merely trying to account for Mr. Santorski's drowning. As you probably know, he was said to be an excellent swimmer and an experienced waterman."

"You're saying he must have been drunk, or something, to ride into the Easy Street Basin? I know. It doesn't make sense. Jay was an athlete—he was in incredible shape. There's no way he could have just *drowned*. But why drugs? Why not alcohol?"

"Your guess is as good as mine."

The frustration returned to the girl's face. "Did you find something that led you to think it's an overdose?"

"Look—we'll just have to wait for the autopsy findings, I'm afraid. To say anything else—particularly in the newspaper—would be pure speculation. And grossly unfair to your roommate."

Sue Morningstar's eyes had fluttered involuntarily at the word *autopsy*. "You're putting me off."

"Not at all. I'm telling you the truth."

"If it's just a drowning, Detective, why did the Nantucket police put *you*—their star investigator—onto the case?" the reporter burst out.

"I'm hardly a star, Miss Morningstar. I just happen to be the only person available right now. And whenever there's an unexplained fatality, we open a file. This is strictly routine. If you want to interrogate somebody, try your roommate, Dr. Cohen. He's given you a false impression, I'm afraid."

The girl's stocky form sagged, defeated, into her chair. "I should have known Barry would exaggerate," she muttered. "He always loved to shit on Jay."

Merry leaned across the desk. "Why, exactly?"

Sue gave a dismissive bark of laughter. "Jealousy. Jay was everything Barry will never be. It was painful just to see them in the same room."

"Did that make the atmosphere in your house . . . somewhat tense?"

The reporter's eyes narrowed. "Are you interviewing *me*, now?"

Merry shrugged. "I was hoping you could tell me something about Jay. It might help us learn why he died."

Sue thought for a moment, her eyes fixed blankly on the middle distance. Then she drew a shaky breath, filled with the echo of tears. "Jay was a remarkable person. I know that's easy to say when somebody's dead, but in this case it's even true. He knew intuitively how to help people. He could sense what made you tick, and what drove you crazy, and he always tried to bring out the best in you. Around Jay, I felt . . . confident. Happy. As though I were pretty and smart and the best person he could possibly be with. Nobody could make me feel like Jay. Nobody ever will again." The strong chin quivered, the brown eyes crinkled, and suddenly Sue Morningstar dissolved in tears.

Merry cast about frantically for a box of tissues, and came up with a small crumpled packet in her father's bottom drawer. She offered them hurriedly to the reporter. "I'm so sorry."

"I have to say that all the time, too," Sue retorted angrily. Her voice was like a lash. She accepted the tissues and pressed one against her nose. "*I'm sorry.* The stock phrase for bereaved survivors. God, I hate journalism. Brutality pretending to be sensitive. Exploitation dressed up as public interest. It sucks, and so do I."

"Like detective work," Merry told her, "the ugliness is an occupational hazard. If you can still recognize the truth, you're doing fine. When you cease to notice, it's time to get out."

Sue nodded abruptly and blew her nose. Merry waited for the girl's breathing to grow calm again. Then she said, "Barry Cohen didn't like Jay. Did he ever try to throw him out of the house?"

"Unfortunately for Barry, Jay was a model housemate. Clean, quiet, and always ready to cook dinner for anyone who was home. Which was rarely Barry. *He* lives at the hospital."

"I understand Barry broke up a practice session one night."

"Harley's band, you mean? I guess you already talked to him. Yeah, that's Barry. Mr. Killjoy."

"Did that make Jay angry?"

"He never even got angry, much," Sue said thoughtfully. "And when he did, it was at inanimate objects—ATM machines that didn't work, engines that failed, traffic jams. Never at people. Certainly not Barry."

"Jay just took his parties elsewhere."

"I suppose."

"Did he party a lot?"

She hesitated. "What's a lot? I mean, that's a subjective term."

"Did he drink heavily, or use drugs recreationally?"

"I thought you were waiting for the autopsy results," Sue said bitingly.

"I am. I'm talking about what you saw, as someone who knew and . . . loved . . . Jay."

The girl flinched at the word, and looked away. "He'd go out for a beer with a bunch of scallopers once in a while. But I never saw him completely plastered."

"Scallopers. Owen Harley?"

She nodded.

"How close do you think the two of them were?"

"I never really thought about it. They seemed to work well together, and Jay loved Owen's band. That had a lot to do with Margot, of course."

"Margot—Harley's singer?"

"Jay was *obsessed* with Margot."

If so, Merry thought, then he was the second person to be described that way. Howie Seitz had used the same word for Owen Harley.

"Why?"

A simple question, which Sue Morningstar might have answered thoughtlessly. Instead, she chose her words with care. "I don't want you to think that what I'm going to say springs solely from jealousy. I *was* jealous of Margot, and still am, if it comes to that. But I think I understood the dynamic between them just as clearly as if I'd never cared about Jay at all."

"Go on," Merry said.

"Margot had some kind of hold over Jay. I'm certain of that."

"You mean—blackmail?"

"No. I mean that she inspired in him some sense of obligation. I don't know what it was. He would never tell me. But he knew that I saw their relationship for what it was. Calling it a sexual attraction was too simple, although there was plenty of that, God knows. Margot can set fire to a room just by walking into it." Sue hesitated, then shook her head. "It goes back to what I said earlier. That Jay knew how to help people. He *wanted* to help people, Detective. It was how he defined himself, I think. But it went even deeper with Margot. He was out to save her life, and she didn't want to be saved."

"You don't like her, do you?"

"That's the least of what I think of Margot. If I could get her off this island tomorrow, I would."

"Why?"

"Because she destroys the people she needs the most. And she uses everybody. Do you think Jay meant to her one-tenth of what he meant to me? Not even remotely. The only person Margot St. John cares about is Margot St. John. She is passionately involved with her own pain. She's made a kind of altar to it."

Sue's voice had a sharp edge of bitterness.

"And nothing is ever enough for her, Detective. If you want to talk about risk, talk to Margot. She pushes the envelope every day."

"Did you ever see her use drugs?" Merry asked.

Sue Morningstar gave her a long, perceptive look. Then her eyes widened with comprehension. "Oh, no," she said despairingly. "Not heroin. Not *Jay*."

Chapter Fourteen

Merry found Laurie Hopfnagel, the manager of Ezra's, sitting in a small, elegantly papered closet furnished with a desk and computer. Hopfnagel was tall and lean, with the sleek hair and shrewd eyes of a domesticated ferret. She rose and extended her hand when Merry's name was pronounced by a helpful underling; but Merry sensed the cordiality was forced.

"You're here about Jay, of course," Hopfnagel said briskly. "Such a tragedy. But your colleague, Officer Seitz, learned all we had to tell yesterday afternoon. I'm not sure what more I can do for you, Detective"—she glanced at her watch—"and I'm afraid this *is* one of our busiest days."

"I won't take much of your time." Merry looked about for a chair, but there was none in the tiny space; so she stood firmly before the restaurant manager's desk and took out her notebook.

Laurie Hopfnagel subsided into her chair. "Very well."

"Officer Seitz reported that you believed Mr. Santorski was stealing tips."

Hopfnagel's roving gaze abruptly stilled. "I did. Yes. I've

informed the proprietors of as much. But now that Jay's dead, I'm not sure what you can do."

"If you can prove the claim, you might be able to recover the sum from his estate," Merry said smoothly. "Roughly how much money do you believe disappeared?"

The woman hesitated, then looked down at her folded hands. "It's very hard to say, of course. I'm not really certain."

"But you're confident enough of Jay's culpability to have reported him to the owners?"

"Yes. They were aware of the discrepancies. There had been . . . complaints. From the other workers. About the disappearance of certain sums."

"I see," Merry said. "When did you inform the owners of your suspicions?"

"Yesterday evening."

"After Jay's death." After he was unable to refute the charge. Merry began to see a method in Laurie Hopfnagel's madness. If she had stolen the money herself, the late Santorski was a convenient scapegoat.

"I wasn't really certain before," the woman said, "and with Jay dead, I never can be, can I? And I'm sure the proprietors won't want to pursue the matter so far as to place a lien on his estate. That would be . . . in very bad taste, don't you think?"

"Taste? I really couldn't say." Merry watched her woodenly. "Just what exactly focused your attention on Mr. Santorski, Ms. Hopfnagel?"

"He was . . . secretive. A loner. Out for what he could get."

"Really?" This was a decidedly different picture of Jay from the one drawn thus far. "Did he ever seem unwell? Or as though his judgment was impaired?"

"Impaired? You mean . . . less than sober?"

Merry let Laurie Hopfnagel pursue that thought for herself. She watched the woman consider and then reject it—almost regretfully, it seemed.

"Jay was in excellent physical condition. That's what

makes his death so odd. He was the last person I'd have thought would drown. Do you think he was drunk, then?"

"We can't make any sort of statement about his physical state until we have the results of the autopsy."

"Of course." The shrewdness had returned to the small black eyes.

"When did you first notice that money was missing?"

"You're very kind to concern yourself, Detective, but I hardly think it's necessary." Laurie Hopfnagel rose again from her chair. "The owners have decided to let the matter drop."

How convenient, Merry thought.

"And now, if you'll excuse me—" The manager extended her hand.

Merry ignored it. "Could you tell me, please, what Jay earned per hour in his position?"

"Per hour? I think he probably earned around twelve dollars."

"You're kidding!"

"That's the going rate for waitstaff," Hopfnagel said stiffly. "Dishwashers earn slightly less. You may not be aware of this, Detective, but it's expensive to live on Nantucket. Getting service help is even harder. We have to pay them the earth. And in the summer months, give them housing into the bargain."

Of course, Merry had never realized that Nantucket was expensive. She had merely been born here.

"And how many hours per week did Santorski work?"

"He was part-time. A six-hour shift, three nights a week, with occasional overtime."

Merry did a swift calculation and nodded. "Roughly two hundred dollars, before taxes. Thank you. That's very helpful."

"I can't think why you should need to know," Hopfnagel retorted, the gentility stripped from her voice.

"Bank accounts," Merry supplied comfortably. She had no lingering illusion that Jay Santorski had stolen tips. But she had a fair idea who *had*. "We can compare his usual earnings with his weekly deposits, and get a handle on just how much of your staff's money went into his pockets."

"He probably spent it," the woman said bitterly. "I don't think you'll find anything."

"Neither do I," said Merry, with a steady look, "but I wouldn't be doing my job if I didn't try. One more thing, Ms. Hopfnagel."

"Yes?" Visible irritation. Perhaps a touch of fear?

"When did Jay Santorski leave the restaurant Thursday night?"

"I told your colleague. Around ten."

"You let everyone go early?"

She nodded.

"When would he normally have left?"

"Maybe an hour later."

"Thank you very much. You've been *so* helpful. And don't hesitate to report thefts in future, Miss Hopfnagel. We can work wonders if we're given timely information. Your average pilferer is usually more lucky than clever."

Laurie Hopfnagel merely smiled, and looked down at her desk.

Merry took the only available table, one with a view of the kitchen's swinging door, and looked forward to a chat with her waiter.

He introduced himself as David—a shining-faced, red-headed twenty-year-old wearing a suspicion of sideburns. When Merry had ordered a platter of fried oysters and some hot tea, she seized the moment and asked David whether he had known the dead scalloper.

"Oh, yeah—we're all wearing black armbands today." He pointed to his crape-encircled bicep. "I still can't believe it. I mean, he was younger than me! And he knew the water! Jay was the last person who should have drowned."

"So I understand." Merry fished for her police indentification in her voluminous purse, and presented it for David's admiration. "I'm investigating Jay's death."

The waiter frowned. "I thought . . . it was an accident."

"I'm sure it was," she replied, with more certainty than she felt. "But we still have to rule out any other possibility."

"Oh." He glanced over his shoulder at a florid man in a checked blazer who was gesturing frantically. "I've got to get that guy some ketchup. Could you wait a minute?"

Merry could; and after a tedious interval spent surveying the attire and conversation of her nearest neighbors, David returned. He deposited a plate of oysters and stood before her, tray dangling.

"I don't know what I can tell you," he began doubtfully.

"What sort of a worker was Jay? Did he do his job well?"

The waiter shrugged. "As well as any of us."

"Did you spend time with him outside of work?"

"Not really. He had his own group of friends. But I liked him," he added hopefully, as though liking Jay might win him a particular prize. Merry's good opinion, perhaps.

"Did most of your coworkers like him?"

"I guess." The waiter's eyes drifted away from her, probably anxious in the event of a summons.

"You never heard anything that might suggest otherwise?"

"No."

"Did Jay ever seem less than himself when he reported for work? Or did he call in sick a lot?"

His brows knit. "Not that I can remember."

Merry sighed inwardly and picked up her fork. "Well, thank you, David. You've been very helpful. You've got a good crowd here today—looks like the storm hardly affected Ezra's."

"Yeah. Last night was dead, but now that the weather's changed, we can't seat people fast enough."

"Good tips?"

"That'd be a change." He brushed at a crumb of bread on her tablecloth and smiled suddenly. "I haven't seen many of those this fall."

Merry looked innocently around the room. "You mean it's been slow?"

"That, or people are stiffing us." He glanced at the man in the checked blazer, whose jaws were working at a massive bite of hamburger. "You wouldn't believe how cheap the tourists can be."

The Whalers won the superbowl, forty-eight to fifteen. The dispirited Boston English trudged off the field through the renewed rain, helmets dangling from chilled fingertips, while Will and his buddies carried Coach Victor at a run toward the goalposts. Jorie found Will among the knot of boys caught in a full-throated yell, and felt a faint surprise. He looked so much like the rest of them. She thought of Will as someone set apart—someone whose thoughts were entirely his own. She turned to see whether Paul had noticed, but Paul was already walking toward his truck. Teeth chattering, Jorie followed.

The two boys could not have been more different from each other. Paul was tall and lean, with gray eyes and blond hair falling over his collar. He was very fair, while Will had the skin of a waterman, tanning quickly and staying dark well into winter. Will's black hair and blue eyes made his rare smiles somehow all the more startling. Paul used to smile a lot, Jorie thought as she watched him striding ahead of her. He used to laugh in a way that took her by surprise, as though he understood something funny that no one else saw. Lately, however, he had grown remote. Impossible to talk to. He hadn't wanted to come to the football game today—the high school no longer interested him—and yet, Jorie thought, Paul had no other world. He seemed adrift. Most of his friends had left Nantucket for jobs or colleges on the mainland. His dad had thrown him out of the house six months ago, and now he lived with five other guys in a place on lower Orange Street. Jorie had been there. It was falling down on its foundations, shingles missing, roof patched, shutters hanging awry. An old Confederate flag discarded by a forgotten summer tenant blocked the sun from Paul's window. It was a depressing place, frightening to Jorie; she had not gone back.

She was often worried about Paul, even afraid for him. At times she believed she loved him; at others, she knew that what she felt was merely the intense attachment of a seventeen-year-old, and that her life would go far beyond him.

"Want a ride?" he asked her as she reached the truck. "I'll take you home, if you like."

"Aren't you going to the party?"

"Party?" He stopped short. "No—no, I don't think I want to hang out with a bunch of high school kids, thank you very much." He pulled his keys from his jeans and shoved them into the driver's side door. But Jorie didn't walk around to her side of the truck. She stood there, willing herself not to shake with the cold, and studied him intently.

"Where were you today, Paul?"

"What do you mean?" He opened the door in her face, using it like a barrier.

"You said you were going scalloping. Will and I were out on the water today for two hours. We never saw you once."

"I did some work for the cops."

"The cops?"

He nodded, his eyes on the ground. "They wanted the Easy Street Basin dredged. In case any of Jay's things ended up on the bottom."

"Jay? You mean the guy who drowned?"

"Yeah."

"He was a friend of yours, wasn't he?"

Paul shrugged. Jorie edged around the open car door and touched his arm tentatively. "I'm really sorry, Paul."

"He just screwed up, that's all."

"Did you find anything?"

"Where?"

"In the boat basin."

"Nah. Just a lot of junk. Waste of time. Are you getting into the car, or what? Because I don't have all day."

Hurt, Jorie glared at him, and for the first time saw the strain on his face. His blue eyes were ringed with shadows, and he was trembling slightly, too, despite the heavy jacket he wore on the water and off. With sudden understanding, she put a name to his restless unease.

"You're using again, aren't you?"

"None of your goddamn business."

Jorie turned as though she had been struck and walked quickly away. She kept her head high and stared blindly at the empty field, lips moving with stifled abuse. He had *promised* her. He had *promised*.

"Jor!"

The word was torn and desperate.

"Come on, Jor! I didn't mean it!"

She walked on.

"Detective. As promised." Dave Haddenfield saluted Merry with a green plastic Gatorade bottle and ushered her into his tiny office. Now that the game was safely won, the assistant coach exuded affability.

"Congratulations," Merry said.

"Thanks. It's really Victor's win—the man's a legend. But if you went to high school here, you know that."

"Yes. He even coached my brother." The thought of Billy suited up to play—had he really been as young as Will Starbuck?—brought a faint spasm of pain. Maybe it was Coach Victor, and all those football Saturdays, Billy had been thinking of when he tackled the grenade.

"You wanted to talk about Jay," Dave Haddenfield prodded.

"Right." She settled her notepad on her lap and uncapped her ballpoint pen.

"I couldn't believe he died that way. It doesn't make sense."

"So everyone says." She felt the coach's eyes on her face, and made a show of scribbling something on the pad. Let him formulate the question in his own time.

"But you still think it was an accident?"

Bingo. Merry looked up and smiled. "I was hoping you could give me your sense of Mr. Santorski."

Haddenfield took off his glasses and wiped the thick lenses with the edge of his sweatshirt. "Is there something . . . wrong . . . with Jay's death?"

"What do you mean?"

"I wouldn't have thought a simple drowning would require an investigation."

"Mr. Santorski's death is unexplained. As such, it requires that some questions be asked."

"I see. So you're *not* considering it an accident."

"Saying it was an accident doesn't exactly *explain* how it happened," Merry elaborated.

"Let's talk plainly, Detective." Haddenfield resettled the glasses on his nose. "Was Jay in trouble when he died?"

"What sort of trouble?"

Haddenfield hesitated. "I suppose you've heard about the Save Our Harbor campaign?"

Whatever she had expected, it was hardly this.

"No. I hadn't. Would you like to tell me about it?"

"It's Owen Harley's brainchild. I'm surprised you haven't come across a flyer or two at Mitchell's Book Corner, or posted on the Hub bulletin board. They're soliciting donations from everybody still breathing. Jay was helping Owen canvass the local landowners and landscape designers."

"About the harbor?" Merry's confusion showed.

"About voluntary fertilizer limitations. Or even an outright ban for properties in the harbor watershed. They were going to bring it before the selectmen at the next Town Meeting."

Like any number of historic New England towns, Nantucket was still governed by a Board of Selectmen and a Town Meeting, at which a number of citizen initiatives were either passed or defeated by two-thirds majority. The two-day political powwow, held every April at the high school, was a forum for public debate and a general ratification of the island's way of life. Merry had tangled once with the selectmen over an unscrupulous real estate development, but she thought they might consider the case of the harbor without police prodding. If the island's most vibrant feature was allowed to decline, more than tourism would suffer.

But what did that have to do with Jay Santorski's death?

"A fertilizer ban," she mused. "I don't quite understand your concern, Mr. Haddenfield."

"It's Owen Harley. He's a bit extreme, Detective. An aging hippy, if you know what I mean. I wouldn't be surprised to hear that he had involved Jay in something . . ." He paused. "Criminal."

"Criminal."

"Yes. I've heard Owen talk about sabotaging the homes of people who refuse to comply with fertilizer reduction."

The image of Jay Santorski huddled over a homemade pipe bomb drifted through Merry's mind. Partly to suppress a wild impulse to giggle, she said, "And would this be before or after they won approval at Town Meeting?"

Dave Haddenfield stiffened. "I'm sorry you find this amusing, Detective. Jay is, after all, dead."

"Jay *drowned* in the harbor, Mr. Haddenfield."

"I know that. I'm merely suggesting that his death might have occurred in pursuit of something . . . unscrupulous."

"I see." Merry looked down at her notepad. Any theory, however bizarre, was worth remembering. "I'll keep that thought in mind. Did Jay's friends know about his involvement with Save Our Harbor?"

"His friends? They weren't the sort to be interested in political causes."

"What were they like?"

He shrugged. "Some of them were involved in music—people he knew through Owen—and some of them were scallopers. Or biologists, like Hannah Moore."

This was a name Merry hadn't heard. "Hannah Moore?"

"She sits on the Save Our Harbor steering committee. Hannah's married to a local real estate guy—big bucks, and I hear she knows how to spend it. Hasn't been too much in evidence lately, however. Hannah and Owen don't see eye-to-eye."

"Because she's not a revolutionary, I suppose. Few wives of real estate moguls are. Was Jay friendly with her?"

Haddenfield smiled. "It was the other way around, Detective. For a married woman several years his senior,

Hannah Moore conducted a scorched-earth campaign in her pursuit of poor Jay. If she hadn't made herself so ridiculous, it might have been funny. Instead it was just sad. Jay didn't give a damn about anyone but Margot."

"Ah, yes. Miss St. John. It sounds as though Jay had his hands full."

"I suppose," Dave Haddenfield said thoughtfully. "But neither of them seemed to make him happy."

"You're the first person to suggest that Jay wasn't a happy guy. From everything I've heard, he was Mr. Sunshine. Did you think of him as moody?"

He studied her expressionlessly for several seconds. "So that's it," he said finally. "You think he killed himself. I admit, it's the only thing that makes sense. Why would a perfectly capable guy of twenty-one, a guy comfortable with boats and the water, drown to death?"

"Because he fell into thirty-eight-degree water at the dead of night with too many clothes on."

From the coach's silence, Merry was certain her deflection hadn't worked. The idea that Jay Santorski had gotten drunk and killed himself over a woman (or two) would be circulating in a matter of hours.

"What did you think of Jay, Mr. Haddenfield?"

"I envied him," he said simply.

"Why?"

"He had everything in the world. Good looks, intelligence, more than enough money, a great education. He knew what he wanted, and he barely had to lift a finger to get it."

"And now he's dead," Merry said flatly.

"Yes. It's bizarre. I can't get used to it." He lifted his glasses from his nose and rubbed wearily at his eyes. They were red-rimmed—from wind? Or sleeplessness?

"Did you like Jay, Mr. Haddenfield?"

"It was impossible not to."

"Barry Cohen doesn't think so."

"Oh, well, *Barry*—he had a lot of reasons to dislike Jay. Most of them having to do with Sue. But you'll have to ask them about that."

"I already have."

"That's probably why Jay was planning to move out."

Merry looked up from her notepad. "He was?"

"He was going to live with Margot. In the Baxter Road house. Jay said the place was too isolated in winter for Margot to be alone; she was frightened at night. The whole thing made Sue absolutely furious."

"Really?"

"They had a huge fight about it at three o'clock in the morning. Woke the whole house. Didn't she tell you?"

"No."

"I suppose I can see why not. Pretty embarrassing for her."

"You've had a difficult time of it in that house, Mr. Haddenfield, with so many tensions among your housemates."

At this, the football coach smiled. "It wasn't a healthy situation. It sounds brutal—but Jay's death will probably help."

In the end, it was Rafe da Silva who dropped Will and Jorie at the post-game party. He pulled up in a parking space outside the coach's house and turned off the ignition.

"You're sure you're warm enough?" he asked Jorie, a small furrow between his brows.

She nodded.

"Give her your jacket, Will, just in case."

"Really, Mr. da Silva—I'm fine."

"You don't look fine," Will said, and shrugged out of his coat. Before she had time to protest, he draped it around her shoulders, fingers cool against the back of her neck. She felt herself flush stupidly. "We'll find you some coffee inside."

"Tea," she said. "Decaf."

She was sitting in the middle of the front seat, legs straddling the gearshift, between Will and his stepfather. Will leaned around her to shake Rafe's hand, with that strange male formality, as though he and his dad were strangers on an elevator. She had never seen Will kiss anybody—other than a peck on his mother's cheek—and she wondered, suddenly, whether he ever had.

"Tell Tess I'll be home by midnight," he told his stepfather. "I'll walk. It's only a couple of blocks."

"And how will Jorie get home?"

"It's okay," she said quickly. "I'll call my mom."

"Look," Rafe said reasonably, "*I'll* walk home right now, and we'll leave the truck parked here. After the party, Will can drop you at your house, Jorie, and save your mom the trip. Easier every way around."

Jorie glanced at Will. His dark blue eyes looked wary.

"What about Paul?" he asked her. "Aren't you seeing him later?"

"I'm never seeing Paul again," she said distinctly.

"Okay, then." Rafe handed Will the keys and opened the car door. "Try to be back by one, buddy."

"I will, Dad." The boy's words were for his father, but he was looking at Jorie.

She drew the collar of Will's jacket close to her throat. "Don't ask me now," she said. "I want to be happy for a while."

Will flashed his fleeting smile. "Then let's go."

Chapter Fifteen

By the time Merry arrived home Saturday evening, she was sick to death of the subject of Jay Santorski. She had talked to people for hours, with that blend of official interrogation and sympathetic shop designed to elicit the fullest response—or so she hoped. She wanted to lie on her couch and watch a movie, with Chinese food for company; but Peter would have flown in the food from Hyannis, and picked it up at the airport, and that much effort was beyond her. She considered calling the dangerous Margot St. John—Sue Morningstar had given Merry the girl's number—and then decided against it. There was a limit to how many questions even *she* could ask in one day.

As she made her way back toward the station, Merry saw that the end-of-the-year darkness had fallen as completely as a blindfold over Nantucket town. Main Street was closed to traffic during Christmas Stroll, and despite the penetrating cold, a desultory crowd moved purposefully along its cobblestoned length. Lights shone out from frosted shop windows and crimson ribbon twined along the horsehead hitching posts. The chorus of a Christmas carol drifted to Merry's ears as she stood before her car, keys in hand. The sights and the sounds made her feel unutterably lonely. Abruptly she stuffed the keys back in her purse and left the car behind on Chestnut Street. Tonight she would walk, and try to forget drowned scallopers and their destructive habits. Tonight she would have her own Christmas Stroll, Peter or no Peter.

She started at Nantucket Looms, with a lingering survey of their braided rag rugs, the color of pomegranates and eggplant, the color of the sea. They had gone in this year for selling wool—and with a sense of surprise, Merry saw the calligraphed placard propped in front of the bins. *Island Merino from Mason Farms*. Had Peter told her he was selling wool to the store?

Had Peter told her much of anything, lately? Or had she simply stopped paying attention?

John Folger sat with his back to the warm glow of 21 Federal's fireplace. The bar was alive with faces—elegant, vividly happy—and a buzz of laughter and clashing cutlery drowned the voices in his head. He glanced sideways at a well-dressed foursome drinking Scotch under one of the restaurant's handsome oil paintings—a racing yacht, keeled-over, with all its flags flying. They were off-islanders come for Christmas Stroll, and privileged in holding reservations for one of Nantucket's best tables. The two women were bottled blondes with ropy gold chains at their necks and well-manicured hands, so similar they might have been sisters. They gazed with artificial adoration into the eyes of their men, who had adopted the daring mode of banded-collar shirts under their Armani jackets.

Well-being circulated among the four like an expensive scent. John turned away and took another swig of his beer.

He had watched the waitstaff pace through the changes of the lunch crowd, the late afternoon aperitif drinkers, and now the dinner surge. He had been sitting at the bar all afternoon, nursing a succession of microbrews. He was *not* drunk—he never allowed himself to be drunk, particularly in uniform—but he was profoundly miserable.

He could not see his way clear. He could not go back. And so he waited, like a man with a terminal disease, for other hands to decide his fate. If he could remain in the warm glow that lived here between the fireplace and the sage-colored walls, all destiny suspended—

"Like another, Chief?"

Tommie the bartender, his expression inscrutable. He had succeeded the day barman—Alonzo Madeira—whose careful dark eyes had betrayed even less. Off-islanders meant little to John Folger, particularly at this time of year; but people like Tommie mattered. They would wonder why he had drunk away the afternoon, and they would begin to talk. There would be a tidal wave of talk breaking over his head in a matter of days; he knew that now.

He had been a fool to involve Meredith. Dirty work should be handled alone.

"I'm worried about Dad, Ralph."

"It's Saturday night, Meredith Abiah, and Christmas Stroll into the bargain. It's high time your father had a little fun. John's old enough to find his way home."

"That's not what I meant. But where is he, anyway?" Merry sliced a hunk of Jarlsberg and laid it on a cracker. Despite the Mayhew House's ample oysters, she was ravenous again. Once she had quit the gaiety of Main Street, her feet had carried her instinctively to her grandfather's house. Ralph Waldo had poured her some Harvey's, put a match to the fire, and listened without comment while she stumbled through an account of her day.

"I believe your father has asked a lady of his acquaintance to dine," he said now, and settled himself in his favorite chair.

"No way." The cracker halted in midair, three inches from Merry's open mouth. "Dad's on a *date*?"

"Don't look so appalled."

"I'm not! Really. I'm pleased. Who is she?"

"Someone he met during that computer course he took at the high school last summer."

"And it's taken him this long to ask her out?"

Ralph Waldo regarded her sardonically. "It took him five years to ask your mother to marry him, my dear. John was never a precipitate human being."

"No," Merry mused, and sipped her sherry. "Which is why I'm worried. He called me back from Connecticut as though a bomb were about to explode, Ralph—and now, every time I want to talk to him, he's unavailable. It's just not like Dad. He's acting—cagey. As though he's hiding something."

Her grandfather reached for a tray table resting near her chair and pulled it toward him. A variety of arcane objects were arranged on the rectangular surface, and his aged hands moved among them fondly. "Hiding something. About the young man who dabbled in heroin?"

"And about Matt Bailey. Bailey's office has been thoroughly cleaned out, Ralph. It's like the guy never existed. Dad has to know something—" She stopped abruptly, her eyes on the torpedo-shaped wooden mold around which her grandfather was methodically weaving strips of cane. "Is that a lightship basket you're making?"

"It is, Meredith. And if success anoints my efforts—you shall have it for a wedding gift."

"Where did you learn to do that?"

"Another course," he said briefly, "in September. You've learned very little about the habits of the Folger men since moving a few blocks away, Meredith. We do not allow ourselves to stand still. We stride forward, toward the twenty-first century."

"With a babe and a basket under each arm. I suppose Emily Teasdale roped you into this?"

Emily Teasdale, librarian emerita of the Nantucket Atheneum, was the friend of Ralph Waldo Folger's twilight years, as he himself might have put it. She was also, to Merry's infinite regret and rage, the grandmother of Roxie Teasdale, a young schoolteacher brutally murdered the previous spring.

"I owe Emily many things, but not my interest in lightship baskets," Ralph replied with dignity. "I came to them entirely on my own. When you reach the age of eighty-five, Meredith, and are still blessedly in command of your wits, you cast about for honorable work. Particularly of a winter evening. I ruled out needlepoint and pornography, not to mention chess with the Wharf Rats, and settled instead on this. Lightship baskets are so peculiar to Nantucket—and in their origins, so peculiar to men, who first devised them—that it seems a man might do worse with his idle hours than to fashion a thing of beauty."

"You have to teach me someday."

"Tell me what's troubling you about the scalloper's death," he said, looking up from the fan of canes.

"Nobody who knew him seems to think he was a drug user."

"That's not so very unusual."

"It is in a small town like this. *Somebody* should have noticed. And then there's the problem of Matt Bailey."

Ralph Waldo's right eyebrow shot skyward. "I thought your father told you not to worry about him."

"That's why I am."

"I see."

"Ralph, why would Dad be lying to me?"

If she had expected him to protest and reassure her, Ralph Waldo was destined to disappoint. "Is he lying to you, then?"

"I think he must be. Or, at the very least, withholding information. He insists Bailey's absence is unconnected to Santorski's death. But I just found a connection today. The kid died with a matchbook in his pocket that had Bailey's phone number on it."

"Ah," her grandfather said comprehendingly, and continued weaving. "Does John know?"

"If he does, I'm the last person he'll tell," Merry shot back bitterly.

Ralph pursed his lips. "And you're wondering why."

"Shouldn't I? Have *you* ever heard of bringing a detective onto a case, and then stonewalling her?"

"Repeatedly. It's common practice in some large urban areas, I believe."

"But not here. Not between Dad and me."

"Merry," Ralph said patiently, "imagine for a moment that John is not your father. Consider his behavior purely from the standpoint of a police investigation. Why would he withhold certain information from you?" Her grandfather's fingers came to rest on the wide wooden drum of the basket mold, as though he were cradling an infant. "So as not to prejudice your findings, perhaps."

"Or because he doesn't trust me to handle the truth," she retorted.

Ralph dismissed this with a wave. "His calling you home from Connecticut should put paid to that fear. Your father trusts you more than anyone else on the force, Meredith Abiah, whether he tells you so or not. You dwell far too much on the mistakes in your past, my dear, and far too little on the successes. Which are considerable."

Merry was silent for several minutes, her eyes on the fire declining in the grate. Ralph Waldo's fingers recommenced their difficult work, and the wind howled around the eaves of the Tattle Court house.

"Let's say, for the sake of argument," she persisted, "that Matt Bailey was running an undercover drug sting operation. And that his agent was Jay Santorski. What if their cover was blown? And their target was a particularly nasty individual, dealing in heroin? Santorski's death, apparently by overdose—which may have been administered against his will, while his wrists and ankles were bound—suddenly makes sense. So does Bailey's disappearance. Matt's scared to death, and on the run."

"I thought you people had sworn off drug operations for a while," Ralph said, his eyes suddenly grave.

"So did I." Merry let all that was unspoken hang in the air between them. "Maybe that's why Dad doesn't want to talk about it."

For years, the Nantucket force had prided itself on undercover work like Fred McIlhenney's. However successful last year's bust, it was in general a perilous and volatile game, with success dependent upon two things:

the worth of the agent planted in the drug dealer's midst, and the secrecy enshrouding the operation.

Like McIlhenney, Bailey had run an undercover op or two—the most recent ending in failure the previous winter. Bailey lacked McIlhenney's flair for discretion. He was also plagued with what he called bad luck, and Merry privately considered bad judgment. Bailey had been careless and blown his agent's cover; and the agent himself, in a desperate bid to shore up his target's confidence, had started snorting cocaine with abandon. By Valentine's Day, the agent was in detox and the target had fled to Mexico.

John Folger had not been pleased. Neither was the DA, Dan Peterson. And he had very nearly aborted McIlhenney's operation, although Bailey knew nothing about it and could hardly have jeopardized Joey Figuera, whose true identity was more closely guarded than Salman Rushdie's home address. McIlhenney had objected, and pled the case for calm—and in the end, he'd busted Marty Johansen.

Bailey, however, was relieved of all drug-enforcement duties.

In theory.

"I didn't think Dad could be rash enough to let Bailey handle something dangerous again," Merry said.

"You don't know for a fact that he did," Ralph pointed out. "You don't even have the results of the autopsy. Young Jay might have died for entirely innocent reasons."

"With needle marks on his arm and Bailey's phone number in his pocket. I don't like it, Ralph."

The Santorski drowning was beginning to look like a classic Bailey screwup. Jay's profile fit the working one for undercover agents. The young man had appeared at random on the Nantucket scene, and worked his way almost immediately into a circle known for its drug use. He had taken a minimally paid laborer's job on a scallop boat, and another part-time at a local restaurant, much as Joey Figuera had done. He had hung out at the typical places that islanders frequented, struck up conversations, asked questions, and looked for some action.

And he had Bailey's phone number in his pocket.

Had they met periodically in the darkness of the moors, Jay edgy and troubled, Bailey his usual overconfident and deeply stupid self? Had Bailey tried to control Jay's growing affection for Margot St. John, or told him to spy on his new friends, or equipped him with a voiceactivated tape recorder and microcassettes, like the one presently hanging from a fishing line in Clarence Strangerfield's office?

Merry set down her sherry glass with ringing finality. "I understand what you mean, Ralph. If Santorski died completely by accident, Dad would see no reason to mention that he was on the police payroll. Why risk the negative exposure? Not to mention the DA's outraged questions. So he decides to keep that crucial fact from me, and hopes I'll declare the death a simple drowning. But I can't be the neutral party he wants, Ralph. I keep finding facts that don't fit the neat solution. I'm not sure that I *want* to, anyway."

"What do you mean?"

"Say that Santorski *did* drown by accident. If he died with heroin in his veins, and he was working for Bailey in any capacity, the Nantucket force is *morally* responsible for his death. We can't dodge that truth. His mother, at least, deserves better."

"Wait for the autopsy report, Meredith," her grandfather counseled gently.

"Dad hasn't left me much choice, has he?"

"You okay?" Will asked Jorie.

She was sitting silently beside him in Rafe's truck, the deep island darkness flowing around them. And something else was lingering there, between the seat and the dashboard—something Will felt in the very tips of his fingers. Anxiety. Nerves. Was Jorie afraid to be alone with him?

"Looks like it's clearing," he attempted. "Stars coming out behind the clouds."

"I think Paul is using drugs." Jorie's voice was very small, like a child's.

"Paul's always been using drugs," Will said, more sourly than he had intended. There had been a time when he had liked Paul almost as much as Jorie; but that was years ago now, and Will was growing older. "Why do you think his dad threw him out of the house?"

"I mean *real* drugs."

A chill rose along Will's back. "Like—what, exactly, Jor?"

She shrugged, and looked out the car window. "I don't know. Heroin, maybe."

It fell like a curse between them, harsh and ugly. "You're kidding," Will said, shock in his voice. Images of needles and hollow-eyed rock stars rose before his eyes. "*Heroin?* Where would Paul get heroin?"

"I don't know," she said again. "Hyannis, maybe? Or from his friends?"

"What friends? *We're* his friends."

"Used to be," she said, turning now to look at him. "We *used* to be his friends. But he has others now. Paul isn't interested in high school kids anymore."

Will's heartbeat accelerated. He drove around the Rotary and took the road to the airport, where Jorie and her mother lived. "Does that include you, Jor?" he asked her in a conversational tone.

"I guess it does." She was trying not to cry.

"I'm sorry," he said, and bit his lip. "He's a total loser, Jorie—"

"What did you do with that needle, Will? The one you found today?"

He hesitated.

"You didn't show it to your dad, did you?"

"You think it was Paul's?"

"I don't know! But what if it was? What if he threw it into the harbor, so nobody could find out? You saw how he put the rocks in the bag. He wanted that stuff to stay on the bottom."

"Nobody's going to know about Paul," Will said, and reached across the gearshift for her hand.

Jorie gripped his fingers tightly, then let them go. "Tell me the truth, Will. Did you show it to your dad?"

"I threw it away," he lied, and turned the truck into her driveway.

Chapter Sixteen

It was nearly midnight, and Margot St. John was afraid.

She was often afraid in the old house sitting high on the Sconset bluff. Most of the neighboring places on Baxter Road were deserted in winter, when the little town's population dove to a mere two hundred, and the wind tore relentlessly at the tips of the dune grass. Everywhere Margot looked, she saw blind windows, shuttered against the dark and the rain. She had turned out the lights in her own kitchen finally, a gesture of solidarity with the gale.

Her arms were locked around her knees as she sat at the bare kitchen table, and her long hair fell across her shoulders like a shroud. From time to time, she tipped back a bottle of Jack Daniel's and swallowed a mouthful of fire. Her birthday celebration.

Two years ago, when she'd turned twenty, they had all gone out for dinner together in Cambridge. Katia had wanted to work late that night in her office at the Harvard *Crimson*—she was just a staffer then, but already fiercely dedicated—and Jay had carried her bodily away from her desk and out the door. Katia had refused to submit to such high-handed behavior, staying stiff as a board while Margot teased and Jay pushed her gamely through the darkened streets.

"You love pasta," Margot was insisting. "And it's my birthday! The *Crimson* is a volunteer job, for God's sake! You don't have to make it your life—"

On one street corner, where they stopped to rest Jay's arms, was a knot of boys. Typical Cambridge boys—polyglot, multiracial, wearing hip-hop clothes and knit hats pulled down on their foreheads. One of them asked if they wanted to buy some smack. Margot had no idea what they meant; now, that vanished naiveté almost made her laugh aloud. Jay took Katia's arm, and started to tug her purposefully toward the opposite corner, when suddenly she broke away.

"How much?" she asked.

"Thirty bucks."

"Let's get out of here, Kate," Jay said, taking her arm again.

But she was already fishing in her purse.

Later, standing in the restaurant doorway, he asked her—urgent, low-voiced, and worried—what the hell she had been doing. "If a cop had seen you, all of us would be in jail right now. You may not care about that yourself, but you should think about what it might do to your friends."

"I didn't ask to come with you tonight."

He turned away, scowling.

"There's a story in this," Katia insisted passionately, her blond hair sliding from behind one ear. " 'Heroin in Harvard's midst.' Do you realize how easy that was tonight? And those kids were maybe twelve. It's urban crime on the edge of the Ivory Tower. That's a story I've got to write. But I've got to find some students who are junkies, first."

"Are you out of your mind?" Jay demanded. "You can't print that. You'd cause enormous problems for a lot of people who just want to destroy themselves in peace."

"Just watch me," Katia said. With that crazy, distant light in her eyes. "It's got nothing to do with you."

And from that day forward, all their lives had changed. Some of them had even ended.

A sharp rap at the door jolted Margot out of reverie. She stood up, trembling uncontrollably, and stared down the length of dusky hall.

Another knock, pounding this time, and the door shuddered. "Margot! *Margot!*"

It was Owen Harley's voice.

Swallowing a sob, she ran to the door and pulled it open. "Owen! I tried to find you yesterday. You weren't home."

He stepped inside and stood looking down at her, just as Owen always did, as though he were viewing her under a lens. "You've been drinking."

"It's my birthday." She tried to smile, and dissolved in tears instead.

And for the first time in their unsteady acquaintance, Owen Harley reached out and took her in his arms. He stood awkwardly, his embrace wooden, and she derived very little comfort from his touch. She backed out of it as soon as possible.

"I've got to talk to you, Margot," he said tensely.

She nodded and led him to the vast emptiness of the living room. There was a sofa there—a camelback, upholstered in a blue damask that had faded to the color of the house's gray shingles. Margot's narrow silk dress, a violent gold overlaid with green veins and bloodred poppies, looked impossibly brilliant against its bulk, as though she had disappeared into an early Matisse canvas.

"Jay didn't just drown."

She looked at him dully.

"He was shot full of heroin when he went into the water."

She squeezed her eyes shut.

"Margot, his arm had tracks on it! The police are asking all sorts of questions. They were over at my place today. Can't you go home? Get off the island for a while?"

She shook her head. "That's ridiculous."

"It's not, Margot. Believe me. You don't want to be here when they find out that Jay was dating a woman who used . . . needles. It would be better for you. To leave. Trust me."

"I mean it's ridiculous to say that Jay shot up before he died. He never would have."

"He must have."

She shook her head violently, her face filling with rage. "It's a lie. A lie, Owen! To make his death seem tawdry and despicable. To drag him down to my—to make people dismiss it. But Jay didn't use needles. He never would have. *I know.*"

Owen dropped to her side and placed his hands in supplication on her lap. His bearded face, ravaged by weather, had a terrible pleading in it. "That police detective had no reason to lie. Jay was shot full of something when he went into the water. You've got to get out, Margot. Please. For me."

"For you?" Her frown deepened. "Would it make you happy if I left, Owen?"

"I'm never happy without you," he said, with sudden appalling intensity. "Not in my boat, not in my bed—not even on the water. You've destroyed the deepest love I've ever known, my love for the sea. You've made me unquiet, Margot, and I'll never go back again."

"Don't, Owen—"

"But I'd send you away in an instant, if I thought it could keep you safe. There's something worse going on than either of us understand."

"There's nothing worse than Jay's death."

He gripped her knees harder, and she winced. "I want you out of it."

She stood up without a word and walked away from him, up the stairs to her bedroom. When she returned, she held a flat manila envelope in her hands, extended as with a peace offering. "He left this for you."

"What?"

"Jay. Thursday afternoon, before he went to work. I was supposed to give it to you at our rehearsal session that night. I forgot."

He stared at the envelope, then took it and opened it. A square of paper, overlaid with the bars of a graph, slid into his hands.

"Is it important?" Margot asked.

"I have no idea."

"Maybe he was coming to talk to you about it. When he rode into the basin."

"Maybe he was," Owen said dismissively, and stuffed the graph back into the envelope. "Will you go home, Margot? At least for a little while?"

"That was the last thing he asked me to do for him," she insisted. "And I failed."

Chapter Seventeen

Paul Winslow was sitting at the lunch counter of Congdon's Pharmacy on Main Street when he saw Will Starbuck walk through the door.

The Christmas Strollers were out in force, and Congdon's was mobbed, so that a regular customer like Paul had been forced to jockey for his bacon and eggs. A wall of bodies hid him from Will's view for a moment. Paul huddled over his fork and kept his eyes on his coffee mug, hoping the moist heat and lack of floor space would discourage the other boy. Paul's head was pounding, and when he reached for his coffee cup, his fingers shook. One booted foot maintained a restless tatoo against the lower rail of his stool.

"Paul."

He turned uneasily and met Will's dark blue eyes. "Hey. What's up?"

"Not much. Didn't get to talk to you yesterday."

"No. Too busy chasing a ball around a field." Paul's voice was more cutting than he had intended.

"You were wicked good, Paul. Nobody this year can touch you."

Paul had quarterbacked last year's superbowl game. Will hadn't even played.

"Yeah, well—that was last year, wasn't it? I'm not a kid anymore." Paul swallowed hard, his eyes flicking from his half-eaten eggs to his half-empty coffee cup. The mingled smells of frying food and wet sweaters were beginning to turn his stomach.

Will ignored the sneer. He continued to stand next to Paul's stool, one hand tucked in the pocket of his jeans jacket, the other still holding his keys. He eased closer to Paul every time somebody brushed past to pounce on an empty counter seat, and the nearness of his body was almost suffocating.

"I figured you'd be out on the water today," Will said, "but Jorie thought I'd find you here."

"Jorie? What's Jorie know about my life?"

"And here you are, keeping Congdon's in business on Christmas Stroll weekend."

Paul closed his eyes and rested one hand against his forehead. It was beaded with sweat. "What do you want, Starbuck?"

"Why aren't you out making money, Winslow, instead of burning it on breakfast?"

"Why does everybody think I've got to scallop every goddamn day?" Paul exploded. "Can't a guy sit out a nor'easter anymore?"

Will cocked an eye at Congdon's plate-glass window. Beyond it, the damp cobblestones of Main Street shone like pewter in the freshly washed light. "Looks pretty sunny out there to me."

Paul half rose from his seat, wanting to slam the other boy's complacent face; feeling the press of bodies around them, he sank back down. "There's no money in scalloping anyway," he muttered viciously. "I'm quitting as soon as I sell my boat."

"Really?" said Will. "I thought you loved that old tub."

Paul did not reply. A large woman in a bright yellow plastic slicker vacated the seat next to his, and Will slid into it.

"Coffee, Milo," he said to the short-order cook behind the counter. "And some two percent, please."

"Two percent! Like it matters!"

"I'm not the person you should be pissed off with, Paul."

"Oh, go to hell."

Will accepted a coffee mug and a small pitcher of milk. Milo leaned across the counter and said conspiratorially, "You gotta order food, Starbuck. I can't let you have the seat today unless you do. You didn't even wait in line."

"Give me some toast."

"Dry," Paul said, in a mincing tone. "No butter. He's in training for the big time."

Will swiveled slightly to study his profile. "So tell me, Winslow, what're you planning to do once you sell the boat?"

Paul shrugged and shoved his half-eaten breakfast away. The nausea had a firm grip on his entrails now, and he couldn't hide the shaking. Would Will notice? Would he understand it if he did?

"You gonna go to the mainland? Try college? Or sell drugs up at the high school?"

Paul's head shot up, and the hands he had clenched around his coffee cup flexed dangerously. "What the hell does that mean?"

"I hear you're a real pro. Got the turkey tracks to prove it."

"Jorie's been talking too much."

"Jorie's pretty upset. I thought you should know that."

"I don't really care."

"You ought to. But I guess you don't care about much, right? Hurt your girlfriend, cut loose your old buddies, waste your cash on drugs while your business goes down the tubes—"

Paul shoved at Will hard, all his anger in his shaking hands. Will landed in a sprawl at his neighbor's feet.

"Hey!" Milo barked with a shake of his spatula. "Watch that kinda action, Winslow, or you're not coming back in here. You okay, Starbuck?"

Will scrambled to his feet, menace in his dark blue eyes. "I'm fine. Give this guy my toast, okay? I think he could use it." He reached across Paul for the keys he'd left on the counter. "And listen, Paul old buddy. Keep away from Jorie, understand? I won't let you screw up her life. She deserves a lot better."

"Like you, for instance?" Paul jeered.

But Will was already out the door.

Merry Folger had also awakened early and walked through the weak sunshine into town. Her large and satisfying breakfast was consumed at the Fog Island Café, a mere block from the Water Street station; and so Will and Paul's lunch-counter fracas went unnoticed by law enforcement.

Merry planned to retrieve her car and drive out to Sconset in search of Margot St. John—but the girl was unlikely to be awake at eight A.M. And so, after tucking into poached eggs, black beans, and wheat toast, washed down with a flood of strong black coffee, Merry strode the short distance to her office and settled down to study Jay Santorski's bank statements.

Her desk was littered with copies of them. The originals had been sealed in plastic evidence bags, tagged as to their date and place of origin, and dropped in the evidence locker.

In the last three months of his life, Santorski had deposited cash to the Pacific National Bank every Friday. One week the balance was increased by about four hundred dollars, and the next, by a little over six hundred, and so on.

Merry picked up the phone and dialed Owen Harley's number. To her surprise, he actually answered. After the usual civilities, she got directly to the point.

"How much were you paying Jay Santorski?"

"We had agreed to a flat fee of two hundred bucks a week. That's not much, but nobody's making money scalloping these days. I usually gross around five or six hundred a week, but gas and boat maintenance have to come out of that. And I pay a shucker to open the scallops before they're shipped to New Bedford. That runs into some money."

Which meant Harley wasn't doing much better than his dead mate. What did he live on? Merry wondered. Grant money from Woods Hole?

"And Jay had his part-time job at the Mayhew House," Harley added, breaking into her thoughts.

"So he did. Thanks, Harley."

Merry already knew that Jay had made about two hundred dollars a week at Ezra's. The two salaries combined accounted for his four-hundred-dollar deposits. But where had the extra two hundred come from, twice a month?

His mother?

Stolen tips from the Ezra Mayhew House?

Or payments from Matt Bailey?

Fred McIlhenney, Merry knew, had paid Joey Figuera three hundred dollars a week for almost a year. Next to that bill, Jay's drain on the police discretionary funds would have been negligible. Bailey had got him cheap.

"I'm sending the plastic bag to the state crime lab for fingahprint analysis, Marradith," Clarence Strangerfield said from her doorway, "and the latex gloves. The forensic fellers may be able to lift some prints from the inside o' the glove tips. The hypo and cassette I've dusted myself."

Merry looked up from the bank statements and smiled at the crime scene chief. "You sure hit the ground running. And?"

"Wiped clean."

"That in itself is highly suspicious."

"I agree."

"How'd the autopsy go?"

"I fainted three minutes aftah the butterfly incision."

"Poor Clare! Were they kind to you?"

"Tolerahbly so. Waved some ammonia undah my nose. After that, I sat up and watched the rest of it. Poor young fellah." Clarence's basset-hound eyes looked mournfully at his shoes.

"Nothing earth-shaking, when they opened him up?"

"Not so's I could tell. Some air in the lungs, so we know he went into the watah breathin'. Pathologist says he died o' respiratory collapse, plain as that. He's sending a full repahrt along with the results o' the bloodwork. We should have 'em both in a couple o' days."

"Thanks for going over. And for taking care of the plastic bag."

"Not a'tall. Where'd yah find it?"

"It came from the harbor bottom."

"Sounds like the title of a Gahdzilla movie. Anything else yah need done?"

Merry bit her lip and considered. "File the lifts, Clare, and send the hypo on to Boston with the gloves. I want the needle examined."

"For heroin residue?"

"And blood. We should try to have the DNA scanned."

"I'm not sure there's enough for that."

"We'll never know if we don't ask."

"You want a DNA sampling from Santorski's body, too?"

"Of course. What does the Chief say? You can't take evidence from a body once it's underground? Or something like that."

"He's wrong." Clarence grinned. "Yah can. This'll mean delaying the corpse's release for burial."

Merry grimaced. "I'd have remembered that minor detail when it was far too late. You're dependable as a rainy day, Clare. Do you ever go home?"

"For meals," he replied with obvious complacency. "I'm ready to roll that cassette o' yahrs, Marradith, if yahr done with flatterin' an old man. Got yahr tape recordah?"

Merry pulled open her desk drawer. "It never leaves my side."

"Never mind the gloves. We know it was clean." Clarence handed her the microcassette with a flourish. "I'll let you do the honahs."

She dropped the tape into the recorder and pressed PLAY. "Let's hope it's not an anticlimax."

White noise. Then a beep. Then a man's voice, offhand and harried. *"Yo—I'm on my way over, but I'm gonna be a little late. See you in thirty."*

"Answerin' machine," Clarence said conversationally. "I coulda put money on it."

Beep. White noise. A dial tone, strident and abruptly cut off.

"Someone who didn't want to leave a message," Merry murmured.

Beep. A woman's voice, this time.

"Hello?"

"Hey . . . I was afraid you were out."

(Another man, different from the first, his voice slightly ragged where the other was casual.)

"No, I was in the tub."

"Alone?"

"Of course alone. Where are you calling from?"

"The Club Car."

"What happened to Cambridge?"

"I came back early. Look, I need to see you. Right away. It's urgent."

A pause, while the woman considered. *"You missed me* that *much?"*

"Stop kidding around. It's about your husband, and it's serious. I've got enough dirt on the bastard to hang him high, ha—"

Beep.

White noise.

. . . *to hang him high, hang him for good?* Is that what he was going to say before the machine cut him off?

The white noise went on for a long time. Merry glanced up at Clarence, hit the FAST-FORWARD button, then pushed PLAY. More white noise.

"Sounds like that's it."

Clarence sat down heavily on the edge of her desk. "Yahr tellin' me somebody cared enough to send *that* to the bottom o' the hahrbah?"

"Yes," Merry said slowly, "and I think I know who."

"You recognized the voices?"

"Didn't you?"

Clare simply looked at her.

"The last guy was Matt Bailey," she said, as though it were obvious, and rewound the tape.

"I think what happened," Merry said to her father, "is that the machine picked up after two rings, right as the woman got to the phone. Most of them do that, once there are messages already recorded. The machine assumes nobody's home, and answers more quickly. So the woman didn't quite get there in time."

She and Clarence were standing in John Folger's office now, the cassette in a recorder on the Chief's desk. He had listened to the fragmentary words twice through.

"Uh-huh," her father said. "I'm not an idiot, Meredith. What's your point?"

"So her whole conversation was recorded. She might not have known that until the final beep, when the machine clicked off. Then, in the middle of this intimate conversation with poor Bailey, she realizes it's all on tape."

"So why doesn't she run downstairs and rewind the tape? Erase the whole thing, if it's such a calamity?"

"I've thought about that. Somebody *else* got there first."

John Folger scowled. "I'm not following you. We know she was alone."

"No. We know she *thought* she was alone. What if someone came in while she was running the bathwater—someone she never heard? Her husband, the one Bailey mentioned. Maybe he was the guy with the wine, who was going to be a little late. He said he'd be back in half an hour, and we have no idea how much time elapsed between the first message and the third. He's standing downstairs, humming to himself as he unpacks his wine bottles—and then he hears the phone ring. Hears the machine pick up."

"And hears the conversation broadcast by the recorder," Clarence finished.

There was a moment of pained silence.

"Depending on what the conversation really meant," the Chief said slowly, "that might have been unfortunate."

"Indeed," Merry said cheerfully. "It might have been a disaster. Our unknown guy could have marched upstairs and yanked his wife off the phone, demanding an explanation. Or he could have quietly picked up the receiver, and listened to the rest of the call. Or maybe he ignored it, because it wasn't important—only then why did the tape end up in the harbor?"

"You think he took the cassette out of the recorder while the woman was still on the phone," her father said slowly, "and eventually dumped it in the sea. That makes absolutely no sense."

"I don't yet understand why he did that," Merry conceded, "but for now, it's my theory, and I'm sticking with it."

"I'll be interested to know when you've got something more like facts, Meredith. So far, this is a bunch of cockamamie bullshit."

"Or would be, if the guy on the other end of the line wasn't Matt Bailey," she observed distantly.

"I think perhaps I oughter be goin'," Clarence murmured, and propelled himself to the door. The Folgers' battles were legendary around the Nantucket force.

Merry waved distractedly at the crime scene chief's back, then pulled up one of the two captain's chairs facing her father's desk and sat herself down. "Come on, Dad. Time to come clean. What was Matt Bailey's phone number doing in Jay Santorski's pocket? And how did Bailey get mixed up with a jealous man's wife?"

"I know nothing about Matt Bailey's love life," John retorted stiffly.

"But you agree that his disappearance takes on an interesting complexion in the light of this tape," she persisted. "Who knows—Bailey might be the next thing we dredge up from the harbor bottom! And what was he doing in Cambridge, anyway? Vacation time? A conference with the ex-wife about little Ryan? Or was it something to do with his latest drug sting operation?"

John Folger's face assumed the wooden look Merry remembered from Friday night's pie-eating session at Tattle Court. She knew, then, that even the tape's revelations had no power to jolt him into speech. That suddenly, she lost her patience.

"Matt *was* running an op with Santorski—wasn't he?"

"Where the hell did you come up with that idea?"

"Oh, for God's sake, Dad—"

"Nothing on this tape would suggest the slightest connection to Santorski's drowning."

"The cassette was found on the harbor bottom, in a bag with a hypodermic needle! Jay Santorski had needle marks in his arm!"

"That's neither here nor there. What I just heard was a personal conversation. It can have nothing to do with Bailey's work."

"What *was* Bailey's work, anyway? I can't find a trace of it in his office. Even his filing cabinets are clean."

Her father's eyes dropped to his desk, and he made a little play of aligning his blotter. "It's highly unprofessional, Meredith, to crossexamine your chief about another detective's caseload."

Merry's breath caught in her throat. "Jay Santorski is dead, Dad. *Dead.* Bailey's nowhere to be found. We're not talking about a caseload. We're talking about a disaster."

"That boy fell into the basin and drowned," her father replied doggedly. "His death has nothing to do with me."

With me. There it was—a denial of responsibility, a desperate shifting of blame. That swiftly, Merry knew her father's guilt. She felt his corrosive fear. And worse, she recognized his cowardice.

He was using her to save himself. The knowledge terrified and enraged her. She took a step back from the desk.

"You called me home as a blind."

Her father looked at her then. A self-righteous stranger stared out of his beloved blue eyes. "I never asked you to meddle in Bailey's business, Meredith."

"No. You asked me to play dumb. The one thing I'd never expect from you."

Chapter Eighteen

Merry left her father without a backward glance, and ran upstairs to call Howie Seitz. He picked up on the third ring; she heard the roar of Patriots football in the background.

"I need you to check the airport passenger lists for Bailey's name," she told him tersely. "And the ferry offices. Find out whether anybody answering his description left the island Thursday."

"Okay." Seitz's voice was reluctant. "But there's a million people answering his description, Mere."

Medium build, clean-shaven face, brown eyes and hair. Howie was right: it was hopeless.

"I'm putting out an APB for his car."

"Should have done that a couple of days ago. Chief know about all this?"

"No."

"Okay. I'll get on it, Mere."

"Thanks, Seitz."

She cradled the receiver and looked around for her keys. In all the years she had known him, Matt Bailey had never kept a conquest to himself. If anybody knew the name of the woman on the tape, it would be Bailey's friends—the Potts brothers, Tim and Phil.

An ancient Land Cruiser, fenders rusted, guarded the Pottses' closed garage door. Huddled shapes outlined against the rear windshield suggested dive tanks and fishing rods. Tim and Phil liked to surf-cast for blues out on Smith Point.

Merry parked the Explorer on the verge of Liberty Road and picked her way across the Pottses' saturated lawn. A curtain twitched at the front window, and then Tim's koala-bear face appeared at the storm door.

"Detective Folger," he said coolly as he pushed it open a few inches and leaned toward her. "To what do we owe this honor?"

From the sound of his voice, it was more like an intrusion.

"How are you, Tim?" Merry asked.

"Fine." A neutral shading to the word, pregnant with anticipation. "Anything wrong?"

"I need to talk to you."

"Come on in."

She followed him into the Pottses' darkened hall and glanced around, blinking. Blue light flowed from a television screen in a room to the left; Merry heard the unmistakable accent of Arnold Schwarzenegger.

"We rented a movie for Ryan," Tim explained. "Ryan Bailey—Matt's son. He's parked in front of it with a bag of chips and a can of soda."

An action film would hardly have been her choice for comforting an abandoned little boy, but maybe guys understood these things better. Merry would have rented something from Disney, and discovered too late that Ryan had outgrown it.

"Want to talk in here?" Tim stood uneasily in the doorway of the room to the right of the hall. Merry was hardly in the habit of paying house calls around the force, and it occurred to her that this might be a bad thing. Maybe she should extend herself, and socialize more with people from work. The notion made her inexplicably depressed.

"Is Phil around?" she asked, taking a seat on a lumpy couch.

"Went into town." Tim remained standing, his arms folded across his chest. He hadn't forgiven her, it seemed, for yesterday's rebuke about Paul Winslow.

"Listen, Tim—I won't waste your time. I want to talk about Bailey."

Tim looked over his shoulder as though she had shouted abuse at the top of her lungs. "Try to keep your voice down, Mere. We don't want to upset the little guy. He's worried enough as it is."

"Sorry. Are you . . . worried, Tim?"

"About Matt?" Something flickered across his face—anger or wariness, Merry couldn't be sure. "Somebody has to be. Everyone else is acting like it's perfectly normal that the guy drops off the face of the earth."

"I know. But the Chief said you wanted to wait a few days before calling Bailey's ex-wife."

"I figured that's what Matt would want. Jen might use this as an excuse to take Ryan away from him—and that would kill Matt."

His vehemence surprised Merry. She had assumed that Matt Bailey was incapable of strong feeling. His relationships never lasted more than a few weeks. But perhaps a child was different—easier to love.

"Do you know where he is, Tim?"

"If I did—"

"I'd be the last person you'd tell."

"Again, I have to think of what Matt would want."

"Meaning, that his feeling for me ranks somewhere below his ex-wife."

Tim didn't bother to answer her directly. "What do you want, Merry?"

"Was Bailey running an undercover drug sting operation with Jay Santorski?"

Tim flinched, and looked away from her, toward the room's single window. "I don't know."

"At least tell me why Santorski had Bailey's phone number in his pocket when he died."

"Did he?"

Merry nodded. "And Bailey left town the same night Jay went into the harbor."

"Are you suggesting Matt killed him?" A flare of anger.

Merry tried to answer calmly. "No. But I'm beginning to wonder why no one else does. Including the Chief. I have to assume it's because the joke's on me. And all of you know exactly where Matt is, and why."

"I haven't the faintest idea what happened that night," Tim said, pointing a finger at her for emphasis, "or why Matt ran. But maybe he doesn't want to be found."

"Look. Don't lie to me." Merry's voice was taut with frustration and anger. "I've had enough of lying. I could dissect a corpse in Bailey's office, it's so clean. Not a shred of paper to show what he might have been doing, or where he's gone. Somebody tidied up after him. Was it you? Or the Chief?"

"It wasn't me."

"This is starting to look like a cover-up, Tim."

"I'm not much interested in threats, Mere. You should know that by now. I'd better get back to Ryan."

"Wait—" Merry held up her hand. "Protect Bailey if you must. I don't care. I'll figure it out eventually."

"You always do. No matter how late in the game, and regardless of the cost."

The sarcasm in his voice was like a lash. He was thinking, Merry knew, of the people who had died last spring, and the knowledge made her flush as though she had suddenly been stripped naked.

"Tim—I need your help. We found a tape on the harbor bottom, not far from the jetties where Santorski's body was. It's a recording of Bailey's voice. From an answering machine."

He stopped halfway to the open door. "Bailey's on tape? With Jay?"

So they *had* known one another. "Not Jay. A woman. I thought you might be able to identify her voice." Merry reached for her purse.

"You have it here?"

She nodded.

Tim looked suddenly wary. "Does your dad know about this, Merry?"

"Why do you ask?"

"You know why. I'm not about to get between you two."

"He's already heard the tape."

"Did he tell you to play it for me?"

"No," Merry said unwillingly. "I thought of that on my own. You and Phil are Bailey's best friends on the force. You'd be likely to know if he was seeing anybody."

"He wasn't. At least, not that I heard."

"You couldn't prove it by this tape."

Tim looked at her narrowly. "You think it has something to do with his disappearance?"

"Yes."

"I don't even begin to understand what's going on, Mere."

"Neither do I." She pulled her microrecorder out of her purse and pressed the PLAY button. "I just want you to listen to this."

Beeps and voices. Tim leaned over the recorder.

"It's the third message," she told him.

"Hey," the disembodied voice began, *"I was afraid you were out."*

"No. I was in the tub."

To Merry's disappointment, Tim's face showed nothing like recognition at the sound of the unknown woman's voice.

"Alone?"

"Of course alone . . ."

"Tim! That's my dad! Did he call? Where is he?"

Ryan Bailey, standing in the doorway, his thin face filled with hope.

"I forgot to shut the door, Mere," Tim said guiltily. He stood up and reached for the boy. "It's not your dad, Ryan. It's just a tape."

"How'd you get it?"

Tim looked helplessly at Merry.

"Ryan," she said, coming to a swift decision, "do you think you could listen to this all the way through? It might help us find your dad."

"Sure." Ryan shrugged, trying to hide his disappointment. "But he's just talking to Hannah."

"Hannah?"

The name jolted through Merry like an electric shock. There couldn't be *two* women with that name involved in this mess.

"Dad really likes her a lot. I saw him kiss her once, when they didn't know I was there."

I've got enough dirt . . . to hang him high. Of course.

Merry studied the twelve-year-old intently. She had to ask, just to be sure. "Do you know Hannah's last name, Ryan?"

"It's Moore," Tim Potts said, his voice incredulous. "Hannah Moore, the biologist. She's married to that real estate guy who lives out in Pocomo. But how she knows Bailey, I can't begin to tell you. Hannah's way out of his league."

Hannah Moore swept her long black hair away from her face and into a knot at the crown of her head. She secured it with a pair of number-two lead pencils and then bent over the microscope in front of her. Her lips moved soundlessly as she counted something. Then she straightened, seized a third pencil, and scribbled numbers on a pad.

"Got it nailed down? Got it all figured out?" her husband asked, from his position in the doorway.

She looked up, her face expressionless, and met Charles Moore's eyes. Then she looked back down at her notepad and continued writing.

In the first year of their marriage, Sunday had been reserved for play. They had taken long walks over the moors together; had browsed for books in the local shops; had bicycled to the old military bunker at Tom Nevers Head, and eaten sumptuous brunches at Chanticleer. All that had changed with Hannah's growing obsession for her work. Now she spent more hours in her Quonset huts than she did in the house. It had been a long time, Charles thought, since she had greeted him with a smile. Much less run to throw her arms around him with helpless joy.

But helpless joy had never been much in Hannah's line. He would have settled for grudging lust.

He wandered around the interior of the lab his money had built, disturbing piles of paperwork and fingering the labeled slides. He peered into tanks with blatant ignorance, and stirred the bubbling waters with an idle fingertip. He did it deliberately, hoping to provoke.

"What exactly do you want, Charles?" she burst out, finally, at the end of her short patience. He whirled to face her.

"A return on my investment," he said. "Some gain for expenditures expended."

Silence. She set down her pencil.

"We aren't doing very well, are we, Hannah? Our projects seem to have failed miserably."

"Our projects didn't take a hurricane into account."

"No. But that doesn't explain the state of our marriage. Now does it?"

Her tongue clicked with irritation, her eyes rolled. "I really don't have time for this, Charles. I'm trying to finish a grant application. I'm low on funds, as you very well know."

"That's no fault of mine," he said gently. "I've beggared myself for you, Hannah. And to little purpose. Is that why you're going to this party tonight? To meet fund-raisers?"

"The da Silvas are friends. Their son Will practically lives here."

"You have no friends, Hannah. Only prospective backers." Charles reached over and released the pencils from her hair. It cascaded darkly about her shoulders, and he sighed. "Such a beautiful face. And yet there's no heart behind it. How did Jay die, Hannah?"

She did not answer immediately, but he was prepared to wait. Charles was very good at waiting. He had outlasted every rival for Hannah's attention, and he sometimes thought she had simply rewarded him for endurance, as though it were a prize genetic trait she might replicate under controlled conditions.

"He drowned."

"Really. How unfortunate."

"For Jay, perhaps."

"You're singularly unmoved."

Something flickered in her face—a trick of the light, or a current in the air between them. It could never have been emotion.

"But you know," he said conversationally, "I learned that much from the talk in town. That Jay drowned. What I wanted to know, Hannah, was *how he died*. I don't have to ask you why."

The sound of tires crunching over gravel drifted through the Quonset hut's thin walls. Hannah peered beyond him, as though he were invisible, and said, "It's Paul."

"Paul?"

"Winslow," she said patiently. "The scalloper."

"You mean the addict, don't you? I suppose I'd better see him."

"There's no need to do me any favors, Charles." Hannah closed her notebook, supremely indifferent to his gaze. He realized that she would leave, that easily, without admitting she had ignored his questions. He crossed to her swiftly and seized her wrist. It twisted painfully in his grasp.

"Know this, Hannah," he told her softly. "I won't be around much longer. Until spring, perhaps, or at the outside, summer. Then you'll have to find someone else to buy into your dreams."

"You sicken me, Charles." Her wrist slid away from his fingers.

"Why? Because I no longer believe your lies? Or because I haven't the stomach for death?"

These questions, like the others, she didn't bother to answer.

Chapter Nineteen

Merry drove aimlessly for a while after she left Tim Potts, following Liberty Street out of town and then heading toward the South Shore, where empty miles of native heath undulated beyond her windshield. She found herself finally at Cisco Beach, an empty expanse of graying sand with nothing but surf on the horizon. Rank upon rank of curling waves were hurrying toward the beach, punctuated by a solitary figure—man or woman, Merry couldn't tell—trudging along the waterline in a red parka. A retriever dashed forward and back, turned tail and leaped high, its tongue lolling crazily. As Merry watched, a stick hurtled through the air, and the dog dove after it into the churning sea. Merry shivered involuntarily. The water must be deathly cold.

How, exactly, did it kill you? Like a gentle form of sleep, numbing the senses completely until consciousness and life slipped away together? Or did the mind resist, denying the inevitable with increasing horror? How long would it have taken young, athletic Jay to lose the battle with the boat basin?

He was a good swimmer. He was familiar with Old North

Wharf. He wouldn't have simply fallen in and drowned, unless his body was completely beyond his command.

Which left two possibilities.

Jay Santorski had so much heroin in his system when his bicycle went into the water, he never even thought to swim back to the wharf.

Or Jay Santorski was carried by boat—the boat that Howie's Irene had heard at three A.M.—to the end of the jettied channel, and left in the frigid water to die. A half mile at least from Old North Wharf, too far to swim back in his heavy clothes and shoes. Even without heroin in his bloodstream, his chances would have been slim.

But if a boat had carried the scalloper to his death, why hadn't it carried him just a little farther—beyond the harbor and out into the Sound, where the approaching nor'easter might have sent his body miles away from the scene of his murder? Why leave him to be discovered a few hours later, in the very path of the approaching ferry?

As a warning, perhaps. A cautionary example. Which brought Merry to Mystery Number Two.

Had Jay Santorski died because of Matt Bailey?

She pulled her hands out of her pockets and worked her way down the dunes to the beach. Began to trudge, like the figure in red, with her head down and her eyes on her shoes. She wished, suddenly, for a dog—Peter's dog, Ney, who was almost her own—and a stick to charm him with.

Whenever Merry tried to cut a new path through the maze of what she knew and feared about this investigation, she inevitably ran smack into the wall that was her father. John Folger was deliberately concealing the truth about Bailey and the scalloper. The simplest explanation was that a drug sting had blown up in Bailey's face; Jay, his agent, had been killed; Bailey had run; and John Folger intended to keep the whole thing secret from both the DA in Barnstable and the interfering press. He had destroyed Bailey's files and denied that any undercover operation had ever taken place.

Why hadn't he just declared the kid's death an accident, and left Merry in Greenwich?—Because he knew a coroner would find the needle marks on Santorski's arm, and decayed heroin in his bloodstream. Or because Bailey might turn up and blow the careful fabric of lies.

Or because the Chief had too much integrity to follow through on a cover-up, regardless of the consequences. But if that were the case, he should have told Merry the truth.

Which might mean that the truth was even worse than she had imagined.

Are you suggesting Matt killed him? Tim Potts had asked, accusingly. Was it even possible?

If Bailey feared for his own life, perhaps. Or if Jay had posed a threat to Bailey's security.

What if Bailey had been *dealing* drugs, instead of running a sting—using his police powers to dispose of confiscated cocaine and heroin taken in raids? Maybe he was Margot St. John's dealer, and Jay, infatuated with Margot, decided to turn Bailey in. Bailey realized his danger Thursday night, called Hannah Moore to tell her he was leaving the island, and met Jay one last time at Old North Wharf.

Merry shook her head in frustration. The theory didn't fit. It was Jay who had needle marks in his arm, after all; and when Bailey called Hannah Moore, he talked more about coming back early than getting out of town. He'd talked, in fact, about her husband. And something he'd found in Cambridge.

She came to a stop on the sand, her eyes fixed on the churning waves. The nor'easter had thrown a considerable amount of seaweed back up on shore; a few dead fish were trapped in the wrack, smelling pungent in the chill air. Merry recorded the odors and sounds with one half of her mind; the other followed Matt Bailey through his purposeful, obscure convolutions. He had been investigating Hannah Moore's husband during his time in Cambridge. He had learned something damaging. That much was certain from the tape. Jay Santorski knew Hannah Moore. And Jay Santorski had left a brilliant career at Harvard—which, the last time Merry checked, was still in Cambridge—to work on the island where Hannah Moore lived.

If her theory was correct, and Bailey was linked to Jay

by the common thread of a heroin sting, then perhaps Charles Moore was the target. And if he had overheard Bailey's phone conversation with his wife, Hannah, he knew all about the sting.

Why kill Jay, then, and not Bailey? Why sink the tape and the hypodermic on the harbor bottom?

She was trapped in a pocket of the maze. But something—apprehension, instinctive knowledge—told Merry that her father was sitting at its center.

The red-jacketed figure darted back down the beach, the dog barking at its heels. A hood was flung back, and hair streamed out in the wind—dark brown hair with red lights, like Peter's.

Merry no longer asked herself why she had left Peter so precipitately Friday morning. She knew now that she had had no choice. Her role in the drama was preordained, and central to its resolution. She sensed dimly that a kind of freedom might lie beyond it. She would never again regard her father's opinion as of paramount importance, or look for self-worth in his grudging words of praise. She had touched his feet of clay. If even John Folger was fallible, then his daughter could err in peace. And find courage to go on.

She shoved a hand in her pocket and fingered Matt Bailey's spare set of keys. She had won them, after lengthy debate, from Tim Potts. Bailey's apartment would probably look as pristine as his office; but Merry had to search it anyway. Regardless of the evils it might reveal.

Feeling unutterably lonely, she took a last look at the sea, and turned back to her car perched high on the bluff.

Matt Bailey lived in a two-bedroom condo on Sparks Avenue, not far from the fire station, the supermarket, and his son Ryan's school. Merry hesitated before the dark red front door, eyeing its brass dolphin knocker—a remnant of Jennifer's good taste, probably—and listened. Only the heavy silence of inoccupancy. She unlocked the door and slid inside.

She had expected Bailey's house to feel dusky, like the dim cave of a hibernatory animal—the atmospheric extrapolation, perhaps, of his office at the station. Instead, it resembled nothing so much as a Pottery Barn catalogue. Jute rugs were scattered across bare hardwood floors; the windows were dressed in beige roman shades, tightly furled to admit the gray light; an overstuffed couch covered in blue denim dominated the middle of the room. There was a cart for the TV and VCR, and a tidy pile of newspapers stacked near the door for recycling.

Merry crossed to these, and flipped through them briefly; the Sunday Boston *Globe*, back issues of the *Inky*. All had been read, refolded, and arranged by date.

It was unfortunate, Merry thought, that she had never bothered to visit Bailey before. She might have known, then, whether the almost obsessive tidiness everywhere in view was as much at variance with Bailey's habits as the present order of his office. But she knew very little, in fact, about Matt Bailey, and she had never wasted much time in the study of his character. He was uninspired by work, insecure about his standing within the force, and prone to bragging about his exploits. Since his wife's fulminating departure for the mainland three years ago, he had seemed incapable of sustaining a relationship. He specialized in women twenty years his junior, who were wowed by the fact that he carried a gun. Bailey was the sort of person, in short, whom Merry detested automatically, without having the slightest inclination to prove herself wrong.

They had got off on a poor footing—Bailey resenting what he considered favoritism in the Chief's awarding of cases, and letting it be known that Merry was nothing but a quota filler in the force's Affirmative Action program. She, for her part, had never made any attempt to disguise her contempt. She had made it a cause célèbre, as though ridiculing Bailey were a prize skill, a game in which she was particularly adept. She'd prided herself on despising the man, because she needed to place a gulf between them. Her sense of self-worth depended on it.

He was incompetent; she was not. He was lazy; she was

driven. He was a putz who couldn't think his way out of his own clothes at night; she had solved every crime her father had handed to her.

Only she hadn't, had she?

The Osborne case had completely defeated her. And too many people had died because of it. Merry had very nearly been killed herself—and on occasion, when her thoughts were particularly black, she believed this a miscarriage of justice. Having failed to save the others, she should probably have died with them. A certain tragic balance would then have been struck.

Better yet, she should simply have let Matt Bailey handle the serial killer case. Then she might have triumphed over him at a distance and been satisfied.

She glanced around the room, saw what might be a coat closet door set into the space below a flight of stairs, and beyond it the kitchen. She should check any closets first; he might keep a shoe box filled with tax returns. Or his personal diary, in which every fact about Hannah Moore's life or Jay Santorski's death might be recorded. Who knew? Stranger things had happened.

The bedroom closet held only a quantity of clothes, some luggage, a dusty set of golf clubs, and a year's worth of *Playboy*. The dresser drawers were filled with underwear, socks, polo shirts in need of washing, and four pullover sweaters. Wherever Bailey had gone last Thursday, he hadn't taken much with him.

The door under the stairs did, in fact, lead to a closet. Merry peered under the hems of parkas and overcoats, and found to her delight that Bailey apparently had no affection for shoe boxes. He had, however, invested in a black metal filing cabinet—sturdy, two-drawered, and refreshingly official. She sat cross-legged on the floor, heedless of dust, and pulled on the handle.

Locked.

She pushed herself to her feet, and made for the kitchen junk drawer. Anything—a metal nail file or a paper clip—might work. But the Bailey junk drawer seemed to hold only a corkscrew, a set of measuring spoons still powdered with aged cinnamon, a roll of tape, a Phillips screwdriver, and a quantity of grocery store coupons long out-of-date. Merry eyed the screwdriver, and abandoned it as unlikely.

Next, she tried the bathroom medicine cabinet. Nothing but laxatives, Band-Aids, and ibuprofen.

In the bottom drawer of the sink cabinet, however, she hit pay dirt. Two bent bobby pins—probably discarded and forgotten by Bailey's ex-wife, whom Merry remembered vaguely as having long brown hair—were wedged at the very back, between a rolled-up heating pad and a box of condoms. Merry seized them without a pang of guilt for having rifled Bailey's bathroom domain, and ran back to the recalcitrant filing cabinet.

Only then did she see the keys to the file drawer, perched innocently above her head on the closet shelf. Stifling a curse, she grabbed them and opened the first drawer.

A short inspection revealed this to contain mostly documents pertaining to Bailey's private life. He was surprisingly methodical, with files for Ryan's medical visits, his artwork, his report cards by year; files for taxes, and charitable deductions, credit card statements and bank accounts. One file held a yellowed marriage certificate, a decree of divorce, and Bailey's passport—or what remained of it: an envelope marked with the Department of State's return address.

Merry looked at this thoughtfully, and set it aside.

Then she picked up the bank accounts.

A swift survey of Bailey's checking deposits and withdrawals showed a depressing pattern. He regularly lived beyond his means, and spent the last week of the month completely in the red. The Pacific National Bank had something they liked to call overdraft protection—essentially a line of credit that kicked in when the account holder was overdrawn—and Bailey regularly resorted to it. From what Merry could see, he rarely paid it back. He was in considerable debt to his friends at Pacific National.

She pulled a copy of Jay Santorski's bank statement

from her purse and tried, as best she could, to coordinate his bimonthly cash deposits with Bailey's withdrawals.

There was no correlation whatsoever.

Merry sat back on her heels, deflated. Either Bailey had never used Jay as an agent, or he'd taken the money from a different account—the police discretionary funds, which only the Chief could authorize. If that was the case, Merry's father was involved in this mess up to his eyeballs. And he'd ordered the paper trail destroyed.

Alternatively, a small voice inside her argued, Bailey and Jay had nothing to do with one another. Jay's extra two hundred dollars came from somewhere else—his mother, perhaps—twice a month like clockwork. Or maybe he *had* got it from stealing tips.

Merry laughed that idea out of town. She was placing her bets on Laurie Hopfnagel for responsibility in *that* case.

She returned the bank statements to their file and closed the first drawer.

The second one contained only one manila folder—but it was remarkably thick. Inside was almost a ream of typewritten paper.

Merry glanced at the first of the double-spaced pages, and knew suddenly why Bailey had spent so much time at his office computer, despite his light workload. His body had reported to duty, but his mind was elsewhere. Matt Bailey, it seemed, was a frustrated writer. The file drawer held a book-length manuscript.

Mike Prescott reached for the smooth butt of his nine-millimeter Browning and trained it unflinchingly on the man cowering in the warehouse's corner. He was a hard cop, and a ruthless one, and he had wanted Joey the Mark at his mercy for two years, ever since his partner had died screaming in a hail of bullets. Joey the Mark had pulled the trigger that put Jim Buckley down. All because of a sting that had gone sour. Now, Joey was feeling the terror that had filled Jim's last moments; and Mike wasn't about to show him mercy. . . .

What did they always say—write what you know? Bailey must have believed it.

Merry scooped up the pages, tucked them under her arm, and went home to read in peace. Her visit to Margot St. John would have to wait until tomorrow.

Chapter Twenty

"Have a scallop, Merry," Tess da Silva urged, handing her a plate and a napkin.

The skillet-seared morsel slid from a toothpick into Merry's grateful mouth, and she sighed with pleasure. "Is this wrapped in bacon?"

"Pancetta. Much better. Try the phyllo, too, it's got roasted peppers and chèvre in it."

"How can you do this after working all weekend?"

Tess grinned and kissed Merry on the cheek. "In the past two days I made a ton of money, and I get to take the next three months off. Who wouldn't celebrate?"

"Three months," Merry murmured. "That's just—*indecent*, Tess. Nobody takes three months off, anymore."

"Except Peter."

"That doesn't count," Merry protested. "He's never really working. You have to be bone-tired to appreciate three months' vacation. And you, Tess, are positively glowing."

It was true; work, or something else—her marriage, perhaps?—agreed with Tess Starbuck da Silva. Merry had rarely seen her look better. She was approaching forty-five, the mother of an eighteen-year-old son, and she managed a restaurant and catering business all by herself. But her odd yellow eyes—tiger's eyes, Will called them—were alive with fun, and her face, though lined, radiated warmth. Tess wasn't beautiful, as she may have been at twenty; but she was happy. And somehow that was enough to make her infinitely attractive.

"I'll tell you a secret," she said now, leaning toward Merry. "I'm pregnant."

Merry's jaw dropped. "You're kidding! That's wonderful, Tess. I'm so happy for you both. Rafe is such a great dad."

"Yes he is. As Will can attest."

Merry slipped one of the phyllo triangles off a plate and eyed Tess's abdomen. "So how are you feeling?"

"Better than I expected." Tess turned swiftly as Will passed with a trayful of wineglasses, and took one for Merry. "I hope this suits. Rafe seems to have disappeared."

A shout of laughter filtered toward them from the Greengage's bar, and Merry smiled. "He's probably sharing the good news with his fishing buddies."

"Then we can sit and talk." Tess drew her toward a pair of Windsor chairs arranged near the dining room's comfortable hearth. "I'm glad you came, Merry. But I'm sorry it's at the expense of your vacation."

"Me, too."

"Peter stayed in Connecticut?"

"He should be in New York by now." Merry glanced at her watch. "In fact, he should be fifth row center at Carnegie Hall, listening to the Emerson String Quartet. He's been looking forward to it for months."

"I take it he wasn't thrilled you left."

"He was utterly furious."

"And now you're feeling guilty."

"Is it that obvious? Of course it is." Merry set down her glass and reached for the fire iron. Prodded a log until it rolled a flaming underbelly skywards, the glow reflecting in her green eyes. "The damnable thing is, Tess, that I had only two choices. I could feel guilty about ignoring my dad, or guilty about abandoning Peter. And I chose to abandon Peter."

"Inducing guilt is usually a woman's trick," Tess observed.

Merry laughed. "Probably both of them would be appalled at this manifestation of their feminine sides."

"Men never understand the sense of obligation women feel to the people they love—how it drives us and shapes our days. Riddles us with conflicting loyalties."

"Oh, Peter understands it. He accused me of valuing my father's good opinion more than I value his."

"And do you?"

Merry looked away. "I've been asking myself that all weekend. It's not that I value it more—" She hesitated, then went on. "It's rather that I can't control the impulse to perform. I've been trained to do that. It's almost involuntary."

"I don't understand. Trained by your father, or by your job?"

"Ever since my brother Billy died—you've heard about that?"

Tess nodded. Billy had died saving Rafe's life in Vietnam.

"—I've been trying to replace him. Trying to be my father's . . . not son, exactly, but his heir, I suppose. I don't know why I bother. I never will be."

"Billy couldn't have handled that killer last spring any better than you did, Merry," Tess said quietly.

Merry felt suddenly exposed in the glare of the other woman's awareness, and drew a shuddering breath. "Let's not even go into that. It was hardly my finest hour."

"A lot of people would disagree."

"A lot of people don't know the whole story."

"They know you were almost killed. That means something to nearly everybody on this island."

Merry reached for her wineglass and took a sip. "Yeah. It means I got lucky. Three other people didn't. And I feel responsible for them—and for their families, Tess—*every goddamn day*. I see their faces at night when I turn out the light. And I can't help knowing that I failed. My father knows it, too. He must think about it each time he has to give me a case."

Tess frowned. "But you got the guy in the end. Has he been tried yet?"

"Sometime this summer."

"Will you have to testify?"

"Of course. Lawyers from both sides have already deposed me. I had to go to Boston just last week for three solid days of questioning, before I was free to spend some time with Peter. It just never ends." She was gripping her wineglass so tightly the stem suddenly snapped between her fingers.

"Oh, God, Tess—I'm so sorry—"

"Never mind." Tess took the broken glass gently from her hands, and set the pieces on a cocktail napkin. "Mexican blown wineglass, eight ninety-five at Crate and Barrel. We break a dozen every week, believe me."

"I'll replace it—"

Tess waved this away. "I didn't understand how awful that case was for you. I thought you had won, in the end."

Merry smiled lopsidedly. "I won the war. But I lost a battle. And I can't quite get over that."

"You've got to. For your own sake, and for Peter's. Does he understand how that case has affected you?"

"In moments, maybe. Right now he's convinced that the real problem is marriage. He thinks I'd do anything to avoid his family, our wedding, and all the commitment it entails."

"And would you?"

"No. Yes. I don't know." Merry looked up from the flames and met Tess's eyes. "I love Peter more than anyone on earth, Tess. But his whole world intimidates the hell out of me. I keep waiting for him to wake up and realize I'm completely inadequate."

"For what?"

"For being a *Mason*!"

"That sounds positively medieval. You're not marrying into a dynasty, Merry, and I doubt Peter would want you to think so."

"You haven't met Peter's mother. To Julia, the most important thing about Peter is that he's the only surviving Mason male. He's got to carry the family into the twenty-first century, and for reasons she can't begin to fathom, he's chosen *me* to carry with him. From the moment I shook the woman's hand a few days ago, it was obvious I'd failed her personal test."

"A handshake was far too plebeian." Tess's lips twitched. "You should have kissed her on both cheeks instead."

"You see? I'll never manage it!"

"I wonder," Tess said softly, "if you're afraid of the easy out."

"The what?"

"The easy out. Look—you feel like you failed at your job. We won't argue, for the moment, whether you did. But marrying Peter would be one way to admit defeat. You could quit the detective work, take an easier desk job, or turn in your badge altogether. Be a housewife. Have children. Change the whole tenor of your life."

"I could." The expression in Merry's green eyes grew remote. "Sometimes that all sounds terribly attractive, Tess. Very safe, and very comfortable."

"And you would always think you'd taken the easy out."

"I probably would. On the other hand"—Merry smiled—"I'd hate to give Julia Mason the satisfaction of walking away."

"I imagine Peter has something to do with that, too."

"Why is love such a pain in the ass, Tess?"

"That's what makes it interesting. Look at me—I'm riveted."

"Shouldn't you be circulating genially, making everybody feel special, like the perfect hostess?"

"I'm counting on the food to do that for me." Tess sighed and settled back in her chair.

Merry suddenly gripped her arm. "Who's that gorgeous woman dressed all in black?"

Tess glances over her shoulder. Her expression hardened slightly. "That's Hannah Moore."

"What?"

"Hannah Moore. She's a biologist, lives out in Pocomo . . ."

"I know all that. Can you introduce us?"

"You want to meet Hannah?"

"More than I've ever wanted to meet anyone in my life. This week, at least."

"Well, then—" Tess stood up. "I warn you, she's a piece of work. I only invited her because she's been so generous to Will. He's volunteering at AquaVital in order to research his senior project."

"AquaVital?"

"That's Hannah's scallop farm. And her lab."

Tess led Merry across the room to the small knot of men gathered around the marine biologist. They were engrossed in conversation—or rather, the men were hanging on every word that fell from Hannah Moore's mouth. Her shining black hair was gathered meekly at the nape of her neck, to fall carelessly over one shoulder. Her strong hips were encased in narrow black wool to the ankles—an almost nunlike effect, but for its caressing exposure. She wore no jewelry, but her lips—so expressive at their corners of a mocking cruelty—were painted a glowing terracotta. Hannah Moore was the picture of power, Merry decided, both carnal and mental.

"Hannah!" Tess exclaimed, with what Merry instantly judged to be forced warmth. "I didn't see you come in. How good of you to join us. Is Charles here?"

"No," Hannah said.

If Tess was disconcerted by the brevity of the woman's answer, she never betrayed it. "Let me introduce you to a dear friend of mine. Hannah, this is Meredith Folger. Merry, Hannah."

"Hello," Hannah said coolly, and turned back to her coterie of men. "The implications of my work, of course, are obvious."

"Of course," one of the men echoed, his eyes fixed soulfully on Hannah's sweeping cheekbones. She might have been a young Faye Dunaway, Merry thought, or someone even more exotic. She looked as though she had Slavic blood.

"Once the scallop's DNA is genetically altered to permit

digestion of the brown tide phytoplankton, we've killed two birds with one stone."

"Exactly," chirped one of the faithful. "You'll be able to clean up the harbor *and* restock it with marketable shellfish."

"The AquaVital tigerback," Hannah agreed smoothly.

Larval tigers, Merry thought, with a *frisson* of recognition. So the tigerbacks were Hannah's. Owen Harley hadn't bothered to mention that.

"My scallops' distinctive stripes immediately announce their provenance on the world market. You know, I assume, the price that Nantucket Bay scallops command."

"But isn't that a price determined, in part, by scarcity?" a tall, raffish-looking fellow in a wine-colored sports jacket asked.

Hannah shrugged. "There will probably be an adjustment downward in price as supplies become more plentiful. That's the natural effect of market forces. But there will always be a premium attached to scallops taken from these waters."

"If your program is so attractive, Hannah, why did the Shellfish and Harbor Advisory Board cancel your grant money last week?"

The biologist turned on the man in the wine-colored jacket as though he had emitted an offensive smell. "The people at SHAB haven't got any guts. They're afraid of risk. I'm looking for investors who thrive on it."

Despite her wariness, Merry was impressed. Hannah Moore was talking about a potentially arcane subject—genetic engineering and phytoplankton—and making it sound like a Wall Street stock offering. Her presentation and style were calculated to sell, and apparently it was working. The raffish-looking man raised his wineglass to Hannah in grudging salute.

"Nobody's ever accused you of lacking guts, my dear. I'm almost inclined to invest myself. The question is whether my partners will be."

"I can Express Mail an informational package to New York tomorrow," she said imperturbably.

Her opponent hesitated, then gave way. "Why don't you do that?"

As if by mutual consent, the admiring chorus broke up and re-formed around a tray of biscotti. Hannah glanced at Merry, and managed a stiff smile.

"I'm sorry. That must have sounded terribly boring."

"Not at all. I found it fascinating."

This elicited no response. Afraid that the woman might walk away, Merry said quickly, "Tess tells me you're running a shellfish farm."

This garnered the slightest of frowns. "It's more of an experimental laboratory, in fact."

"That explains the word *DNA*. I thought I heard you mention it."

"Yes. I'm trying to breed a superscallop—one that will thrive in the harbor's current conditions."

"Well, amen to that," Merry said with false fervor. "I'm just sick about the harbor's decline. I've been reading your literature."

"My literature?"

"From Save Our Harbor. Aren't you on the board?"

Hannah's brows knit faintly. "Philosophical differences forced me to resign."

"Oh, no! And your work holds such promise, too!"

"I'm glad you think so. The Save Our Harbor people disagreed."

"You don't mean Owen Harley?"

Hannah sipped noncommittally at her wine. "Owen thinks we need to address the nitrogen problem before we can ever hope to boost the scallop harvest. He's made the people of Nantucket the scallop's natural enemy. I believe that harbor degradation is a fact of modern life, and that we should force the scallops to deal with it themselves. Imposing fertilizer limits or septic field renovation is merely a short-term solution."

"It's a pity that Owen is so shortsighted," Merry said regretfully. "But I suppose he's terribly distracted right now with Jay Santorski's death. He and Owen were very close, I understand."

"You knew Jay?" Hannah's tone grew, if possible, even colder.

"Not really. Did you?"

"Yes. I wasn't impressed."

Not for Hannah the desire to speak well of the dead.

"I'm surprised to hear that," Merry managed. "Do you mean personally? Or professionally?"

"Both. Jay was bright, of course, but too arrogant to know his own interest. He turned down chances that might have made his career. What he needed was a lesson in humility. And a bit of independence. He was afraid to test limits." The gray eyes, when they met Merry's, were unabashedly mocking.

"Unlike you."

"Exactly. Jay was fundamentally a coward."

She spoke with an unguarded bitterness, and for a moment Merry wondered just how much wine Hannah Moore had consumed.

"That's a pretty strong word to throw at a dead man," Merry said quietly. "Everyone I know thought he was selfless to a fault."

Hannah laughed abruptly. "Jay was an interfering, high-handed, arrogant son of a bitch. Selfless doesn't even come into it."

This, from the woman Dave Haddenfield had described as hot in pursuit of the dead scalloper. Had Jay's disinterest embarrassed and enraged her enough to create this scorn?

"Well—he was young. Who knows what he might have become?"

"For someone who never knew Jay, Ms. Folger, you've got a pretty glorified idea of him."

"Oh, call me Merry," Merry gushed shamelessly. "Where are you from, Hannah?"

"LA. By way of Columbia."

"You studied marine biology there?"

"My doctorate is from Harvard."

"So that's how you ended up on this coast."

"After a stint at Woods Hole, yes."

"Just like Owen Harley and Jay! What a small world. Did you ever run into them over there?"

Hannah's gray eyes narrowed. "Once or twice. Last summer."

"And you've been on Nantucket . . . how long?"

"Three years."

"You're married to an islander, aren't you? Is that why you settled here? True love?"

She shrugged. "I had done all I could at Woods Hole."

"But where did you meet your husband?"

Hannah held her glass against her black cashmere sweater, as though the wine might shield her. "Charles has family in Cambridge. Harvard is in Cambridge, Ms. Folger, in case you didn't know. Is there anything else I can tell you about my personal life? My clothing size, perhaps? Or what I eat for breakfast?"

Merry affected astonishment. "Oh, dear—have I been nosy again? It's my worst failing, Hannah. I'm so sorry. I'm famous for asking too many questions—I guess it's just a habit acquired at work. Matt Bailey always says—"

"Who?" The biologist almost choked on her wine.

"Matt Bailey. My colleague at the police station. Matt knew Jay pretty well, too, I gather."

"You work at the police station?" The gray eyes had quite lost their mocking detachment.

Merry smiled apologetically. "Didn't Tess mention that? I suppose not. Yes, I'm a detective, Ms. Moore, and I'm investigating Jay Santorski's death. So why exactly *did* you think he was an interfering, high-handed, arrogant son of a bitch?"

Hannah set down her wineglass. And without another word she walked away.

Will Starbuck backed out of the Greengage's kitchen with a tray of chocolate-dipped biscotti held carefully in both hands. His mother's food was disappearing at an astonishing clip. Will sighed with relief as he successfully negotiated the swinging double doors, and turned toward the living room—where he ran smack into Paul Winslow's father.

"Hey, there," Jack Winslow said, reaching for the tray as it slid precariously in Will's grasp. "Don't fumble the ball, Will!"

"Mr. Winslow." Will ducked his head. "I didn't see you there. Would you like a biscotti?"

"A what?"

"Chocolate-covered cookie."

"Sure. Say, Will—you did us proud out there yesterday."

"Thank you, sir. You saw the game?"

"Reminded me of Paul's better days." Mr. Winslow was a large, affable man with commensurate appetites; he crunched an entire biscotti into his mouth while Will waited politely, tray extended. From the expression of false jollity on the man's face, Will knew the conversation wasn't over.

"Listen, son," Winslow said confidentially, "have you seen Paul lately?"

"Yeah. He was at the game, too. And he was having breakfast at Congdon's this morning. I said . . . hello."

"How'd he seem to you?" The man kept his eyes on the tray, as though debating among its offerings.

Will stiffened slightly and averted his eyes. "Okay, I guess."

Jack Winslow looked at him then. "Is he still using drugs?"

"You'd better ask Paul about that, sir. I really wouldn't know."

"Then I assume he still is." Jack shook his head, and Will could feel the frustrated rage. "Ever since his mother and I divorced—no, make that *ever since I remarried*, he's been like a stranger. When I think of how Marion loved that boy—hell, how much *I* love him—I could shake every bone in his body."

"It can be hard getting used to a new parent," Will said carefully.

"You seem to have managed it pretty well!"

"But my father died." Will shifted the platter from his

right hand to his left, wondering why he was saying all this to Jack Winslow. "Death is different. It feels less like it's your fault."

Jack Winslow's face froze. "You think that's what Paul feels? That we divorced because of him?"

"I have no idea what Paul feels. We're not that good friends. But he's sure trying to punish somebody. Maybe it's you—or maybe it's himself."

"Maybe it's both."

Will did not reply. He had seen Winslow's new wife; she was twenty years younger than Paul's mother, and she was expecting her first child. What nineteen-year-old boy wouldn't resent the new family he had never chosen, and grieve for the one he had lost? Will understood it completely. His own situation was utterly different.

"Paul needs friends, son," Jack Winslow said haltingly. "Good friends. People he can count on when things are tough."

Since he can no longer count on his parents, Will thought. But he only said, "He probably needs a father more." And then flushed at his own rudeness.

For a moment, Jack said nothing, his jaws working at the hard biscotti. "I suppose I deserve that. I thought kicking him out of the house might knock some sense into him. But it may only have hurt him more. First his mother leaves, and then I abandon him. . . ." Winslow's eyes met Will's, with almost a sense of shock, as though he had forgotten the boy's presence. Then his expression changed, and he clapped Will lightly on the back. "Get going with those cookies, son, before I eat the whole tray."

"Yes, sir. Enjoy the party."

By the time Will worked his way around the room to his mother's chair by the fire, it was empty. Merry Folger, however, was sitting there with her gaze bent on the flames. She looked up and smiled.

"Hey, buddy."

"Hi, Mere. Want a biscotti?" He thrust the tray toward

her like a blocking tackle, hoping food would deflect her attention from the needle he'd found on the harbor bottom.

"Biscotti. Sure. I've eaten everything else in the house." She chose one and turned it in her hands, studying the layer of chocolate and cookie as though it might tell her fortune. "Thanks, by the way, for saving that plastic bag."

Will swallowed hard. Jorie's face, and the memory of the lie he had told her, rose painfully in his mind. "No problem. Did you . . . find anything important?"

"Could be. I'll let you know if I can." Merry studied his face. "You look spooked, Will. What's up?"

"Nothing."

"Okay," she mused, "I've said that myself on occasion. Sometimes I even mean it. Other times, I'm just avoiding a topic."

He shrugged and looked away in embarrassment. "I meant, nothing to do with you, Merry. Or that bag."

"Oh. Girl trouble?"

Will gave up and perched on the arm of Tess's empty chair. "Sometimes I think it's girl trouble. Other times I think it's just life."

"That's another thing I've often said. This wouldn't happen to be the girl with the big doe eyes and the jeans torn out at the knee?"

Surprised, Will nodded.

"Caught you staring at her yesterday. She in your class?"

"Yeah."

"But she's already taken by Paul Winslow."

"How do you know Paul?"

"He did some dredging for us yesterday. In the boat basin."

"Paul?! With the *police*?!"

"I know." Merry smiled sardonically. "It's not often a junkie will get within five feet of a uniform, much less volunteer for the job. But he knew Jay Santorski."

"The dead scalloper." Will's mind was reeling. "You *know* about Paul?"

"I know what the marks on his forearm mean. He wasn't

wearing a jacket yesterday, despite the freezing rain. I guess dredging is warm work."

"Not that warm," Will said.

"How do you know Paul?"

"He was a year ahead of me in school."

"And his girlfriend?"

"I'm not sure Jorie's his girlfriend anymore."

"Well, that's a relief. If you care about her, keep her out of Paul's clutches. It's a hard road back from where he's gone."

"Paul used to be a good guy," Will protested. "He just needs help right now."

Merry looked at him searchingly. "Do you know where he gets his drugs, Will?"

"No. And I don't want to." But perhaps, he thought privately, he ought to find out.

Chapter Twenty-one

Margot lay in bed alone and waited for the sound of fog horns that never came.

It was a moonlit night, and no blinds fell across her window. Far below and beyond it, crashing on the deserted Sconset beach, was a sea the color of mourning. Sankaty Light's sweeping beam swept across its face, offering terrifying glimpses of waves caught in the act of curling. The sea was never still, never slept. It teemed with untold monsters. There were more of them at night.

Since sleep was denied her, she wished for the comfort of fog—its formless blanketing death. Both fog and sleep were lost somewhere over the Atlantic. Grief tore at Margot's entrails, famished and unrequited.

Why had Owen told her to go away? He must know that she was waiting for Katia and Jay. Margot had seen the open wound of love in Owen's face when he pleaded with her that afternoon. Or perhaps it was a hint of hate. He had always been jealous of Jay. Was that why he insisted Jay's arm was punctured by needles? To deepen her present misery?

She had seen Jay the night he died. There were no

marks on his arm. Jay had never used heroin. He thought of it as death.

Margot pushed herself out of bed and felt her way downstairs toward the kitchen phone. She still knew Jay's number by heart.

Sue Morningstar, groggy with sleep and her own bottomless grief, answered on the fifth ring. It was just as Margot was beginning to speak that something—the rising wind? an unquiet ghost?—blew open the front door.

Chapter Twenty-two

A layer of torn cloud partly screened the face of the moon when the last ferry rounded the end of Brant Point, but the light was strong enough to trace a wavering path across the calm seas of the harbor. Peter Mason stood in the bow in the darkness, following the path with his eyes. The gale winds had dropped, but the air was raw. Tomorrow would probably bring fog.

The ferry slid past the Easy Street Basin and the pilings of Old North Wharf. A moored dory bearing a blazing Christmas tree amidships bobbed gently in the steamship's wake. An overwhelming sensation of coming home filled Peter's soul, buoyed him on its current, and made him grip the ferry rail with quiet happiness. Everything he had ever loved was in this small place.

A phrase of a late Beethoven quartet jangled in his brain—much as the Emerson String Quartet might have played it. Or was playing it, even now, to a pair of empty seats in the center of Carnegie Hall's fifth row.

A klaxon sounded; the loudspeaker boomed. Vehicle drivers were ordered to the lower cargo decks. Peter gave a last look at the moon's path, felt the ferry hull lurch against its obdurate berth. Then he bid farewell to the darkness and went in search of his car.

He was not an unforgiving man, nor yet an obtuse one. He understood the importance of Merry's work, to herself and the people she served. He recognized the burden under which she had labored for much of the past year, and with a lover's peculiar intimacy he knew the demons that haunted her. But if Peter was capable of insight and forbearance, he was nonetheless a man prey to easy wounding; he had been betrayed in love before. As he watched Merry purposefully packing her things in Greenwich, and enduring the silent drive to La Guardia Airport, he had begun to wonder whether he was *too* kind, *too* forbearing, and in the end supportive to his own detriment. The women he loved had a tendency to take Peter Mason entirely for granted.

So he did not call Merry Folger from the Steamship Authority terminal. He merely drove his car down the boat ramp, through town, and straight out Orange Street, ignoring the turning into Fair and her above-the-garage domain. He did not allow himself to question his behavior as he shot out of the Rotary toward Polpis, and the hundred acres of Mason Farms, where the cranberry vines lay frozen and colorless under the December sky. The effort it cost him to thrust Merry firmly out of his mind was evident in the frown that creased his brow, and the unblinking nature of his gaze as he stared at the floodlit road beyond his headlights. For what, then, had he come home?

He told himself that there was no purpose to spending a week alone in New York. That he had work to do, although this was the time of year when his farm demanded the least attention. In fact, he had spent all of six hours in Manhattan, and came away dazed by traffic and the great city's magnificent decay. He had been too long an island-dweller; the urban landscape hurt his eyes. He longed for isolation, for silence pierced by birds, for an inner peace made manifest in the singular curl of a wave.

He did not come home for Merry.

If anything, he came home to deny himself her presence. In this he thought to find the answer to the loneliness he carried around like a bit of shrapnel. It had occurred to Peter that he needed Merry too much. It might even be this considerable need that was stifling her spirit, making her balk at marriage and the endless toll of years. If Peter feared anything, it was that he might lose Merry forever. So he decided to leave her first.

There was a danger in dependency upon any one human being; it laid the soul open to abuse. He would pull back. He would let go. And in this distance, he would find his strength.

It was just possible that she would notice.

Peter wanted Merry to comprehend how much he mattered. He wanted her to die for lack of him.

As an impulse—as an operative plan—it was the very reverse of his usual supportive self. It appealed to his love of discipline, his self-sufficient ideal. Both had kept him a relative recluse on Nantucket for the decade before he had met Meredith Folger. Returning to them now was like another sort of homecoming. He was safest when he was alone.

And as he turned into the hummocked terrain of the moors, nothing above but the stars thrown like so much salt across the sky, Peter smiled.

There was no one to greet him when he pulled up before the old house. He had given his housekeeper, Rebecca, the week off. Rafe had driven out daily to tend the sheep and feed the dog, who barked frantically as Peter shoved open the front door. He spent a moment fondling Ney's ears, while the dog's tail thumped rhythmically against a bench that stood in the hall; and Peter noticed, as always when he saw Ney again after a brief absence, that the dog was growing old. The knowledge twisted in his heart.

He stooped to pick up his mail, and read through it as he walked toward the kitchen. Bills; credit card offers; contribution requests from Princeton (so necessary at the end of the year); and a postcard from his friend Sky Tate-Jackson, showing a statue of Buddha reclining. Sky had been traveling with his wife through Asia for four months now, and the postcards came like fragmentary thoughts, long after their posting in obscure places, full of talk about weather and vistas that Sky had already forgotten. The impulse to write while on vacation, Peter thought, had much more to do with the person traveling than the person to whom he wrote. Postcards were the wanderer's last tie to a life he no longer believed existed—and a threat that he might someday return.

He read the words on the back of the Buddha, a faint smile flickering over his lips, and then turned to a long white envelope with a preprinted label and no return address. Another solicitation for money, he thought; and he was not disappointed.

Dear Friend of the Head of the Harbor, it began. *A recent study released by an interdisciplinary team of noted Woods Hole scientists has found an appallingly high level of nitrogen in the waters of Nantucket Harbor.*

It was high, Peter argued mentally, but not appallingly so. Nothing like the problem in Chesapeake Bay or Long Island Sound, where Georgiana and her children sailed all summer. He had read a copy of the Woods Hole report. He had felt obliged to do so—he fertilized his cranberries several times a year, and the runoff of nitrogen through his bog system and its related wetlands probably fed straight into the harbor.

Nitrogen is contributing to the decline of shellfish and plant life throughout the Head of the Harbor. The barrier shore of Coatue, prized by islander and seasonal resident alike for its unspoiled beauty, is severely affected. But measures can be taken to control the destructive impact of nitro-

gen in our waters. Won't you join with us now, before Nantucket's island beauty is silenced forever?

Since when were scallops and eelgrass vocal, Peter wondered irritably, and glanced up at the letterhead for the name of the person who had so mangled his mother tongue.

Under the rubric "Board of Directors" he found several names he recognized. Owen Harley he knew through Rafe. And then there was Mac McIntyre, one of Nantucket's selectmen, and Sally Forsyte, who owned a local plant nursery. *That* was interesting; they'd won over a landscape designer to the cause of nonfertilization. It was only natural, he supposed, that they would try to recruit Peter Mason, one of the island's commercial growers. He scanned to the end of the list, then backtracked to a name that seemed familiar.

Jay Santorski.

Then words tugged at his brain, but no face obligingly surfaced. *Jay Santorski.* How did he know that name?

And then it came to him—the scalloper who had ruined his vacation. Peter frowned, and looked back at the list.

Below Santorski was another name Peter knew.

Hannah Moore.

It seemed for an instant that his heart stopped, and then recommenced beating with a painful jerk. Hannah Moore. He hadn't thought of her in years. A curious expression came over his face—a look of caution and faint excitement, as though he saw temptation clearly and debated its purpose. If Hannah Moore was crusading for the environment with Merry's dead scalloper, Peter might put their long-dead acquaintance to some practical use.

And he might teach Merry a lesson into the bargain.

He read through the petition to its closing plea for funds, then refolded it carefully and tucked it into the pocket of his jacket.

He knew he'd come home for a reason.

• • •

The telephone jerked Merry out of an abyss of sleep. She groped for the receiver groggily—aware, despite the haze of interrupted dreams, of the quickening of her heart. It could only be Peter, fresh from Carnegie Hall.

"Detective Folger?"

A woman's voice. Merry's heart came down to earth.

"Speaking," she muttered, and dragged a hand through her hair.

"It's Sue Morningstar. I'm sorry to call so late—"

"That's okay." Merry glanced at her bedside clock, and read a quarter past midnight. She must sound like she'd walked out of a tomb. "What is it, Sue?"

"Margot St. John just called me."

"Morgot called *you*?"

"Yeah. Ironic, isn't it? I guess I'm the person she thinks of most when she thinks of Jay. She'd heard about the drug overdose thing."

Merry sat up. "From whom?"

"Owen Harley. He told her Jay's arm had needle marks on it. When it came out of the harbor. Did you deliberately lie to me yesterday, Detective?"

"I'd call it more of an omission," Merry said reasonably. "Some things, believe it or not, are confidential in an investigation."

"Except when you're talking to Harley." Sue didn't attempt to hide her bitterness.

"Harley didn't have a reporter's notebook or a story deadline when I interviewed him. What else did Margot say?"

"She insisted Jay had never shot heroin. That he never had needle marks on his arm."

"She didn't see him the night he died," Merry objected. "Two people have told me she was practicing all evening with Owen Harley's swing band. Did she say anything else?"

"I didn't talk to her long. Someone came in and she had to hang up."

A small trill of apprehension ran along Merry's spine. "Roommate?"

"She doesn't have one—she's house-sitting for an off-islander. But her friends drop by at all hours."

"I see."

"Detective—I'm worried about Margot. I know that's hard to believe, given how much I dislike her. But she sounded . . . afraid. Spooky, in fact."

"Spooky?"

"She said someone called Katia had come for Jay, and they would both be back for her soon."

Again, the insistent trill. "Was she as high as a kite?" Merry asked sharply.

"I don't know."

Merry sighed and closed her eyes. "Look, Sue—you can't stay up all night because Margot St. John is seeing things. She probably sees things all the time. You're just the one who got the call."

"Okay." Sue Morningstar sounded relieved. "I'm sorry I bothered you, but—"

"You didn't bother me. I'll drive out to Sconset tomorrow and talk to Margot. Then I'll call and let you know how she is."

"Good night, Detective."

Merry hung up the phone and looked blearily around the room. She had fallen asleep over Matt Bailey's manuscripts—like their author, they were less than riveting—and the scattered white pages shone like ghosts in the steady moonlight. She gathered them into an untidy sheaf, then got out of bed to draw the blinds. At the window she stood a moment with her hand on the sill, staring out at the beckoning night; and felt as though she were the only person alive. She'd had no word from Peter in nearly three days. He must be very angry, then, and nursing his anger in private.

She walked into her small kitchen. Drinking a glass of water in the dark, with only a leaking tap for company, she heard Sue Morningstar's voice in her head. *Someone called Katia had come for Jay, and they would both be back for her soon.*

Margot had asked for help, until her plea was interrupted. Merry shivered, and felt her thin nightdress waft against the back of her legs. Almost human in its caress.

She tossed the last of the water back into the sink and went in search of her clothes.

The drive out to Sconset was probably absurd. Merry raced as though all the hounds of hell were at her heels down the deserted length of the Milestone Road at one o'clock in the morning. The moon shone so brightly on the macadam that she barely needed her headlights, and the undulating folds of the moors stretched to either side like a piece of rumpled bed linen. She might almost have been dreaming, with the dreamer's pell-mell sense of urgency. But as her car slowed at the outskirts of Sconset, turning almost of itself toward Baxter Road, it struck her that even Margot St. John might consider her visit a trifle bizarre.

The girl was probably asleep.

Merry halted the car in the middle of a street turned spectral by moonlight, and weighed her options. She suddenly felt very foolish.

If everything about Margot's house looked perfectly normal, Merry decided, she would turn around and go home. She would drink a glass of wine, which never failed to send her straight to sleep. She would ascribe her behavior to excessive tension and the power of midnight suggestion; and she would undertake never to answer the phone after twelve, whoever the caller. That done, she put the car in gear and crawled toward the address Sue Morningstar had given her.

Margot St. John's house was the only one on Baxter Road that still had lights shining in the windows. It was as though all the life of Sconset had been obliterated in an instant by the cold hard light of that December moon.

She stood blankly on the brick steps for a few moments, listening to the stillness. Her ears were straining for the sound of some movement beyond the storm door's glass—some rustle or snatch of music that might betray a covert habitation. But there was nothing. She glanced first over one shoulder and then the other, registering the dark desertion behind neighboring windows. Their blind panes reflected fitful snatches of moonlight. Even Betsy Osborne's old home, three doors down from this one, was shuttered and silent. The Markham family, who now owned it, had moved to Back Bay for the school year. Merry's eyes drifted over the freshly shingled Markham facade, and she shuddered.

A broad swath of light swept across the fronts of the houses and was gone. Sankaty Light carving up the night, from its sandy height at the end of Baxter Road.

Merry dismissed the ghosts of last spring and turned back to the storm door. Her eyes focused on a tear in its screen—a curious rip formed of two lines at right angles to one another, just beyond the latch, as though someone had forgotten a key, and had forced an entry with a pocketknife. She pressed Margot St. John's bell and waited for the echoes, hollow in the stillness. Then she crept quietly around to the rear of the house.

Here was a deserted deck, with a cheap green lawn chair. Someone—Margot, perhaps?—was in the habit of sitting there, legs propped up on the railing, and staring out to sea. Like all summer things caught in the shore wrack of a different season, the chaise looked conscious of being past its prime.

The lighthouse beam swept by her once more, dazzling her eyes.

Merry turned and looked out over the deck's rail.

Here was the sea itself, rolling from Portugal to the foot of the Sconset bluff. The curling surf gleamed phosphorescent under the brilliant moon. A boardwalk, feet buried in the dunes, led from the deck on which Merry stood to the bluff's eroding edge; and then a staircase, tangled with beach plum and *rosa rugosa* in the summer months, plummeted crazily to the beach below. Spectacular. A site to die for, even in the wintry dark. But the house itself was what the real estate industry would have labeled *a smart buyer's investment opportunity*. Particularly in the present climate of soaring home prices. Its condition verged on the shabby.

At the back elevation, a scattering of double-hung windows, asymmetrical and out of proportion to one another, revealed the house's age. Modern architects were rarely so thoughtless of appearances; even their asymmetricality looked intentional. Four stumbling chimneys, and a fanlight in the peak of the roof. Sliding doors from kitchen to deck. A decrepit loggia tottering under the weight of a pathological wisteria vine, dormant now and crabbed.

The lighthouse beam again, as inexorable as the waves.

She mounted the deck steps, ignoring the embarrassed chaise longue, and peered through the sliding doors into the kitchen. It was sunk in darkness, but her straining eyes picked out a jumble of every sort of canned good and grocery box, thrown willy-nilly about the room in a paroxysm of rage. She drew a sharp breath and bit her lip.

Someone had gone through the pantry like a whirlwind, tearing food from the shelves and overturning chairs. Broken crackers were stewn underfoot, paper toweling trailed dizzily from a countertop, raspberry preserves smeared the tiles.

And a pile of white powder—flour?—spilled obscenely across the sink.

Just beyond the kitchen's side door, almost as an afterthought, she saw the trailing length of terry-cloth robe. A foot extended beyond it.

It was a slender foot, and long, the pale skin almost translucent. The foot of a relatively young girl.

The hair rose slowly along the back of Merry's neck. It was possible, she supposed, that Margot St. John had merely passed out from a too-intense tango with heroin. But she knew instinctively that the girl was dead. The second sense that had sent her down the moonlit Milestone Road had proved unerring. It led straight through the right-angled tear in the storm-door screen directly to Margot St. John's corpse.

Merry closed her eyes and pressed her forehead for a moment against the cold, smooth glass of the door. And then, quite deliberately, she returned to her car and with a single call set in motion the forces that would rouse her crime scene team from their well-deserved sleep.

Chapter Twenty-three

"Bashed her head in," John Fairborn said matter-of-factly. He brushed back a matted length of dark hair and pointed to a shard of bone that emerged sickeningly from the victim's scalp. "Sharp-edged object, probably metal, swung from above and behind her. By a right-handed person."

"That sounded just like all the murdah books," Clarence Strangerfield called approvingly from the front hallway, where he was on his knees dusting the door for fingerprints.

The official response to death had transformed the silent, dreaming house. Strong lights, mounted on metal stands, glared from the center of every room. Camera bulbs flashed. Howie Seitz—who had seen two friends dead in a matter of days—was stoically dusting the kitchen's scattered canned goods and cereal boxes for latent prints. Upstairs, Nat Coffin was similarly engaged. Evidence collection would take them both hours to complete.

A young uniformed policewoman was crouched with a large sketchpad a few yards from Margot St. John's body. Triangulating the position of the corpse, Merry thought, remembering her own early days as a uniformed rookie. Ten years ago, now.

"She couldn't have fallen backwards and hit her head on something?" she asked Fairborn.

"Like what? The edge of a garden hoe? I don't see one lying around, do you? Besides, the angle of the wound suggests a downward slice. She would have had to have fallen on your garden hoe upside down."

"Okay," Merry said mildly, "I was just checking. Any idea how long ago it happened, Doc?"

"Hour or two at the most. She's barely cooled. And no rigor to speak of." He thought a moment, lips pursed and gaze wandering, as though the stench of blood had no power to affect his senses. "But time of death is a crapshoot. I often wonder why anybody bothers to ask."

"You know why we ask."

"The persistence of hope over experience."

Merry stared down at Margot St. John's lifeless face. Her staring eyes were full of unsaid words, a secret she had nearly divulged. They reminded Merry of a clock whose pendulum has stopped, freezing one moment in perpetuity—and of something she had almost forgotten: a girl's terrified gaze, dark with kohl, shining in the light of Federal Street.

"I've seen this girl before."

Howie looked up from the box of soap powder he was dusting, suddenly alert.

"She was frightened of something. I know it," Merry insisted.

Fairborn closed his medical bag and retrieved his coat. "Looks like she had reason to be."

What had Dave Haddenfield said? That Margot wanted Jay at the Baxter Road house for protection as much as anything else? "I meant to talk to her this morning. I should have."

"You can't save everybody, Meredith." The doctor's voice was uncharacteristically gentle. "Where would I be for business?"

"Get out of here, Doc."

He swung his jacket over his shoulders and grimaced. "I should have left this in the car. There's always an unpleasant odor of blood after one of our little chats."

"It matches your clothes, then." Merry followed the doctor to the door.

"Not to mention my hair. I only hope the ladies waiting in my office tomorrow don't have a highly developed sense of smell. It could induce more than morning sickness." When he wasn't on call for the police, Fairborn maintained a thriving gynecological practice.

"Take a shower, Doc," Merry advised. "*Before* you get back in bed."

Fairborn gave her a lazy smile. "You ever notice these murders seem to come in a rush?"

"We don't know that the drowning was a murder," Merry objected carefully.

He waved that away. "We go for months with nothing, and then . . ."

"Boom. Like plane crashes. In threes," Clarence observed from his position by the door.

Threes. Just like last May. Merry frowned at the crime scene chief, and misunderstanding her message, Clarence thrust himself to his feet.

"Let me open the door farh yah, Doc. Wouldn't wancha destroyin' the evidence."

When Fairborn had slid behind the wheel of his teal-blue BMW and roared away, Merry wheeled on Clarence irritably. "Why do we call that guy in, anyway? He never tells us anything except what we already know—that the victim's dead. I could have recited that bit about the sharp-edged metal object before I even made a call to the station."

Clarence didn't bother to answer this directly. "Didja see the needle mahrks on her arm?"

Merry nodded. "No surprise there."

"They were a lot mahr pronounced than that young fellah's we pulled outta the harbah."

"So was her habit, from what I hear. But why kill her?"

Merry's eyes traveled thoughtfully around the house's barren interior. Very little furniture, fewer pictures on the walls, and a set of sheets serving as curtains on the front windows.

"I wouldn't think there was much money in the case," Clarence offered skeptically.

"It's weird, isn't it?" Merry agreed. "This girl was supposed to be house-sitting. But it's as though she never really inhabited the place at all. Not a shred of anything personal, except in her bedroom."

"House-sittin', huh? I'da thought it was somethin' less respectable."

Merry turned. "Why?"

"There's men's clothing in one o' the closets upstayahs." Trust Clarence to make a quick survey of the house, and draw his own conclusions. But she had done a survey herself, while waiting for his van to arrive.

"There are no men's toiletries in the bathroom. The clothes could belong to the house's owner—left here off-season. Or . . . Seitz?"

Howie's curly head poked around the kitchen doorjamb. "Yes, Detective?"

"Run upstairs and tell me whether the men's clothes in the guest-room closet could belong to Jay Santorski."

"Speakin' o' that young man," Clarence volunteered while they waited for Seitz to fulfill his commission, "I traced that 617 phone numbah."

"From the matchbook?"

"Ayeh. Registahed to a woman in Cambridge by the name o' Purcell. Catherine Purcell. Elderly widow. She still summahs on the island."

"You spoke to her?"

"Had to. Otherwise, we'd nevah know why Santorski had her numbah, would we?"

"And?"

"Mrs. Purcell had never heard of 'im."

Disappointment made Merry's tone a little sharp. "You needn't sound so triumphant, Clare. That's not exactly a rabbit you've pulled out of your hat."

"But she told me somethin' that *might* be of interest."

"Yes?"

"The address of her summah house on Nantucket. I could discuss the mattah with her house-sittah, she said." The gleam in Clarence's brown eyes was unmistakably self-congratulatory.

"Don't tell me. Let me guess."

"318 Baxtah Road. Yahr standin' in Catherine Purcell's front hall, Marradith."

Howie chose this moment to call over the upstairs banister. "Couldn't be Jay's stuff. Wrong size."

"Too small?" Merry asked, remembering the lifeless Michelangelo.

"By about four sizes."

Merry looked back at Clarence. "So if the home owner is a widow, and the clothes aren't Jay's . . ."

"We're dealin' with an unknown quantity."

Merry looked for Howie. He was just galloping down the stairs. "Seitz! Did Margot have a frequent male visitor, by any chance?"

The patrolman frowned. "None I ever heard of."

Merry sighed in exasperation. "Maybe he's a *sporadic* male visitor. Or maybe we're making a mountain out of a molehill."

Clarence pursed his lips. "Could fly ovah on weekends from Bahston."

"Leaving corpses in his wake." Sunday was, after all, the end of Christmas Stroll. A good time to head back to the mainland, particularly if the holiday hadn't gone as planned.

"Any reason to think he had a tempah?"

Merry shrugged. "Other than the victim's tendency to crash on her friends' couches rather than turn up at home, I couldn't really say. We don't even know this guy's name."

"Might find it on somethin' lyin' around the house."

"If we can find anything in this chaos."

"Ayeh," Clarence agreed, "not yarh usual breakin' and enterin'. Don't often see a burglah who raids the pantry and leaves the stereo in the neighbahin' room. Looks like a crime o' passion to me."

"Or a drug-crazed rampage. He—or she—was searching for something."

"Heroin?"

"Why not? There's a lot of white stuff spilled. Flour in the sink, powder on the bathroom floor." Merry considered this theory in silence, then shook her head dismissively. "Margot died because she knew something. I'm sure of it."

"About young Jay's death?"

"Possibly. Or maybe they both knew too much about something else."

Merry left Clarence standing in the hall, and took a last look at Margot St. John's face. A paramedic from Cottage Hospital was just about to zip a black body bag over the tangled mass of auburn hair. Merry saw that he had closed Margot's eyes. She felt curiously relieved.

"There must be a property manager, Clare," she said briskly, and turned away from the corpse. "Someone to call when the pipes break in January, or a tree falls on the garage. A real estate agency, maybe, or a local handyman. They could probably tell us a lot."

"I'll get onto it, Marradith."

"Hey, boss," Nat Coffin called urgently from the top of the stairs. "Look at this. I found it in her bedroom."

Merry and Clarence glanced upward.

"It's an ATM slip dated Saturday. Somebody tried to pull a hundred bucks out of Pacific National Bank. Insufficient funds, it says."

"That slip of paper you were hoping for," Merry told Clarence. "Although with our luck, it probably belongs not to an unknown male, but to Margot herself. Everything about her screams insufficient funds."

"Make a copy o' the account numbah," Clarence called upward, "and check it with the bank."

"Detective Folger?"

This time it was Howie, standing white-faced in the kitchen doorway with a can of stewed tomatoes held gingerly in one gloved hand. A damaged can, apparently. Even at the distance of twenty feet, Merry saw the dried smear where the tomatoes had leaked from the seam.

"I think I just found our murder weapon."

When the shrouded body of Margot St. John had been loaded onto a gurney and wheeled away to the waiting ambulance, the small crowd of Sconset residents still lingered on the fringes of the scene. All were bundled into coats and wore hats against the perpetual Sconset wind. By this time, the moon had set somewhere over the mainland, its cold hard light giving way to dawn.

The scattered knot of men and women was silent, from apprehension and something like respect. This was a moment culled from television time: the snarling bursts of a police radio from one of the assembled cars or vans; the flashing red and blue lights; the tramp of strange feet across the barren lawns. As regular as a heartbeat, the powerful beam of the Sankaty Light swept them all like a scythe. They were mesmerized by the strange familiarity of what they saw, and felt themselves borne along by the cinematic drama, mere flotsam in the tide of official business.

One of them paced alone, along a narrow strip of sandy roadbed a hundred yards from the scene. Even in the dark, his nervous tension should have screamed a warning to the police officers milling in and out of Margot St. John's house. But their gaze was focused inward; and when they moved under the eyes of the curiosity-seekers, their majesterial bearing suggested that they were unconscious of observation. Like actors, Paul Winslow thought, who pretend they're playing to an empty theater.

He was shuddering like a leaf as he propelled himself up and down the sandy strip. His hands were clenched tightly in his pockets. His lips were bitten raw. Every now and again he glanced at the violated house, its windows blazing and its front door flung wide; and his eyes were like those of an animal glimpsed fleetingly in the headlights' glare.

Paul was terrified and wild.

After the body was driven away, a woman he recognized from Saturday's dredging at the Easy Street Basin—a lifetime ago, it now seemed—strode down the front path and tossed her purse in a gray Explorer. Then she began to move among the assembled crowd, extending her hand in greeting, a notepad at the ready. She wore half-glasses, and her face was white with exhaustion. She was asking them about Margot, Paul knew. Asking what had happened that night. Whether anyone had heard or seen anything at all.

He stood, muttering, undecided whether to risk the encounter. In his present state, he couldn't trust himself. He might break down and sob; he might plead for mercy and salvation. In any event, he would fall into a trap.

The impulse to run overcame him. He fought it. If he ran, they would be after him like wolves.

And silently, almost imperceptibly, he began to back away, down the length of Baxter Road, toward the enfolding darkness at the base of Sankaty Light.

Chapter Twenty-four

Charles Moore's house in Pocomo looked almost abandoned Monday morning when Peter pulled the Range Rover to a halt before the door. He sat in his car for a moment, staring through the rain at the peeling clapboard facade; then he pulled the keys from the ignition and got out. Hannah had done well for herself. He had always supposed that she would.

He didn't bother to mount the front steps or ring the bell. Instead, he followed his instincts toward the water. His first sight of the Quonset huts that housed the labs on the edge of the marsh slowed his progress a little. The love—or some more mercenary emotion—that Hannah had lavished upon them was immediately apparent, and stood in sharp contrast to the neglect endured by the rest of the property's buildings. Peter concluded from this that Hannah suffered from diminishing resources. She was a fastidious creature, but her funds would go first to her work.

His footsteps crunched on the gravel path, and to give Hannah warning, he coughed. Another man might have hallooed foolishly, and sent the marsh birds skyward with his antics; but Peter could not shed his breeding, even for the sake of a role.

"Is someone there?" a low, impatient voice called from the middle hut.

"I'm looking for Mrs. Moore."

"Come in, then."

He pushed open the door and peered around the edge. A sea of glass-sided cases met his eyes, green water bubbling with plentiful gases, humidity clouding the fettered air. "Hannah?"

When she thrust her swivel chair away from the lab table, and her long black hair raked across her shoulders, it was as though ten years had never passed.

Or almost.

The same taut frame, control screaming from every line of her body. High cheekbones, merciless gray eyes, the long, nervous fingers that were always moving. Even her feet, Peter thought as he glimpsed the strong toes she had shoved into black leather sandals, had changed very little. Only Hannah would wear Italian platforms in the dead of winter, in the middle of a marsh.

Ten years, however, had pulled the skin more sharply over her bones and had turned her firmly adrift in the doldrums of thirty. She would never again be a luminous ingenue with a face like Paulina Borghese—if indeed she ever had been.

But she was looking at him now, and so he schooled himself to show nothing like calculation in his eyes. He refused to be taken at a disadvantage.

"My God. Peter Mason." She half-rose from her stool. "I never thought I'd see *you* again."

"Why not? It's a small island."

"And you can avoid whomever you choose. I made certain you'd avoid me. You have for long enough. What brings you here?"

He smiled, but didn't move from his position by the doorway. "Several things, in fact. Belated congratulations on your marriage."

"Entirely unnecessary." She dismissed the absent Charles

Moore with one hand. "I'm not likely to be married for long. What else?"

"Curiosity."

"About what? Not my marriage, I hope. I may be bored, but I'm not desperate."

Peter ignored the taunt. He gestured vaguely around the lab. "Curious about all this. I'd like to know what you're doing, Hannah, with your brains and your money."

"Why?" she asked, suddenly wary. "Why now? You've never cared about scallop culture before. Or my brains, come to think of it."

"Untrue. I found both quite fascinating when we last knew each other. We each had our passion for growing things at the edge of the sea. You might call it our common ground."

"You just wanted to get inside my pants."

"Did I?" Peter sounded intrigued, as though the notion of Hannah's pants, and all they lovingly caressed, had never entered his head. Hannah's eyes hardened, and she stood, if possible, yet straighter.

He reached inside his suede bomber jacket and pulled out an envelope. "I received this in the mail a few days ago. I thought you might be able to explain it."

She accepted the envelope without a word, and scanned the letter it contained. The faintest suggestion of a smile hovered about her lips. "I see they've even provided a thoughtful box at the bottom of the page, designating your contribution. How dreadfully gauche." She handed the letter back to him.

"They? I thought I saw your name on the letterhead."

"Old stationery."

Peter reached into his jacket again and withdrew a small postcard overlaid with slanting script. "Then I suppose you're not responsible for this."

She took it between two fingers, as though it might carry disease. " 'Stop the destructive fertilization of your cranberry bog, Peter Mason, or suffer the consequences.' " She looked up at him, and amusement flooded her face.

"What I would like to know is, *destructive to whom?*" Peter said. "Certainly not the cranberries. They're flourishing. And I don't even use chemicals. I'm entirely organic."

"Nitrogen is nitrogen. You must know that fertilizer runoff is killing the harbor." Hannah returned the postcard indifferently. "And that, my friend, sounds like a threat."

He laughed. "What are you planning to do—chain yourselves to the bog at harvesttime? Slaughter my sheep?"

"Eviscerate your dog, perhaps. But I told you I'm no longer a member of Save Our Harbor."

There was an edge of malice to her voice that Peter didn't like. But he kept his demeanor purposefully light. "They probably drink cranapple juice at their committee meetings, too. And never consider the irony."

Hannah regarded him speculatively. "Are you laughing in the face of terrorism, Mr. Mason?"

"I don't take threats very seriously."

Her eyes met his, and after a moment, she nodded. "I remember. Threats were always useless where you were concerned. I must explain that to Owen Harley. He's probably responsible."

"Owen? I can't believe he'd write this."

"Why not?"

"I know him. He's too sane."

She laughed harshly. "Sane? What a curious word to use. People are never sane about what they really love. Besides—that card could have been written by a preadolescent hooked on dime-store novels. That's just about Owen's mental age."

"You don't like him. Is that why you quit the harbor group?"

"I don't like inefficiency," Hannah said.

"Ah." Peter looked around the lab, saw the gleaming stainless steel, the unclouded glass. Efficiency took money to maintain. "It's odd, Hannah. That they should pick me to harass. I disturb nobody. I live very quietly in the middle of my farm. I barely go out for a loaf of bread."

"Yes." Hannah leaned against her lab table and folded her arms across her chest. Her gaze was intent, and cruel. "A housekeeper to buy your groceries, a Rafe to run your sheep. Even a policewoman, I understand, to provide companionship. Why should anyone like Owen Harley trouble so solitary and powerful a person as Peter Mason?"

"Because he enjoys harassing people?"

"He wants funding, more likely. Owen is a child of the sixties. He has a great passion for community consciousness. Save Our Harbor was inevitable."

"But my bog isn't on the harbor."

"It borders Gibbs Pond, however."

Peter shrugged.

"You're not an idiot, Peter, even if you did waste your time studying history at Princeton," Hannah said impatiently. "Anything you put into your bog eventually drains into the groundwater that ends in the harbor."

"But at least my fertilizer goes to produce an island product. They should attack the owners of all those trophy homes in Shawkemo, who are tearing up the dunes to plant luxurious lawns."

"You operate on a much larger scale. Any commercial grower does. I'm sure Bartlett Farms got a similar message."

"Maybe they paid up." Peter secured the letters within his coat. "I suppose I should make a hasty and improvident donation to the Save Our Harbor fund. Or should I call it the 'Save My Cranberries' fund?"

Hannah's gaze sharpened. Her usual response to the hint of money. "Call it what you like," she said. "It'll still be a lost cause."

"Really? Is the harbor that bad?"

"Of course not. Compared to the Chesapeake or even Long Island Sound, it's in fairly good shape. I was talking about Owen Harley, and his desperate band of legislative revolutionaries. The things he's advocating—low-cost loans for septic field renovation, voluntary limitations on fertilizer use, and dredging the head of the harbor—are incremental. They mean *years* of waiting before the harbor rebounds, much less the scallop population. I want a more immediate return on my money."

"So why do you bother with all this?" Peter looked perplexed and waved a hand at the bubbling tanks. "I thought you were under contract to provide scallop spawn to the shellfish board."

"Oh, them." She dismissed the shellfish board with a flick of her black hair. "Hurricane Edouard relieved me of *that* obligation. Forget the spawn, Peter. Mere numbers mean very little if the harbor degradation continues. I'm on the brink of something much more exciting now. Something that could make me a fortune."

Her smoky voice was tremulous with passion, and for an instant, he remembered what it had been like, God forgive him, when he *had* wanted to get into Hannah Moore's pants. A bare three weeks of exhilarated longing, of blinding desire, ten years ago when he had been rebounding wildly from a broken engagement. And then he had understood what she was.

"Are you willing to talk about it, Hannah," he asked her now, "or is it too much of a trade secret?"

The passion faded, and she averted her eyes. Considered in silence for the space of a few heartbeats, and then looked at him searchingly. "What do you do with your money these days, Peter?"

At last, he thought, they had come to it. He moved closer to her and caught a faint scent of hyacinth. "Besides throwing it away on lost causes, you mean?"

Her gray eyes were difficult to read. They had grown hazy with hope and doubt, blunting her habitual calculation. "Let's go down to the docks," Hannah said abruptly. "No one will hear us there."

Having returned to bed at dawn, Merry overslept that Monday morning. Her rest was fragmented by an overpowering anxiety; fitful dreams, in which something vital and unknown had been left perennially undone, were punctuated by glimpses of Margot St. John's pleading dead eyes. When at last Merry roused herself, and went groggily in search of coffee, it was already nine o'clock. She abandoned breakfast, and drove purposefully to the Water Street station. The only cure she knew for nightmares was a headlong plunge into work.

Several reports sat waiting on her desk when she arrived around ten o'clock. She set down her purse and took up the first of these—from Nat Coffin, Clarence's assistant. Paul Winslow, Merry read, had vanished without a word from his group house on Orange Street. Nat's highly correct account of his morning acquired a querulous tone at this point; he had badly wanted to talk to Paul. It was Paul's account number that Nat had found on an ATM slip in Margot St. John's bedroom.

A sensation of doom, lingering from her broken night, swept over Merry. Paul's flight—however it had been occasioned—could only look like the desperate beating of a guilty bird against the bars of its cage. She set the report aside, called Nat at his desk downstairs, and told him to check the airport and ferry terminals for a passenger of Winslow's description.

The second report was from Howie Seitz, apologetic where Coffin had been self-righteous. He had yet to locate Matt Bailey's car.

Merry turned this news over in her mind, the single sheet of paper idle in her hands. Her late-night foray into the world of Bailey's fiction had suggested a more novel escape route than his aged VW bug. Bailey's hero, the trigger-happy Mike Prescott, was in love with a dangerous woman, whose husband had threatened to kill him. When things blew up in his face, Prescott stole an expensive yacht and fled through a storm to the Caribbean.

She must ask Tim Potts whether Bailey knew how to sail. And send Howie down to the Town Pier, to inquire whether a boat of any description had gone missing. Few vessels were still in the water at this time of year, and a theft would be fairly obvious.

But first, she owed her grandfather a visit. Somewhere along the moonlit length of Milestone Road, driving slowly behind the ambulance that had borne Margot St. John to the Cottage Hospital morgue, Merry had been visited by revelation. Like Paul—or was it Saul?—on the road to Damascus. Bailey, she was certain, had been involved in a drug sting. Her father, she was equally convinced, had known all about it. And neither would have conducted the operation without a legitimate paper trail. The disappearance of that trail from Bailey's office and home hardly meant that it had been destroyed. John Folger might be many things at present—a prevaricator, a lone wolf, a coward dressed up in Authority's clothing—but he remained a stickler for procedure. That was why he had called Merry home, and launched an investigation, when a man of less compunction would have declared Jay's death an accident.

If she was correct, then the paper trail still existed. And Tattle Court was the only place her father would trust with his more shameful secrets.

As she slipped out of the station's side door, and turned her steps toward her childhood home, Merry hoped against hope she was wrong.

Chapter Twenty-five

"Meredith Abiah." Her grandfather's face emerged from the corner of the living room, dappled with shadows thrown out by his reading lamp. Despite the earliness of the hour, the house was dark; a mark of the gloomy weather and the declining year. He closed his book, one forefinger trapped carefully between its pages. He was reading Patrick O'Brian, Merry noticed inconsequentially, *Fortune of War.* Aubrey and Maturin held captive in Boston, and killing Frenchmen with abandon. He must have read it several times already. But what had he told her once? "A man my age has no time for new acquaintance. He's too busy taking leave of his oldest friends."

Where would she be, she thought with heartache, when Ralph was truly gone? Left to make her own peace with a father she no longer knew?

"To what do I owe this pleasure?" her grandfather asked. "A desire to play hooky?"

"Oh, Ralph," she burst out, "everything's awful."

"This wouldn't have to do with young Peter?"

"Peter?"

"Ran into him this morning over at Marine Home.

Looking fit, but given to an unwonted taciturnity. Have you two traded words?"

Peter was home. And he had never called her. Unsettling; worth consideration, at another moment; but perhaps there would be a message on her machine when she got back to her apartment tonight. He could have arrived late—and unlike Sue Morningstar, would be hesitant to wake her. When *had* the last boat from Hyannis docked?

"What were you doing at Marine Home?" she asked Ralph.

"Looking at gas grills."

"You prefer charcoal."

"But I cannot resist a sale. And everything, as you know, is marked scandalously low the week after Stroll." He tossed the O'Brian on a table and, both hands braced against the arms of his chair, struggled to his feet. Merry extended a hand involuntarily—to shield herself from his pain, perhaps. "Now tell me why you are here, my dear, with that desolate expression on your face. Has Peter hurt you?"

"No, Ralph—or at least, not in any way I can't handle. But I need your help."

The white eyebrows furled acutely over his vivid blue eyes. "In what way?"

"Has Dad brought home any files lately? Say . . . since Thursday or Friday?"

"I don't know. Files?"

"Big green hanging ones. From the station."

"We didn't use those in my day. Now let me think. Friday." He studied the worn braiding of a rag rug at his feet. "This wouldn't have to do with your interesting theories about the death of that young scalloper?"

"Ralph—there's been another murder."

He stared at her wordlessly for the space of an indrawn breath. Then he closed his eyes and sighed. "You certainly make it hard on an old man, Meredith. Help is not what you need. You're asking for betrayal."

"I'm trying to save my father," she said tersely. "He's so far in, he can't find his way out."

"Out of what? Surely you don't believe him capable of..."

"Murder? Of course not. But of covering for the incompetence of a subordinate—yes. Undoubtedly. He's done it often enough for me."

"You were never incompetent, my dear." Ralph touched her blond head lightly. "Merely unlucky. A state that can descend upon anyone. As it has descended upon your father."

"You know what he's done." Apprehension tightened her mouth. "He's told you."

"Poor John has never breathed a word. Only come into the house preoccupied and bleak, and left it in much the same fashion. I have never been able to encourage his confidence, Merry. That is one of the sadnesses of our life, lived for so many years in an equable harmony. Something prevents us from opening our minds to each other. The work, perhaps, divides us."

"I thought the force was your greatest bond."

Ralph shook his head. "I could not wish upon any son the burden of filling his father's shoes."

She had never viewed John Folger in this light—as struggling himself to live up to an elder's good opinion; and it changed, without warning, Merry's entire perspective on her history with her father. He was merely repeating a pattern he had himself undergone. He was teaching her as he had been taught. It was for Ralph—long detached from authority and its fears—to offer her unquestioning love. The certainty of acceptance, and forgiveness of her sins. The board of selectmen would never hold him accountable again.

As they would certainly hold John Folger, when the present tragedy came fully to light. Whether her father feared Ralph's unspoken judgment more, was a question Merry chose not to ask.

"I understand," she said gently. "Forget I even asked. Just look the other way while I ransack the house."

"That won't be necessary," Ralph replied. "He hid them under the bed. In your old room."

. . .

What Merry found, amid the dust bunnies and scraps of paper that invariably collect beneath the best of mattresses, was the entire contents of Bailey's office filing cabinet. She thrust aside his expense account records, the endless justifications of past investigations bungled, and spared only a moment for his collected correspondence. What she wanted was hidden innocently in a slight folder with the words *Tiger Op* on its tab.

Larval tigers, she thought irrelevantly, and settled down cross-legged to read.

The first piece of paper was a report, dated November 13 of that year, and addressed to the chief of police. It detailed Bailey's initiation of an unlooked-for and valuable contact only a few days before. The contact, who remained nameless, was "a college-educated white male working seasonally as a scalloper, who approached this officer to propose the joint incrimination and arrest of a heroin trafficker operating on Nantucket Island."

Jay Santorski, almost certainly. Jay had sought out the police, then, rather than the reverse.

Scribbled at the bottom of Bailey's initial report were the words *Looks good—go ahead. Offer two hundred biweekly for his help, if he'll take it.* And the initials *JF.*

There it was, the absolute proof of her father's complicity in an operation almost certainly gone bad.

Overcome with defeat and anger, Merry set the file aside. She could not read any further without affording John Folger a final chance. She would go back to the station and confront him in his office. He might, just possibly, tell her the whole story, now that Margot St. John had been murdered, too.

Murdered, too.

The girl had died because of John Folger's cowardice.

Merry thrust herself to her feet, her face set in the impassive lines of rage; gathered up the file; and left Ralph sitting mournfully, with O'Brian for comfort, in his corner of the shadowed living room.

. . .

She found the Chief poised at the foot of the station's stairs. It was as much as she could do, to approach him as though everything were fine. As though nothing had changed.

"Meredith." He kept his eyes on a sheaf of paper. It trembled slightly in his hands.

"Chief. Do you have a minute?"

"I've already sent a preliminary report about the girl over to Dan Peterson," he said, forestalling her. "I'll let you know his decision on jurisdiction."

As the District Attorney for the Cape and Islands, Dan Peterson disposed of all homicide investigations. He usually preferred to assign them to the three-member state police force resident on-island; but on more than one occasion, Merry had found her way around that preference with surprising agility. This was not one of those occasions.

"I don't care about jurisdiction," she replied. "I want off this case."

He looked at her woodenly. "You mean—the drowning?"

"I mean the *homicide*. Margot St. John was murdered because she knew Jay Santorski. I'm more certain of that than of anything in my life. Which means neither of them died by accident."

"I suppose we'd better talk about this in private."

He led her down the short hall to his office without another word, and faced her across the desk, as though its broad, familiar bulk might offer courage. "You've made some pretty absolute statements. Before we even discuss your resignation from the investigation, I want to know what you've learned."

"Nothing you'd probably consider important. Except that I can't work under these conditions."

"Conditions?"

"This . . . deliberate obscuring of the truth." She drew a calming breath. "You need to hand this one to somebody else. Somebody who can investigate it objectively. You should have done that from the beginning."

He glanced out the office's sole window somewhat desperately, as though contemplating flight. "I thought *you* might be objective, Meredith."

"More objective than yourself, at least?"

"Just tell me what you've got."

She began to pace in front of his desk, ticking off the facts on shaking fingers.

"Jay Santorski had a promising future in marine biology. He was liked and respected by most people who knew him. He was infatuated with a young singer named Margot St. John, who may have introduced him to drugs, and who died a brutal death last night.

"I've also learned that Jay was friendly with Matt Bailey, who disappeared the night of Santorski's death. The last recorded words out of Bailey's mouth implied that he had been working in Cambridge—where Jay Santorski attended Harvard. The house in which Margot St. John was killed belongs to an off-islander named Catherine Purcell, a resident of Cambridge. Her phone number was written on a matchbook found on Santorski's corpse, but Catherine denies knowing him. From this I can surmise two possibilities: Catherine is lying; she knew Jay Santorski well, and the two of them arranged for Margot to house-sit on the island; or Margot St. John herself once lived in Cambridge, where she met Catherine, who never heard of Jay in her life. And for some reason Jay intended to call the woman."

John opened his mouth to object, but Merry held up her hand. "Please, Dad. You asked for facts. I'm trying to deliver."

"Go on."

"Matt Bailey, in that odd recorded conversation, was talking to a woman his son, Ryan, has identified as Hannah Moore."

This was news to the Chief. He flushed darkly.

"You will remember Bailey told Hannah point-blank

that he had discovered something in Cambridge that was damaging to her husband. I know that Charles Moore has roots in that town; Hannah told me so herself, only last night. She met him in Cambridge. Interestingly enough, the dead Jay Santorski also knew Hannah Moore."

"Is that all?" her father asked impatiently.

"Not quite. There's the part that fits even less neatly into the facts as related. Jay Santorski and Margot St. John were both friendly with a young islander named Paul Winslow. Like Jay, Paul is a scalloper; like Margot, he is a heroin addict. Paul Winslow's ATM receipt was found at the scene of Margot's murder. He has disappeared from his group house, and his parents haven't heard from him. We've notified the ferry terminal and the airlines."

John threw up his hands. "My God! The part that doesn't fit neatly! It sounds like the key to the whole case!"

"If you factor out Bailey. And Hannah Moore. And a tape and hypodermic found on the harbor bottom."

Her father still stared out the window, apparently mesmerized by a helmet-haired blonde who stood in animated discussion, a lightship basket over one arm, on the corner of Chestnut and Water Streets. Her beefy, middle-aged conversant in the duck-hunting boots threw back his head and bellowed with laughter.

Shouldn't the tourists have gone home by now? Merry thought irritably.

"You'd think the tourists would have gone home by now," her father muttered. Then he turned away from the window and slumped into his chair. He looked older and more hopeless in that moment than Merry had ever seen him. She felt a surge of fear and pity supplant her blinding anger.

"Tell me about this Hannah Moore," he said bleakly.

A concession, of sorts. He had accepted the tie to Bailey. "She runs a lab and shellfish farm out in Pocomo. Her husband is supposed to be a wealthy real estate mogul. Hannah volunteered for an organization founded by Jay Santorski and his scalloping captain, Owen Harley, called

Save Our Harbor. There's some suggestion that Hannah pursued Jay romantically, and was rebuffed."

"Then by all means, let's haul her in!" the Chief retorted bitterly. "Hell hath no fury, and so forth. She probably shot Jay full of his girlfriend's heroin, and then waited two days to bash the girlfriend on the head."

"I didn't say that, Dad—"

"Then what are you saying? That she killed them over a disputed point of political activism? The fact that this woman knew Santorski professionally means nothing whatsoever. A lot of people have been interested in scallops throughout the history of this island, Meredith, and they've managed to coexist without killing each other."

"Hannah's hard up for funds to continue research," Merry persisted. "What if her devoted husband found a lucrative sideline?"

"Dealing heroin?"

"Why not? Cocaine once looked like an option to a famous car designer who needed cash."

"And you think Jay Santorski found out about it, and was going to turn him in?"

"Maybe Charles Moore's drugs were destroying Margot, and Jay didn't like it. He went to Bailey, fingered the heroin dealer, and Bailey went to Cambridge. I'm assuming Moore's suppliers are there. The information checked out, and Bailey called Hannah Thursday night to warn her. Only something went wrong. Jay was injected with an overdose of heroin, Bailey went underground, and the answering machine tape went into the harbor."

"That still makes no sense. All they had to do was erase it."

"Agreed," Merry admitted. "I can't explain the tape, yet."

"You can't explain a lot of things. How anyone could overpower that athletic young scalloper long enough to get a needle in his veins—"

"I think he was bound. Wrists and ankles. Pending the autopsy report, of course."

Her father was silent a moment. "Pending the autopsy

report, why don't you just accept that he might have shot himself full of his girlfriend's drugs, and died as a result? It's the simplest solution."

"And the most palatable. Right?"

He shrugged.

"At the very least, we ought to check the Moores' alibis for the night in question."

"You never did like Bailey, did you, Meredith?"

"No. But neither am I responsible for what he's done in this case. Isn't it time you told me all about it?"

For the space of several heartbeats, John Folger said nothing. Merry watched a range of emotions cross his face, and held her breath. Then he shook his head almost imperceptibly, as though he had come to some inward decision.

"Type up your report, Detective," he said. "I'll place it in the file. I'm still not convinced these deaths are related. Jay Santorski ran with a dangerous crowd. He dabbled in risk, and he died. The girl was probably killed for her drugs by that Winslow fellow."

"And Matt Bailey?"

"Will have to explain himself when he finally turns up. As I'm sure he eventually will."

Merry thought with pain of Bailey's operational file, tucked even now into the depths of her purse. She had no choice but to read it. She had offered her father a chance: he had thrown it away.

"Don't do this, Dad," she pleaded.

He made a show of collecting some errant papers, shuffled them into a neat square. Precision and efficiency; form over substance. "Your resignation from the case is accepted."

"What will it take?" Merry burst out. "Matt Bailey's body on a plate?"

The furious blue eyes came up to meet her own for the first time in that painful, pointless interview.

"It'll take *proof*, Meredith. You've given me nothing on which I could base an arrest—and I've had enough of your celebrated *instincts*. We know where they got us last time."

The previous night, Merry had contained her rage for the sake of the crime scene crew. She had concentrated on evidence collection, the pathetic tally of death; she had suspended feeling and walked through her appointed role. Today, however, she was alone with the memory of Margot St. John's untimely end. Her pointless waste.

She felt herself flush. "I screwed up last spring, Dad. Fine. I won't deny it. But unlike you, I never did it *deliberately*. Two people are dead—one of them because of *you*. Because you knowingly and persistently denied your investigating officer the background to this case."

"Remember where you are, Detective. And exactly who you're talking to."

She laughed bitterly, and turned toward the door. "Those are two things I can never forget. You're the man I've looked up to—my entire life—as the embodiment of integrity. As a professional ideal. And in a single weekend, you've smashed that god into pieces at my feet. I'll never regard you in the same way again, Dad. And that's another kind of death we've got to deal with."

Chapter Twenty-six

Merry left her father sitting morosely behind his desk, and strode out into the chill December day with her purse slung over her shoulder. On the sidewalk, she hesitated; where to read Bailey's ugly dossier? Her office was out of the question. Lunch somewhere—the casual exposure of the stolen file on a gaily clothed table—was impossible. The mere thought of food set her stomach to churning.

She began to walk toward the Easy Street Basin. So what if the wind off the water was freezing? It would slap her out of anger. Focus her energy. Sharpen her senses.

And no one was likely to contest her possession of the Basin on such an untempting day. If Owen Harley turned up in his wet suit and long johns, so much the better. She was becoming expert, Merry reflected, on the killing of numerous birds with a single deft toss of her stone.

"Jorie!"

She stopped short in the parking lot of the high school, her arms full of books. "Paul?"

He had pulled an old Whalers baseball cap over his

shaggy blond head, and his faded blue eyes looked at her warily from under the brim. His hands were shoved into the pockets of his jacket—a Tommy Hilfiger navy and yellow striped windbreaker, too light for the chill air sweeping over the island in the nor'easter's wake. Jorie remembered when Paul's father had given him the jacket, which he had desperately wanted, right after the superbowl game he had quarterbacked last December. That was well before the disappointments of April, and his failure to get into Boston College, and the fatal decision to spend his savings on a used scallop boat and assorted controlled substances. Jorie's throat constricted as she looked at Paul, his shoulders hunched against the wind whistling around the school parking lot. He probably hadn't eaten or slept in days. He looked, in fact, like the sort of derelict she would normally cross the street to avoid.

But she remembered who he had been, and made no move to go anywhere. "What are you doing here?"

Paul took a step toward her, then stopped short. "I wanted to see you."

"Well, I don't want to see you." She shifted the books to her left hand and gripped her purse strap tightly with her right, as though he might attempt to steal it.

"You don't understand," he said in a rush. "I've been trying to quit. That's why I was so edgy Saturday, why I snapped your head off. And then there's the whole thing with Jay dying . . . I haven't used a thing since Thursday night, and I feel as though there's a rat in my stomach eating its way out." He closed his eyes tightly and crouched down all of a sudden, almost falling to his knees. The hands he reached to the damp macadam were shaking.

Jorie dropped the books and knelt down beside him. "Paul! Should I get a doctor?"

"No!" He spat out the word and opened his eyes, struggling to focus on her face. "They'll tell the cops. I know they will. Just get me to my car. It can't last much longer."

"You need help. There are things you could take—things that would—"

"—Make me think I'm on heroin?" he said bitterly. "Fool me out of being a junkie? That's the last thing I need. Heroin's all I can think of, and it's driving me nuts."

"Then let's get you some help," she argued.

For an instant the wild blue eyes managed to fix their gaze. "Don't," he said urgently. "I'm afraid."

"Of what? The police?"

Paul shook his head violently.

Jorie's stomach knotted and she glanced around desperately. None of the other kids was interested in the sight of her talking to her boyfriend, even if their decision to sit on the wet surface of the parking lot looked a little odd.

And then Jorie saw Will, standing like a statue in the midst of a dispersing crowd of their friends. His eyes were locked on her face, and his expression was unreadable.

"Don't move," she said fiercely to Paul; but he was rocking back and forth, arms folded over his abdomen, and his eyes were closed again.

She ran, as quickly as her ill-fitting clogs would allow, and grabbed Will's arm. "It's Paul."

"No kidding. I had hoped it was his better twin."

"He's really sick, Will. He says he's been trying to quit. I think it's killing him. And he won't let me go for a doctor." She was pleading, as though he had already refused her what she had not asked. "He says he's too afraid."

"Of what? A hospital?"

"The cops, I think."

Will's dark eyes stared unblinkingly into hers, as though he could see through everything and always would. He started to say something, then dismissed the thought with a grimace and walked away. Jorie clattered behind him, fighting a sharp spurt of tears.

"Hey, buddy," Will said softly, and hunkered down near Paul's face. "Let's get you on your feet."

"Take me to my truck."

"Why? You have something you need in there?"

The sudden harshness in Will's voice was like a slap across the face.

Paul's eyes flew open and Jorie saw the anger blaze—

anger not just at Will, or at her, or at the desperation of his choices—but anger at himself. In such a mood, she realized, he could be dangerous.

"Come on." Will grasped Paul's arm and lifted him bodily from the macadam. That single act told Jorie all she needed to know about Paul's weakness; a few months earlier, Will could never have gotten close enough to lay a hand on him. "We're going to *my* car."

"Where are you taking him?" Jorie asked.

"To the hospital, of course."

"*NO!*" Paul flailed wildly. "I won't go there, you bastard! They'll tell the police!" He broke free of Will's grasp.

"Please, Will," Jorie urged. "There must be somewhere else."

The three of them stood for a moment, Paul swaying and ashen.

"I suppose we can't take him home to his dad."

"That would be the same as taking him to the hospital."

"And your mom would do the same."

Jorie nodded miserably.

"So would mine. But we can't just dump him at his place on Orange Street. He needs someone to take care of him."

"What about . . ." Jorie searched for possibilities, and discarded most of them. It had to be an adult, but one who wouldn't interfere. "What about Hannah?"

"Hannah?! She wouldn't take care of anybody! You know that!"

"But she wouldn't turn Paul in to the police, either," Jorie reasoned. "And you and I could watch him in one of the huts until he's okay. We can say we're over there for our senior project. Nobody'll think twice."

"You're probably right," Will said thoughtfully. "But will Hannah let him stay?"

"I hope so." Jorie reached for Paul's arm and felt him slump against her heavily. "Come on, Will—Hannah's our only hope."

• • •

But it was Charles Moore who met them in the driveway of Aqua-Vital. They had forgotten about Charles.

He was driving out in his dented blue Mercedes, the top down despite the cold, and a slight breeze ruffled his silver hair. He hit the brakes as he pulled abreast of Will's truck.

"Hey, kids! 'Fraid you're out of luck. Hannah's gone out. You don't usually come on Mondays, do you?"

"No," Will said. "We thought we'd just stop by and talk. But that's okay, we'll see Hannah Friday."

Moore smiled and looked beyond him. "Is that Paul? Why aren't you out on the water earning a living, young man?"

This sally was greeted with silence.

"Paul's not feeling well," Jorie volunteered hurriedly from her place between the two boys. "So it's probably good that Hannah's not here. We can get him—home now."

"What is it? The flu?"

Paul didn't respond. He drifted in something like a stupor.

Charlies Moore set his parking brake carefully and thrust open his door. Jorie drew an involuntary breath; where they rested in her lap, her hands balled into fists.

He walked around to Paul's side and leaned in the open window. "He looks pretty bad. Maybe you should bring him into the house."

"That's not necessary," Will said quickly. "We'll get him home."

The good-humored ease of Moore's expression hardened into something more acute. Concern? Or comprehension? "Has he been able to tell you . . . what's wrong?"

"Not really."

The man's gaze shifted slowly from Paul to Will. Then he nodded slightly. "Home's probably the best thing. I'll tell Hannah you stopped by."

Back in the Mercedes, he smiled at them jauntily. "Go ahead and turn around after I clear the drive."

Will watched in his rearview mirror until the Mercedes had shot past them toward the Polpis road; then he looked at Jorie. "What do we do now?"

"We could hide him in one of the huts. Hannah'll be back soon. We could ask her then." She spoke quietly, as though her voice might disturb the boy beside her; but from the look on Paul's face, he was beyond the reach of words.

"Mr. Moore wouldn't like it if he knew."

"Maybe he won't know."

"He lives here, Jorie. He'll know. Besides, Hannah's hardly an angel of mercy. We were stupid to think this would work."

"So what now? Paul looks really bad. What if he dies, Will?"

"He won't die. He might *wish* he had, by the time this is over, but . . . how about a hotel?"

"We'd need a credit card."

"I haven't got one."

"I could take my mom's, and forge her signature," Jorie offered doubtfully.

"No way. Besides, she'd get the bill. And then what would you tell her?"

They were both silent, and Will's front teeth worried at his lip. "We'll have to take him to Peter's."

"Who's Peter?"

"Peter Mason. He's a friend of mine. Rafe works for him. It's only five minutes away."

"You mean, Mason Farms?" Jorie's voice was incredulous. "He's the guy who's going to marry the cop, right?"

"Uh-huh. But Peter'll help. He's not like a parent, and he always knows what to do. It's got to be better than taking Paul back to his place. He'll only get sicker there."

"I think this idea sucks," Jorie said firmly. "Peter'll tell his girlfriend, and Paul will never forgive me."

Will glanced at her over his shoulder, then eased the truck's fender toward a stone wall that ran along the drive. "That's the best news I've heard all year. Then maybe he'll leave you alone."

"You'd like that, wouldn't you?" she shot back. "You don't give a shit about Paul."

The dark blue eyes stayed fixed on the road. "But I care a lot about you, Jor."

She swallowed hard, aghast at the surge of joy that greeted his words; and then remembered the other boy beside her. "I wouldn't have asked for your help if I'd thought you were going to hand Paul over to the cops, Will."

"Peter isn't even home. He's gone to New York and he gave Rebecca the week off."

"Rebecca's the girlfriend? The cop?"

"The housekeeper. The place'll be empty."

"So how will we get in?"

"I know where Peter keeps the spare key."

Jorie mulled this over, then shook her head. "It's too risky. We can't go with you. You've got to take us back to town."

"Where, exactly?"

"Anywhere!"

"The middle of Main Street? The graveyard? What?" Will shook his head. "I can't do that, Jor. You'll never be able to handle him alone. I'm sorry, but we're going to Pete's. You've just got to trust me."

Trust, Jorie reflected, had never been very important to Paul.

Matt Bailey had gone to Cambridge, Merry learned from his file, because his unnamed contact had sent him there. The heroin traveling through Nantucket's drug underground had its origins in a network of enterprising Dominican Republicans, long-established in the multi-racial fringe of the university town. The unnamed source's girlfriend—a promising young Harvard student and *Crimson* reporter—had been researching the story. She had befriended the youngsters pushing drugs on the Cambridge streets. She had followed the network from its end point in the ghetto, to some of the more rarified neighborhoods of Boston; she had identified the primary dealers, who were anything but Dominican, although quite often Republicans.

And she had been about to publish her piece when she had died quite tragically, the victim of her own fascination. A heroin overdose.

"And her name was Katia," Merry murmured to herself, "although Bailey may never have known it. But how does the road lead from Cambridge to Nantucket?"

She read on. And picked up the trail near the back of the slim file, on a typed list that detailed four purchases of heroin. The buyer had been Margot St. John. The dealer, Charles Moore.

It was all there: dates, amounts, and purchase prices. Jay must have observed the sales, Merry thought, or wormed the facts out of the girl; but he seemed never to have bought any drugs from Moore himself. That, Merry supposed, had been intended for another day, with a police entourage in attendance. Jay's life had ended first. Much as the unknown Katia's had done.

Who betrayed him? Margot St. John, in a moment of incautious talk?

Or Bailey himself, during that taped conversation with Charles Moore's wife? Merry was inclined to award Bailey the responsibility; an error of this magnitude was entirely in keeping with the course of his life.

But the answer would have to be found outside the green arms of the official folder. It ended abruptly two nights before Santorski's death, when presumably Bailey had departed for Cambridge.

Two items of interest remained. One was a succinct history of Charles Moore's life. The other was a list of contacts Bailey hoped to debrief during his trip to the mainland.

Moore had deep roots in the Cambridge community. A trust-fund orphan, according to Bailey's notes, he was raised by a patrician aunt and her banker husband in a large house not far from Harvard Square. His résumé included St. Paul's and Harvard; a minor post at the uncle's bank; and a brief stint in Washington during the Vietnam War. At the age of twenty-five, with canny foresight, he had purchased a quantity of slum properties in the more degraded sectors of Cambridge. The gentrification of the seventies and eighties had done well by Charles Moore. In the early nineties, he had retired with Hannah to the house in Pocomo, which had been in the Moore family for three generations.

Hannah's maiden name, Merry was pleased to note, was an unceremonious and pedestrian Steinmetz. She was Moore's second wife; his first marriage, to an Irene Lewis, had ended in divorce only a few months previous to the Nantucket move.

Hannah the Home-Wrecker, Merry thought. The appellation suited her.

But a swift survey of Bailey's Cambridge contacts banished Hannah Moore's specter to the fringe of Merry's mind. For another woman's name leaped clamorously off the page. *Catherine Purcell.* Catherine Purcell, whose Cambridge phone number had drowned in Santorski's pocket Thursday night. Catherine Purcell, in whose Baxter Road house Margot St. John was brutally murdered.

Catherine Purcell—whom Bailey identified, in his rapid, looping script, as Charles Moore's widowed aunt.

It made sense, Merry thought, that Moore's clothes were still hanging in the house's closets. He probably even possessed a set of keys.

Chapter Twenty-seven

"Lookin' for me?" Owen Harley shouted across the boat basin's chop.

Merry jumped involuntarily and slapped Bailey's operational file closed. "Owen. Hello."

He guided the scallop boat carefully between the bevy of wooden dories still bobbing in the shallows off Easy Street, and moored up at his private slip. He looked more grizzled than ever this afternoon, with the hood of a dirty gray sweatshirt pulled up over his ears. His face, too, was weary unto death. A bad day for the delivery of ill tidings. Merry summoned her flagging courage; the duty had to be faced.

Harley cut the engine. "Got news about Jay?"

"Sort of." She frowned involuntarily.

"So do I, as it happens. C'mon up."

Merry followed him within, and took up her familiar position before Owen Harley's million-dollar view. She drank in the emptiness of the ragged channel as it curved past Brant Point, and tried not to remember Margot St. John's pleading dead eyes. They had followed her relentlessly throughout the day.

Harley showered and exchanged his working clothes for a set of comfortable black sweats. Their monochrome drape lent a peculiar elegance to his weathered frame, as though its angles and crags had been willed to him by Papa Hemingway. In the background, Billie Holiday sang the blues.

But Merry turned away from the window's peace. "I've got bad news. It's Margot."

"Margot?"

They had never actually discussed the fact of Margot—either her occasional tenancy of his sofabed, or the tension she had caused between Owen and Jay. In fact, as far as Merry and Harley were concerned, Margot might never have existed.

"Someone killed her last night."

He lifted a hand to his face, where it hovered uncertainly for a few seconds before dropping again to his side. Then he turned and slumped into a chair.

"I'm sorry," Merry said.

No answer. Owen Harley rocked forward, as though he had been kicked in the abdomen. Merry reached out a hand, then withdrew it without touching him.

"There's no good way to say it. But I thought I ought to come myself, instead of telling you over the phone."

"How long?"

Merry didn't understand him. "How long . . . what?"

"How long has she been dead?"

"We're not sure. We think since late last night, around midnight, perhaps."

"Oh, God." The rocking ceased, and he came to rest with his chest against his knees, arms locked around them as though he were afraid of hypothermia. "I saw her on Saturday."

"Where?"

"At the house. I went out there to talk to her." Harley looked up at Merry, his face more terrible for its lack of tears. "I told her to get out."

"Of what?"

"This—mess."

Merry looked around and found a chair. She pulled it close to Harley's huddled form and sat down.

"When you told me about the needle marks on Jay's arm, I was afraid. He was close to Margot, and Margot was an addict. I wanted her to leave town before you people caught up with her."

"When we talked on Friday, you never mentioned her name."

"I know."

"You should have. We might have been able to protect her. Margot wasn't the person we wanted."

"Don't say that, damn you! Nothing could protect Margot. She was a moth caught in a flame. It's amazing she lived this long!"

Merry shoved a hand through her blond bangs, sticky with humidity, and sighed. "Look. I'm sorry. That was unfair. But it makes me crazy, Owen, when I'm an hour too late. I went to talk to Margot last night, and all I found was a body."

"You found her?"

"Yes."

He went very still. "How—did they do it?"

"They?"

"He. She. It."

"Margot was hit on the back of the skull with a sharp metal object. She probably never even felt any pain." Merry kept the fact of the tomato can out of her story; it lacked dignity, and could have no significance for Owen anyway. "The kitchen was pretty torn apart, as though her killer was searching for something."

"Heroin," he said bleakly. "Of course."

"Was Margot likely to have had a supply of it in the house?"

"No. She lived from fix to fix. Bought it when she had the money."

Merry asked the next question more from curiosity than a need for confirmation. "Do you know where she got her drugs, Owen?"

He put his head in his hands, and his shoulders began to heave.

She went over to the small galley kitchen. The mugs, she remembered, were stored in the cupboard to the left of the sink. She filled the kettle with water and searched about for tea. By the time she had found it, Owen Harley had recovered enough to sit up. But his eyes were fixed on the gray line where sea met cloudy sky, miles beyond his window. Merry doubted whether he even saw the knife of a sail moving slowly against the horizon.

The Billie Holiday record—an actual LP, not a remixed CD recording—came to an end. In the silence, the tea-kettle's whistle shrilled.

"I don't know why I'm grieving," he murmured at last. "Maybe now she's at peace."

"She wasn't before?"

"Only when she was high." He closed his eyes. "What a waste of a life. And what a life to waste."

"You loved her, didn't you?"

He nodded dismissively. "Oh, yeah. She was one of the rare ones. Torn by guilt, and by memories she couldn't silence—but in those few moments when her mind and body soared, Margot was like nothing else on this earth."

"Did she know how you felt about her?"

"Probably not. I never, ever, touched her. And I think she grew to trust me. She knew I was her truest friend."

"What about Jay?"

A flicker of anger, that swiftly passed and left Owen's face as ravaged as before. "Jay was good at saving things. Or at wanting to save them. He wanted to save the harbor, and the scallop population; he wanted to save Margot; he may even have wanted to save me." Owen paused for consideration. "All because of his failure to save the one person who really mattered."

"A girl named Katia."

His eyes flicked up to Merry's face. "You've heard of her, then? She was Jay's girlfriend and Margot's college roommate. Katia haunted them both."

That single fact explained a lot of things. Merry handed Owen the mug full of scalding tea, and he drank it obediently, as though it had already cooled. "Margot made a phone call yesterday morning, Owen. To Sue Morningstar, one of Jay's old housemates. She told Sue that it was Katia who had come for Jay, and that they were both coming back soon for her."

"A presentiment of death? She was probably out of her mind."

"She hung up when someone came through the front door. We don't know who that was. We found the storm door unlocked, but the screen had been slit."

"Margot never left the front door open. She was afraid of violence."

"—but it may have been opened by a key. Who had a key to her house, Owen?"

"Jay."

"Anyone else?"

"I don't know."

"Have you ever heard of a man named Charles Moore?"

"Hannah's husband? Of course. Margot was house-sitting for his aunt."

"How did that arrangement come about?"

"I assume it happened back in Cambridge. Margot must have known her there."

"Charles Moore didn't set it up?"

"I don't know."

"Okay. Let's try something else. Who were Margot's friends?"

"Me. Jay. A kid named Paul Winslow. She met Paul when he came to hear us play one night in September, just after Jay came to the island. They had drugs in common."

"So I've noticed. Did she spend a lot of time with Paul?"

"Not really."

"Tell me about him."

Owen looked at her searchingly. "Is there a good reason for asking? You think Paul killed her when he couldn't find any heroin in her house?"

"Someone murdered her yesterday. Maybe it was a random homicide—but I think that's unlikely, given Jay's death."

"Jay shot heroin and then drowned."

Merry didn't reply.

"You think Margot knew something about his death?"

"I think it's possible. Any ideas?"

The vague expression of misery turned suddenly acute. "My God. That's what I wanted to tell you. This news about Margot put it out of my head."

"What is it?"

He rose and went over to his desk. "Jay left something behind him. A message from the grave."

Merry felt a cold finger move up her spine. Between Margot's dying words and Owen's present ones, she was beginning to credit the supernatural. "What sort of message?"

"A spectrogram."

"A what?"

"The image made by a mass spectrometer. It's a machine that analyzes samples of things—organic compounds, generally—and charts their chemical structure."

He handed Merry a manila file. "Take a look."

She slid the sheet of paper from the folder and stared at it uncomprehendingly.

"It's some sort of graph. Of what?"

"The chemical makeup of a scallop's tissue, I think."

"What does that mean? And why did he have it?"

"I have no idea. You'll have to ask Mel Taylor, Jay's thesis advisor over in Woods Hole. This must have come from his lab at the Rinehart Coastal Research Center. Jay wouldn't have access to a mass spectrometer here on the island."

"Rinehart." Merry's eyes were fixed on the spectrogram, as though it were the Rosetta Stone. "Jay went over there the day before he died. You think that's when he got this?"

"It must be."

"How did it get to you?"

"Jay gave it to Margot. The night he died. She was supposed to bring it to our practice session, only she forgot."

"So she *did* see Jay that night," Merry murmured. Margot's insistence on the absence of needle marks on Jay Santorski's arm gained sudden credibility. "Did Margot tell you whether it seemed urgent to Jay?"

"Not directly. But she felt that she had failed him, by forgetting the spectrogram. She thought he came over here Thursday night to discuss it with me."

"And fell into the boat basin." Merry waved the bar graph under Owen's nose. "Why would this be important? Do you think it's part of his thesis?"

"Could be. Or it could have more to do with that paper you found in his bike pack."

"Larval tigers," Merry said slowly, "and a sketch of the Horseshed." Hannah Moore, again.

"None of it makes any sense," Owen said.

"But it will. There's reason behind all of it. May I have this?"

"By all means." He stood up abruptly. "And now I've got to get going. Get the morning's catch over to the openers."

Which really meant he wanted Merry to get going, and take her misery with her. "Just tell me what you know about Paul Winslow," she said quickly. "Then I'll leave you alone."

"Paul's a kid. He's right out of high school. He's angry at his parents for splitting up, and angry at himself because he thinks he caused the divorce. He's angry at a variety of colleges for refusing him admission, and angry at the world because he's decided he's a scalloper and there are no scallops in the harbor."

"Is he angry enough to kill somebody?"

"That I don't know. But I'd find it hard to believe."

"Where would he go if he was in trouble?"

"Can't you find him?"

Merry shook her head.

"Oh, man . . . this just gets worse, you know?"

No reply to this seemed necessary. At the door, however, Merry turned and said, "Are you sure you should be alone today?"

A faint smile. "I'm not going to end it all by slipping overboard, if that's what you mean."

"I just thought you might need someone to talk to."

"I'd rather talk to myself. Or God, if He's listening. Is there going to be a service? For Margot?"

"I don't know. Her body will be flown to the state crime lab for further . . . investigation. Once it's released to her parents, they're free to make arrangements. I'll keep you posted."

"Thanks." Owen reached around her and pulled open the door. "For everything. If someone had to find her, I'm glad it was you."

Chapter Twenty-eight

At the moment Will Starbuck drove away from AquaVital and headed toward Mason Farms, Peter Mason was saying good-bye to Hannah Moore in front of a Main Street eatery, after a prolonged and provocative lunch.

The morning's conversation on the Pocomo dock had turned into a tour of the entire AquaVital lab complex. Peter was more impressed than he had expected by the scope of Hannah's work. Shellfish culture, he knew, was a mix of simple techniques, lots of time, and boundless hope—rather like the business of raising cranberries. Water, rather than soil, was the preferred medium, of course—but success was just as dependent upon the forces of nature.

Hannah was determined to circumvent those forces, he soon realized. She was playing a little at God in the marshland at the head of the harbor.

This wasn't immediately obvious, of course. Most of AquaVital's outer trappings were exactly like any other shellfish farm. In the shallows just off Pocomo, Hannah had launched a series of wooden rafts that resembled window screens—square, steel-meshed frames designed to protect young scallop spawn during its setting stage. She had staked netting around a group of eelgrass beds to protect established scallops from predators; but netting and rafts could do nothing against wind and wave, as Hurricane Edouard had taught her.

Back in the Quonset huts, she led him to an array of large tanks. "This is where my tigerbacks spawn," she said. "Seawater is pumped in from the dock area, and the temperature is raised a few degrees, which tricks mature scallops into believing it's time to reproduce."

"Like forcing bulbs."

"Sort of. Then, while the young are still in the free-swimming larval stage, which lasts about two weeks, they're kept in these tanks"—she gestured toward another bank of bubbling vats—"and fed single-celled phytoplankton I grow over there, in a different tank."

"The one with the domed cover?" It was bright yellow, and looked hermetically sealed. Two valved chambers permitted entry to the tank, presumably by gloved hands.

"I want to keep contaminants away from the algae," Hannah explained. "I'm extremely careful about how I feed my spawn."

"I see. And then?"

"They metamorphose—that's when they finally start looking like scallops—and grow large enough to set."

"I don't see anything that looks like a scallop." Peter peered into the larval tanks.

"Come over here."

Hannah was already across the room, and holding up a long, cyclindrical mesh object.

"What's that?"

"A Japanese onion-bag net. It's used to set the spat."

"The what?"

"Spat. Shellfish spawn. They clamp on to the netting after the larval stage and grow to seed size. This net is suspended in an upweller—a tank that pumps highly oxygenated water to the scallops, making them grow more quickly."

"And since there are no natural predators in the tank, and a ready source of algae courtesy of Ms. Moore, the survival rate must be very high."

"Yep."

"How do they get back in the harbor?"

"Once the seed is several millimeters in size, it's placed in these mesh pearl nets. I string the nets from long lines tied to the pilings out there in the harbor. That usually happens in late spring, and I leave them in the nets until fall. Then they're released throughout the harbor. Unless a hurricane wipes out the pearl nets first."

"Like Edouard."

She smiled bitterly. "That storm cost me three million seed scallops. And my grant money from the town."

"Ouch."

"It doesn't matter. Those tigerbacks were failures, anyway." She dropped the onion-bag netting back into its tank. "Usually these nets would be tied out in the harbor. But the seed you see here is only experimental."

"In what way?"

She hesitated, openly assessing him. "You're obviously familiar with the harbor degradation."

"As a demon fertilizer, I ought to be, don't you think?"

"How much do you know?"

"I read a copy of the Woods Hole report."

"Ah. Then you know about brown tide."

"The phytoplankton bloom that chokes the feeding systems of bivalves."

"*Aureococcus anophagefferens*. A dinoflagellate first observed in1985 in Narragansett Bay, then in the Peconic and Great South Bays of Long Island. It grows rapidly, turns the water brown, blocks out light, and causes widespread destruction of eelgrass on the bottom. Vast populations of scallops and oysters in those waters no longer exist."

"They're ceasing to exist here, as well."

"But it's a reversible phenomenon. If you can get rid of the brown tide, the scallops come back. The problem is, we still don't know how to predict or control these blooms."

"I thought they were due to sewage."

"Perhaps. But algal blooms are as old as the seas. They've existed from time immemorial. They will probably occur long after our civilization and its pollutants are gone."

Peter folded his arms across his chest and studied Hannah's expression. It was perfectly controlled, which bothered him. He knew that she was attempting to play him like a fish—because she needed money? Or for some other reason?

He said: "You're hoping to get rid of the algae."

"I've done it," she replied. "Here, in the lab."

"How?"

"How isn't important. It's results that matter."

"If I'm going to give you my money, I'd like to know what for."

Hannah looked at him shrewdly. "*Are* you going to give me your money, Peter?"

He shrugged. "Depends on what I hear."

She seemed to come to some sort of decision. "All right. I'll tell you. A few years back, two researchers at Stony Brook isolated some seawater viruses that seemed to control the growth of brown tide algae. We're only beginning to understand how viruses work in the world's oceans—a teaspoon of seawater contains literally a hundred million different ones—but I've taken the research one step further. Do you know much about viruses?"

Peter shook his head.

"They're parasites, of course, and they often kill their host organism. We've seen that with HIV. Over time, a virus will mutate quite readily, adjusting itself to prolong the life of its host. That mutability makes viruses the devil to combat—HIV changes shape with almost every attempt to conquer it, for instance. But viral mutations can also be useful. Sometimes, we can influence viruses to serve our ends."

"And you've . . . influenced . . . yours?"

"Last year, I filtered out one of the brown tide-eating viruses. I exposed it in massive quantities—far more than is likely in nature—to my tigerback scallop spawn in its larval stage. In my first trials, the virus invaded the spawn and killed it. But with repeated exposure, the virus itself mutated slightly until the latest batches of tigerbacks could tolerate it. Virus and spawn seemed to adapt to one another. And when I studied the young scallops, I found a remarkable thing."

She moved closer to Peter, and he read the passion buried deep in her gaze. "*My tigerbacks had genetically altered.* Their feeding systems were capable of ingesting *Aureococcus anophagefferens*. Peter, I've created a super-scallop in my laboratory. It's the answer to everybody's problems."

There was a dubious silence. Then Peter drew a deep breath. "That's a remarkable story, Hannah. You must have investors flocking to your work."

Her eyes slid away from his and once again, he felt that she was withholding something. "Not exactly. Investors want tangible results. I've only just reached the point of confidence in my trials, and I haven't been able to test these tigerbacks in the harbor waters. The ones I released over the past few years were failures as far as brown tide is concerned. But come spring, I'll have this seed strung out on the pearl nets. By fall, they'll be ready to set. The following summer, millions of my mutated tigerback scallops should be clearing the harbor of the brown tide."

"You need eighteen months," Peter said, comprehendingly. Then he peered through the lab's shoreward window, assessing the pilings that thrust at intervals through the Pocomo shallows. Far across the harbor lay the protected barrier beach of Coatue, its trailing fingers lacing the sea at almost predictable intervals; to the left, barely glimpsed, was the sprawl of town. It was a spectacular piece of property from any point of view—and it would never have been beyond Hannah to marry for real estate.

"It's fortunate that your husband owned all this prime water acreage. —Or is that *why* he's your husband?"

She didn't answer him.

"The taxes must be astronomic," he mused. "Has Charles ever been tempted to sell?"

Hannah flinched. "Of course. Real estate is his business, and I don't have to tell you that home values are skyrocketing right now. This house has been in Charles's family for several generations, but it costs the earth. If Charles is going to sell, now's the time."

"Hard to blame him," Peter said. "This part of the island is a summer resident's dream. Harbor views, without the fear of erosion. It's relatively sheltered, except for the occasional nor'easter."

"The same conditions that make it ideal for scallop culture," Hannah said softly.

Peter turned his back on the water and looked at her speculatively. "Has he talked about it?"

"Charles is always talking. Whether he follows through is another matter. He likes to think that threats will keep me in line."

"Is that what he needs? Coercion?"

She shrugged. "We've grown apart. People do. Charles feels that I've drained him of capital to little purpose. I feel that he's shortsighted. It can make for unhappy dinner table conversation. Sometimes I think he'd sell just to spite me."

She momentarily lost control of her expression, and Peter glimpsed the desperation and anger—the sheer violence of will—that animated Hannah Moore. Then she walked abruptly away from him and out of the Quonset hut. After a moment, Peter followed her.

"How did you do it, Hannah?" he asked her.

"Locate the virus?"

"No. Alienate your husband."

She looked at him speculatively. "Why do you want to know?"

"If I'm going to back your work, I want to do it with my eyes open."

At that, a smile flickered around her lips. "Alienating Charles was as easy as breathing, Peter. He can't bear the fact that I love my work more than him. I told him the truth back in Cambridge, before we ever married—but he didn't believe me. Now he does."

"Let's go get lunch," Peter suggested. "And you can tell me the rest."

"You really want to know about my marriage?"

"Not your marriage. The virus."

And so Peter was parting from Hannah Moore late that afternoon in front of Arno's when a voice behind him said, "Peter."

He glanced over his shoulder and saw Merry.

She was standing stock-still on the sidewalk roughly ten paces away, and her eyes widened as she looked from Hannah to himself. He recognized the strained expression she generally adopted when she was determined to appear casual; but perhaps her emotion had nothing to do with his return to the island, or his apparent intimacy with Hannah Moore. She was, after all, involved in a case; and Merry rarely spared a thought for anyone when her work engrossed her.

"Hello, Hannah," she said, to his surprise. "Nice to see you again."

"Hi." Hannah pulled up the collar of her sheared beaver coat against the cold, and gazed at Peter, as though Merry hardly existed. "Think it over. But not for too long. I have to seek funding from *someone* in the next few weeks, and I'd like it to be you." Her voice deepened slightly, as though she had just invited him into her bed—which, upon reflection, perhaps she had.

"I'll be in touch," he replied; and with a lingering caress from her gray eyes, Hannah Moore walked away.

There was an awkward pause as Peter watched her go; then he turned to Merry, and waited for her reaction.

"Ralph said he'd run into you." Her voice was determinedly neutral.

"Right. At Marine Home." He reached into his pocket for his keys. "Can I drop you somewhere?"

"Oh—no, thank you." Merry took a step toward him, and then stopped, as though bewildered. "What's wrong with you, Peter?"

"Nothing. Anything wrong with you?"

"Why haven't you called me?"

"I figured you were busy. The drowning." He kept his voice deliberately indifferent, and watched her black eyebrows furl. She looked exhausted, and worried, and as though she needed nothing so much as a kind word; and for a moment, he wished profoundly that he could take her back to Mason Farms and keep her there until she slept. But the impulse rankled as soon as it came; he would not be supportive to his usual fault. Merry needed to make her choice. Happiness with him, or misery with her work.

"That's not true, and you know it." She was angry, suddenly. "You're trying to punish me for leaving Greenwich, aren't you?"

"You're under stress, Meredith." He said it quietly enough, but he'd given the words an edge that could hardly be missed.

She brushed back her bangs in frustration. The winter day had turned cold, and the early dark was settling over the town; a light veil of snow whirled from the sky, and settled like lace on her hair. "Okay. Fine. Behave like a child if it makes you feel better. I have more important things to do than watch."

"As usual."

She rolled her eyes and started to walk past him. He tried to stop her, but she wrenched her arm angrily out of his grasp.

"One more thing, Peter," she said, her voice brittle with anger. "Your lunch date. Hannah Moore. She was a little too cozy with both Matt Bailey and Jay Santorski, one of whom is missing, while the other is dead. Think about that before you call her again, okay? Just a word from your friendly neighborhood police officer."

"What do you know about Hannah, Merry?"

"Not enough. But believe me, I will."

She was twenty feet away from him now, and moving fast.

"Merry—"

No response, not even a sign that she had heard.

Peter stood there, alone in the thickening snow, with his feet slowly turning to ice.

Chapter Twenty-nine

By Monday afternoon, most of the lingering Christmas Strollers had at last departed for Westchester and Litchfield and Back Bay and Georgetown, taking with them a raft of shopping bags gaily strewn with colored tissue, framed canvases wrapped in brown paper, and gold chains strung with diminutive lightship baskets.

They left behind a slight sensation of anticlimax. Shopkeepers marked down clothing and pillowcases and china teapots made of basket-weave porcelain, then posed disconsolately before their plate-glass doors, and sighed as they surveyed the empty cobblestones beyond. Managers of restaurants harried their waitstaff, and made baleful and secret decisions over who should remain and who would be let go. The concierge at the Ezra Mayhew House spent an entire morning directing repairs to the garlanded decorations around the hotel's front door, which had been partially destroyed by Friday's nor'easter, undeterred by the fact that Christmas, although three weeks away, seemed already to have come and gone.

A west wind bustled anxiously among the sodden shingle houses, as though it, too, had someplace better to be.

The scallopers were still plying the waters in their small open boats, with their steel gantries rocking above them like an army of empty doorways, and attempted with every hurl of the dredges to defy the course of nature. Owen Harley was among them; but he was seen to drift without decision, his winches stilled and his gaze fixed on the dying bottom.

Only the Unitarian minister, whose Christmas Eve madrigals were to be this year a thing of surpassing beauty, regarded the end of Stroll with complete complacency. His singers would devote more time to their music. They would follow his eyes intently as he stood at the fore of the church, and rose slightly on the balls of his feet to command the opening phrase. He smiled with satisfaction, already feeling the glow of winter candlelight and the faint inhalation of breath that preceded the burst of sound. He was unaware, it seemed, of the seasonal death of tourism, or of the insidious decay of the harbor's waters, or of the brutal ends to two young lives. He was attempting to decide which sweater vest to wear beneath his gray tweed jacket.

The parking lot that comprised the bulk of Steamboat Wharf was conspicuously empty. Not for December the frantic jostling of an August day, when tickets bought eight months before were fingered like pieces of the true cross. The weekend hordes had come and gone, and left a single car becalmed in the post-holiday silence. A shabby old VW bug the color of faded denim, it sat in the wharf's small front parking lot overlooking the terminal. Its windshield was cracked and spotted with rain, and one wheel hub had been replaced by an unpainted panel that gleamed through the morning fog like a bare bone.

Mona Baldock pushed back the hood of her navy-blue Steamship Authority slicker and stared narrowly at the car. It was not one she had flagged off the ferry ramp from the first boat that morning, or the single boat this afternoon; and when she considered the matter, she was almost certain that it had been parked in its spot for several days. Mona glanced at the ferry terminal doors, where her boss's head was bent over an unlit cigarette. He hated people using the wharf's lot illegally. So Mona started to walk toward the car.

It was possible to send unaccompanied vehicles over to Nantucket for a small fee, although it was a practice the Authority discouraged. It was more common in summer, when ferry reservations were tight, and cars sometimes traveled standby. The owners would cross on a morning ferry, and an Authority employee would bring their cars over at midnight, or early the next morning. The owners were expected to retrieve their vehicles from the terminal lot a few hours after arrival. The VW, Mona realized, had been overlooked in the rush of Christmas Stroll crossings.

She was maybe two yards from the driver's side door when a sudden gust off the water buffeted the car. A smell so foul, so unlike anything Mona had ever experienced, wafted over her. She let out a small yelp, turned her back on the car, and bent double as though from a blow. Then she fled without a backward glance toward the safety of the Authority's offices.

Running into Peter Mason with the Faye Dunaway-esque Hannah Moore on his arm was probably the only fitting end to what had been an utterly lousy day. After leaving Owen Harley, Merry had spent most of the afternoon attempting to reach Margot St. John's parents. She had succeeded at last in wresting the father from a business conference in Manhattan. He was annoyed at the interruption, and then devastated by the news. Merry had never before been forced to endure a grown man's sobbing over the telephone, and she hoped never to experience it again.

It didn't help, Merry thought, that she was tired and seemed to have a cold coming on, or that her jacket still smelled faintly like Owen Harley's fishing shack. It was just Fate's kind of joke, to throw Peter her way when she was at her most defenseless.

Walking now into the police station without a glance to left or right, almost oblivious to the calls of greeting thrown out by her colleagues, Merry wondered what plans Hannah had for Peter Mason. She wanted his money, of course—but would Hannah Moore stop there?

"Detective!"

"Hey, Seitz. Any news of Paul Winslow?"

Howie shook his head.

"Come on up to my office."

He followed her there, rendered mute by the black look on her face, and waited while she fished out a phone book. "Call this number, and ask for Will. He should be home from school by now. Then ask him for the name and number of Paul's girlfriend. She might have an idea where he's gone."

"Okay," Howie said briefly, and lingered in the door. "You all right?"

"I'm just *fine*." Merry slammed the phone book on the desk for emphasis. "How 'bout you? It can't have been easy to see Margot like that."

Howie averted his eyes. "I didn't sleep at all. And right now, I feel like hell."

"Then go home after you make that call. By the way, Seitz—anything come in from the state lab about Santorski?"

"Clarence thinks it'll be a few more days. Wednesday, maybe."

"What do those people do with their time, anyway?"

"Clare dusted the plastic coating on the bike chain," Howie said helpfully. "It's got a bunch of prints on it, some of 'em smudged—"

"That's really great, Seitz. That's just what I needed to hear."

"—and two of them, a thumb and forefinger, match the lifts he took from Jay's body."

Merry's restless rifling of her desk papers stilled, and she looked up. "You're kidding."

"No, I'm not."

She came around the desk like a banshee and caught the patrolman in a bear hug. "That's fabulous, Seitz! That almost certainly means the bike accident was faked. You realize that, don't you? Somebody cut the chain and tossed bike and all into the water, after they dumped Jay out by the jetties."

"Speaking of dumping," Howie said quickly. "I followed up on that information of Irene's. You remember—the woman on Old North who thought she heard a boat in the middle of the night. I asked Harley where he kept his scallop boat's key. He hung one on a hook just inside his door. Jay had another. It wasn't found on his body."

"And it wasn't in his room. Someone took it after Jay was bound hand and foot, and used the boat to get rid of him. It's probably resting comfortably on the bottom of the boat basin."

" 'Fraid not, Mere. Harley found it in the ignition Friday morning. He thought Jay had left it there Thursday afternoon, and he was pretty pissed at Jay's stupidity. He didn't go out on the water that day because of the nor'easter, so he took the key upstairs and never thought of it again. It was only about an hour later that the Coast Guard pulled Jay's body out of the water."

"Any prints it might have had will be botched beyond recognition," Merry said bitterly.

Before Howie could reply, Clarence Strangerfield peered around his elbow from the dimly lit hallway. "Howie. Marradith."

There was an expression of gravity in his soulful brown eyes that even Howie couldn't miss. The patrolman sidestepped into Merry's office and Clarence's round form filled the doorway.

"What is it?" Merry asked.

"Matthew Bailey."

"You've found him?"

Clarence nodded.

Merry pushed back her desk chair, her eyes trained on the crime scene chief's face. "It's that bad?"

"Ayeh."

"Dead."

"Several days."

Merry closed her eyes. "Oh, God. Poor little Ryan. Have you told Tim Potts?"

"He's calling the boy outta school right now."

Her eyes flew open. "You're not going to make him identify his dad?"

"O' cahrse not." Clarence lowered himself creakily into a free chair. "Matt was stuck in the trunk of his cahr. All folded up in a tight ball. It was a vee-dubbyah, Marradith, as you'll remembah, and they don't have much trunk space. In the front, where a narmal cahr's engine'd be."

Merry exhaled deeply and shoved a hand through her bangs.

"Who found him?" Howie asked.

"Steamship Authority. They thought somethin' was funny 'bout the cahr. Then they got near enough to smell it . . ."

"At least it's been pretty cold," Howie said lamely.

"That'll help the doctahs."

"How did he die?" Merry asked Clarence.

"I'm thinkin' the same way as young Jay."

"Injection?"

He nodded. "Same blue colah to the skin, same wide-open eyes. Maybe poor Matt even died the same night, who knows? Certainly not Fairbahrn. What with the decomposition o' the body . . . but I'm sendin' it straight ovuh to Bahston."

"Does the Chief know?"

"Went to him furhst. But you're handling Santorski's death, Marradith," Clare said steadily, "and I thought you ought to know. Whatevah the Chief decides."

The Chief, Merry thought, had decided to accept her resignation from the investigation of Santorski's drowning. But she didn't need to spell that out for Clarence right now. Like her, he was probably in official ignorance of Santorski's undercover drug work for the Nantucket police; but he was too wise not to make a sum of these troubling parts.

And if the crime scene chief was doing that, so were

Howie Seitz and Tim Potts and everybody else on the Nantucket force.

"Did you find anything else in the car?" she asked him distantly.

"Some trash. Couple o' soda cans and some old potatah chip bags. We vacuumed for fibahs, o' cahrse, and we're sendin' the clothes to Bahston."

"Right." Merry turned her back on Clarence and Howie, her eyes fixed on the patch of Federal Street she could see from her window. She should feel a mix of emotions, she knew—sorrow for a fellow human being, outrage at the death of a colleague, sympathy for Matt Bailey's young son. Instead, she felt only fear. And this time, it was for her father.

The scene outside John Folger's office might have been scripted from a television drama. Sue Morningstar, notebook in hand, had pinned Janelle Taylor against the Chief's door. Merry stopped short a few feet from the pair, pitying them both.

"Detective Bailey has been dead some time, isn't that correct?"

"I couldn't say."

"The *Inquirer & Mirror* has learned that he was, in fact, missing since last Thursday, and that nothing was done to find him. Could you comment?"

"No. I really think, Ms. Morningstar—"

"Are the murders of Margot St. John and Detective Bailey linked to the mysterious drowning of a young scalloper Thursday night?"

"You'll have to wait for the Chief's statement." Janelle smoothed her cardigan flat over her hips, an admission of nerves.

"When is he planning to speak?"

"Hello, Sue." Merry advanced with her right hand extended. "I should have called you about Margot. Please forgive me. I haven't had a spare moment to think."

Sue whipped around like a dervish. "Detective Folger! Thank God! Maybe now I'll get some real information."

"I'm afraid I've got to see my father."

"But, Detective—"

Janelle slid away from the door, and Merry slipped inside. A tide of protest harried her footsteps.

John Folger was sitting motionless at his desk. The blotter and in-box were cleared of paper. He looked up when Merry entered the room, then averted his eyes. "You heard."

"Me and everyone else on-island, by dinnertime."

"Who is that girl?"

"Sue Morningstar. Santorski's roommate. I'd say she's out for blood."

He did not reply. His eyelids flickered, as with an overpowering weariness.

"What're you going to do, Dad?"

The Chief shrugged. "That's up to Dan Peterson. He'll probably turn all three investigations over to the state troopers."

He was right, of course. It was the DA's only feasible decision, once Bailey's ties to Jay Santorski were public knowledge. An undercover operation gone wrong would taint the Nantucket force; they could not be trusted to investigate their own. And the deliberate delay and obfuscation—which must inevitably come out once the matter fell into other hands—would destroy the Chief's authority.

"That's not quite what I meant." Merry steeled herself to the unpleasantness. "I asked what *you* were going to do."

Her father stared at her blankly.

"The press will savage your reputation." She jerked her head toward the door. "That girl out there is just the beginning. We can expect the Boston television stations in another few hours. What are you going to say?"

"I don't know." His head sank into his hands. "I just don't know."

"You'll have to resign."

That got his attention. The blue eyes met Merry's own,

blazing. "For one mistake? After a lifetime of service any man should be proud of?"

"After three murders, Dad. After all the lies and denial."

The blaze in the eyes faded. "I can brave it out. The people on this island believe in me. They should, by God. I've never been anything but a figure of trust."

"Which is why you'll have to go." Merry walked slowly toward her father's chair, then crouched down by his side. "Someone has to tell you this, Dad. Better it should come from me than from Dan Peterson. Or the selectmen. Or, God forbid, the barracudas of the press." She reached for his hand.

He shook it away. "Get out of here, Meredith."

She reared back as though she had been slapped. "Do you think I like this? It tears me apart. I've hated this whole business from the moment you tossed it in my lap."

"It'll blow over," he muttered. "It'll be resolved. The one thing that ties these three deaths together is heroin. The girl took it, the boy was trying to stop it, and Bailey got in the middle. Bill Carmichael should make short work of it."

Bill Carmichael was the head of Nantucket's small detachment of state troopers. He would have Merry's case in the morning. A sharp access of bitterness—the recognition of the entire weekend's futility—brought Merry to her feet. "I'm sure Bill will tie things up nicely, Dad, once you give him those files you've got tucked under my bed. But it won't save your job. Bailey's work was for nothing."

"You've seen those files?" A flush spread over his cheeks; of anger, or shame, Merry couldn't say.

"Charles Moore will get off scot-free. He should have been rolled up long ago. And would have been, if I'd read Bailey's reports Friday night."

The flush deepened. "It's always about you, isn't it, Meredith?"

"No, Dad," she said with a ragged laugh. "This time, I'm afraid, it's entirely about *you*."

Chapter Thirty

As he swung into the semi-circular drive before his old saltbox, Peter's headlights arced over Rafe's pickup, sitting silent and empty in the early December darkness. The truck's presence puzzled him. He had called Rafe that morning, to tell him that he was back from the mainland and no longer needed a twice-daily attendance on the dog and sheep. Rafe had welcomed him without much comment, and then mentioned casually that he had just seen Merry. At the thought of her now, Peter frowned involuntarily.

He had wanted to hurt her, and he had succeeded. The question was whether he could repair the damage.

If he left her alone, it would seem as though he didn't care how callously he tore in half the fabric of their lives. If he called her tonight, he gave her the infinitely enjoyable opportunity to hang up on him. Neither option was particularly attractive. He had the choice of being a jerk, or a weenie.

Peter sighed in frustration and parked the Range Rover in front of his door.

"Rafe! Rafe, buddy!"

No answer. Peter looked toward the darkened windows of the barn, and then, after the barest hesitation, began to walk toward its broad double doors, calling as he went.

"What do we do now?" Jorie asked Will desperately as they stared at the master of the house from Peter's guest-room window. "You said he was away for the week!"

"He was!"

"Oh, right! You *want* Paul to end up with the cops!"

The sound of breaking glass brought both their heads around. Paul, shuddering beneath a mound of blankets, was tossing and turning feverishly. One outflung arm had overturned his water glass, resting on the nightstand by the twin bed.

"Margot! Margot! Wake up, baby, please! Jesus, the blood!"

Jorie stared at Will. Her eyes were wide and very dark, as if the pupils had drunk in every scrap of available light. Will gripped her arm just below the shoulder, as though his touch might comfort them both. "Who's Margot?"

"I don't know."

Paul lurched over the pillows again. "Got to get outta here . . . police! Police!"

His lips looked blue, and as they watched, his teeth began to chatter. And yet beads of sweat stood out on his forehead like sap running from a wounded tree.

Released from the spell of Paul's words, Jorie darted to his side and began to gather up the bits of broken glass, heedless of her fingers. "Get a towel," she said to Will tersely. "It's run into the rug."

Will darted toward the bathroom in the hall, grabbed something terry—a washcloth, as it happened—and raced back. He knew what Peter's housekeeper, the absent Rebecca, would say about the mess, and the liberties he was taking with Peter's things. For an instant he wished profoundly for her stern presence, the bright blue eyes snapping beneath short-cropped, iron-gray hair; Rebecca of the capable hands and economical speech. Then he simply wished he had never known Paul Winslow, or cared enough to help him.

"Here." He thrust the cloth at Jorie. She pressed it hard against the plum-colored rag rug that Peter had probably bought, at breathless expense, from Nantucket Looms.

"What are we going to do?"

Paul's mutterings had declined to incomprehensibility, but his thrashing was wilder than ever.

"We can't take him out of here now," Will said. "Peter's seen the car. He probably thinks it's my dad, come to feed the sheep."

"So will he look for him before he thinks of the house?"

"Maybe. Ney's out there, and that might make him think Rafe is, too." Will had sent the dog careening joyously in pursuit of a ball before he allowed strangers to invade Peter's domain.

"One of us should watch at the window. See where he's going. Then we could smuggle Paul down the stairs and get away before Peter finds out." Jorie's whisper had all the urgency of trench warfare. She was remarkably adept at plotting deception, Will observed; why had he never noticed it before? Probably part of her impulse to protect Paul. Something feminine and desperate.

As if he understood Will's thoughts, the raging form on the bed rose up suddenly like a force of nature and hurled himself toward the door, dragging bedclothes and Jorie after him. The girl was clinging to Paul's legs, crying out. She might have been a fly.

"Let me go, dammit! I didn't do it! I didn't do it!"

Raw, unearthly screaming, as though he were some great beast mortally wounded. Will seized Paul's arm, and was flung violently away. He crashed against the bed frame, and felt pain stab upward from his hip. He was cursing suddenly, too, with a grave fluency, too aware that Paul's noise must be audible at some distance.

And then, like approaching doom, Will heard footsteps clattering heavily on the old wooden stairs.

. . .

"I think he should go to the hospital," Peter said firmly, "and then we should call his parents."

He had dealt with Paul in an efficient, if slightly brutal fashion, by dragging the young man bodily to the barn and lashing him with a rope to one of the central support pillars. There Paul was allowed to rave to his heart's content, while the blankets Jorie had wrapped around him slipped inevitably to the floor. The other three had stepped outside the barn door to discuss his fate, and the slight distance between themselves and their delirious charge came as a considerable relief.

"We can't tell his parents," Jorie said miserably. She was close to tears, from exhaustion and fear. "His parents don't want to know anything about Paul."

"They should." Peter spoke gently, but Will knew from long experience that he was not to be trifled with. "They've unleashed him on the world. They've got to pick up the pieces when he crashes."

"His dad's already thrown him out," Jorie argued.

"I don't know," Will broke in. "I think his dad is real worried. He asked about Paul last night, at my mom's party. I think we should call him, too."

Jorie threw up her hands. "But they'll go to the police!"

"The police?" Peter looked to Will for explanation.

"Paul's scared of being turned in to the cops."

"For possession of heroin? I'd say his problem at the moment is *non*-possession. What he needs is a detox center, and fast. There are ways to make this process a lot more manageable."

"He's really scared," Jorie insisted.

"He's a lot more than that. He's a raving lunatic. I don't think Paul's choices count for very much, at the moment. I'm sorry, Will, but you brought this problem to my house, and I have to do what I think best." Peter's expression was uncompromising.

"I know, Pete. I tried to tell Jorie—" Will stopped in the midst of what felt like a shifting of blame, and stood straighter. "Paul's dad is in the book. His name's Jack Winslow."

"Thanks." Peter held his gaze for an instant, but Will read in the hard gray look nothing like forgiveness. As always when he was very angry, Peter had retreated behind a barrier of calm. "Speaking of parents, you two ought to call your own. But let me get an ambulance first. There's no way that guy is going anywhere in either of our cars."

As Peter walked across the yard toward the house, the dim outline of his figure swiftly swallowed in darkness, Jorie took a tentative step after him. Then she turned and looked at Will.

"I'm so sorry . . ."

He nodded once. "Pete'll get over it. The important thing is to take care of Paul."

At his words, a strangled cry came from inside the barn, and the sound of booted feet pounding on the straw-strewn floor.

Jorie shivered, her face turned toward the sound. "I've never seen anybody this way. It's so *horrible*. Like watching torture."

Will took her hand, so lightly that he might have been Ney, nosing her palm for a forgotten treat.

"I'm sick to my stomach, Will. I can't stand this anymore."

He heard the break in her voice, and knew that she had begun to cry. He could have let her weep in peace, her face averted, with only the empty moors surrounding them for witness; but instead, his breath suspended, Will took her in his arms.

She shuddered once and then began to sob in earnest. They were still standing like that, an island in the midst of Paul Winslow's ruin, when the ambulance arrived.

Peter Mason stopped pacing the length of the hospital corridor when Jack Winslow walked in. Although they had never met, Peter knew immediately what the man was there for. His florid face was awash with anguish and disgruntlement. A small woman with weary eyes followed him like a shadow. As almost an afterthought, Peter noticed that she was pregnant.

"Mr. Winslow." Will Starbuck rose slowly from the bank of seats outside Paul's door.

"Hi there, Will. Jorie." Jack came toward them uncertainly, as though it hurt to see them. "And you must be Peter Mason."

"Yes. We talked on the phone." Peter held out his hand, and Winslow took it.

"This is my wife, Nicole."

The second wife, according to what Will had told him in the car ride over to the hospital; the stepmother Paul could not accept. This woman was probably twenty years younger than Jack Winslow, her hair a faded blond the color of pickled pine. She looked as though she felt as much beyond the situation as Paul's dislike had forcibly placed her.

"Where's Paul?" Winslow asked.

Peter gestured toward the closed door behind him. "They've given him something to quiet him."

The something was methadone, but Peter saw no reason to play the role of doctor. Winslow nodded, and stared vaguely at the closed door.

"I think you can go in."

Winslow hesitated, reached for the doorknob, then let his hand fall back to his side. "I'd like to talk to Will and Jorie first. Honey, why don't you go get some coffee?"

This, to the unfortunate Nicole. She slipped away without a word or a backward glance; and Peter wondered, suddenly, why she had come at all. But Jack Winslow had already forgotten her; his eyes were fixed on Jorie and Will.

"What in the hell did you two think you were doing, trying to take care of Paul yourselves?" The words came out in a spattered rush, throttled with anger. "You might have been hurt. And then what would I have said to your parents, miss?"

Jorie flinched, but did not reply.

"Or to yours, young man? And why you had to go and involve Mr. Mason—"

"Excuse me, Mr. Winslow," Will broke in, his voice cracking in a way it hadn't for years, "but the last time we talked, you told me Paul needed friends. Jorie and I tried to be that, tonight."

"Then you went about it in a damn-fool way," Winslow retorted. "You should have called me."

"Maybe so." Will's dark blue eyes looked almost black in the hospital's fluorescent lights, and his cheeks had turned a dusky red. "But that's not what Paul wanted."

"The hell with what Paul wanted! Paul hasn't been in his right mind for months! Who knows if he ever will be? What he needs is to be committed! Someplace where they can take care of these things!"

"That's not fair!" Jorie cried.

"Look, Mr. Winslow—" Peter broke in.

But it was Will's voice that cut through them all. "I don't think you understand what he's trying to do."

Jack Winslow gave a sour bark of laughter. "Oh, that's rich! I don't understand, is that it? I'll tell you what Paul's trying to do—he's trying to make *me* feel guilty, and kill himself into the bargain, so we can all see just how much we failed him!" He shoved a finger under Will's nose for emphasis. "Well, I'll tell you right now, Will Starbuck, I'm not buying it. I gave that kid everything—everything! And I'm not going to crawl to his side and beg forgiveness for something that was inevitable."

"His drug use, you mean?" Peter asked, frowning.

Winslow dismissed the question with a sweep of his hand. "I'm not talking about that."

"You're talking about the divorce," Will said.

"Yes. The divorce. Which happens in probably half of all marriages these days. What makes Paul so different from any other kid? Why does *he* always have to play the victim? He's got to grow up, and he's got to do it now. Because I wash my hands of him." Winslow turned and headed for the door.

"You did that a while ago, mister."

Will's quiet voice stopped Paul's father in the middle of the corridor.

"What did you say?"

"I said you gave up on Paul a long time ago. You don't even understand what tonight means."

"Will—" Jorie reached for his arm, but Will ignored her.

"Your son is trying to break a habit that was about to kill him. He probably tried the wrong way, because he's proud and he's broke and he's got nobody to turn to; but what he's done is incredibly brave." Will walked down the hallway, stopping inches from Winslow. "Before you came here tonight, I thought there might be hope for you and Paul. That you might be proud, even, of what he's tried to do alone. But I can see that I was wrong. You're just like he is. Too afraid to admit that you made a mistake, or that maybe there's room for forgiveness. You'd rather lose your son than lose face, wouldn't you?"

Jack Winslow looked for an instant as though he might strike Will, and Peter almost stepped between them; but then something died out of the older man's eyes, leaving only the mark of defeat.

"Somebody's got to bend here, sir, or you'll both lose," Will continued, more gently. "And forgive me for saying so—but this time it's got to be you. Paul needs a dad more than anything else. Certainly more than he needs friends. But he's in no position to ask for help. Jorie and I have to do that for him."

There was a silence, while Jack Winslow studied the linoleum floor. Nicole Winslow chose that moment to return with two cups of tepid coffee. He took one from her, and sipped it absently.

"Are you going in?" she asked softly.

He nodded.

"I should probably wait here."

"You do that," he said, and handed her his cup.

• • •

When Jack Winslow finally emerged from his son's room, and walked slowly down the corridor with his wife and a doctor to discuss Paul's options, Peter clapped a hand on Will's shoulder. "Ready to go? I don't think there's anything else we can do tonight."

Will's face, when he looked up at Peter, was flushed and contentious. He had been arguing with Jorie in a fierce whisper for the past few minutes, and from the gleam of decision in his eyes, he had prevailed.

"We need your advice."

"About what?"

"Paul. When he was raving at your house, he said some weird things."

"Ravers often do."

"We don't know whether it's important or not." Will glanced at Jorie. She refused to meet his eyes.

"Come on," Peter said. "Get it over with."

"He kept talking about Margot." Will's eyes went to the waiting-room television, suspended in the far corner. "We just saw the news. Somebody named Margot was killed last night in Sconset."

Peter looked sharply at Paul Winslow's door.

"I think we ought to tell Merry," Will persisted.

"Merry?" His heart sank. He was going to have to call her after all. But would she, in fact, hang up on him?

Chapter Thirty-one

Merry did not hang up on Peter.

She listened without warmth or comment to his brief explanation, and then, for the second night in a row, she put down the phone and crawled out of bed straight into her clothes. Bill Carmichael of the state police might be in charge of the case by morning; but until then, Merry felt duty-bound to contain the situation. It would be nice to think that Paul Winslow was going nowhere before morning, when he was scheduled to be sent to a detox center on the mainland; but as calm and reason returned on the wings of methadone, he might decide to run.

Before she left her apartment, Merry called the Water Street station. She didn't have a reason to hold Winslow—the mere presence of his ATM slip near the murder scene was hardly enough—but with his friends dying like flies, the boy would need a guard for as long as he remained in Cottage Hospital.

A strong wash of moonlight led her through the silent streets. As she drove, Merry's lips moved unconsciously over a stream of whispered thoughts. She had been so intent upon simply locating Paul Winslow that she had never debated the notion of his guilt. Could he have been so desperate for heroin that he wrecked Margot St. John's house in a fruitless search for drugs? Had he brought the steel edge of a tomato can down upon her head with vicious force, simply because she had denied him what he needed?

Merry was certainly meant to think so. And that thought alone stilled her roving mind.

Peter sat alone in the dark at Mason Farms, looking first at the silent phone and then at the shadows of the dormant *rosa rugosa* vines the moonlight threw across his bedroom wall. He was thinking about Merry Folger. He had deliberately left the hospital before she arrived; the glare of fluorescent light was antipathetic to delicate negotiation.

What had Will told Jack Winslow—that somebody had to bend, if a bond was not to break? In this instance, it was unlikely to be Meredith. She had no reason to bend at all. She had simply done what she believed to be her duty, and he had punished her. For the crime, perhaps, of regarding his claims upon her attention as less important than those of her work. Or for having been unapologetic for doing so. But was this so wrong? If the roles were reversed, would not her strident claims on his time be regarded as unreasonable? Selfish, even? She had struggled for some time now with the warring attractions of love and duty; and rather than helping her make them compatible, he had forced her to choose. It had been brutal, and childish, and entirely understandable. But he was done now with childish things. The brutal and the understandable were far too lonely at the end of the day.

A rising wind tossed the shadows on his wall. Outside, the leafless vines rattled like a handful of bones.

Paul Winslow was asleep when the night duty nurse quietly opened his door. A light still shone on his bed, and a television flickered overhead in the corner, but the boy's body was slack. His face was turned toward Merry, the lips slightly parted, and he looked, she thought, like the last person to have suffered the torments of the damned that evening. It was painful to destroy the utter peace of his repose, but she did it without a second thought.

"Mr. Winslow." Merry shook his shoulder gently. "Mr. Winslow."

His head rolled down to his chest and stayed there. She shook him a bit harder. The eyelids fluttered.

"Mr. Winslow, it's Meredith Folger, of the Nantucket police. We met at the Easy Street Basin."

He squinted at her vaguely, then rubbed his eyes. "What time is it?"

"Just after ten. I'd like to talk to you about the death of Margot St. John."

Comprehension and pain came flooding into his face at once. *Macbeth does murder sleep,* Merry thought suddenly, remembering her grandfather's mangled quotation of a few nights past. Paul Winslow thrust himself up against the pillows.

"You're a cop?"

"Don't you remember? You did some dredging for me the other day. After Jay Santorski drowned."

He looked around him wildly, seized for an instant by pure panic. Merry almost attempted to restrain him forcibly, afraid he might take flight, but decided instead just to sit down. There was a chair waiting by the side of Paul's bed, and she slid into it almost casually.

That seemed to calm him. He sank back against the pillows and took a ragged breath, his eyes fixed on her face. At least, he was probably thinking, she hadn't come to arrest him.

Merry folded her hands on her lap and looked at him steadily. "Did you know that Margot was dead?"

Paul nodded once. "I saw you at the house."

For an instant, Merry imagined him hiding in a closet while she stood on the back deck, peering into Margot's ravaged kitchen. Then she dismissed the notion. "You saw me?"

"Last night. When they took her away. You came out right after the stretcher thing."

"Gurney," she corrected automatically. "So you were standing in the crowd."

"On the edge of it."

"I'm sorry we missed you." As though it were a party, and she had arrived too late for conversation.

"How did she die?" Paul asked, swallowing hard.

This time, Merry didn't bother to skirt the truth. "Someone bludgeoned her with a can of tomatoes."

He winced and looked away.

"I know. It's horrible and silly at the same time."

Paul nodded and plucked at the hospital bedsheet. It was rough, starchy polyester, and blindingly white under the harsh lights. "Why are you here?"

"Because we found an ATM slip dated Saturday in her bedroom, Paul. It had your account number on it."

From the blank disinterest on his face, he had missed the point of her words.

"The kitchen was torn apart, every sort of packaged food pulled down from the shelves, flour spilled out on the floor. Sugar in the sink, and baking soda, and talcum powder in a mess upstairs." She waited, hoping the words would sink in. "Her killer was looking for something, Paul. Do you know what that might be?"

"Smack?"

"That's what we thought, too." Merry reached across Paul's lap and lifted his left wrist in her hand. The unforgiving light picked out the graffiti of needle marks. "I guess you've been looking for smack yourself. Did you think Margot might have it?"

To her surprise, he laughed. "That'd be a change."

"What do you mean?"

"I was the one who supplied *her*."

Merry's black brows furled suddenly. Paul Winslow's name had never appeared in Matt Bailey's operational file. "I thought you were brought in here tonight half out of your mind. Desperate for a fix."

"That was a choice, ma'am. I decided to get myself clean. What heroin I had went into the harbor Saturday morning."

He had called her *ma'am*. God, she must be getting old. "Paul—I'm going to be blunt. You're in a bad situation. You were a friend of this girl's, your property was found in her house, and you've said you were at the scene on the night in question. You're a known heroin addict. As was Margot."

"Okay," he said, and clasped his hands together. Merry saw that they had started to shake. "I guess I need a lawyer."

"You do."

He smiled. "I shouldn't even be talking to you, right?"

"Probably not. And I should have read you your Miranda rights."

"Only if you're charging me."

"True."

"So I guess you're not."

Merry sat back and gazed at Paul steadily. "Not tonight. There's a small matter pending."

"Like linking me to the murder weapon?"

Merry raised one eyebrow.

"You never will." He said it without bravado, as a bald statement of fact. "I didn't kill her."

"Then why were you hiding from the police?"

"Because somebody else did." The words were sharp with fear, and a bit of rage. "They killed Jay, too. So who's left? *Me*. I'm not about to end up dead in the harbor. I'm getting clean, and I'm getting out."

Merry leaned toward him, her green eyes piercing. "Why would someone kill your friends, Paul?"

He shook his head violently. "I don't know. Maybe because Jay wanted Margot to quit using. And they didn't like it."

"Who's *they*?"

As she expected, her question went unanswered.

"Your theory might explain Jay's murder," she persisted, "but once he was out of the way—why kill Margot?"

Paul shook his head again, his eyes fixed on the humped shapes of his toes beneath the blinding sheets.

Merry sighed. "Look—I understand your fear."

"I'm not afraid! I'm just not stupid! They're two different things!"

"Okay—okay." Merry thrust out her hands to stem the tide of wrath. "If you're not afraid, you should be. Whoever killed Margot wants us to think she was murdered by *you*."

Paul's blue eyes flashed up to hers. "But you don't think that. You believe me."

"I don't think much, Paul, and I believe even less."

"You've got to believe me! I wasn't even near Sconset!"

"When?"

"Whenever it happened! I hadn't seen Margot since Saturday morning, when we had breakfast. Before the dredging."

"But you were there when her body was taken away. Why, Paul?"

For the first time, something like caution flickered across the boy's face. "Just wanted to see her."

"At dawn? Did you often show up at Margot's house at that hour?"

He shrugged and averted his eyes. "Sometimes."

Merry's frown deepened. The atmosphere of frankness was slipping away. Paul was concealing something—out of fear, perhaps, or embarrassment. Or guilt. Had he gone to the house earlier in the evening and seen Margot's body? And waited around until someone else came? Was it possible he had witnessed the murder? Or was he just afraid to tell Merry what he had wanted from the girl?

Time to get tough.

"Paul, you said you supplied Margot with heroin. Did she pay you for it?"

"Sometimes. Usually she was broke."

"That could be damning in a court of law. If a jury decided that you were trafficking in an illegal substance—or conspiring to traffic—you could get five to twenty years in prison. It's a much heavier charge than your basic possession."

"We were just friends!" he protested hoarsely. "I wasn't trying to make a buck off the stuff. I just passed it on at cost, when she needed it."

"Maybe so," Merry conceded, "but a good prosecutor will turn that story against you. You're in trouble, guy, and there's no way to sugarcoat it. I wouldn't want to see you spend the next ten years in prison."

His face had been pale when she first entered the room, but at the moment it looked positively ghastly.

"It might help your situation if you decided to assist the police."

"I didn't kill Margot!"

"Maybe not. But you might be able to lead us to whoever did."

The boy went very still.

"You got your heroin from someone. It didn't just materialize out of thin air."

"I'm such a chump," Paul muttered. "Jesus, what was I thinking of?"

"You were thinking about murder. I want to talk about dealing. Who's your supplier, Paul?"

He hesitated, then shook his head. "I just want out of this. It's gotten too weird."

"I know. I can help you do that."

"They'll kill me."

"They? *They* wouldn't be Hannah and Charles Moore, would they?"

Paul looked around desperately, as though his enemies were closing in. "I'm supposed to fly to the mainland tomorrow. Go into detox. I can't deal with this right now."

"You're not going anywhere unless I say so."

"Bullshit! My dad told me!"

"Your dad didn't know you were implicated in a murder."

"I'm not!"

"As of early this morning, buddy, you most certainly are."

Galvanized by fear, he kicked off the covers and swung his legs out of bed; but the IV tube threaded into his right arm abruptly stopped him. "Christ," he breathed, and reached for the aluminum trolley by his bedside.

Before he could stand up, Merry pressed a buzzer to summon the nurse.

"Two people are dead, Paul," she argued fiercely. "If their killer thinks you're a liability, nothing on God's green earth is going to save you—"

"You think I don't know that?"

"—except me."

Brave words, but they had the power to make Merry shudder. She had failed to save the last man who had trusted her, after all.

A nurse appeared at Paul's doorway and smiled at them both. "Those officers you were expecting are here, Ms. Folger. They're in the waiting area."

"Great," Merry said. "We've decided to place Mr. Winslow in protective custody. They'll be standing guard outside his door."

Paul fell back on his pillows with a curse.

Merry reached into her purse and found a business card. She wrote her home number at the bottom and dropped it on the bedside table. "Use that anytime," she told Paul.

"I guess I'm not going into detox." His voice was bleak.

"You wouldn't be any safer there," Merry reminded him as she turned to go. "If someone wants to find you, kid, believe me, they will."

Chapter Thirty-two

Tuesday morning, John Folger finally capitulated to the growing crowd of reporters, video cameras, and mobile broadcast units snarling traffic on Water Street.

He had almost avoided his office altogether, but Ralph Waldo's silent disapproval urged an early departure from Tattle Court. He had scheduled a conference call with Dan Peterson and Bill Carmichael for eight o'clock in any case; and so seven-thirty A.M. found him toiling through the strident knot of journalists, who juggled their takeout breakfasts from Fog Island in one hand and their microphones in the other.

"There will be a statement at nine o'clock," John barked, with something of his former imperiousness; then he shut the station door firmly in their unreconciled faces.

Sue Morningstar, the girl who had known Santorski, was still among them. She looked, John thought, as though she had camped outside all night, sacrificing a shower and a change of clothes for the public's right to know. Or her own.

For a few moments he stood immobile before the front

reception desk. Behind him, the 911 response station's lights blinked reassuringly. What *did* the public need to know, exactly?

Jay Santorski's voice as John had last heard it—apprehensive and young—drifted through his mind. He closed his eyes sharply against the memory. Perhaps Merry was right, and he had no choice but to resign. To tarnish his unimpeachable record of service—nearly thirty-five years, counting his stint as a detective under Ralph—with the indelible admission of an unwitting guilt. It had all been a mistake, a juggernaut of error.

Should a man's whole life be sacrificed to a single miscalculation?

Not without a fight. John stood a little straighter and smoothed his mustache. He would not go quietly into that great good night.

Merry, too, had arrived early for work. Her virtue was rewarded, as virtue rarely is, with a faxed copy of the state pathologist's autopsy report on Jay Santorski. It sat innocently on her desk, inviting her to delve further into a case she was about to relinquish. She pulled out her chair and stared at it, debating. By rights it should go directly to Bill Carmichael.

"Hey, Mere," Howie Seitz said from her doorway. "Clare got the crime lab's results on the plastic bag you found in the harbor."

She looked up, a faint line creasing her brow. "Yeah?"

"No prints on the hypo. They managed to pull two off the inside of the latex gloves, and they match a couple of lifts from the outside of the plastic bag."

"What did the needle contain?"

"Seawater."

"*Sea*water?" she echoed, and snatched up the pathologist's report. While Howie waited, she skimmed it avidly. "I guess drugs are no longer the point, Seitz."

"What's it say?"

"There was no heroin in Jay Santorski's body. Drugs didn't kill him." She sat down heavily in her chair, mind racing.

"But you can't detect heroin in an autopsy anyway." Disbelief from Howie, as though she had announced that Jay was still alive.

"You can't. It decays to morphia. Clarence specifically asked the state crime lab to screen Santorski's blood for it, and it wasn't there."

"So what *was* in his bloodstream?"

"Nothing they could detect." She flipped to the third page of the pathologist's report and shoved it under Howie's nose. "There's a lot of technical jargon that boils down to one conclusion. Jay drowned."

"I knew a former member of the U.S. Crew Team who died of a heart attack," Howie offered conversationally. "He was thirty-three."

"This wasn't a heart attack."

"So it *might* have been an accident. He could have just . . . been dropped overboard, and unable to get back."

Merry shook her head. "That might have worked if he were drugged, Howie. But not when he was in command of his senses. Why didn't he kick his shoes and parka off, and head for shore? Even in cold water, he might have made it. He was a triathlete. He took care of himself. He wouldn't just slip beneath the waves. Not without help."

"And there *are* those needle marks," Howie mused.

"The pathologist couldn't explain them."

"Isn't there a Dorothy Sayers plot—"

Merry looked up, aghast. "You've read Sayers?"

He grinned. "Why do you think I became a cop?"

"Because you had no other option!"

"Oh, ye of little faith, and less imagination," he retorted imperturbably. "Chief Inspector Parker was my hero from way back. Anyway, there's this plot where a nurse goes around killing people with a syringe. Only the syringe is empty. She's injecting air. And the air bubbles actually stop the heart."

"That's a myth," Merry said dismissively. "Or at least an exaggeration. To make it work, you need a huge syringe, and even then, it rarely results in death. Besides, they'd have found air bubbles in Jay's bloodstream and heart valves, even hours after death. There's no mention of those here."

Howie flipped through the report. "Any mention of fibers in the wrist and ankle abrasions?"

"No fibers, but the areas of greatest trauma to the skin are compatible with the wrists having been twisted against each other. There's even some subcutaneous bruising above the right anklebone, as though the left had worked against it. The considered opinion is that Jay was bound with an undetermined substance."

"Maybe he had just strength enough to work his hands and feet free, before the cold overcame him and he drowned."

"Maybe," Merry said slowly. "But I'm not convinced. There's something else at work here, I know it. We have to consider Bailey."

"Because Bailey died the same way," Howie reflected, "only Bailey didn't drown."

Merry nodded. "Remember the color of their skin?"

"Blue." Howie shuddered.

"We thought it was from exposure, or maybe from the heroin itself. The lab thinks it shows cyanosis—oxygen deprivation."

"They were killed by cyanide?"

"The pathologist would probably have found that." Merry folded the report, slipped it into her purse, and headed for the door. "I've got to go talk to Fairborn right away, Seitz."

"There's a press conference in ten minutes," he objected.

"At which point, the case is no longer ours. If my dad asks, just tell him I'll be back in an hour."

• • •

"Cyanosis? From drowning?" John Fairborn returned the pathologist's report to Merry and grimaced eloquently.

"Not exactly. There's Bailey's murder, too. He didn't die in the water."

"No," Dr. John agreed. "I'd have guessed heart failure there."

Fairborn looked fresh from eight hours of sleep. He wore a white lab coat crisp with starch, and he was smoking a post-breakfast cigarette on the back porch of his house. His office was in the converted garage. When Merry found him, Fairborn was dictating rapid-fire notes into a handheld tape recorder. His hapless nurse was expected to transcribe and file his thoughts regarding each day's round of patients. Judging by the pace of Fairborn's patter, the poor woman probably arrived at five A.M.

"Does it say there the lungs were paralyzed?" he asked, and took another drag on his cigarette.

"Not explicitly." Merry thumbed through the lab's report. "There was air in them, so he went into the water breathing. What concerns me is not the ultimate cause of death, but the precipitating factors. Blue skin and needle marks. He must have been shot full of *something*."

"Cyanosis by way of a needle. It could be any number of things," Fairborn mused.

"I'm sure it could," Merry said patiently, "but it would be helpful if you could narrow the options a little."

The doctor thought for a moment and then shrugged. "Okay. Let's start with the commonplace. Anesthesiology."

"Anesthesiology," Merry repeated slowly. "Yeah? So?"

Fairborn tapped some ash into a planter and narrowed his eyes against the smoke. "An anesthesiologist sometimes uses drugs that produce mild cyanosis. And you can find them in most hospitals every day."

"What kind of drugs?"

"They're generally curare-based."

Merry frowned. "Wait a minute. Isn't that the stuff from South America?"

Fairborn laughed, a rare event. "Originally, yes. Indians

used to rub it on their arrowheads. It shows up in Golden Age detective fiction a lot."

"Do you read Dorothy Sayers, too, Doc?" Merry asked suspiciously.

He ignored her. "Nowadays curare is produced in any number of drug labs under a variety of trade names, for use in the operating theater. A controlled amount will temporarily suspend the workings of the lungs, for example, during surgery. Or a certain dose will serve as a muscle relaxant. It's a highly useful substance, actually."

"A deadly poison?" she asked skeptically.

"Even aspirin is deadly if it's abused, Merry. All drugs are poison—it's just a matter of dosage."

"And semantics," she said. "So this stuff is injected into the bloodstream?"

"Hardly. That would kill a man."

They were both silent a moment, considering Jay Santorski's punctured veins.

"Is it detectable?"

"Only in the tissues, through spectrographic analysis. The Golden Age detectives didn't know about that."

"But access to curare must be controlled."

"It is. Although most controls can be circumvented by a nimble mind."

Merry tapped Fairborn's arm with her half-glasses. "If you wanted to get your hands on curare, Doc, where would you go?"

"To a doctor who could prescribe it. But he'd have to be a pretty good friend—and the kind who doesn't ask questions. Or I'd steal it from my average urban hospital. That would require some inside knowledge, of course."

Unbidden, Barry Cohen's face rose before Merry's eyes. "Would it be available in a local pharmacy?"

"Most things are. But as for curare specifically . . ." He shrugged. "I can't help you. You'll have to research that yourself."

Merry sighed and gazed pensively at the doctor's dormant flower beds. He was a careful gardener; at least six inches of straw were heaped over the perennials, and burlap encircled the leafless rose canes. "This changes the whole perspective of the case."

"Does it? Santorski is just as dead. Someone still killed him."

"But it's no longer a drug bust gone awry. Anyone with a grudge might have committed murder. I have to rethink everything."

"A drug bust? I thought it was just an overdose."

Merry smiled faintly. "That's what we were all meant to think. Look, Doc—could the state crime lab sample the tissues for curare?"

"If they haven't already released the body."

Merry's eyes widened with apprehension. "Oh, man. Can I use your phone?"

"Hey, Starbuck," Paul Winslow said.

Will nodded from the hospital-room doorway. "You feel good enough to talk?"

"Come on in." Paul tossed a copy of *Sports Illustrated* on the floor and ran his fingers through his blond hair. It had been washed, Will noticed. Paul's entire appearance was newly scrubbed and wan. His blue eyes were restless, and the skin beneath looked bruised.

"Where's Jor?" he asked.

"Busy. I just came over on my lunch hour."

The truth was, Jorie's mother had forbidden her to see Paul; but Will couldn't tell him that. He pulled up a chair and sat down next to the bed. "What are those two cops doing outside?"

"The detective put them there."

"Merry Folger?"

"Yeah."

Will flushed, remembering his whispered dispute with Jorie the previous evening. If Merry had taken charge of Paul, it was primarily Will's fault.

"She's calling it protective custody," Paul explained. "In case somebody tries to kill me."

Will sat back. "You're kidding."

Paul eyed him steadily. "Two of my friends are dead."

"That guy Santorski—"

"And Margot. His girlfriend. She was a friend of mine, too. Somebody killed her the other night."

The girl from the newscast. Paul had been screaming about her; screaming about blood. "I thought the scalloper drowned."

"Shut the door, buddy."

He did as he was told, and came back to Paul's bedside.

"Margot was a user," Paul said. "Jay was trying to get her to stop. The cop thinks they were both killed, and maybe I'm next."

"Because . . ." Will let the word die away, and took a deep breath. "Because you know where to get heroin, right?"

Paul nodded. "I used to get Margot's for her."

Will considered this in silence. Then he said, "If I were you, Winslow, I'd get out of here."

The blue eyes slid away. "Oh, I'm okay. My dad's shipping me off to this place in the Berkshires. Sort of a poor man's Betty Ford. It'll be great. Listen, Starbuck—"

"Yeah?"

"You know this cop?"

Will's stomach tightened. He didn't want to explain why he had betrayed Paul to the police last night. He wasn't exactly sure himself. For Paul's own good? Or because he wanted him out of Jorie's way? Probably both. Today's visit was a form of penance.

"I know her pretty well," he replied. "She's Peter Mason's girlfriend. We were staying at Peter's last night, before we brought you here."

"I remember. There was a dog, and a barn, and this guy who scared the shit out of me."

"That'd be Pete."

"So what's she like?"

"Merry?" Will frowned. "She's pretty cool, actually. She caught the serial killer last year. Remember?"

Paul shifted restlessly under his sheets. "Do you trust her? I mean, if she made a deal, do you think she'd keep it?"

"Yeah." Will put all his conviction in the single word.

Paul closed his eyes and, despite the warmth of the room, shivered involuntarily.

"You want to sleep now?"

"I want to think," he said, "and it's almost time for my meds. That's what they call them here—meds. I'm not drugged out, I'm *medicated*. Sick, huh, Starbuck? Reality's all in what you call things."

Merry called the state crime lab, and learned to her relief that Jay Santorski's body was still in the morgue. She asked the pathologist to sample both the scalloper's and Matt Bailey's tissues for curare-based drugs—or any other common pharmaceutical capable of causing respiratory failure. Intrigued, the pathologist agreed.

On her way back to the station, she stopped at Cottage Hospital, which—in the form of Barry Cohen, its chief resident—insisted that all drugs removed from the dispensary were strictly accounted for. Even Merry's *suggestion* of laxity bordered on the offensive, Barry implied, and it was with a fixed expression of displeasure that he showed her to the door. She toyed briefly with the notion of Barry killing Jay out of an uncontrollable desire for Sue Morningstar's undivided attention; but since the doctor had no reason to murder Bailey, much less bludgeon Margot St. John with a tomato can, she abandoned the idea. Not without some wistfulness.

At Congdon's Pharmacy on Main Street she received a highly documented response to her inquiry about curare. All prescriptions were registered in the pharmacy's computer, and a painstaking search by generic and name-brand drug type showed there were no prescriptions registered for curare-based substances. A survey of the shelves showed that none was even kept in stock.

It was, Merry reminded herself, a long shot. Dr. Fairborn had only been guessing at the substance that had killed the two men. In fact, any number of things might have been pumped into the veins of Jay Santorski and Matt Bailey. But what?

What, other than the pursuit of heroin, did the two men have in common?

As she stood in the wind of Main Street, her keys hanging idle in her hand, the answer suddenly came.

Hannah Moore.

Chapter Thirty-three

Despite the veil thrown over Jay Santorski's identity, Matt Bailey's operational file made perfectly clear that the scalloper had volunteered to collect evidence against Charles Moore. Merry had assumed, all along, that Jay's role was a passive one; that he had gleaned information from the doomed Margot St. John, and merely passed it on, a willing conduit, to the authorities charged with drug-law enforcement. But Merry had neglected the hallmarks of what was, she saw now, a virulent obsession; she had failed to correctly interpret the signs. Jay Santorski had loved a girl named Katia. Katia had died too young, in suspicious circumstances, with a blot forever attached to her name. Jay had dropped out of Harvard. He had followed Margot—who was addicted to the heroin that had killed her roommate—to Nantucket. And he had set purposefully about his revenge.

Jay had used Bailey, not the other way around.

He had no intention of wreaking havoc in any personal, violent way. What Jay wanted was to witness Charles Moore's ruin. He intended to strip this most respectable of men of his patrician heritage. Of his name. His fortune. And even his wife.

Jay was acquainted professionally with Moore's wife, who needed money for her research—money Moore earned from the sale of illicit drugs. Jay would have used his relationship with Hannah to shadow Moore. He would have infiltrated the household with his handsome, athletic body; charmed husband and wife with his intelligence and humor. He would have attracted and rebuffed the predatory Hannah, Merry thought, out of sheer enjoyment for the sport.

He would have laid a thousand snares, collected his damning information, and awaited Bailey's move.

Only something else—something equally consuming—had intervened. And diverted Jay from his single-minded purpose. So that the day before his death, he had abandoned scalloping with Owen Harley, and spent arduous hours on ferries and bicycles in pursuit of an unexplained scallop spectrogram.

Larval tigers, Merry thought. *Viral morph/unobserved phenomenon.* And then, *Tiger Op*. The notation on Bailey's operational file. Was tiger simply their symbol for Hannah Moore? Or was its significance more complex?

The only person left who might be able to tell Merry was Jay's thesis advisor, Dr. Melrose Taylor.

She pushed aside the incalculable, and surveyed instead that familiar mental landscape, dotted with the figures of Jay, Matt, and Hannah. The impetus to murder lay somewhere among them, like a dragon unwittingly roused. Had Jay discovered Bailey's relationship with Hannah—so implicit in that last hurried phone conversation—and felt betrayed? Had he accused Bailey of compromising their operation, and the two come to blows?

They could hardly have killed each other, simultaneously, Merry reflected with irritation. One had ended in the basin, after all, and the other in the trunk of his own car.

She would have to retreat.

To the tape itself.

Merry had assumed, all along, that it was Charles Moore who had interrupted that last, and most interesting, phone call between his wife and Matt Bailey. She had pictured him arriving home too soon, while Hannah huddled over the receiver in a bath towel, damp and cooling. But Merry saw, now, her own stupidity. She had focused on identifying *Hannah*'s voice, instead of the man's at the beginning of the tape. . . . What if that first message—the harried voice informing Hannah that the caller would be late—had been Jay, and not Charles Moore?

She considered this possibility with rising hope.

Fresh from his conference with Mel Taylor at Woods Hole, Jay calls Hannah Thursday morning and arranges to see her after work that night. He's sent home early from Ezra's, and so he rides out to Sconset and entrusts the spectrogram to Margot, with strict instructions that it should be passed on to Owen Harley. Jay stays at Margot's longer than he intended, and so he calls Hannah again from the Baxter Road house. He tells her he'll be a little late, but he's on his way; that's the first message the machine recorded. Jay is nervous about the meeting—his voice sounds a little harried. But whatever Jay learned at Woods Hole the previous day is too important to put off.

He walks into the Moores' kitchen while Hannah is still in the tub. Takes off his coat, shakes the ubiquitous rain out of his long hair. And then he hears the disembodied voices broadcast by the answering machine. (Merry adjured herself to find out where the Moores' answering machine actually was. Somewhere on the first floor, almost certainly, since Hannah failed to recognize that her conversation was being recorded.) *Jay listens as Bailey foolishly gives Hannah the power to warn her husband. And he sees months of work—of calculated fury—in pieces at his feet.*

He forgets the business of the spectrogram—the meaningful discussion about Hannah's work—and snatches the tape from the answering machine. He runs back out into the night. He pedals away on his rickety old bicycle, which he has ridden from the Baxter Road house.

The theory explained one thing, Merry thought with

satisfaction—why the Moores had not simply erased their unfortunate tape. It had been stolen by an adversary first. But how had it ended up in a bag on the harbor bottom? Jay would have kept the thing, as evidence of Bailey's complicity. He would have turned it over to the police, and demanded immediate action.

Except, Merry thought with a chill, that he had drowned before he could.

She went back to her office and braved the huddle of journalists grouped at the door.

"Detective!" Sue Morningstar cried. "Does the Chief's decision to give your case to the state police signal a lack of confidence? Are you considering resignation?"

"Am *I* considering—" Merry stopped short, drew breath, and struggled for calm. "The disposition of cases is decided by the district attorney. You'll have to refer your question to Dan Peterson." She pushed her way to the door, fuming inwardly, and dangerously close to tears. Without even looking for her father, she fled up the steps to her office and slammed the door.

On her desk was a note from Bill Carmichael, requesting the case files. She ignored it, and reached for a Cape Cod phone book.

Two disconnections and three misroutings later, she reached Dr. Melrose Taylor in Woods Hole.

"Jay?" the scientist cried. "Of course I'd love to talk about him. Can you get over this afternoon?"

Merry glanced at her watch. She could just make the afternoon ferry to Hyannis, rent a car, and drive to Woods Hole. She had a few phone calls to make first. And the case files to send over to Carmichael. If one has determined to circumvent the district attorney's reallocation of one's case, it is important to present the appearance, at least, of helpful compliance.

"I'll be there around four," she told Taylor.

• • •

The storm that had been building all morning broke just as Merry was halfway across Nantucket Sound, out of sight of both the island and the Cape. She bore with being lost in a raging sea by reminding herself of the countless Folger generations that had rounded the perilous Horn, and arrived safely off the coast of China. Then she put down her book, forced her way through the swinging doors of the middle deck, and stepped out into the tearing wind. The Sound was a churning mass of viscous wave that looked almost solid. A sickly yellow light gleamed palely in its thrashing curves, the reflection of a hidden sun.

It was unlikely, Merry thought, as she gauged the storm's fury, that she would get back to the island that day. Unless she were willing to fly.

At the mere thought, she shuddered.

As the storm swept over the huddled gray buildings of Nantucket Island that afternoon, Peter Mason stepped out of his Range Rover and raced rapidly down the gravel path to Hannah Moore's lab. He thrust open the hut's door and ducked inside, shaking rain from his dark hair.

"Peter!" Hannah stood up, smiling, and opened her arms wide. "How *lovely* to see you. What brings you out on such a dreadful day? You must be chilled to the bone!"

She wore a pair of tortoiseshell glasses today that turned her unapproachable beauty ever so slightly academic. Still compelling, of course—but more honest. Hannah as she truly was, not the practiced and shining public relations expert. For a moment, recognizing the unvarnished dedication to science lurking somewhere behind those glasses, Peter was stirred to pity. She would not like hearing what he had to say.

"I came to talk about my investment."

"You did?" she asked cautiously. She had been refused before.

"I'm prepared to back fully half of your operational costs for the next eighteen months," he said. "My support should serve as a springboard for additional investment—a consortium, perhaps, to cover the other fifty percent. Can you tap into that kind of venture capital?"

"With you on board? Almost certainly." She didn't waste time in effusive thanks, but, lost in calculation, began to pace in front of her bubbling tanks. "This is exactly what I've needed. Something I can hold up as an emblem of investor confidence. It'll make a world of difference. When can we finalize?"

Peter's lips twitched. "You're welcome, Hannah."

"Oh, Peter—you must know I'm grateful beyond words. You've given me lifeblood. I won't forget it."

She moved to him swiftly and kissed him full on the mouth. He stiffened, and took a slight step backward.

Behind the glasses, Hannah's gray eyes turned suddenly mocking. "Don't worry. I won't scare you away. Or try to compete with the little cop. I value your . . . patronage . . . too much."

"Thank you." A host of long-forgotten images—scenes from a summer ten years ago when he had toyed with the notion of Hannah Moore—flooded into his brain. She had always valued patronage over love; it was her most chilling quality.

"I'll call my lawyer," she said. "Could you meet with him tomorrow?"

"Provided you can resolve one difficulty."

"Yes?"

Peter walked over to the hut's window and gazed out at the storm. Marsh grass bent double by a vicious wind, waves churning like molten iron on the blackened shore. The sort of afternoon best spent indoors, with a book and some sherry for company. And Meredith, of course. Where was she now? Consumed with the disaster that had overtaken the police force? Peter had watched the newscasts. Thursday's edition of the *Inky* would be all over it. And much as Merry had disliked Matt Bailey, Peter knew that she would be anguished at his violent death—the unnecessary ugliness of it. She would sleep badly, eat little, and spend her waking hours silently obsessed with the details of the case. He had lived through these things before. His usual role was to listen—to feed her soup, and make her laugh; to hand her stolen comfort that invariably made her feel guilty.

Only this time, she had not called.

"What difficulty?" Hannah asked him.

He turned away from the window. "I talked to Charles this morning. At his real estate office."

She gripped the back of her desk chair with both hands. "What could you possibly have to say to Charles?"

"He owns this estate. I wanted to know whether he intended to keep it."

"What did he tell you?"

"That he plans to put the place on the market this spring."

"This spring."

"After Easter. It's the best time to list a house, he says."

"Easter." She was repeating his words as though they were a French lesson, and she a very bad student. "He can't."

"Hannah—" Peter took a step toward her. "You must understand my position. I'll back you in your present circumstances, but not with the prospect of the lab's closure in a matter of months. I can't agree to any commitment until the matter of AquaVital's future is decided. That's something you and Charles have to discuss."

She released the desk chair, and clenched her hands into fists. "These threats. Like a chain around my neck."

"It didn't sound like a threat to me," Peter said gently. "It sounded like a promise."

Jack Winslow turned away from the storm filling the hospital window and gazed down at his sleeping son. He felt all the terrible burden of tenderness that dreaming children—regardless of their age—invariably provoke in a watchful parent. Jack had held his love for Paul at bay for so many months, in the belief that only a determined hardness would shake the boy from disaster; and now that he had let go—had admitted how precious Paul was, how irreplaceable—he felt weak and old. He wanted to take the thin body in his arms and cradle it, as he had done so many years ago. He wanted the boy's young face to turn against his own in sleep, and lie there, gently breathing and certain, an eternal two-year-old.

Paul's eyelids fluttered and opened. For an instant, before comprehension returned, they were filled with a nameless fear.

"Hey, buddy," Jack said quietly, and touched his shoulder.

Paul thrust himself upward against his pillow, yawned hugely, and shook his head. "Hi, Dad. What's up?"

"We've got the word to go."

"You mean, I can leave?"

Jack nodded. "You're coming home. They've given me some medication. Then tomorrow we'll fly to the mainland."

"I'm going to the clinic?" The fringe of sleep dissipated and was gone. "What about the cops?"

"They left a half hour ago."

Paul shuddered uncontrollably, pulled the sheet tight around his body, and stared at the empty doorway. "Shit," he muttered.

Jack's brow furrowed. "I thought you'd be happy."

"Could you leave me alone for a minute, Dad? I've got to make a call."

His father hesitated.

"A minute, max. Then I'll get dressed and we can go."

"Okay. I'll be outside in the hall."

Paul waited until the door had closed behind Jack Winslow. Then he reached for the phone.

Four unanswered rings, and a forwarding to dispatch.

"Police."

"I'd like to speak to Detective Folger." Paul's heart was racing, and his mouth felt dry—sensations to which he was well accustomed, although rarely in the absence of drugs.

"She's out of the office. May I take a message?"

Paul thought for a moment. "No," he said, and hung up.

Chapter Thirty-four

"You mean Winslow's been *released*?" John Folger cried in outrage late that afternoon.

Dr. Barry Cohen drew himself up to his full five feet eight inches. At Cottage Hospital, doctors were king—and police chief, too, if it came to that. "We released Mr. Winslow into the custody of his father, who will be admitting him tomorrow to a state-approved rehabilitation center in the Berkshires. It was all perfectly in order, I assure you."

"Why weren't we notified?"

"But you *were*." Cohen made a play of consulting his clipboard. "At noon today. We understood that Detective Folger—your daughter, I believe—was in charge of Paul Winslow's case. She was duly consulted, and referred us to the state police. It was *they* who authorized the patient's release."

John glanced at the anonymous clock face high on the hospital walls. After four, and Winslow could be anywhere. He closed his eyes in frustration. "Give me the kid's phone number. And his home address."

• • •

The Woods Hole Oceanographic Institution's Quisset Campus was an impressive grouping of low-storied buildings fronting Vineyard Sound. There was a bicycle path running along the water, and a decorative pond set like a jewel in a small garden, now bleakly dormant. Under the present veil of storm the campus looked depressed, as though it wished to be left alone; Merry felt vaguely guilty as she mentioned Melrose Taylor's name at the security gate, and progressed in splendid isolation down the sweep of tree-shrouded drive.

Taylor's lab was located in the Rinehart Coastal Research Center, a mere stone's throw from the bike path and ornamental pond. He was a small, bird-headed man with a shock of white hair, peering intently through an electron microscope at the mitochondria of some unfortunate sea creature's cell. When his assistant announced Merry's presence in the hushed tones appropriate to a chapel, Taylor ignored her just long enough to shoot a micrograph of whatever he was seeing.

"That's it," he said, pushing his lab stool away from the scope's controls. "Develop it and file it with the others, Lori, before I leave."

"What about the tissue?"

"File it." Taylor cocked his head and smiled at Merry. What was visible of his body was tanned, she noticed, as though he had recently been in the tropics; and although he was probably around her father's age, he gave the impression of greater youth.

"Mel Taylor," he said, rising and extending his hand.

"Meredith Folger."

"*Detective* Meredith Folger."

"Yes, *Doctor*."

He laughed, and motioned her to follow him through the jungle of test tubes, Bunsen burners, and saltwater tanks, to a minuscule office where journals and computer printouts were stacked shoulder-high. "Find a seat, if you can."

"Thanks," Merry said, glancing about ineffectually. She set her purse on the floor and perched on the edge of a file cabinet.

"This stuff has been here for years," Taylor explained apologetically. "Long before my time. Like the mountain, it waits for Mohammed. And we're happy to come."

Merry reached for her notebook and half-glasses. "This must be something like Mecca, I suppose, to a marine biologist."

"Yes. Although my own degree is in the aquatic sciences—a slightly different emphasis."

"How so?"

"Civil engineering, rather than biology. I studied at MIT before Harvard deigned to hire me."

"I see," Merry said uncomprehendingly.

"No you don't!" Taylor said roguishly. "And it doesn't really matter. I've never really done anything like civil engineering in my life. I study the physiological and genetic regulation of dinoflagellates—their patterns of growth and migration worldwide. It's partly geography, partly a desire to muck about in boats, and mostly a yen to cut things up and paste them back together. What can I do for you?"

"Tell me about Jay."

Taylor's jocularity instantly fled. It was followed by an expression of such sadness that the little man seemed to age before Merry's eyes. "Poor kid," he said. "Was it really heroin?"

"How did you ever get that idea?" Merry asked, astonished at the rapidity with which investigative theory traveled.

"Owen Harley called me over the weekend to tell me about Jay's death. He said he'd heard Jay was on drugs when he went into the water. I couldn't believe it." The scientist shook his head. "I absolutely could not believe it."

"The autopsy results have pretty much ruled out heroin," Merry told him. "If that's any comfort."

"Then what was it? Alcohol?"

"No. Actually, Doctor, the confusion surrounding Jay's death is largely why I'm here. I hoped you could tell me why he visited you the day before he died."

Taylor frowned. "I thought that visit was something of a secret."

"I found a piece of paper in Jay's room that had your

name on it." Merry reached in a manila envelope she had brought with her from Nantucket and retrieved the paper. "Do those words mean anything to you?"

Taylor scanned the two lines. "The *Albatross IV* is the Fisheries Service research vessel. I did a stint on it a few weeks ago—as Jay was aware. He met the boat when it docked last Wednesday. I was surprised, not to mention pleased. Jay is—was—one of my favorite students at Harvard."

"You hadn't expected to see him."

"No. But he came on a matter of some urgency."

"Larval tigers?"

Taylor smiled. "Jay asked me to look at a scallop under the electron microscope. The tigerback. He'd found it in a Nantucket lab, and thought it might be a sport."

"A what?" Merry said.

"An organism genetically different from its parents. A mutated offspring. Anyway, we looked at it under the EM, and failed to discover much that was striking. So I ran a liquified sample through our mass spectrometer and compared the results to a control sample of common bay scallop."

Merry reached in her purse and withdrew the image of colored bars Jay had left with Margot St. John before his death. "Is this the spectrogram that resulted?"

"Yes. That's the tigerback."

"But what does it tell you, exactly?"

"The chemical composition of the tigerback's tissues. As represented by bands on the graph." Taylor gestured vaguely toward a machine dominating one counter of the room beyond the small office. "The mass spectrometer is a remarkable bit of junk, Detective. There are about ten million organic chemicals in the world, and an infinite number of combinations of them in nature. The spectrometer tells us which chemicals are present in a sample, in what configuration—and the spectrogram gives us a molecular footprint, as it were. An identifiable signature. You must have run across the spectrometer before—it's used quite often in police work."

"By the FBI, and the state crime lab," Merry observed. "Not by small island police departments. So this graph is the scallop's footprint?"

Taylor nodded. "Did you find it in Jay's room, too?"

"He left it with a friend the night he died. The friend was murdered a few days later."

Taylor's frown deepened. "And you think they were both killed because of *this*?"

"I have no idea. But the fact that Jay's death followed hard on the heels of his visit to you is one reason I'm here today. Is there anything in this graph, Dr. Taylor, that's worth the taking of a life?"

He sat back and stared at her. "Not in this image, per se. But perhaps in the mutation it documents."

"You'll have to explain that, I'm afraid."

"You've heard of the tigerback scallop?"

Merry nodded. "It was bred in the AquaVital lab on Nantucket."

"By Hannah Moore."

"Are you acquainted with her?"

"Only by reputation."

A circumspect answer—but the very fact of Taylor's discretion told Merry more about Hannah's reputation than a more direct answer might have done.

"Dr. Moore," he continued, "has taken the genetic engineering of the bay scallop remarkably far, I must say. The tigerback represented in this image has been fundamentally altered in a manner that could revolutionize shellfish farming and, indeed, solve one of the major problems associated with it—the destruction by brown tide of bivalve grounds up and down the East Coast. You can't pinpoint it under a microscope, but the evidence is in the tissue."

"Brown tide." Merry clutched at the single phrase she remembered from her first conversation with Owen Harley. "That's the algae that thrives on nitrogen."

"One of them, yes. There are millions of different algae, Detective—diatoms, dinoflagellates, prymnesiophytes, or chloromonads." He hesitated, and then smiled faintly. "But you don't need to know all that. The point is this: brown tide phytoplankton—*aureococcus anophagefferens* chokes the feeding systems of bivalves. That includes scallops. Hannah Moore changed the genetic structure of the tigerback in such a way that it can now digest the algae that used to kill it."

"She told me that herself," Merry said. "I see how it could revolutionize the scallop problem. But where's the danger?"

Taylor stood up. "Let me show you something. I've only been sure of it today."

He led her to a saltwater tank sitting near a window. Beyond it, rain lashed in great sheets against the docks, turning the pilings black and sodden. "These are some adult tigerbacks. Jay brought them over in a plastic bag last Wednesday."

Merry peered into the water and saw the familiar scallop shape, its dusky brown shell ribboned with streaks of orange and yellow. "Striking," she said.

"And unique to Nantucket. They're tagged as island produce by the fact of their shells. Deciding to mutate *these* was a brilliant marketing move on Dr. Moore's part. And it may eventually help us eradicate the problem she's created. We can find her monsters and destroy them."

"Destroy them?"

The scientist's bird-like head tilted at her speculatively. He gestured to a neighboring tank. "This, Detective, is *aureococcus anophagefferens*."

"It looks like muddy water."

"Exactly. The algae turns the tank opaque. In certain places—the bends of Coatue, for example—the bottom of your harbor looks exactly like this."

Merry grimaced.

"I've been feeding the tigerbacks this brown tide algae for the past week," Taylor said. "Their feeding systems show no sign of suffocation."

"So it works!"

"Yes."

"Then what's wrong?"

"Exactly what Jay suspected. An unforeseen eventuality.

Once successfully ingested, *aureococcus anophagefferens* interacts with a bacteria present in the cells of the scallop itself, and produces a neurotoxin. We've never observed this particular phenomenon before, because the scallops usually died in the act of ingesting the algae."

"And now they're dying afterward?"

Taylor shook his head. "The toxin has no effect on the tigerback itself. That's fairly usual when a bivalve feeds on toxic algae. There are any number of them adrift in the seas, Detective, and scallops have been ingesting them for millennia. But the toxins *do* remain stored in the scallop's tissues. I found the brown tide neurotoxin there just this morning, in significant quantities, when I ran the scallop tissue through the spectrometer."

"And?" Merry prompted, her mind racing.

"The toxin can be passed on to any organism that eats it. You must have heard of paralytic shellfish poisoning—when someone gets a really bad clam?"

Merry nodded.

"PSP, as it's known, is fairly rare in these waters. It comes in the wake of what's called a *red* tide—a toxic algal bloom—and if it's observed, shellfish beds are usually closed to fishing."

Red tide. She *did* remember the term vaguely. "There was something on the Georges Bank once, I think."

"In 1990. A group of fishermen ate toxic mussels." Taylor turned away from the saltwater tanks. "The first documented outbreak was in '72, along the Massachusetts coast. More incidents have occurred since—in California, Turkey, Alaska, Asia."

"Is the damage to the beds permanent?"

"No. Once the algal bloom subsides, the shellfish gradually shed the toxins. The beds can reopen."

"And this is happening," Merry attempted, "because of increased nitrogen runoff."

"Perhaps," Taylor temporized. "The pollution of coastal waters is at an all-time high, and so are the toxic blooms; but they have existed forever, and it may be that we are simply able to monitor them better now than we did fifty years ago." He shook his head. "I'm inclined to think it's nitrogen runoff, myself. Take *pfiesteria piscida.*"

"*Fis* what?"

"It translates roughly as 'fishkiller.' A dinoflagellate that emits a deadly neurotoxin when a fish passes by, literally stripping the tissue from the bones. It was discovered only a few years ago, and since then, millions of fish in the Carolina estuaries have died. Now it's migrated into the Chesapeake. The scientists studying *pfiesteria* have linked it to fertilizer and sewage runoff."

"Does it affect humans?"

"Seems to. Local fishermen working in infested waters claim to have suffered skin lesions, mild paralysis, and memory loss. They equate the experience with Alzheimer's."

Merry winced and held up her hands. "Okay. You've convinced me. But what does our brown tide algae do?"

"To the scallop? Nothing."

"To a person who *ate* the scallop."

Taylor folded his arms across his chest, considering. "The observations on this are so new, I can only extrapolate from other algal neurotoxins. Initially, you'd feel a tingling on the lips and gums. In a few minutes, that would spread to the legs and arms. Your speech would become incoherent; you'd feel light-headed and nauseated. In severe cases, respiratory depression or arrest might occur."

Respiratory arrest. In the middle of the boat basin. She knew, now, how Jay Santorski had died. And she thought she knew why.

"You only felt certain about the existence of these neurotoxins this morning," Merry probed. "What drove Jay to talk to you last week?"

The bird-like eyes grew sharper. "Hannah Moore tried to recruit Jay for AquaVital. She wanted to hire him once he got out of school. She was very . . . persuasive, from what I understand."

"And Jay?"

"—Had decided to refuse her. He mistrusted Moore's approach. Jay had studied long enough with me, Detective, to suspect that Nature usually knows what it's doing. There was a reason, he surmised, why scallops died before they could digest brown tide. Because a greater evil might result if the scallop *lived*."

"A deadly pairing," Merry mused. "Like bleach and ammonia."

"Sort of." Taylor was amused.

"Did Jay know about the toxins when he left here Wednesday?"

"Oh, yes. When I said I wasn't certain until this morning, I simply meant I hadn't reproduced the phenomenon in my own lab, under more controlled conditions."

"I see. And what was Jay going to do with the information?"

"Well—" Taylor threw up his hands as though the answer were obvious. "He was appalled at the implications. If Dr. Moore released these mutated specimens in the harbor in large quantities, as Jay thought she meant to do, the devastation to the scallop industry—and indeed, to humans consuming the shellfish—might be incalculable."

"But surely Hannah would recognize that!"

"I imagine she's working frantically to find a way around the problem." Taylor smiled sadly. "Isolating the toxin. Trying to control the interaction of scallop bacteria and algae. Looking for ways to alter the scallop further genetically—it could take years of research. But she's pressed for time and money. In the meantime, one of these"—he gestured toward the tank of tigerbacks—"might slip into the harbor."

If Taylor had anything to do with it, Merry thought, the mutated tigerback would be blotted out of existence. Even in death, Jay would confound Hannah's work; he had charged a man of obvious reputation and integrity with safeguarding the truth.

"How strong is this toxin, Dr. Taylor?"

The scientist's face grew sober. "In general, shellfish neurotoxins are about fifty times stronger than similar plant toxins—curare, for instance."

"Curare," Merry repeated, and her hand clenched in a fist. She remembered the blue tinge to Jay Santorski's face, the apparent paralysis of the eyelids. It was clear what had happened.

Jay had returned from Woods Hole late Wednesday, alive to the horror of all that might happen if Hannah's scallops were allowed to slip into the harbor waters. He called her that night or early the next morning and demanded to see her after his shift at Ezra's. In his anxiety, Jay may even have mentioned his trip to Woods Hole.

Merry wouldn't put it past Hannah Moore to have had a needleful of toxin ready and waiting for Jay mere moments after ending her phone call. His flight from her house later that night, answering machine tape in hand, merely confirmed the need to kill him; she had Charles Moore's cash flow to protect, after all, as well as her life's work.

Merry swallowed hard, and fixed her eyes on Taylor's face. "So if someone *had* isolated this toxin, and if it *was* injected directly into the bloodstream . . ."

The doctor said nothing for a moment, simply stared as though she were an unobserved phenomenon herself. "You thought Jay died of an overdose. Was that because of a needle mark?"

Merry nodded.

Mel Taylor sat down heavily in his chair, all the energy drained from his body, and put his face in his hands.

Chapter Thirty-five

"Starbuck."

The voice, low and urgent, came from the shadows beneath a venerable elm tree that shaded Will's front lawn. He looked up from his bicycle lock, eyes straining through the torrential rain and darkness of late afternoon, and said, "Paul?"

The blond head emerged, followed by Paul Winslow's lanky body. "I've been waiting for you."

"You should have gone inside. It's wicked wet out here."

Paul huddled into his Tommy Hilfiger jacket. "I didn't want anyone to know I was around."

Comprehension dawned. "Did you sneak out of the hospital?" Will's voice dropped to a whisper, and he glanced uneasily over his shoulder at the lighted windows of his house.

"They let me go. I'm flying to the mainland tomorrow."

"So what are you doing here?"

"Can we talk in my truck? It's parked down the block."

Will hesitated. He had told Tess he was riding over to the Atheneum to do some research for a history term paper, and she had asked him to be back by seven. But it wouldn't take long to talk to Paul. He probably wanted to know about Jorie. She hadn't seen Paul since Monday night. "Okay."

He followed the other boy hurriedly to his battered old truck, both of them ducking as if they could avoid the streams of rain. The streets were deserted; Nantucket off-season felt like a theater set ready for striking. Behind the blank windows of the empty houses, there would be no one to watch Paul Winslow's furtive return.

"What's up?" Will asked as he slid into the passenger seat. The interior of the truck was stale with cigarette butts, the smell intensified by rain.

"I need your help. And I haven't got much time."

"Neither do I. I've got a term paper, and my mom wants me home in an hour and a half."

Paul drew a deep breath and reached into the small space behind the driver's seat. "You ever worked a video camera?"

Will's brow furled. "Once or twice."

"It's my dad's. A Sony. Should be pretty simple." He handed the camera to Will, who hefted it consideringly.

"You want to take *pictures*?"

Paul rubbed anxiously at the fogged windows. "I don't know if it'll work tonight. But I can't wait until tomorrow—my plane leaves too early, and you've got school."

"What are we taping?"

"A drug buy," Paul said, and put his key in the ignition.

Thirty seconds later, a second car sprang to life. It kept a casual distance behind the two boys—almost indistinct, but for its headlights piercing the rain-lashed darkness.

"Seitz? Thank God you're still there."

"Detective! How'ya doin'?"

"I've been better," Merry said. Her voice faded for an instant against the howl of the storm as it crossed the telephone wire. "The ferries are out and I just flew in from Hyannis."

"No way." Howie's voice was disbelieving. "In *this* storm?"

"I kissed the ground when I arrived. Just like the Pope."

"What were you doing in Hyannis?"

"Woods Hole, actually. Look, Seitz—I need you to pick me up."

"With a thermos full of hot buttered rum."

"Forget that. Just bring your gun."

"Merry—"

"It's better to ask forgiveness than permission, Seitz. Trust me. I've got this case sewn up. But I need proof, and I can't wait for Bill Carmichael to move."

"Does your dad know about this?"

"I'm not sure he's earned the right to know."

The baldness of that statement silenced Howie for several seconds. "You're really going to get me fired one of these days," he complained.

"Or promoted." She was growing impatient. "If you can't come, Seitz, I'll understand. Really. I shouldn't ask you to share my risks. I'll just take a taxi. But for God's sake call dispatch for me and send out some backup."

"Where?"

"To Hannah Moore's place. Pocomo."

"Stay there," Howie ordered. "I'm on my way."

Half the Moores' windows were glowing against the storm when Paul Winslow pulled around the gravel drive. He was alone in the front seat. Will had jumped down at the gate, video camera in hand, and was creeping up under cover of darkness.

Paul looked toward the water, and saw a light shining dimly from the middle Quonset hut. Hannah was still working. That was good; he didn't want to see her. The important thing, now, was to get in and out before she finished up for the day.

The drug buys usually took place in the Moores' study, a room at the rear of the house. Charles Moore's cherry bookcases, commissioned by some nineteenth-century ancestor, contained a drawer with a false bottom. He kept his supply of heroin in its depths. Will's task was to secrete himself in the hedge below the study window, and film the transaction through the glass.

Paul set the truck's hand brake and thrust open the door. He had called Charles before recruiting Will. The man had greeted him with a burst of cynicism, and the suggestion that they meet before dinner. Charles had written Paul off as one of the damned—taking his supply of poison to the mainland detox center.

He drew a deep breath, and ran up the front steps.

Catching Charles red-handed on film was important, of course. But Paul was here tonight as much for Margot St. John as for himself. He had stood in the shadows outside her window as Margot's murderer brought a tomato can down on her skull. He had watched the systematic destruction of the kitchen. And later, it was Paul who had gone back into the house and made certain Margot was dead.

He had wept, briefly, over her lost young body, before the terror of the place and the increasing pool of blood had driven him, shaking, from the room, to stand in agonized solitude not far from Sankaty Light. He could not leave her alone; but neither could he go to the police. And so he had stood there for nearly four hours, before the gurney and its wasted burden were gone.

Margot's ravaged face would not leave Paul alone. It was inconceivable that her murderer should go unpunished—or worse, that someone else should be held responsible for the crime. Paul had watched the brutal business, and he knew the murderer's weakness. Fingerprints had been left behind.

He had come here tonight for something like proof, and he would not leave until he had it.

A faint movement grazed his peripheral vision. Will, ducking around the far corner of the house, his feet slipping momentarily on the rain-soaked ground. So far, so good. Paul rang the bell.

The car that had followed Paul Winslow's truck was parked, now, at the verge of the Pocomo road. John Folger zipped his jacket against the rain, pulled a hood over his gray hair, and tucked a pencil-point flashlight into his pocket. His gun nestled snugly in a shoulder holster. It had been years since he had ventured silently into the field, his own master, alone against the forces of evil; and a heady excitement sang in his veins.

He locked the car behind him and set off, as noiselessly as possible, up the edge of the Moores' gravel drive.

John had expected Paul to make a final feverish purchase of heroin before flying to the mainland. He had waited outside Paul's house, and when the boy went in search of Will Starbuck—Will Starbuck, of all people!—he had followed a sedate distance behind. Kids that age never suspected surveillance; it was like stalking tame deer. Paul would lead him directly to Charles Moore, with heroin in hand. John Folger would arrest a vicious drug dealer, charge him with the murders of three people, and salvage his own career in a single blow. If Bill Carmichael asked, the Chief would credit an anonymous tip—an unnamed source. Or cite his inability to reach the state trooper, who had gone home early in the storm. He'd talk of fearing delay, of Paul's imminent departure, of striking while certain irons were hot. It was the end result that mattered in these cases, after all—not the means to achieving it. That was something Meredith would never understand.

Hannah pulled shut the lab's door and jiggled the knob to make certain it was locked. The rain was coming down in frigid sheets, and with the advancing evening, would probably freeze. They might even get snow.

She wrapped her open jacket close about her body, and trudged purposefully up the path that led to the house. Rain darkened her black hair to ebony, plastered it to her skull; but she was heedless of the wet. Hannah was nursing a cold fury. Peter Mason's money had been hers to command, but for Charles.

Her right hand rode snugly in her pocket, encased in a latex glove. As her fingers closed on the hypodermic, secure in its plastic cap, Hannah smiled. In a matter of hours, she would be free.

Charles was increasingly dangerous. There was the liability of his drug-dealing, first and foremost. She had welcomed the tax-free income, but she had feared his ultimate discovery. The assets of drug traffickers were confiscated by the government, and sold at public auction. Hannah had no legal claim to the Pocomo estate; she lived there on sufferance. Charles's work had set AquaVital at risk.

And then there were the subtle threats. The questions about Jay. The suggestion that Charles knew she was somehow involved.

He was very ill, of course. He had often told her that, come spring, he would not be around to trouble her. She had steeled herself to wait, believing that at his death the Pocomo estate would be hers by right. And then, this morning, he had revealed his betrayal to Peter.

Charles would have to be removed. But he had brought his destruction upon himself. For a man in his condition, in fact, the hypodermic would be a swift release.

Hannah's head came up as she approached the house. It sat on the brow of a small hill, its windows shining with light. The figures in Charles's study were clearly outlined against the room's crimson walls. She stopped still in the middle of the path, oblivious to the cold hard rain. Paul Winslow, buying heroin. The kid would probably be dead in another six months.

It was a complication, of course, but a minor one. She would simply wait for the boy to leave.

And then she craned forward, eyes narrowing against the tumultuous dark. Backlit by the room's golden glow was a dark shape—a head, she was certain of it. A head peering into a black oblong—a hand-held video camera. Indiscernible to Charles from within the room, because of the darkness and the howling wet and the privet hedge that huddled close to the old house's windows—but screamingly apparent to Hannah's eyes.

Paul Winslow, it seemed, was less of a fool than she had thought. And he had just signed his own death warrant.

. . .

"You leave the island tomorrow?" Charles said as he opened the false bottom of the cherry desk's drawer. He extracted a small scale and a large plastic bag filled with white powder.

"Yeah." Paul tugged at the zipper of his jacket. His stomach fluttered nervously, and he found it hard to meet Moore's eyes. "I need some smack for the road."

"How much?"

"Can you give me an ounce?"

Conviction for trafficking in as much as an ounce of heroin, Paul thought, might land Moore behind bars for a good while. What had the detective said? Five to twenty years?

"That's quite a lot," Charles said with an incredulous smile. "You planning to supply all your friends?"

Paul flushed and looked away, to keep the man from seeing the anger in his eyes. "I could be at the clinic for a while."

"With this in your system, I imagine you will be. Where do you think you'll get a needle? They're not going to leave drug paraphernalia in your room."

"I'll find a way."

Charles studied him in silence, and Paul felt his heart quicken. Was Will getting all this on tape? Did their voices carry far enough?

"Can you pay for it?" Charles asked.

"Depends what you're asking."

"Let's say—" He looked into space a moment, calculating, and Paul held his breath. Driving home from the hospital, he had asked his father for some money to take to the clinic. Jack had stopped at an ATM on the way and withdrawn two hundred dollars.

"Four hundred."

Paul exhaled gustily, as though disgusted, then reached into his back pocket. "I can give you two."

"Then we'll settle for half."

"Oh, man—you can do better than that. I'm a good customer. How long has it been now?"

"Six months, at least. But I don't count on you guys having a long shelf life. You're a high-risk clientele, Paul. Look at Margot."

That brought Paul's head up and his eyes fixed on Charles's. "What about her?"

"From what I hear, she was killed by somebody who wanted drugs." There wasn't a trace of duplicity in the man's expression, only the faintest interest in his voice. "Who could that have been, I wonder? *You,* Paul?"

Paul's hands balled into fists at his side, and for one blinding moment he wanted to hurl himself at Moore's complacent neck and choke the very life out of him. But instead he breathed deeply and said, "Let's do this deal so I can get out of here."

"Very well." The man tipped some powder into the scale and smiled up at Paul. "In view of your long association and excellent credit record, I'll give you three-quarters of an ounce. For two hundred."

"Thanks, man." Paul handed him the cash, hoping devoutly he could repay his father sometime.

At that moment, Hannah Moore opened the study door. She held the video camera in one hand. The other pushed Will Starbuck, eyes brilliant in his pallid face, abruptly into the room.

Chapter Thirty-six

"Will," Charles Moore said. "What a pleasant surprise. I thought you had more sense than to adopt your friend's habits."

"He does," Hannah said, and shoved Will so hard that he tripped over the threshold and fell sprawling on the rug at Charles's feet. "He's been taping your little transaction. What were you thinking, boys? That you'd blackmail us? Or just go straight to the police?"

"We're paying off a debt." Paul had gone dead white at the sight of Hannah, but he stooped very carefully to help Will up. "To my friend Margot. Did you tell your husband about her, Hannah? How you smashed her skull in, and left her lying in the mess you made of her kitchen?"

"Well." Hannah closed the study door carefully behind her. "If I wasn't sure you had to die before, I am now." She pulled a vicious-looking needle from her pocket and held it against Will Starbuck's jugular. "Don't move," she said to him genially, "or you'll die in a matter of seconds. I don't want to have to carry a dead weight down to the dock."

Charles Moore was staring at his wife wordlessly. With her wet black hair snarled about her face and shoulders, she might have been Medusa. Something violent and unappeased, and utterly ruthless. "Did you kill Margot, Hannah?"

"Yes."

Her one-word answer to every annoying question.

An expression akin to grief passed over Charles's face. "Why?" he asked her hoarsely.

He was mourning the death of Hannah, Paul thought, which had occurred some time ago; not Margot's graceless passing.

"So that the police would believe Jay's death was drug-related," Hannah said, exasperated. "Isn't it obvious? Besides—I thought she was hiding something. Some kind of evidence. Jay went to Woods Hole that day, and he saw Margot before he saw me. Whatever proof he had, wasn't on him when he died. Now please—get your gun out of the drawer, Charles. You've kept it there for years, in fear of burglars. We have burglars tonight. Okay?"

So that was how it would be. Heroin-addicted Paul, hell-bent on destruction, tries to steal drugs from his dealer's house on the eve of his flight to the mainland. Dealer shoots the crazed addict in self-defense, and to the horror of all kills his newly corrupted friend Starbuck into the bargain.

For himself, Paul didn't care very much; but he hated what was going to happen to Will. Could he tackle Charles before he went for the gun? Not with Hannah holding that needle to Will's neck.

John Folger crept up the back steps, toward the light spilling out onto the porch. Struggling to drag Will Starbuck and the video camera inside, the black-haired woman had been unable to slam the door. A gust of wind had done the rest. John stepped through the opening into the darkened back hall, careful not to slip on the rain-soaked vinyl flooring. He clutched his service revolver in his right hand, and steadied it with the left. Then he crept quietly toward the sound of voices.

For an instant, he wished he had called for backup. Someone dependable to signal as he made his way down the hostile length of hall. Someone who knew what she was doing.

He wished, in fact, for Meredith.

"I *will not* let you kill me, and have my mother think I committed a crime. I won't." Will's words came out with a throttled vehemence. "It's not going to end this way."

"I don't think you have any choice."

Charles reached into the secret drawer and withdrew a small pistol. He held it awkwardly, as though the thing were alien, and stared unbelievingly at Hannah. "You really killed Margot. You killed all of them, didn't you?"

"Oh, Charles. Would you *please* stick to the point? These boys just filmed your little transaction."

"So destroy the film."

"Not good enough, Charles."

"It's yourself you're worried about, isn't it, Hannah?"

"*They're going to the police*, Charles. They'll have you arrested for trafficking, and me accused of murder. Is that what you want?"

"I don't really care anymore," he said, in the voice of defeat. "I'm completely past caring. It's only a matter of months for me, after all. There was a time when I would have done anything for you, Hannah—and did. But that time is gone."

Hannah extended her free hand toward her husband. "You'd better give me the gun, Charles. And stop whining, please. You make me sick."

Charles looked at the two boys—Paul, trembling slightly with fatigue and the need for his medicine; Will, stark and unnaturally bent in Hannah's grasp, his neck recoiling from the tip of the needle. Then he shook his head and set the gun on his desk. "No."

Hannah required only a second to react. She dragged Will, still subject to the needle, away from the door.

And at that moment, John Folger burst into the room.

Howie Seitz didn't bother to park his car in the road. He drove straight up the Moores' drive, tires churning, his heart in his mouth. He had recognized the Chief's car where it sat on the verge—had seen it the same moment Merry Folger had.

"Christ," she had whispered, horrified. "What the *hell* is he doing here?"

Seitz didn't have to ask what she meant. He had heard all about the neurotoxin on the drive from the airport.

They threw open the car doors and ran heedlessly up the front steps. Merry tried the front door, found it locked, and without hesitation fired a bullet into the lock. The door swung open.

They paused an instant on the threshold, listening in agonized suspense for telling voices. And caught the faint sounds of combat from the end of the hall.

Merry outsped Howie Seitz by several yards. She came to a halt in the study doorway, her gun leveled. Across the room, Paul Winslow and Will Starbuck were pummeling a man who must have been Charles Moore. At Merry's feet lay John Folger, sprawled on his back, his right arm thrust upward against Hannah Moore's chest. His left hand was locked around her right wrist, in a desperate attempt to deflect the needle she held poised in her fingers.

How strong she must be, Merry thought distractedly. *Strong and silent as Death.*

At that moment, Will Starbuck broke free of Charles Moore and sprang with a yell onto Hannah's back. She coiled like a snake to face him, and raised her hypodermic.

"No, Will," Merry cried, and aimed her gun. As the needle came down in a shining arc, she pulled the trigger and fired.

• • •

Hours later—years later, it seemed, when she and Howie had given their statements to Nat Coffin, and the gurney had rolled silently away, and Charles Moore was thrust handcuffed into a blue police cruiser—Merry went in search of her father.

He was sitting not in the Moores' well-lit kitchen, where Will Starbuck and Paul Winslow were trading phone calls with their parents and drinking hot chocolate stirred up by a helpful policewoman, but in the darkened and deserted living room. Near his chair was a low table, and on it rested an answering machine.

Merry hesitated in the doorway. John Folger glanced up at her, then looked back at the patch of carpet he had been studying so earnestly. She sighed and turned away.

"Meredith—"

"Yes?" It took all her strength to muster that single word; she was exhausted and shaken by the violence that breathed in her hands. She had never killed a person before.

"Halfway down that hallway tonight, I knew that I had made a mistake. I acted out of pride. And the desperation of an old man."

"You're not that old, Dad. And you probably saved those kids' lives."

"Very nearly at the expense of my own. What was in that needle?"

Merry sagged into a chair not far from his own, and ran her fingers through her hair. Woods Hole was another lifetime ago. "It was a neurotoxin derived from scallops. She killed Bailey with it. And Jay Santorski, of course."

"No," John said decisively. "I did that."

He seemed to think no other explanation necessary. Merry leaned toward him, and said softly, "Of course you didn't, Dad."

"He called me that night. From a public phone in town. He said that Bailey had blown the operation and they would all be hunted down. He wanted help—someplace to go to ground. I told him not to be ridiculous, that we'd call a meeting in the morning. To get some sleep. He said he couldn't go back to his house. So I told him to sleep at a friend's."

Owen Harley's pull-out couch, Merry thought with welling sadness. *Jay was going to ground when Hannah caught up with him. She made it look like he died of an overdose, but she killed him to protect her own work. Did Bailey help her? Did Bailey know what he was doing? Oh, God. Better that we never know.*

"I didn't want to taint the operation by making contact with Bailey's agent," John continued. "You know how it is—absolute secrecy, compartmentalization. Only one person is supposed to see the guy's face. Bailey couldn't keep a secret, of course. He couldn't resist taking me to Ezra's for lunch one day and pointing out that our waiter was also his agent. But inserting myself in his operation on the spur of the moment—that was another level of magnitude entirely. I never thought—"

"You never thought your advice would get a boy killed," Merry finished bleakly. "We never *do* think the unthinkable, somehow. We just have to live with its consequences."

Her father did not reply. His words seemed spent. But he reached for her hand, and gripped it fiercely. "I can't bring the three of them back. But I *can* accept the responsibility for their loss. I'll resign tomorrow."

"Are you sure, Dad?" She turned his palm upward and laced her fingers through his. "You've emerged a victor, tonight. A killer and a drug dealer in one fell swoop. Carmichael will never forgive you."

"I'll never forgive myself," he said starkly. "At least I can go with dignity."

Merry rose from her chair and smiled faintly down at his gray head. "I'll be there to watch you go, Chief. And I'll be as proud of you tomorrow as I've ever been in my life."

"One more thing."

"Yes?"

"I want you to apply for the job, Meredith."

"*Your* job? You've got to be kidding."

"You're the best candidate I know. And I've been all over the state, believe me. There's no one to touch you."

"Then I pity the state."

"There will be a job search, of course," her father continued woodenly. "And the selectmen will have final approval over any candidates. It could take months to find a replacement. Not everybody wants to work out in the middle of the Atlantic, and pay through the nose for the privilege."

"Don't talk about it now."

"Promise me, Meredith."

"I can't, Dad. I can't think about anything."

Except Hannah Moore, lying dead on her own carpet. And the gun still warm in Merry's hands.

Howie Seitz drove her the short distance from Pocomo to Mason Farms through the rain-filled midnight. Neither of them spoke; it was a relief to be silent.

Peter met her at the door. One look at Merry's face was enough, and he reached for her.

If a choice must be made, Merry thought fleetingly as she turned her wet face into his shoulder, then perhaps in that moment she had made it.

"Forgive me," he said, in that hour just before dawn, when the first cawing of blackbirds blends harshly with the pulse of distant surf. "Forgive me for being cruel."

"I'm trying to forgive you for waking me up," Merry retorted. "Do you have any idea how *tired* I am?"

"Yeah. It shows."

"But speaking of cruelty," she added, "I never thought you could be such a—a bastard."

"Then you must think I'm not human."

"Maybe I did. Maybe I still do."

When her voice held so much sadness, there was no clear way to continue.

"I think I wanted you to choose," he attempted.

"Between you and my father?"

"Or your work. Whatever it is that your father represents."

"Why is that so necessary?"

"It isn't. It just seemed that way last week."

"It never was before."

Peter shrugged helplessly and smoothed her blond hair. "I don't know. For stupid reasons, probably. Because I'm a guy."

Merry snorted. "And guys want their women to adore only them, is that it?"

"Under the eyes of their critical mothers? Yes. They do. I'm not saying it's particularly fair or enlightened, but for a few short days last week I really wanted you to be the picture-perfect model of a Mason fiancée."

"Discuss wedding gowns and flower arrangements, and whether we should honeymoon in Maui or slosh all over Venice. That sort of thing."

"Exactly! I wanted you to glow a little, and badger George for stories about my childhood, and page through my prep school scrapbooks. Completely egotistical, I admit—but was it so much to ask?"

"You wanted me to be Alison."

"No," Peter said, confounded, "that is something I will never want, my love."

Merry considered this a moment in silence. "I was hardly picture-perfect. But you know, Pete, I never will be."

"Me neither. Apparently."

They each attempted and discarded a variety of words.

"You shouldn't have to choose," Peter said finally. "You should be able to manage a complex life. You have the skill and the passion to do it, God knows."

"But you'll keep feeling this way—shortchanged, somehow—for as long as I try," Merry countered. "I don't know what the answer is. I can't convince you of something you don't feel in your gut. Sometimes I think you just don't trust me to love you enough."

This was so true, it took his breath away.

"But then, I do the same thing," she continued. "I keep

waiting for you to walk away. I thought you'd done that, Monday."

"With Hannah Moore."

"Hannah Moore. Oh, God, Peter—all that intelligence and beauty, that fierce will to *be*. I tore away her soul without a second thought."

"And sent it to the lowest rung of hell, I hope. You *will* not feel guilty about this, Merry. You will *not*."

"I don't feel guilty." She propped herself up against the bed frame and smoothed the quilt over her knees. "I feel dangerous—and awed. After last night, very little separates me from the Hannahs of this world. We both know now what it is to take a human life."

A few hours later, she was established in front of his fireplace in a terry-cloth robe and slippers. Itzhak Perlman played a Bach partita somewhere in the house, and the singing reach of the violin brought tears to Merry's eyes. She drank Peter's excellent coffee, and tried not to consider the day.

"When will John do it?" Peter called from the kitchen. A marvelous scent of warm muffins wafted through the doorway.

"Probably at nine A.M. He'll call a press conference—triumphantly present the gist of last night—and then, with understated drama, he'll resign."

"You'd better get in the shower, then."

"Yes." She set down her coffee mug. "I cannot fail him now. I wonder if Ralph will be there."

Peter muttered something unintelligible, probably an assent, from the other room.

Merry stared out over the wintry moors, which were blanketed with fog in the aftermath of the storm. Peter's sheep were milling there aimlessly, like soggy bundles of sweaters on stumpy legs. She watched them and allowed her mind to drift; she remembered any number of things. How improbably young her grandfather had looked when he turned over the force to John; the way her grandmother, Sylvie, had wept with mingled pride and sadness when Anne Folger pinned the chief's badge on John's starched uniform shirt. She saw herself three years later, a lanky thirteen-year-old standing next to Ralph on a blustery October day, while her father ordered a team of dredgers to comb Madaket Harbor for his wife's body. She remembered target practice out at Tom Nevers in the failing light of late summer evenings, her first service automatic, her father presenting her police academy diploma, a perfect surprise in a perfect day.

And how for years, she had never felt completely certain that John Folger approved her choice of profession. He had finally laid that question to rest.

Or perhaps, at last, *she* had.

She got up and followed the scent of the muffins. "Let's run away, Peter. Skip the press conference. Take off into the blue like the irresponsible beings we are."

"Want to go back to Greenwich?"

"Don't tease." Merry ran her fingers through his damp hair and scowled at him. "Bring up New York, and I'll be on my knees."

"Running away won't help," Peter said quietly.

"Oh, *would* you shut up! Sometimes running away is utterly delightful. I think I'm due for a bit of running."

"I think you should stay and apply for the job."

Merry picked a burst cranberry from the top of a muffin. "Don't be ridiculous, Peter. I can't follow my dad in the force. The selectmen would never allow it."

"They appointed John when Ralph Waldo retired."

"Times were different then. I can hear the arguments now—*a new broom, a clean sweep, some fresh blood*. And they'd be right to say it."

"You've got more of a standing in this community than you realize, Merry. People admire you—and what's more, they trust you."

She regarded him dubiously. "Are you being selfless again?"

"Oh, probably."

"Do you have any idea how much time it would take to run the entire force?"

"I've tried not to think about it. What matters is that you've been working toward this your entire life, whether you admit it now or not."

She was silent for a while, the muffin forgotten.

Chapter Thirty-seven

John Folger, the chief of Nantucket's police for more than twenty years, resigned his position at nine A.M. on Wednesday, December 11. It was remarked that he had chosen an odd moment for his decision—on the heels of a dramatic drug bust and the closure of a vicious homicide investigation—but perhaps, the island sages said, the Chief knew when to leave. Better men than he had waited for failure to force their hands. John had departed at the peak of his powers.

Most of the force's twenty-odd members gathered to hear him. His father and daughter stood by his side. Sue Morningstar, who covered the final press conference for the *Inky Mirror*, was certain she saw a tear on Detective Meredith Folger's face; but perhaps it was an effect of the numerous flashbulbs. Afterward, Sue tackled Merry in the station hallway.

"This was all about *scallops*? Not about heroin at all?"

"I'll give you an exclusive, Sue. Come on upstairs."

• • •

Weeks passed. The Unitarian minister's Christmas madrigals were declared a magnificent success, and he appeared quite splendid in a *Nantucket Magazine* photo spread, wearing his cranberry-colored sweater vest. He rang out the year with the church's famous bell, on a January night of brittle coldness.

The decorations came down slowly from the Mayhew House's walls. Laurie Hopfnagel departed for a job on the mainland.

Shops closed. Shop owners flew gladly to the Virgin Islands. Bad weather set in, in earnest, and the ferries were docked as often as they ran. The cobblestones of Main Street were covered in snow, and schoolchildren sledded gleefully down its abandoned length.

The state crime lab's analysis of tissue from the bodies of Jay Santorski and Matthew Bailey proved that both died from a massive dose of neurotoxin, derived from scallops and injected into the bloodstream. Hannah Moore's fingerprints—lifted from the gloves found on the harbor bottom—tied her conclusively to the murders.

The bodies of the two men were finally released for burial. The story was eventually displaced by others—like Fred McIlhenney's masterful appearance in the witness box and Marty Johansen's conviction on charges of cocaine possession. But a registered nurse in Boston—and one orphaned twelve-year-old boy, pulled abruptly from school and relocated to Newton—found it impossible to forget Hannah Moore. Or the men they had lost.

Paul Winslow left his clinic in the Berkshires and applied to Boston University, claiming an interest in law.

Jorie Daugherty applied to Georgetown, and accepted Will Starbuck's invitation to the Prom.

Will applied to Princeton. It is as yet uncertain whether he will be accepted there; but a glowing alumni recommendation from Peter Mason may help.

The *Inky Mirror* promoted Sue Morningstar, on the strength of a New England journalism award for a three-part series covering the Toxin Murders, as they came to be called.

When Sue moved out of the house on Pilot Whale Drive, Barry Cohen lacked the heart to replace her. He continued to deliver babies during low-pressure systems, which were frequent and prolonged that winter.

Charles Moore's estate running down to the sea was quietly put up for sale. The Quonset huts were dismantled and hauled away. A large quantity of scallop spawn was discreetly destroyed—although some of it found its way to Dr. Melrose Taylor, and the Rinehart Coastal Research Center.

Charles Moore died in prison.

The Board of Selectmen's search for a new police chief is ongoing. Clarence Strangerfield was named acting chief in mid-December, and has considered applying for the position; but he is uncertain whether Meredith Folger has already done so, and he regards the question as delicate. Clarence is aging himself; and he has a vague notion that what the force needs is young blood. He has no wish, moreover, to compete with a woman he has loved and respected since her birth.

And he misses his evidence room, where Nat Coffin is presently wreaking havoc.

Merry Folger and Peter Mason departed the island themselves in late January, for a long-delayed vacation in Manhattan. And as they were browsing among the bewildering wealth of china patterns displayed about Tiffany's upper floors, Merry suddenly stopped short and clasped Peter's hand.

"That looks like my grandmother Sylvie's," she said, pointing to a plate encircled with birds and flowers, vaguely Japanese.

"It does?"

"You hate it, don't you?"

"Not at all. I'm merely surprised. It's so . . . so . . ."

"Elegant? So unlike me?"

". . . so much what my mother would have chosen," Peter finished, with a smirk.

Merry's black eyebrows furled dangerously. "Don't make me hurt you, Peter. I must and will have it."

"Then Sylvie's it is." Peter turned the plate to the light, enjoying the porcelain's thinness and delicate wash of color. "Does this mean we can finally set a date?"

About the Author

FRANCINE MATHEWS has worked as a journalist and as a foreign policy analyst. She has written four novels in the mystery series featuring Merry Folger, including *Death in the Off-Season, Death in Rough Water,* and *Death in A Mood Indigo*. Under the name Stephanie Barron, she is the author of four novels in the bestselling Jane Austen mysteries, *Jane and the Unpleasantness at Scargrave Manor, Jane and the Man of the Cloth, Jane and the Wandering Eye*, and *Jane and the Genius of the Place*.

She lives in Colorado, where she is at work on a suspense novel, *The Cut-Out*.